Cherry Baby

The *New York Times* once called Rainbow Rowell 'talented enough to be uncategorizable'. She writes novels, comics and short stories. She's a #1 *New York Times* bestseller several times over, wrote an Indies Choice Book of the Year, and is a three-time Goodreads Choice Award winner. The thread that runs through all Rowell's work is her sunlit, knife-sharp empathy and unflagging sense of humor. She writes about life – and usually love – in a way that feels painfully, wonderfully real. Visit rainbowrowell.com to learn more.

Also by Rainbow Rowell

Slow Dance
Scattered Showers: Stories

THE SIMON SNOW TRILOGY
Carry On
Wayward Son
Any Way the Wind Blows

Landline
Fangirl
Eleanor & Park
Attachments

Cherry Baby
a novel

RAINBOW ROWELL

PENGUIN MICHAEL JOSEPH

UK | USA | Canada | Ireland | Australia
India | New Zealand | South Africa

Penguin Michael Joseph is part of the Penguin Random House group of companies whose addresses can be found at global.penguinrandomhouse.com

Penguin Random House UK,
One Embassy Gardens, 8 Viaduct Gardens, London SW11 7BW

penguin.co.uk

First published in the United States of America by HarperCollins 2026
First published in Great Britain by Penguin Michael Joseph 2026
001

Copyright © Rainbow Rowell, 2026

The moral right of the author has been asserted

Penguin Random House values and supports copyright.
Copyright fuels creativity, encourages diverse voices, promotes freedom of expression and supports a vibrant culture. Thank you for purchasing an authorized edition of this book and for respecting intellectual property laws by not reproducing, scanning or distributing any part of it by any means without permission. You are supporting authors and enabling Penguin Random House to continue to publish books for everyone.
No part of this book may be used or reproduced in any manner for the purpose of training artificial intelligence technologies or systems. In accordance with Article 4(3) of the DSM Directive 2019/790, Penguin Random House expressly reserves this work from the text and data mining exception

Designed by Nancy Singer
Set in 11.75/16pt Adobe Caslon Pro
Typeset by Six Red Marbles UK, Thetford, Norfolk
Printed and bound in Great Britain by Clays Ltd, Elcograf S.p.A.

The authorized representative in the EEA is Penguin Random House Ireland, Morrison Chambers, 32 Nassau Street, Dublin D02 YH68

A CIP catalogue record for this book is available from the British Library

HARDBACK ISBN: 978-0-241-68842-7
TRADE PAPERBACK ISBN: 978-0-241-68843-4

Penguin Random House is committed to a sustainable future for our business, our readers and our planet. This book is made from Forest Stewardship Council® certified paper.

Cherry Baby

Chapter 1

'*No*.

'I said *no*. Not now.

'Steven, *please*, I'm begging you ...

'No –

'No –

'I know what you want, but I just –

'I'm wearing *black*, Stevie. I just want –

'For *once*, I just –'

Cherry's phone chimed. She ignored it. She was trying to hold an overgrown dog at arm's length while she got out the door.

Trying unsuccessfully. Stevie was too big and too *eager* to be contained – she pushed forward, tail-wagging, brown eyes pleading for affection. Stevie had human eyes. Like a gorilla.

'Okay, *fine*.' Cherry gave in, lifting her arms. 'Fine, fine, fine.'

Stevie leapt forward, rubbing her big head against Cherry's black pants, first one thigh, then the other.

'I know ...' Cherry sighed and patted the dog's broad back. 'You're a good girl, Stevie.'

Stevie was a two-year-old Newfoundland–Great Pyrenees mix. (Some people called this a 'NewfiePyr.' Cherry was not one of them.) She was huge and white, with black spots around her eyes and ears – and she was as fluffy as a sheep or some sort of mountain goat. There were dog owners who actually collected their Great Pyrenees' fur and made *sweaters* from it. (Again, Cherry was not one of them.)

Stevie looked like a polar bear wearing a burglar's mask, and she was probably the nicest dog who'd ever lived. Her full name was Stevie Nicks. Cherry's ex-husband had named her.

Cherry's phone chimed again. She kept ignoring it. Stevie was still trying to push closer. She was always like this when Cherry had been at work all day.

She wedged her head between Cherry's legs and charged forward. This was apparently a show of submission – it was one of Stevie's favorite moves – but Cherry had short legs, and the dog practically knocked her off her feet every time she attempted it.

'Stevie!' Cherry shuffled back, trying to find her balance. 'Jesus!' Her phone double-chimed, two texts landing one after another.

Stevie was between Cherry's legs and also wrapped around her knee. (She was as long as a Chinese dragon.) It was too much.

'That's it – *house*!' Cherry ordered. 'You have to go to your house, I'm sorry. I can't do this right now.'

Stevie heard the word 'house' and dutifully trotted over to her wire kennel. The dog was well trained, Cherry would give Tom that. She handed Stevie a probiotic treat and closed the door. The kennel took up half the small front room they used as a foyer.

Cherry reached for a lint roller and started at her wrists. She was covered in white hair, even in places that Stevie hadn't touched. There was hair in the *air* in Cherry's house. It was a full Pig-Pen situation. Maybe Cherry should change her clothes . . .

Or maybe she should just stay home.

She didn't really want to go to a concert by herself. She'd planned to go with her friend Stacia, but Stacia had flaked out, and Cherry couldn't think of a *single* other person who might want to take the extra ticket.

Cherry was thirty-six. Her friends didn't go to concerts anymore – they had kids. Or they watched prestige television. Or they liked to get to sleep early so they could make it to spin class or whatever this year's version of spin class was. *Cherry* didn't even go to concerts anymore.

Tom hated concerts. He didn't care about music, and he didn't like people. Anytime Cherry had tried to take Tom to a concert, he'd spent the whole night frowning at everyone, and he didn't even realize he was doing it. Tom had resting uncomfortable face.

Cherry started with the lint roller again at her shoulders. Her phone chimed.

She'd bought tickets for this concert on the day that it was announced. Goldenrod was her favorite Omaha band. She'd seen them play live twice, before Tom – and before the band had gotten kind of famous and broken up. Tonight was a reunion show. They were going to play their first album straight through. Cherry didn't want to miss it. She was tired of *missing* everything.

Her phone chimed, and she pulled it out of her back pocket to take a look. The group chat with her sisters had thirty-five new messages. Cherry opened it.

The first text was from her sister Honny:

'*THE THURSDAY TRAILER JUST DROPPED! THIS IS NOT A DRILL!!!!*'

Cherry silenced the phone and shoved it back into her pocket. She set the lint roller on top of the kennel and gave Stevie a stern look.

Stevie was looking up at Cherry with needy eyes. Stevie had resting *yearning* face.

'I'm going to let you out,' Cherry said, 'but you can*not* jump on me. And you're not going with me.'

Stevie yearned silently.

Cherry unlocked the kennel. 'Stay down.'

Stevie hopped to her feet inside the cage.

'I'm serious, Steven.' Cherry backed toward the front door.

Stevie looked ready to bolt.

Cherry ran for the door and slammed it closed behind her.

Chapter 2

Cherry parked on the street, as close as she could get to the concert venue – a small club in an industrial part of downtown Omaha. It was raining and already dark.

Maybe it was foolish to go out at night by herself like this. Cherry should at least tell her sisters where she was going, to be safe. (Though that always seemed less like a protective measure than a way to streamline the process later when people were looking for your body.)

Cherry's sisters were still blowing up the group chat – and they'd also started texting her individually, to ask why she wasn't replying. Cherry continued to ignore them. She shoved the phone and her wallet into her pocket and got out of the car, sprinting for the club door.

The young guy taking tickets barely looked at her when he checked her ID. She hoped she was early enough to get a table. The only seating in this place was at a few high-tops near the bar.

Cherry got inside and made a beeline for the last available table, hopping a little to get up onto a stool. *Victory!* she thought, then immediately felt foolish. (When had victory become a chair?) But she felt exhilarated, too, just to be here – to be *out*.

She felt *daring*, to be out by herself.

She felt old ... already ... compared to everyone else here.

She felt fat. (Always.)

She felt kind of cute, in her dark jeans and gauzy olive-green sweater ...

Cherry liked everything she was wearing tonight: Chunky baby blue leather boots that she'd ordered from Denmark. Dangly pink earrings made by a plastics artist she'd found online. A vintage heart-shaped locket that she wore with almost everything.

She had cute clothes – too many cute clothes, probably. She'd taken over their bedroom closet, and then the entire spare bedroom. Tom had had to keep all his shoes and dress clothes in a closet downstairs. (He never made her feel bad about that.) (But also he never wore dress clothes.)

Clothes were important to Cherry – her appearance was important. Every weekday morning, when she rode the elevator to her office on the twelfth floor of the Western Alliance building, she took real satisfaction in seeing her reflection in the mirrored brass doors.

Cherry had always been able to see herself clearly. She had a good eye, and she could turn it on herself. She knew what she was working with.

Like – she had long, thick hair in a beautiful, unusual shade of chestnut brown, and she knew it. She had hazel eyes and thick lashes. Really nice freckles across the bridge of her nose. Dimples. A good smile. Cherry knew all this about herself. She could see it.

Also . . . she was fat.

Not fat like most women think they are. Cherry was *actually* fat. Objectively. And she *knew* it. She could say it out loud. She didn't hide from it.

Cherry came from a long line of fat women. (There were three fat women lighting up her cell phone right now.) She'd been a fat kid, then a fat teenager, and now she was a fat lady.

She knew how she looked, how people saw her – she thought about it constantly. Whatever else Cherry was thinking and doing (which was a lot; if Cherry were a train car, she'd be the locomotive), she was *also* thinking about being fat.

Cherry was so used to thinking about being fat, she hardly even noticed that she was doing it. She was so used to thinking about being fat, she never *thought* about it.

There was dog hair on her sleeve. She frowned and plucked it off.

More people were showing up for the concert now. Cherry watched them pour through the door. The crowd was younger than she was expecting. Weren't these kids too young to know Goldenrod?

Maybe this was just the crowd for every concert here ... Guys with patchy beards. Girls with blunt haircuts and tattoos creeping up their necks and onto their cheeks. Everyone had tattoos now. Literally, everyone. Even soccer moms and elementary school teachers. It must be difficult to be young and rebellious these days – you had to get a tattoo right across your face if you wanted to stand out. You had to wear clothes so deeply unflattering that no one over thirty would dare try it. The girls at this concert were wearing what used to be called mom jeans. Waist-thickening, ass-flattening jeans. Mom jeans and dad sneakers. Cherry didn't have the heart for any of it. She was too old and fat to lean away from her strengths.

She wished that Stacia was here ... or somebody.

In the old days, Cherry would have come to the concert with a big group of friends from work or school.

Your friendships change when you get married. And then they change again when everyone starts having kids. Cherry had been left behind at the kid stage. And now Tom was gone, and it was worse than being left behind – it was like getting thrown back to the start.

Maybe she needed younger friends.

She wasn't the *oldest* person here, at least. There were even a few people she recognized, just from living in Omaha her whole life and showing up in certain kinds of places.

She spotted a guy who used to work at the record store ... back when Omaha had record stores. And a woman who used to work for the newspaper, back when Omaha still had a real newspaper. Sometimes the world was so new, it made Cherry dizzy – and she was only thirty-six. No wonder her mom always seemed confused.

Someone touched her shoulder. A young woman with short, unfortunate bangs wanted to know if Cherry needed the other chairs at her table. Cherry said she didn't. The woman dragged them over to the bar for her friends.

Cherry watched them for a while – then realized she was staring at people like some sort of twentieth-century weirdo. She should stare at her phone, like a normal person. She glanced over at the bar one more time – and right into the eyes of someone who was watching *her*. A man. He smiled.

Cherry frowned. *Was that . . .*

It definitely *was*. She smiled, surprised. The man was already walking toward her. She smiled bigger.

'Russell Sutton!' she said as he stepped up to her table. 'As I live and breathe.'

'Cherry, Cherry,' he said, grinning at her. 'You're a flashback – look at you.'

'Look at *you*,' Cherry said. She *was* looking at him. He looked . . .

Well, god, he looked the same way he always had. Like he'd dropped out of his mother's womb with a good haircut and tortoise-shell glasses. Like he was *born* with that smirk. Russell Sutton of the Fairacres Suttons. Talk about flashbacks. Talk about concussive blasts from the distant past.

'What are you doing here?' Russ asked, smiling with all of his teeth, like he couldn't help it.

Cherry laughed. It was a dumb question. 'I came for the show.'

He leaned on the high-top table. A lock of brown hair fell onto his forehead. 'You know what I mean. I haven't seen you around for *generations*. Are you by yourself?'

'Yeah, you?'

Russ shrugged and swept his hair back with his hand. 'Ish. I came by myself – but you know, I know everyone here. *You're* the fresh face, Cherry. Where have you even been?'

She laughed again. 'Nowhere. Around. I still live in midtown. I still work for the railroad.'

'I didn't know you worked for the railroad – what do you do?'

'I sit in an office and give orders.'

He laughed. 'I'll bet you're good at that. You're married, right? To that guy who does the cartoon? They're making a movie, isn't that right?'

Cherry clenched her teeth. For just a second. She didn't stop smiling. 'That's right – *Thursday*.'

He looked confused. 'They're making it on Thursday?'

'No,' she said. 'That's what it's called. The comic. *Thursday*.'

'Oh.' Russ's mouth quirked down on one side, sheepish. 'Sorry. I've never actually read it.'

'That's –' Cherry smiled for real. 'That's okay.' She shook her head. 'And anyway, I'm actually . . .' She shook her head again and flapped her left hand. 'Divorced.'

Russ stood up a little. 'Oh.'

'I mean, we're *getting* a divorce.'

His face was serious. 'I'm sorry, Cherry.'

'No, don't be. It's . . .' She waved her hand again. 'You know.'

'I've been divorced for three years,' he said.

'Oh. Russ.' Cherry finally stopped smiling. 'I'm sorry.'

'It's okay.' He shrugged. 'I lived.'

His eyes were soft. She smiled at him.

He leaned toward her and bumped his elbow against hers. 'You'll live.'

She laughed a little. 'Thanks.'

'Do you want a drink?'

Cherry looked over at the bar. 'Yeah, but I don't want to lose my seat.'

'I'll get you something,' he said. 'What do you want?'

She bit her lips, humming. 'Nah. I'd just have to go to the bathroom when the show starts, and *then* I'd lose my seat.'

'Oh my *god*,' Russ said. 'Just tell me what you want. I'll protect your seat all night, Grandma.'

She pointed at him. 'Seriously, do you promise? I can't stand through a concert.'

Russ made a face. 'I've stood with you through several concerts, Cherry.'

'That's the problem. I ruined myself with long nights in high heels.'

He grinned again, nostalgic. 'Oh yeah, you did. You used to wear those little pin-up girl shoes.' He held up his thumb and forefinger. 'They made your feet look tiny.'

Cherry kicked his shin with her clunky boot. 'I want a Coke Zero. And you have to come back in an hour to watch my seat while I go to the bathroom.'

'I won't leave your side,' Russ said, loping away from her toward the bar.

Cherry smiled after him. Then tried to shake it off. But her face still felt like it was smiling even with her lips pressed together.

Russell Sutton. Who would have thought?

Chapter 3

Russ brought back a Coke Zero for Cherry and a beer for himself. And he kept his word – he stuck to her table. The opening act had started playing – a local band that never broke out, Sacagawea – but Russ and Cherry just huddled a little closer and kept talking. Cherry told him a bit more about her job. She'd started out as a graphic designer – he knew that – then she got promoted to team leader, then manager, and now she ran the railroad's marketing department. The woman above her *officially* ran the department. But Cherry was the brains of the operation and frequently the mouth, and always the person who made sure that everything got done. (She was a little more self-effacing as she explained all this to Russ.)

Russ had been working in and around government since college. He was the mayor's chief of staff now – even though the mayor was a Republican and Russ was a lifelong liberal. (His grandpa had been governor, back when Nebraska still elected Democrats.) And he was active in a bunch of civic groups. For voter turnout. Literacy. Arts programs in marginalized neighborhoods. He really *did* know half the people in the room – they kept stopping at the table to say hello. He kept introducing Cherry. (*'Do you know my friend Cherry? We were practically roommates at Creighton.'*) Russ still went to a lot of concerts. He still saw a lot of movies. He still ate dinner once a week with his parents. He was still really, *really* attractive.

'Handsome' wasn't the right word for Russ. He wasn't especially tall or broad. His features were kind of sharp. He looked like the token Irish actor on a BBC drama – a little flintier than everyone else and a little more alive. His eyes were dark blue and set deep, and his color was high. When he was excited or drunk, he looked feverish.

He looked a little feverish tonight.

Russ had gotten married after law school to someone Cherry had never met – a Marian girl who worked at the Community Foundation. (Marian was one of the Omaha schools where rich Catholic girls went.) They had one kid, an eight-year-old boy named Liam – he was at Saint Margaret Mary now. Did Cherry want to see a photo? Yeah. She did. She looked at Russ's phone and smiled. His son was a doll. She said so.

Cherry didn't have any photos to show Russ. She wasn't going to show him a picture of Stevie – that would be too sad. (. . . Even if Cherry did have a thousand of them on her phone.) And she didn't want to talk about Tom. She *couldn't* talk about Tom the way Russ talked about his ex-wife – like she was just another thing that had happened in the years since he and Cherry last talked.

'I can't believe you work in *management*,' Russ said. The opening act had finished their set. Goldenrod would be starting soon. 'You were always so creative.'

'I'm still creative,' Cherry said, affronted. She was chewing on ice. She swallowed it. 'There aren't very many people who can be creative *and* practical. It's my magic power, actually. I can make sure the work is good, and I can make sure it gets done. And I can talk to the numbers and money people.'

'Huh.' Russ looked at her glass. 'Do you want another Coke Zero?'

She shook her head.

'Don't you miss being an artist?' he asked.

'I know I'm supposed to say yes, but . . . I think I'm a better executive. I don't think I was *ever* much of an artist.'

'Sure you were.'

She rolled her eyes. 'When did you ever see my art, Russ?'

He shrugged. 'I just don't think you would have been an art major if you were shitty at it.'

Well. That was true. 'I got by,' Cherry conceded. 'But I wasn't an artist.' Not like the other people she went to school with. Not like Tom. 'If I had to go back to design, I'd miss what I'm doing now.'

'I just can't picture you at the railroad,' Russ said. 'As an *industrialist*.'

'I'm not a robber baron.'

He laughed. 'Do you still see Stacia and all those guys?'

Cherry nodded. Minimally. 'Yeah. Same old crowd.'

Russ shook his head, like he was remembering something fondly. Cherry could imagine some of the details.

A guy walked past their table and waved at Russ. Russ waved back.

'Do you ever wish that you got out of Omaha?' Cherry asked.

He cut his eyes toward her. 'What do you mean?'

Cherry looked up at him. He was a bit taller than her, standing by her chair. 'Just ... the same old faces,' she said. 'The same old intersecting circles. Do you ever wish you'd gotten out?'

Russ smiled a little. His eyes looked extra alive. 'Not tonight.'

Cherry ran to the bathroom before the show started, and when she came back, Russ was sitting in her seat. He smiled at her and got up. The band was walking onstage. Cherry climbed onto the chair, clapping. She was so excited for this show. Even more excited now that it was starting.

The first song began – and Cherry immediately felt herself sliding backwards. Back to her early twenties. To her senior year of college, when she'd had this CD on repeat. Goldenrod was the band that made 'Omaha emo' a thing. Simple, pretty guitars. Whiny, breathy vocals. Base-level unhappiness. All of Goldenrod's songs were about being lonely or feeling guilty. The lead singer was a famous depressive. He was wearing a paper crown tonight, playing the first few chords of the song on an acoustic guitar.

God, Cherry *loved* this song. She loved this *feeling*. She laughed a little, just for the joy of it. People around her were whooping.

Russ had moved to Cherry's side of the table, to face the band. He turned to her, smiling, and sang the first lyric – '*I was young, and I was tired, and I was splitting in three.*'

Cherry grinned.

These concerts were all the rage now – bands playing their best-loved albums all the way through – and after a few songs, Cherry could see why. It was *delightful*. Hearing all the songs you wouldn't usually hear at a concert, the not-even-B-sides. Hearing the songs in the precise order that you knew them best.

Cherry kept smiling. She kept tearing up. She kept looking over at Russ – she still wasn't over the shock of *seeing* him again, and there he was, standing right next to her. Standing so close that his arm brushed against hers every time he took a drink. *Russ Sutton, as she lived and breathed.*

There were songs on this first Goldenrod album that had always reminded Cherry of Russ, that she'd twisted to fit her hopeless crush on him – *obviously* she'd had a crush on him – and now he was right there beside her, singing along.

Maybe this was a message from the universe . . .

It *had* to be a message from the universe – it was too strange and specific for happenstance.

Cherry had gone out for the first time since Tom left to do something just for herself – she'd gone out *by* herself for maybe the first time ever – and this strangely perfect night was here waiting for her. A band she loved, an album she loved . . . and a boy she'd once liked an awful lot.

An awful, *miserable* lot.

Maybe the universe wasn't on her side – would a benevolent god send Russ Sutton onto Cherry's path? This ache in her stomach was familiar and delicious, but it had never led to satisfaction, not where Russ was concerned.

And *yet* . . .

There was satisfaction in feeling *something*, wasn't there? In standing close to someone this attractive and exciting? It felt good to *be* attracted. To buzz a little.

Russ shifted his weight and rested his arm on the back of Cherry's chair.

And Cherry let herself enjoy it.

Chapter 4

Everybody was going to the Galway that night.

They were twenty-two and still feeling like they had to go out and drink legally every weekend just because they could – because it's what adults did. Adults drank in bars, not in dorm rooms and basements.

On Friday and Saturday nights, and sometimes on Thursdays, Cherry's friends put on low-cut, high-cropped, slit-up-the-side silky tops, and they went out to the bars.

Cherry was never the most enthusiastic participant – partly because she was too fat to pull off a crop top, but *mostly* because her dad was an alcoholic. Being around drunk people made Cherry anxious, not merry. And being drunk herself didn't improve the situation.

Cherry didn't *get* drunk the way her friends did. She had to drink way more than they did to feel anything at all. Because of her weight, maybe. Or possibly genetics. Cherry could pound shot after shot and never feel soft or silly. She'd feel persistently sober for a couple rounds, then overheated for the next couple, and then – if she kept going – sick.

There was no upside to it. She didn't take any pride in holding her liquor. Cherry didn't want to be one of those women who was always proving she could drink like a man. That seemed ... expensive. And caloric. And sad.

However ... it *was* Friday night. And everyone was going out. And Cherry *liked* to go out. The Galway at least had music ...

She put on a tight dress with a low-cut neck and a full skirt, and offered to drive.

The Galway drew three types of patrons: Creighton University students, career alcoholics, and people who really liked Irish folk music. It was downtown, shoved into a narrow gap between two office buildings. A bar this skinny didn't have any business offering live music. The musicians were always crammed into the back on a plywood riser, and there was nowhere to sit and listen. There was hardly any place to stand.

Cherry dragged Stacia to the stage end of the bar so they could see the band. Stacia was drinking a Moscow Mule. Everybody was drinking Moscow Mules that spring. Stacia didn't care about music, but she knew that Cherry did, and regularly indulged her.

Stacia was Cherry's roommate and one of her closest friends. She was very pretty. On Friday nights, she was hot. Her breasts were *just* small enough to skip wearing a bra, and even though she wasn't tall – just a little taller than Cherry – she had the snakelike torso of an *American Idol* contestant. She was still wearing low-rise jeans to show it off. (Low-rise jeans in 2010!)

Cherry had stopped wearing low-rise jeans the second it became possible. She wore skinny jeans and yoga pants during the week, and on weekends, she wore one of two spendy rockabilly dresses that she'd bought online.

(The problem with rockabilly brands was that they were *obsessed* with cherries. Cherry hadn't worn anything with cherries – or even fruit – since she was old enough to dress herself.)

Tonight she was wearing a yellow dress with a vintage cowboy pattern. It was Cherry's favorite dress – even though the last time she'd worn it out to the bars, some guy as old as her dad had offered to take her for a ride. Cherry always wore this dress with a baby blue cardigan and bright red heels. Her friends told her she looked adorable.

You'd think that going out with her hot, skinny friends and watching them get hit on all night by law school students would be depressing for Cherry ... But she'd be a shut-in if she let herself get depressed by things like that. Cherry had *always* been fatter than her friends. She'd *always* been less attractive to guys. Being mad or depressed about it would be like getting mad at the sun for rising.

It got her down sometimes ...

It ate away at her, constantly, sure. Low-key.

But it didn't get her *down*-down. It didn't keep her from going *out*.

Cherry was drinking Coke. The band sounded like Mumford & Sons but with whistles and bagpipes.

'I like your dress,' somebody said.

Cherry turned to him. It was a guy her age. Dark hair, clean-cut. Round glasses. His cheeks were red, and he was holding a copper mug. He might already be drunk.

Cherry nodded.

The guy leaned toward her. 'I had pajamas that looked like that when I was six.'

'Back in the 1940s?'

'My mom made all my clothes.'

'That sounds nice,' Cherry said, biting down on some ice and looking away.

'You were in my ethics class,' he said.

She looked back at him. That couldn't be right; she'd remember this guy from class. He was good-looking in a way that Cherry would have noticed. She liked his hair – short and wavy, but not clippered. Long enough to fall into his eyes. He pushed it off his forehead. His eyes were dark and sparkling – he was probably drunk.

'I sat in the back,' he said. 'When I came. It was an eight a.m. class – I wasn't built for it.'

Cherry *had* taken ethics at eight a.m ...

'You sat in front,' he went on. 'You're fond of sweaters.'

'You *are* fond of sweaters,' Stacia said. She was standing behind Cherry, grinning.

The guy cut his eyes to Stacia, then back to Cherry. He held out his hand. 'I'm Russ.'

Cherry took his hand. 'Cherry. And this is Stacia.'

'*Cherry*,' he said. 'Is that your swing-dancing name?'

'My what?'

'You know, like ... rockabilly girl. With the dress. *Susie. Dixie. Flo. Cherry.* Is your real name Jessica or something?'

'Her real name is Cherish,' Stacia said, laughing.

Russ made a face like he hadn't expected that. 'Oh god, that's actually sweet.'

'I'm not a rockabilly girl,' Cherry said. 'I'm just a person wearing a dress.'

'I said I liked it.'

'I know you.' Stacia pointed at him.

Russ nodded. 'We had econ together.'

'That's right – your name is *Russ*.' Stacia *was* already a little drunk.

'So, *do* you swing-dance?' he asked Cherry.

She rolled her eyes back up to him. 'You're wearing round glasses. Does that make you a boy wizard?' (She actually liked his glasses a lot.)

'Maybe. Why'd your parents name you Cherish?'

Cherry sighed. 'Why'd your parents name you Russ?'

'It's my dad's name. And my grandpa's.'

Cherry couldn't figure out why this guy was talking to her. Guys didn't talk to her in bars. Unless they were *really* drunk. Or really old. Or if it was getting close to last call and they were lashing out in every direction.

That wasn't to say that guys *never* talked to Cherry ...

She wasn't untouched. Or even unloved. She wasn't a virgin. Cherry had had two boyfriends in high school and one at the beginning of college, and she'd slept with someone else since then. And at least two of those guys had been in love with her. Maybe two and a half.

But none of them had hit on her out of the blue.

Cherry had to grow on boys. She had to wear them down, by being around and being charming. By being surprisingly cute for a fat girl. By smelling good. By brushing her hair against their shoulders when they talked. By having breasts that sat so close to her chin that you couldn't really miss them when you looked in her eyes.

Every guy who had ever dated Cherry had been her friend first – and probably thought at first that she was too fat to date. But then she'd grown on them ... and all the things that they liked about her had crowded out her fatness.

The point was, they hadn't started talking to her in a bar. Or in the student center. Or at a party. They'd never actually *hit* on her.

So this guy, this skinny, good-looking guy with the deep blue eyes, *couldn't* be hitting on her. He wasn't that drunk, it wasn't that dark. Cherry wasn't sitting behind a desk or standing behind a wall. He could see all of her.

'Can I buy you a drink?' he asked. He glanced over at Stacia. 'Both of you?'

'That's okay,' Cherry said at the same time that Stacia said, 'Moscow Mule.'

'Moscow Mule,' the guy repeated. Russ. He was looking at Cherry.

'She's drinking Coke,' Stacia said.

'Coke and ...?'

'Just Coke,' Cherry said.

'She's the designated driver,' Stacia said, like it was funny.

'That's handy,' Russ said. 'I could use a designated driver.' He pointed at Cherry. 'Don't go anywhere. I'll be right back.'

Stacia didn't even wait for him to get out of hearing distance. 'He's *cute*.'

'Is he?' Cherry made herself sound skeptical.

'What?' Stacia shoved her. '*Yes*. You know I like skinny guys with dark hair. He looks like a poet. Or like he's in a band.'

'You just mean he looks pale and underfed. He looks like the third-best-looking guy in U2.'

Stacia made a face. 'You think he looks like the bald guy?'

'Are you talking about the Edge? *No*. I meant – he looks like a *fictional* member of U2, who would still only be the third-best-looking.'

'You just mean he looks Catholic,' Stacia said, tipping her copper mug up to empty it. 'He's cute enough for me.'

'You can have him.'

'I don't know . . .' Stacia teased. 'I think he likes youuuu.'

Cherry made a face. 'You know how this goes. I'm just the approachable person who stands next to your intimidating exposed torso.'

'Shut up, Cherry,' Stacia said. But she still laughed, which Cherry took as affirmation that she *did* know.

'Ladies.' Russ was back with three drinks – two copper mugs and a glass of Coke.

Stacia took a mug, and Russ swung around to Cherry, standing close. 'Trade me,' he said.

Cherry took both drinks, and he took her empty glass, and Stacia's, and pushed into the crowd again. A second later, he was back, standing right in front of Cherry, taking his drink from her.

'Designated driver . . .' he said. Cherry was five-foot-four – almost five-foot-eight in heels – and he was a little bit taller than her, but not too much. (Russ didn't look like the Edge; he looked like Bono.) 'Do you take turns?'

'Nope,' Stacia said. 'Cherry's permanently designated.'

'That doesn't sound fair. That's like when my older brother called shotgun for life.'

'Did it work?' Cherry asked.

He looked in her eyes. 'Yeah. He was bigger than me.'

'She doesn't mind,' Stacia said.

Russ was still looking at Cherry. 'Is that true?'

'I don't drink,' she said.

'She's never even *had* a Mule,' Stacia said. 'She won't even try one.'

'They're good,' he told Cherry.

'I assume so,' she said. 'They come in a special glass and everything.'

'You can *taste* the copper,' Stacia said.

'You really can,' Russ agreed. He nudged his chin toward Cherry. 'Why don't you drink?'

'I like to keep my wits about me.'

'Your wits . . .' he said, stalling out. It sounded so witless that Cherry laughed for the first time.

Russ frowned at her and took a drink.

The Irish folk band kicked it up a notch. They were actually *good*, not just competent. Apparently they were from Kansas City. Their frontman could play every instrument that got handed to him.

A few people had started dancing. Cherry and Stacia – and Russ – got pushed away from the stage, but the three of them stayed together.

Russ seemed actively interested in the music. Not just drinking near it. 'I was hoping you swing-danced,' he said to Cherry between songs.

'Why?' She lowered her eyebrows. 'Do *you* swing-dance?'

He shrugged. 'A little.'

'That doesn't seem like something people do "a little" of. That's like saying you do "a little" karate.'

'Not really.'

'It's a *commitment*,' she said. 'You have to go to a special place on a special night, you have to wear special clothes . . .'

Stacia was listening and laughing at them both.

'You're the one wearing a swing dress,' Russ said to Cherry.

'I just think it's cute.'

He nodded. 'It is cute.'

'I think it's cool that you swing-dance,' Stacia said. 'Is it hard?'

'Not at all.' He was still looking at Cherry. 'I could show you . . .'

'Can you swing-dance to *this*?' Cherry tilted her head toward the bagpipe player.

'Absolutely. Let me show you.'

She wrinkled her nose. 'Better not. I'm the designated driver.'

'What does that have to do with anything?'

'It means I still have my wits about me,' she said.

'Coward.' Russ looked over his shoulder at Stacia. 'Do you enjoy joy, Stacie?'

'It's Stacia,' she said, 'and I *do*.'

'Stacia.' He held out his hand.

She took it. 'Are you sure?' she asked in a flirty voice. 'I'm not wearing a special dress . . .'

Russ pulled her toward him. 'That's purely optional.'

Cherry stepped back to give them space.

Russ guided Stacia through a few back-and-forth steps. He was making eye contact with her, smiling. Stacia was laughing. He held her by her hand and by her beautiful bare waist.

Once they were moving in rhythm, Russ swung Stacia away from him, then reeled her back in. Stacia squealed, delighted. She was clumsier than he was, but that didn't seem to get in his way. Cherry couldn't help but smile.

After a few more moves, Russ wrapped his arm around Stacia, holding her close – then spun her out to the end of his reach. He quickly kissed her hand, then said, 'Your turn, Cherry,' and grabbed Cherry's hand. For a second, he was holding on to them both.

'Do it, Cherry,' Stacia said. 'It's so much fun.'

Cherry let Russ pull her close. 'I don't know how –'

'Just follow my lead.' He was stepping back and forth. His hand was on her hip. She looked down at their feet. 'No,' he said. 'Look at me.' He was already swinging her out away from him. Then back. He took her other hand and swung her to the other side. 'Look at me, Cherry.'

She did. His cheeks were pink, and his eyes were sparkling. He reeled her into him, her back against his chest. 'Relax,' he said. 'Just be momentum.'

'Momentum,' Cherry repeated. Russ's arm was firm around her waist. He must be thinking about how much thicker she was than Stacia. He could definitely feel her belly under his elbow. He put his other hand on Cherry's hip and spun her out again, under his raised arm. Then back into him. Then away from him. Cherry went almost limp, letting Russ push and pull at her. Had he spun Stacia this much? Cherry was getting dizzy. She was laughing despite herself. Every time he whipped her around, her skirt flew out in a circle. She was glad she was wearing tights.

Stacia was watching them, laughing and clapping.

As the song ended – with a furious fiddle solo – Russ spun Cherry gently away and grabbed Stacia's hand and held it over her head, giving her one more twirl. All three of them were grinning. Russ's face was flushed and sweaty. He was holding both their hands.

'That was amazing,' Stacia said.

'I told you it wasn't hard,' he said.

Cherry let go of his hand but couldn't stop smiling at him. 'You did all the work.'

'How did you learn to dance like that?' Stacia asked.

'I took classes in middle school.'

That made all three of them laugh. Russ was still holding Stacia's hand.

Some guy walked over and bumped Russ's shoulder like he knew him. 'Hey,' the guy said, ignoring the girls. 'We're taking off. Everybody's going to your place.'

'Yeah, all right.' Russ looked at Cherry, then Stacia. 'Everybody's going to my place. You coming?'

'Yeah.' Stacia looked at Cherry, eyes alight. '*Yeah*, right?'
'Yeah,' Cherry agreed. 'Sure.'

Cherry and Stacia couldn't really talk on the way to Russ's house, because Russ rode along with them to show them the way. Cherry's other friends came, too; Cherry was their ride home. Russ called, 'Shotgun!' on the way to the car.

He lived in an apartment building not far from Creighton, in kind of a rough neighborhood. Cherry was expecting his apartment to be disgusting – three college guys lived there – but it actually wasn't so bad. There wasn't much furniture, but it was clean. Wood floors, high ceilings. There were already too many people crammed into the living room by the time Cherry and her friends got there. There was rap music playing, and some people were dancing. Cherry recognized a few of them, from classes and her dorm.

'There are drinks in the kitchen,' Russ said.

Stacia and Cherry's other friends – Grace and Elizabeth – headed that way. Russ stuck by Cherry.

He ran his fingers through his hair. 'Is this fun for you?'

'What?'

'Staying sober while everyone around you gets progressively blitzed.'

She shrugged. 'It varies.'

He hummed.

'It beats sitting in my dorm room by myself,' she said, 'and I *do* enjoy being smug and condescending with everyone the next day.'

'You must be really popular.'

'*So* popular.'

He ran his hand through his hair again. 'Do you know what I remember about you, from ethics class?'

'My sweaters.'

'Beyond the sweaters.'

She shook her head.

'When we introduced ourselves on the first day, you said you were an art major.'

'I am.'

'Art majors don't have to take ethics.'

'Ethics are universally relevant,' she said.

He looked amused. '*Are* they?'

'I thought it sounded interesting.'

'So you took ethics as an *elective* . . .'

She nodded.

'I took History of Rock,' he said.

'That also sounds interesting.'

'It was.' The music had gotten louder. 'It was!' Russ shouted, just in case she hadn't heard him. 'Cherry . . .' He leaned closer, his mouth by her ear. He was still shouting. 'I think *you're* interesting.'

She pulled her head back so she could see his face. 'Are you drunk?'

Russ laughed. 'No. I think I'm totally sober.'

Cherry didn't know what to say. She didn't know how to stand. She turned away from him, toward the people dancing in front of the couch.

'Do you want to dance?' Russ asked.

She looked back at him. 'I don't know. Can you swing-dance to Lil Wayne?'

He grinned. 'I mean . . . *I* can.'

He held out his hand. Cherry smiled and shook her head, but she still took it. Russ put his other hand on her hip. What happened next wasn't really swing-dancing – it was normal house-party dancing, with a bit more hand-holding and a few unnecessary spins.

But the *next* song, 'Low' by Flo Rida, apparently *was* a good swing-dancing song. Russ pulled Cherry closer and tried to lead her through some slightly more elaborate steps. She couldn't keep up. They were both laughing. Almost everyone at the party was dancing now – there wasn't space for Russ to fling Cherry around. He held her hip and twirled her right in front of him, so they were eye to eye every time she spun back to face him.

Stacia and Grace and Elizabeth came dancing in from the kitchen. Stacia was holding two drinks. She danced up to Russ, holding out a drink for him, her arm moving with the music. He took it from her, matching her rhythm. He was still holding Cherry's hand. He held it over her head and twirled her away from him, then let go, still dancing – sort of with Stacia, sort of with Cherry – as he took a sip. Grace grabbed Cherry's hand and shouted the chorus of the song at her. Cherry nodded along. '*Low, low, low, low, low, low, low, low.*'

Cherry looked back at Russ. He was twisting down to the floor. Stacia was dancing over him, her arms in the air – halter top riding up so high, you could see the little cross tattooed just under her left breast.

Cherry let go of Grace's hand and backed off the dance floor. She felt a little disoriented.

A girl was standing on one end of the couch, dancing. Cherry sat at the other end and tucked one of her heels under her knee.

She watched Russ dance with Stacia. And another girl. And then with two of his guy friends.

Another song had started before he looked over at Cherry. He held his arms up, like, *What gives?*

Cherry just waved.

Russ stood still for a few seconds, the only still thing on the improvised dance floor. Stacia was right next to him, flicking her hair from side to side, with her arms folded behind her back, pushing her chest out.

Cherry smiled at Russ.

Russ smiled back. He took a step toward her, holding out one hand.

One of his friends – a big guy waving around a beer bottle – stumbled between them. Russ caught the guy. Then started dancing with him. (Boys didn't really dance together. They stood near each other and held their drinks in the air and shouted into each other's faces.) Russ kept glancing past his friend at Cherry.

Cherry got up to use the bathroom – and to steady her nerves. She'd swear she felt Russ watching her as she left the room.

The bathroom was down a hall. It was also less gross than she would have expected. None of the towels matched, and Russ and his roommates used an old picante-sauce jar to hold their toothbrushes – but everything was clean.

Cherry looked in the mirror. She was flushed from her cheeks down to her neckline. Her eyes were extra shiny. She shook her head. Then shook her head again. Then reapplied her red lipstick.

She made a decision:

When Cherry walked out of this bathroom, she was going to stop shrinking away from Russ. When he reached out to her, she was going to reach back.

Against all odds and all her past experiences, this cute, charming guy seemed really interested in her. He'd *literally said* that he was interested in her.

And Cherry was very, very interested in him.

She was going to stop turning away from him in disbelief. She was going to start moving *in*.

She opened the bathroom door and walked out to the living room.

Russ was right where she'd left him . . .

Making out with Stacia.

A couple hours later, Cherry drove Grace and Elizabeth back to the dorms.

Chapter 5

Funny that this used to be an album Cherry would listen to when she was sad. She hadn't stopped smiling tonight since the moment Goldenrod started playing.

She was reminded of how great Russ Sutton was at concerts. Most people *weren't* great at concerts ... They complained or got too drunk or wanted to leave before the encore to beat the rush in the parking lot.

Russ was completely present and engaged. He'd sing along and dance in place. He'd look over at you every few minutes, like, *Isn't this great?* He'd get invested in your options at the merch table. How many shows had they dragged Stacia to over the year they were dating? (The year that Stacia and Russ were dating.)

Stacia had always been game for a concert – she was game for most things – but she didn't *love* music. She got bored at long concerts, especially if no one was drinking, and she didn't like situations where everyone pressed against each other. She didn't like being jostled by strangers. (Jostling was probably more unpleasant for hot girls.) Cherry kind of loved getting lost in a crowd, everyone dancing together like one organism. Sometimes Stacia would leave Russ and Cherry in the thick of it and wait for them at the back of the room or sitting at the bar.

It felt familiar for Cherry to be shoulder to shoulder with Russ Sutton in the dark like this. It felt easy.

'I wish we were closer,' she said between songs. She meant, to the stage.

'We could be closer,' Russ said. He knew what she meant. He shook the back of her chair so it rocked. 'Let's get closer.'

Cherry scrunched up her nose. She didn't want to give up her seat – but she also didn't want to spoil Russ's fun. 'You can go.'

'Oh, does Her Majesty not want to leave her throne?'

She made another face. 'It's not me, it's my lower back.'

'Come on, Cherry. We're still in our youth. We're *Millennials*.'

'And I'm aging like milk.'

The next song started. It was another of Cherry's favorites. Another one she'd played over and over when she was feeling low. '*Unf*,' she groaned. 'I *love* this song.'

Russ's arm slipped from her chair to her shoulders and squeezed. 'Come on. We're moving up.'

Cherry bit her lips for a second, then hopped down off the chair.

'Attagirl.' He tugged her forward.

She let him lead her through gaps in the crowd. Russ had a way of moving like he was on his way somewhere. People always stepped aside for him.

He kept his arm around Cherry, and she kept close to him, all the way up to the front, just a few people away from the stage. Close enough to read the lead singer's ironic T-shirt – OMAHA IS FOR LOVERS . . . *of free parking*.

Russ looked over at Cherry and raised his eyebrows like, *See? I told you this would be great.*

She grinned back at him.

He turned to the stage, already swaying and nodding his head to the music. His arm still in place.

Cherry noticed. And didn't move away. She swayed with him, her shoulder against his chest, letting her head swing back and forth.

They wouldn't have been standing quite *this* close back in college. Russ wouldn't have put his arm around her. But he used to dance with Cherry sometimes at concerts – if the beat was right, and if there was room. By the time Stacia and Russ broke up,

Cherry had learned the basics of East Coast Swing and a little bit of the Lindy Hop.

This was different. Closer. Tighter. Russ's chin was brushing against Cherry's hair, and her hip was solidly against his – and he didn't seem to mind. He didn't seem worried about anyone seeing them. Maybe this was standard Russ behavior these days. *Find a friend. Get cozy. Have a good time.*

It was *not* standard Cherry behavior. It had been a while since she'd felt cozy with anyone.

This was all very irregular for her . . . Beyond irregular – *surreal*.

Cherry was currently singing along to a song, about unrequited love, that had been her soundtrack for the second half of senior year. And the boy she'd been thinking of back then? Was holding her now, *also* singing along, completely oblivious to Cherry's heavy feelings, past or present.

Life was absurd.

If the last year had taught her anything, it was that.

Was the universe *actually* talking to Cherry tonight? Had it sent Russ back across her path as auspiciously as possible? (*'Stop saying "the universe" when you mean God,'* her sister Honny would say.) Or was this night just another *thing* that was happening? A coincidence. More chaos.

Cherry's voice caught on the chorus of the song. Her eyes teared up. She laughed out loud.

Russ looked at her, nodding his head with the music. He gave her another squeeze and leaned over so she could hear him. 'I forgot how great you are at concerts. I missed you, Cherry.'

'I missed you, too,' Cherry said softly.

She hadn't *actively* missed Russ. She hadn't really thought about him in ten years. But now that he was right beside her, she missed him like crazy. Every good and bad memory was rushing back at her. *Concerts. Lunches. Studying in her dorm room. Driving to Broken Bow to visit Stacia's family at Easter.* Cherry had spent a whole year stealing glances at Russ and then squirreling her feelings away somewhere that Stacia – and Russ himself – would hopefully never see them.

And now Russ was here, and Stacia wasn't. (Stacia was married! To another chiropractor! She had three kids!)

The song ended. Russ's hand dropped below Cherry's bra strap. 'How's your back?' he asked, like he'd heard her think the word 'chiropractor.'

'Fine. It won't hurt till tomorrow.'

'Oh, good,' he said, 'I'll be long gone by then.'

Cherry laughed and elbowed his stomach. His arm tightened around her waist. She stood up straighter, instinctively, like she could straighten herself skinny. It had been so long since a man had touched her for the first time ... (She didn't have to straighten for Tom. He knew what Cherry was hiding under her clothes.)

Cherry's favorite song ended. Another favorite song began. Russ kept his arm around her. His fingers were cupped around her side, right in the crease of her belly. She was standing so tall, her eye line had jumped from his chin to his cheeks.

He glanced over at her. 'You okay?'

She nodded. 'I'm good.'

He squeezed her again. 'This okay?'

'It's good.'

He pulled her even closer. Fully against him. If Cherry turned her head, it would be in his neck. She was close enough to hear him singing along. She sang with him.

Now when Russ swayed to and fro, Cherry really did sway with him. They were dancing together. Properly.

He kept glancing at her, singing to her. It wasn't awkward. Because he didn't *make* it awkward. (Russ never got embarrassed, so he was never embarrassing.)

There was only one hit song on Goldenrod's first album, and it had become a hit years after the fact, when it was featured on *Grey's*

Anatomy. The song was practically a cappella – more or less spoken word. Everyone in the crowd knew it. Cherry knew it. It was about being in love with the wrong person.

The lead singer stopped singing during the chorus and let the audience recite the lyrics, pointing the microphone out at them.

Russ and Cherry looked right into each other's eyes and said/sang the words. He put his other arm around her, across her stomach. Cherry stretched another sixteenth of an inch taller. She turned toward him, inside his arms, and touched the placket of his button-down shirt. (Russ was the only one here wearing a button-down shirt.) He noticed her touching him, and his smile quirked up on one side, happy about it. Cherry rolled her eyes, like she thought he was being dumb. She didn't think that. She thought he was being *unbearably* attractive. She thought he *was* unbearably attractive. She'd always thought so – she'd never been able to bear it, especially when he was aiming all of that floppy-haired, blue-eyed *Russ*ness her way.

He was aiming it now. Cherry felt very ... *targeted*.

She flattened her hand against his chest. He was warm. Hard. Russ was still thin and boyish – at how old, thirty-seven? Thirty-eight? Still sharp-jawed and loose through the shoulders. He didn't hold himself up like someone who was divorced. His posture was light. It was difficult to picture him with a kid.

Cherry stroked his chest and Russ stroked her hip. He'd stopped singing. So had she. The song had changed. It was the final song on the record, Cherry realized – the song she knew the least. She'd usually fallen asleep or gotten out of the car before she got to this one.

Russ tilted his head down toward hers, and they swayed, slow-dancing.

When the song ended, so did the album.

Cherry let go of Russ and turned back to the stage, holding her hands above her head to applaud. Russ didn't let go, just shifted a little bit to stand behind her. The crowd was going wild. Truly. Russ's mouth was by Cherry's ear, but she could still barely hear him over all the cheering – 'We should go.'

She looked back at him. She was still clapping. 'Is the concert over now?'

He looked right in her eyes. He was *close* – their chins and noses would touch if Cherry said something too emphatically.

'No.' He shook his head. 'They're going to play more from their other albums.'

'Oh.' Cherry was confused.

'But if we left now, the album would be perfectly discrete. A complete experience with a beginning and an end.'

'That seems rude to the band,' she said.

Russ laughed. 'I think they'll manage.'

She'd stopped clapping.

'If we left now …' Russ said, his eyes gleaming, '… we could *leave* now.'

'*Oh*,' Cherry said, understanding.

She felt a sharp and immediate slice of guilt – even before she felt the thrill.

(The absolute fucking *thrill*. Like someone had dumped a shot of adrenaline down her spine. Russell Sutton, as she lived and *breathed*.)

But the guilt hit first … Why guilt …?

Because of *Stacia*?

Because Cherry had spent a whole year of her life stewing in guilt, knowing she was lusting after her best friend's boyfriend? Knowing she was looking too long and laughing too much, and cracking too many jokes that were meant for him, not for the room …

Stacia had never seemed jealous. Even when Russ and Cherry were dancing together or bantering like vaudeville professionals right under her nose – Stacia never seemed to mind.

She must have suspected how Cherry felt about her boyfriend …

And she must have known that it didn't matter.

It *didn't* matter. Stacia and Russ broke up after a year because Stacia wanted to date someone else, and Russ didn't fall into Cherry's arms for comfort. He moved on. She – Cherry – didn't see him again after that.

That was a dozen years ago. More. It was old news. What did Cherry have to feel guilty about tonight?

Was it *Tom*?

Tom was gone.

'Cherry . . .' Russ said, still looking for something in her eyes.

Cherry nodded. 'Let's go.'

Russ closed his eyes and pressed his forehead against hers, smiling so wide.

Goldenrod started playing a song from their second – more sophisticated, but less iconic – album.

Chapter 6

They agreed to take separate cars.

Russ looked conflicted about it, standing on the sidewalk outside the club. 'Don't sober up and change your mind.'

'I'm already completely sober,' Cherry said.

'This is a really good idea,' he said. Firmly.

'Are you trying to hypnotize me?'

He took hold of both her hips and leaned in close. He hadn't kissed her yet. (Cherry was pretty sure that was an operative 'yet,' that the kiss was near at hand.) 'Don't change your mind,' he said again.

'I'll change my mind if I want to.' Cherry pulled away a bit, so she could really look in his eyes. 'But I won't want to.'

Russ bumped his forehead against hers. He groaned. 'I'll meet you there.'

They were going to Cherry's house. They'd decided that quickly and in a very unsexy way. *My dog will eat Kleenex if I don't come home tonight,* she'd said.

They hadn't discussed what they would be doing at her house. That was clear.

Cherry had never slept with someone on the first date before . . . but this *wasn't* a first date. It wasn't a date, and it wasn't their first time meeting each other. She'd spent more time with Russ than with guys she'd actually dated herself. And she'd liked him more. Wanted him more desperately.

Maybe that should worry her . . . how desperately she wanted this. But – weren't you *supposed* to want? Wasn't desire *good*? Was

Cherry not supposed to sleep with Russell Sutton because she was *too* attracted to him? Was she only supposed to have men that she *didn't* want this bad? To keep herself in check?

(This line of thinking made it seem like Cherry hadn't wanted the other men in her life. Which wasn't true or fair. But she hadn't wanted them like *this*. Never like this.) (Except for Tom.) *(Stop thinking about Tom.)*

Russ beat Cherry to her own house. He was waiting on her porch.

She let him in without wasting time on talk or touching.

Stevie was waiting, too, just inside the door. (Stevie tried to bolt out the front door every time Cherry opened it. She loved running and being chased.)

'Holy shit!' Russ exclaimed.

Stevie was all over them – she was big enough to be all over both of them at once. Jumping and barking. (She also loved new people.)

'Sorry!' Cherry said. 'Don't worry, she's sweet.'

'She's *enormous*.' Russ was backing away with his hands out. Stevie had jumped up onto his chest. She was tall enough to partner-dance with a grown man.

'Stevie, down!' Cherry ordered. 'We don't jump on people.'

'I think we do,' Russ said.

Cherry pushed the dog's shoulders away from him and got between them. 'Stevie! Calm!'

Stevie was jumping on Cherry now.

'No,' Cherry said in a stern voice. *'Down.'*

Stevie stayed up.

'House!' Cherry ordered, pointing. 'Sorry,' she said again to Russ.

Stevie was cowed by the word 'house.' Her tail dropped, and she dragged it toward her kennel.

'Good *night*,' Cherry said, giving the dog a bedtime treat and locking the wire door. She dropped a cover over the kennel so Stevie would know it was time to chill.

'Wow ...' Russ said. 'When you said you had a dog, I didn't think it was Beethoven.'

Cherry laughed. 'Sorry.'

He was looking down at himself, brushing off his shirt. 'How did she drop her entire coat on me?'

'I know, it's terrible. I never wanted a dog.'

He tilted his head up. 'I'd hate to see what dog you'd get if you *wanted* one ...'

She shook her head. 'It was –' She shrugged. 'My husband –' She shook her head again.

Russ's smile softened. 'Cherry.'

'Yeah?'

He held out his hand.

She took it.

'I am so happy to be here,' he whispered.

Cherry nodded. She looked up into his eyes. 'I didn't change my mind.'

He squeezed her hand. '*Good*. Can we ...' He looked around. He was standing near the bottom of the stairs. 'Why do you have a baby gate?'

'For the dog.'

'Smart.' He reached behind himself and unlatched it. Then glanced at Cherry. 'Yeah?'

'Yeah,' she breathed.

Russ led her past the gate – led her up her own staircase. He had a way about him. All of Cherry's anxieties stepped out of his way.

He stopped at the landing.

Cherry motioned toward her open bedroom door. Russ led her inside.

His arms closed around her again, and his head dropped, hovering over hers. 'Hey,' he said in a low voice. He was looking at her face but not in her eyes.

Cherry let her gaze fall to his cheeks. 'Hey.'

'You haven't changed at all.' Russ touched the side of her head. 'Like a flashback, seeing you tonight.'

Cherry hummed.

He petted her hair. 'So beautiful,' he said. 'Like a fucking ... *beacon*. Just ...' He kissed the side of her head. 'Cherry, Cherry.'

Cherry went a little weak at the knees. And between the ears. She hadn't been ready for the word 'beautiful.'

It wasn't that she'd never been called beautiful before – or even that she didn't *believe* she was beautiful. She just never thought that *Russ Sutton* saw her that way.

She was still reeling when he kissed her.

He kissed her.

Cherry made a little blissed-out noise at the back of her throat. She swayed on her feet, and Russ tightened his arms to hold on to her.

When he pulled his mouth away, he was smiling. Cherry smiled, too.

He kissed her again.

She reached out and found his chest. His shoulders. She held on.

Russ was a very teasey kisser. Very brushy. Pulling away constantly to smile and start over. It left Cherry off-balance. Out of breath and laughing at nothing.

He kissed her cheek, then her throat. He nosed along the neckline of her olive-green sweater. 'You and your goddamn sweaters ... I've been wanting to take off your sweater since the first time I saw you wearing one.'

Cherry shook her head like she didn't believe him. (She *didn't* believe him.) Her cheeks were dimpling.

Russ lifted his head. He grabbed her waist, hooking his thumbs in her belt loops and shaking her a little. 'Take it off,' he said in a stern but slightly silly voice. 'Right now.'

Laughter thrummed in Cherry's chest. 'You want me to take off my sweater?'

'*Right* now.' He shook her a little more. 'You're driving me crazy.'

Cherry reached for the bottom of her sweater, her anxiety catching up with her giddiness. (This was it, the big reveal. She wondered if Russ Sutton had ever seen a fat girl naked . . .) She pulled it up.

Russ groaned long and low, and started shaking Cherry's hips again before the sweater was clear of her chin. She laughed and dropped it on the floor.

'*Cherry*,' Russ sighed, manically kissing the tops of her breasts.

Cherry was wearing a very pretty pink bra with extra straps crisscrossing her cleavage. All of Cherry's bras were very pretty. (It put her in a real bind whenever she went to get acupuncture – finding something plain to wear so that the acupuncturist wouldn't think she was making a pass at him.) Cherry was wearing pretty underwear, too. She liked to lean into her strengths even when no one else could see them.

'God, you're just . . .' Russ bit her breast.

She yelped. And touched the top of his head. His floppy brown hair. So different from Tom's. *(Stop.)* 'Russ,' she let herself whisper, playing with his hair.

'This is a very vexing bra . . .' His face was still in her chest. He pulled at the decorative straps with his teeth.

She coiled her fingers in his hair. 'Why?'

'Because it looks so good on, I want it off. But then it will be gone, and I think I'll miss it.'

Cherry laughed again, humming. She was doing a lot of laughing – she might be a little delirious. She was already so turned on, and not because of anything Russ was doing. It was because he was *him*. Everything Russ was doing was on top of the him-ness. (Everything he was doing was too much, really.)

He pulled one of her bra straps down and kissed her shoulder. 'Remember those dresses you used to wear? With the cowboys? And the lassos? The little horseshoe buttons . . .'

Cherry closed her eyes. 'Uh-huh.'

'*Fuck . . .*' He pulled the strap farther down her arm and kissed the newly exposed inch of her breast. 'Were you wearing bras like this under those dresses?'

'I couldn't afford bras like this in college.'

He growled. 'I'm still going to pretend that you were, the next time I think about them.'

She tugged his hair. 'When do you think about my dresses?'

He looked up at her. 'Every time I see a cowboy. You fucking ruined Westerns for me, Cherry. I got turned on during *There Will Be Blood*.'

Cherry laughed. 'Liar.'

He kissed her cheek. 'I'm not a liar.' He kissed her chin. Her neck again. He nosed between her breasts. 'I thought about you,' he said softly. 'I thought about this.'

Cherry swallowed.

Russ pulled the cup of her bra down over her nipple. 'Fuck,' he whispered, and kissed her there.

Cherry dragged her hands down his hair, down his neck. She held on to his shoulders. He was much slighter than Tom. *(Stop.)* 'Russ,' she said.

Russ bit her nipple and sucked. Cherry swallowed again. Her face fell into his hair. He smelled good. Unfamiliar. He was sucking so gently. It was surprising – she didn't think of Russ as gentle.

Everything was surprising. It had been so long since Cherry had been touched, and so very long since she'd been touched by new hands. Bitten by new teeth.

She whined a little. Russ put an arm around her waist and pulled her in closer. His belt buckle pushed into her bare belly. She thought she could feel his cock.

He was trying to pull the other side of her bra down now, but all the fiddly pink straps were in the way. 'Okay,' Russ said, like he was fed up. 'This has served its purpose.' He reached behind Cherry with both hands to unhook her bra. She smiled up into his eyes, letting him do it. He crowded her against his chest, working on it.

'Do you want help?' Cherry asked. They were looking in each other's eyes.

Russ shook his head. 'I want to beat this level by myself.'

She laughed. 'You're so different than I was expecting...'

The clasp opened, and Russ made a noise like '*ha!*' Cherry's breasts fell loose. (She wasn't worried about *this* reveal – her breasts were very good. Round. High. She'd spent all of her teen years worrying about stretch marks and then her first boyfriend had made some rude comment about her nipples – but now that the internet was full of bare breasts, Cherry had seen enough to appreciate her own.) She made room for Russ to pull the bra away.

'How am I different?' he asked, already kissing her naked shoulder.

She touched his hair again. 'You're sweeter.'

He stood up, pulling away from her. Her bra was hanging from his hand. 'You didn't expect me to be sweet?' His eyebrows twitched down. 'Wasn't I sweet to you?'

'You...' Cherry looked at him. At his first-rate face. His expensive hair. Those deep-set blue eyes – even more arresting now that there were some lines around them. 'No, you were sweet.'

He was. Always thinking of Cherry. Asking about her life. Bringing her coffee and treats whenever he brought something for Stacia. And he was *so* sweet to Stacia.

'I don't know what I expected,' Cherry said. 'I guess I didn't expect this at all.'

'But...' Russ dropped her bra. He still looked serious. '... did you want it?'

Cherry's mouth clicked open. Her mind went blank. There were tears in her eyes, she was pretty sure. *Did she want it?*

She nodded her head.

Russ clenched his teeth, and a little muscle jumped under his eye. He pulled Cherry against him with both arms and kissed her, hard. It was still sweet somehow. Tender. His hands were on her back. He was kissing her like . . . like . . .

Well, he was kissing her like he wanted *her*. Not just this. Like Cherry was a very specific person. To him. In his arms. At this moment.

She kissed him back.

When Russ eventually took a breath, they both got a little frantic. He bit her neck. He squeezed her breasts. She started unbuttoning his shirt, and he shook it off, then yanked his undershirt over his head with one hand. (He was the sort of guy who wore undershirts.)

She smiled at his bare chest. At the dark hair across his pecs and down his belly. He was pale. A different shade of pale than Cherry. Than Tom. 'Russ . . .'

He pulled her toward her bed. Cherry unbuckled his belt.

They fell, then climbed, onto the bed. Cherry was on her back. Russ went for her fly. The waist of her jeans cut into her belly. He moved away a little, kneeling over her. 'Take them off, yeah?'

'Yeah,' Cherry said, lying back and sucking in her gut to unbutton her jeans. She hated this next part, but there was no avoiding it. *This* was the big reveal. She couldn't have sex with Russ without showing him exactly how fat she was. (Well, maybe she could – on a dark night with no moon. Or in some sort of glory hole situation.) Her vagina was very inconveniently located for subterfuge.

Cherry pushed her jeans down and decided to grab her panties, too. Russ helped, pulling everything down her legs, pushing them off the bed. Then he looked up at her. Cherry was sitting up a little. Creasing at the waist.

She still *had* a waist. Her sisters all lost theirs after their pregnancies, but Cherry was a blown-out hourglass. Wide hips. Heavy thighs. A belly that hung a little.

'I don't want to hear you complain,' her sister Joy would say. *'You're built like a Lane Bryant lingerie model.'*

'Wait till she has kids,' Honny would say.

And Cherry would think, *That'll be a long wait.*

'Cherry,' Russ said, moving toward her. His eyes were big. His glasses were smudged. 'You're so ...' He touched her hip. 'Okay,' he said, 'we'll just, um ...' He started kissing her, stupidly, his mouth loose and open. *'Jesus,* okay.'

Cherry swallowed. Still nervous. Kissing him back. 'Okay.'

'You don't know,' he said.

His chest was against hers. She reached up to his face, cradling it. 'What don't I know?'

'How bad I wanted this,' Russ said in a husky voice. 'How much I ... You're so ...'

He moved away and got rid of his pants. Got back to kissing her. They were both naked now. Their legs and arms were tangling. He lifted his head up to take off his glasses. Cherry took them from him and reached over to set them on her nightstand. He kissed her ribs as she stretched. He looked younger without his glasses. Open. She laughed.

'What?'

'I've never seen you without your glasses,' she whispered.

'I'm a bad candidate for Lasik.'

She laid a palm over his cheek. 'That's the strangest thing anyone has ever said to seduce me.'

Russ laughed. She laughed with him. 'You laugh a lot during sex,' he said.

'We're not having sex.'

'Okay, you laugh a lot during foreplay.' They were both whispering.

Cherry laughed again. She wrinkled her nose. 'I think I'm just glad that you're here.'

Russ was lying half on top of her. She could feel his cock on her hip. Hard. A little wet. He kissed her again – like he was glad, too. She could feel him smiling. He took a breath and whispered, 'What's our plan for birth control?'

'Oh.' Cherry realized that she hadn't thought about it. *How had she not thought about it?* 'I'm not on anything.'

Russ ran his hand up the inside of her thigh. 'We could just ...'

His fingers got to her vagina. (Cherry was old enough to call the whole area 'vagina'; she hadn't gotten on board with modern precision labeling.) She braced again for him to feel how fat she was. Every part of her, even this one. (Cherry's vagina was *substantial*. She wasn't one of those women with just a hint of lip. A *sliver* of labia.)

His hand curved around her, and his eyes closed. '*Fuck*,' he said – like he was cursing, not suggesting. '*Cherry*.' And then, 'We could just ...'

She hummed. He was rubbing along the seam, feeling how wet she was. Feeling the split. His fingers slid back and down into the canal, the vagina proper. Cherry groaned. '*Fuck*,' Russ said again.

She opened her legs, and his fingers sank deeper.

He looked up at her face. Cherry was still holding his cheek. She kissed his nose. He pumped his fingers, and she made a noise that was half sigh, half whine.

'We could just ...' he said again, swallowing.

'Oh.' Cherry sat up. Suddenly. Her shoulder hit Russ's forehead.

He jerked back, surprised, and pulled his hand away.

'I think I have ...' Cherry leaned toward the nightstand again, opened a small drawer, and came back with a strip of condoms. She and Tom had used condoms, and period tracking – Cherry didn't do well on the pill. But it had been a long time ...

She squinted at a packet, looking for an expiration date. 'A-*ha*,' she said. 'We're in business.'

Russ laughed and grabbed the strip out of Cherry's hands. He pulled her close again, levered her back onto the bed, and pushed his hand back into her pussy. Less gently this time. He rubbed his palm into her clit. '*Oh*,' Cherry said.

'Good?' he asked.

She nodded. It *was* good. She could maybe come like this. Eventually. It wasn't what she was used to. She was used to Tom's thick fingers. Or her own. Not the flat of an unfamiliar palm.

Cherry was worried suddenly that she wouldn't be *able* to come, not on demand like this, even though she really wanted to. Even though she really wanted *Russ*.

Had the clock already started? This was the thing now, right – the woman comes first?

Back in college, it had taken several tries for Cherry to work out an orgasm with the guys she slept with. And coming was come-and-go at first with Tom. Tom's approach to her body had changed over time, as he got to know her better. As Cherry felt more comfortable giving direction, and Tom felt more comfortable taking it . . .

(Cherry knew that she shouldn't be thinking about Tom right now, but how could she *not* think about him? She'd been married to him for *eight years*. He was the only man her body recognized. This was his *bed*, for god's sake.)

'Cherry,' Russ whispered, kissing her cheek. He pushed his fingers in deeper, giving her clit a break.

Cherry groaned. This was a less complicated feeling – she liked being fucked. She wanted more of it. She tried to think of a way to say so that wasn't '*Just do it.*'

She pulled Russ's body closer, spread her legs wider.

He got the message. 'Yeah,' he said, lifting off of her to put on a condom.

Cherry had one more discordant moment when Russ slid into her. Another *Tom! Tom! Tom!* moment –

Cherry wasn't supposed to be doing *this with someone else! No one else was supposed to be in* her body *like this! She* belonged *to someone!*

But he was gone.

Tom was gone.

'Cherry,' Russ said. Between her legs. Holding himself above her torso. His eyes were half closed. 'You're so . . .'

'Russ,' she said, arching up into him.

Russ looked gorgeous. Flushed. Alive. He was already thrusting into her with purpose. It felt amazing.

Maybe the universe knew that Cherry needed the most desirable man in her personal history to fuck her back to life again. (*'Stop saying "the universe" when you mean God,'* she heard Honny say again. But would God have sent Russ Sutton to have sex with Cherry? He *did* move in mysterious ways . . .)

Russ's head was hanging over hers. He still looked like Bono. He grinned down at her, and Cherry grinned back. Both of them were panting.

He reached down between their bodies, but there wasn't room for his hand. He lifted up to make space. Found Cherry's clit again, rubbed it. His forearm was pressed into her belly. He said, 'What do you need, baby?'

Cherry froze. *'What?'*

Russ's hand stopped moving. 'Does that hurt?'

'No. No, it's good.'

He rubbed her clit again, more gently. 'You feel so good . . . I want you to feel good.'

'I want . . .' Cherry said. 'Can I come after?'

Russ smiled. 'You can come whenever you *want*.' He pulled his hand up and dropped onto his elbows, rocking his hips forward. His flat stomach pressed into hers. Cherry felt bigger than him in every way like this – but she felt good. She moved with him. Held him.

Russ was still sweet, even now. Looking in her eyes. He raised his eyebrows like, *Isn't this great?* and Cherry nodded.

Once, back in college, they'd all gone to the grocery store together, and Stacia had left Russ and Cherry in the freezer section to pick out ice cream while she went to get tampons – *'Stay with Cherry, I need to do some lady shopping'* – and a Billy Joel song had started playing over the store speakers. 'Leave a Tender Moment Alone.'

Russ had grabbed Cherry's hand and pulled her close, wrapping his other arm around her waist. They knew each other so well by then that Cherry didn't even ask what he was doing. She just smiled up at him as he rocked her back and forth to the music. She loved the way Russ moved. She loved the way he moved her. He swept her all the way down the aisle, to frozen vegetables, and Cherry was completely at ease when he tipped her back over his arm into a dip.

'I wanted this so bad,' he said now. He was breathing harder.

Cherry nodded again.

'I wanted you,' he said. 'From the moment I saw you. *Cherry.*'

Cherry touched his face.

He kissed her wrist, then lifted up onto his hands. 'Did you . . . Tell me you wanted this, too.'

'I . . .'

Russ's face was flushed. His hips were insistent. 'Tell me you wanted it.'

'I wanted it,' she said.

'*Tell* me.'

'I wanted you.'

He shook his head, like he was trying to hold back. 'From the moment I met you, Cherry.'

'Russ.'

He pushed in hard. 'In that goddamn sweater.'

'I always wanted you,' she said. Guilty. Thrilled. 'I was crazy about you, Russ.' Honest.

Russ bit his bottom lip when he came.

Then he went soft all over and affectionate. Puppyish. Kissing her neck and chest with his mouth open. Cherry didn't expect it. The unabated *sweetness* of him.

He lifted out of her and fell on his side, kissing her shoulders, smiling. Catching his breath. 'Is now "after"?'

Cherry nodded her head. She was *still* reeling.

He touched her with his fingers and then with his palm, and

whispered her name in her ear as she came. Then he kissed her so furiously that she thought they might start all over, but instead they kissed each other half to sleep.

Cherry drifted off with her cheek on Russ's shoulder.

She woke up at three a.m.

Russ was dressed and standing by her bed. He said he had to get home, that he had his kid first thing in the morning. He wanted Cherry's phone number.

She gave it to him, and he kissed her cheek and told her to go back to sleep.

Chapter 7

Yesterday 7:22 PM

Joy

THE THURSDAY TRAILER JUST DROPPED! THIS IS NOT A DRILL!!!

Honny

Oh my God, Cherry – are you seeing this??

It's even worse than we thought.

Joy

It's so much worse that it's BETTER!!!

I mean, the actress playing Baby!! I CAN'T LOOK AWAY!

Honny

That girl isn't even fat – she just has a big head.

Joy

She's Hollywood fat, probably a size 6.

Honny

I think she might be wearing padding . . .

Joy

NO!!!

Honny

Yes! Watch it again, and look at her butt!

Joy

AHHHHH! You're right!!

This is problematic! I'm offended!!!!

Faith

You are so much prettier than this actress, Cherry.

Joy

Like a thousand times prettier!!!

But Jesse Plemons is WAYYY hotter than Tom!

Honny

Agreed.

Faith

Oh, I don't think so . . .

Joy

OF COURSE Tom made sure that a handsome actor was playing him . . .

Honny

IS Jesse Plemons handsome? When Cherry said it was the guy from Friday Night Lights, I thought she meant the other one. Tim Riggins.

Joy

WHY WOULD TIM RIGGINS PLAY TOM??? I AM DYING!!!

Honny

You should be flattered that this actress is wearing padding, Cherry. Your butt is inimitable. They had to use special effects, and they still couldn't match it.

Joy

I kind of wanted Melissa McCarthy to play Cherry :(

Faith

You mean to play Baby.

Honny

Melissa McCarthy is too old – and now she's too skinny. Ozempic strikes again.

Faith

That's unconfirmed. Maybe she lost it the old-fashioned way.

Honny

Starvation?

Joy

Melissa McCarthy would have been great – she has Cherry's dimples!

Honny

Melissa McCarthy has your dimples, Joy. Get over yourself.

Joy

Cherry and I have the SAME dimples!!

Faith

Doesn't it feel kind of weird to watch real people play these characters?

Honny

Were you expecting a cartoon, Faith? We knew that the movie wasn't animated.

Faith

I don't know what I was expecting . . .

I'm so used to seeing the characters in a comic strip, and then suddenly there they were on screen – real people. But not the *actual* real people. It kind of gave me the heebie-jeebies.

JOY

CHERRY, WHERE ARE YOU?? HAVE YOU WATCHED IT YET???

Honny

Text her, Joy.

Maybe she has the group chat muted.

Faith

Shouldn't we be talking about all this on the 'SISTERS' thread, with Hope?

Honny

No dice – this is a fat-girl-only conversation. No skinnies allowed.

Faith

You can't say that about everything, Honny.

I don't like having a group chat called 'NO HOPE.' It's perverse.

Honny

I only named it that so that we don't accidentally hurt Hope's feelings!

Joy

What size do you think Hope is these days? Maybe a 12 or 14?? Does that count as 'skinny'???

Honny

Skinny enough! I haven't been a size 14 since sixth grade.

Faith

None of us have, Honny!

Honny

Well, I rest my case!

Joy

CHERRY! Where are you??? We are DYING to talk to you about this trailer!!

Honny

You shouldn't mute the group chat, Cherry. What if something happened to Mom?

Faith

If something happens to Mom, you guys better use the other thread!

Today 9:10 AM

Cherry

If something happened to Mom, I hope you would CALL.

Joy

CHERRY!!!! THERE YOU ARE!!

Honny

I can't believe you left us hanging for 14 hours!! Have you watched the trailer yet?

Cherry
Nope. And I'm not going to.

Joy
What?? You HAVE to watch it!!

Cherry
I don't HAVE to do anything but pay my bills and feed Tom's dog.

Faith
Cherry! Where were you last night?
We were worried.

Cherry
I went to a concert, and then I went to sleep. Unburdened by Tom's movie trailer.

Honny
I'll bet you were still burdened . . .

Faith
You went to a concert?

Joy
The actress playing you is all wrong, Cherry!!
We think she's wearing padding. And she has hollow eyes : (

Faith
She means the actress playing Baby.

Honny
Oh, she's definitely wearing padding. They scoured the whole of Los Angeles to find someone bigger than a size 2, and all they could find was a fish-eyed British lady with a big head.

Cherry

Unsurprising. Hollywood only ever had three fat actresses, and now they're all on Danish weight loss drugs.

Faith

You're so much prettier than that actress, Cherry.

Honny

That goes without saying.

Joy

I'll say it. You're WAY prettier!!

Honny

You should have had the right to approve your likeness.

Cherry

It's NOT me.

It was never me. And if I watch this trailer, it's just going to be one more thing I can't unsee and that I can't do anything about.

Honny

I guess that's fair . . .

Cherry

Thanks for your permission, Honny.

Faith

Sorry, Cherry. We'll stop talking about it.

Honny

. . . to YOU.

We're still going to talk about it amongst ourselves. We're going to mock this film at every turn.

Joy

Does this mean another group thread???? My life is already too complicated!!

Chapter 8

Today 9:35 AM

Hope
Oh my God, have you guys seen the Thursday trailer? The actress playing Baby is 100% wearing a fat suit.

Honny
Cherry doesn't want to watch it or talk about it.

Faith
She doesn't want to see it and then not be able to unsee it.

Joy
IX-NAY ON THE URSDAY-THAY!!!

Hope
Oh. Sorry, Cherry.

Cherry
It's okay. I know that I can't totally avoid this movie . . . but I don't want to *invite* it into my life.

Hope

That makes sense. I won't mention it again.

Let me just say this . . .

You are so much prettier than this actress. And she has dead eyes.

Cherry

Thanks, Hope <3

Chapter 9

Cherry was *not* Baby.

Baby was a supporting character in a cult webcomic turned blockbuster graphic novel turned major motion picture.

Baby was a drawing.

She looked like Cherry. She talked like Cherry. Sometimes she did things that Cherry did. Sometimes she said the exact same things that Cherry had said.

But Baby wasn't Cherry.

Baby still belonged to Tom.

Chapter 10

Cherry had woken up to more than a hundred messages from her sisters – on six different threads. If she'd tried to ignore them any longer, Honny might have called the police. (Or had Joy do it.) Cherry was very rarely the focus of her sisters' attention, but she was still expected to show up and play her part.

Cherry was the middle child. The third of five girls. In *Pride and Prejudice*, that would have made her Mary – the most forgettable Bennet sister.

Cherry was *not* forgettable. No one would ever call her mild-mannered or receding . . .

Unless they'd met her sisters.

Her sisters were just *a lot*. They were all loud, all confident. All *bossy*. Honny was so bossy, she'd practically usurped Hope as the oldest child. Sometimes it felt like someone had accidentally sent five eldest daughters to the same family.

First came Hope, who was forty-two. She was the sharpest of them. And the biggest goody two-shoes. The most pulled-together. (It figured that Hope would be the one to lose weight.)

Honny came next at thirty-nine. Her name was actually Honor, but everybody called her Honny, like 'Honey.' (*Hope, Honor, Cherish, Joy, Faith* – their names were a whole thing.)

Honny was the pushiest and the funniest. And the most dangerous. As a kid, she'd talk everybody else into doing something naughty and then be the one to tell on them.

Cherry came along three years after Honny.

And then Joy came a year after that. Joy was thirty-five and the most beautiful – she looked like a fat Sophia Loren. She was also the most excitable and the easiest to influence. Joy took Honny's side in all things.

Faith was the baby at thirty-two. She was the most like their mom – which meant she was sweet and sort of humorless, but still very bossy. Faith got her way by making you feel guilty about even questioning her.

Cherry could have been a real Lucy Van Pelt in someone else's family – the Beyoncé, or even the Meg March. But in her own family, she was always relegated to the back seat. Usually the third row.

Part of it was that her sisters had bigger, busier lives than she did. They were all married with kids, and all active in their big evangelical church. (Only Cherry had ventured off the path to righteousness.) With children depending on them and God watching over them, her sisters had a lot more at stake.

And part of it was just that Cherry got tired of shouting over the four of them. She'd learned at an early age to save her voice.

Cherry set her phone on the nightstand and crawled back under the covers, feeling the sheets slide over her bare skin. She'd have to get up soon, to feed Stevie.

That was the best and worst thing about having a dog ... You *couldn't* stay in bed all day. Cherry had been a zombie for months after Tom left. (After Tom hadn't come home.) She'd just been going through the motions. But she had work, and she had Stevie – so there *was* motion. There were weeks when she fed Stevie more consistently than she fed herself.

It was already a half hour past Stevie's usual breakfast time, but Cherry really, *really* didn't want to get up. Or get dressed. Her nakedness was the only proof that something almost inconceivable had happened in this room last night ...

Cherry had slept with Russell Sutton.

Cherry. And *Russ.*

She shook her head every time she thought about it. (She'd been covering her eyes and shaking her head since she woke up.) She wanted to call someone and shout about it – maybe that would make it feel more real – but the only person who would truly grasp the significance was Stacia, and Cherry was *never* telling Stacia.

She couldn't tell her churchy sisters, either. (Much as she'd like to drop it in the group chat.) They didn't believe in premarital sex, let alone not-quite-divorced sex.

Cherry knew that her sisters blamed her divorce on her *lack* of churchiness. If she'd married a good Christian man, he'd still be here. And Cherry would have babies. She'd be fat and happy like the rest of them – instead of slightly less fat and alone.

Cherry pulled the covers up over her head. The bed creaked.

Stevie instantly started whimpering downstairs. She'd slept in her kennel. She must have been listening for signs of life.

'Right,' Cherry said, hauling herself up. She felt self-conscious now, walking through her bedroom stark naked. Thank god she hadn't turned on any lights last night, and that Russ had snuck out before daybreak – Cherry hadn't done anything to change this room when Tom left. (When Tom left, they'd both been expecting him to come home.) His spare change was still sitting on his bedside table … His lip balm. A few receipts. A book of puzzles that he liked to work on when he couldn't sleep.

All of Tom's clothes were still in his dresser – he hadn't asked for her to send them anywhere. His Kansas City Royals cap was still hanging off the lamp by their bed.

Downstairs was worse: Tom's books. Tom's movies. Tom's Nintendo Switch. Tom's boots by the door. Framed photos of Tom and his mom that Cherry had hung up in the dining room. (Tom's fifth birthday party. Tom riding an elephant at the Henry Doorly Zoo.)

Whenever Cherry tried to address this situation – to consider making a plan to start clearing some of his things away – she could feel gravity increasing around her. Just *thinking* about it made Cherry feel so heavy and tired, she'd have to sit down immediately, and sometimes she wouldn't get up again for hours.

It was better for her productivity and state of mind if she *didn't* think about it. That was doable. Cherry could move through her house without making eye contact with any of Tom's things. Or any of the things that were too much theirs together ... Disney World souvenirs. An afghan Cherry had crocheted for him. A Jonathan Adler vase he'd given her on their anniversary. Cherry just didn't let her eyes focus in certain directions.

It was a good thing no one in her family ever came over to visit. Her sisters had kids, so Cherry went to them. Same deal with Stacia. Nobody came to Cherry's house. No one knew how she was living.

Cherry put on yoga pants and a T-shirt – she'd meant to buy a Goldenrod T-shirt at the concert – and went downstairs to feed Stevie.

To make some oatmeal.

To start some laundry and vacuum.

There was no sign anywhere that anything out of the ordinary had happened last night.

Russ hadn't left a note. He hadn't left his jacket. Or a business card. Or a trace.

And Cherry didn't have his number.

Chapter 11

Cherry kind of forgot that the whole world would be able to watch Tom's movie trailer. Including everyone at work.

People who had never mentioned the *Thursday* comics – even when the books were runaway bestsellers, even when Tom was on *The Late Show* – were suddenly very interested in the *Thursday* movie.

Cherry had meetings all day Monday, and every one started with, 'I saw the trailer for your husband's movie!' (Almost no one at work knew that Cherry and Tom were separated.)

'Well, it sure looks good,' someone would say.
'It *does* look good,' Cherry would reply.
'They've got that actress playing you, the one from the thing.'
'Oh, she's not playing *me*.'
'I thought she had a British accent?'
'Acting, I guess.'
'I guess you'll get to go to the big premiere.'
'We'll see.'
'Did you get to meet Kathy Bates?'
'No. I wish.'
'She was great on *The Office*.'
'I agree.'
'Say, did they try to get Alexander Payne for the movie?'
'I'm not sure . . .'
'That would have been cool.'
'It would have.'

'Then they could have filmed it in Omaha – and we *all* could have met Kathy Bates.'

'That would have been *really* cool.'

'Well, you tell your husband that we're all excited for him.'

'I will.'

'Tell him we want to meet Kathy Bates!'

The last meeting of the day ended at 5:15. Cherry felt done in. She was sweating through her blouse under her wool jacket, and she'd rubbed all her eyeshadow off onto her hands.

She stayed in the conference room to gather her papers. And her defenses.

Meg Jones, Cherry's boss, stepped into the doorway. She was wearing a cashmere coat and holding a pebbled leather satchel. She was on her way out. 'You doing okay?'

Meg had been in all the meetings, too. And she was the only other person in the building who knew that Tom was gone.

'Yeah,' Cherry said, waving her hand. 'Fine.'

'Are you sure? Because you look like the stock photo we used for that Employee Health brochure on depression.'

Meg Jones was in charge of all the railroad's communications, internal and external. Cherry was her second in command.

'*When It's All Too Much*,' Cherry said.

Meg nodded.

Cherry started to cry.

Meg sighed and stepped into the conference room, shutting the door behind her. 'I see.'

'Sorry,' Cherry said, fanning her cheeks. 'I'm sorry.'

'Don't apologize. I almost started crying myself when that idiot from legal wouldn't shut up during the planning meeting.'

Cherry didn't believe that Meg Jones had *ever* almost cried. She was the most composed woman that Cherry had ever met. (To be a female vice president at a railroad, you had to make people forget you were a woman at all.)

Cherry got a Kleenex out of her bag. 'You mean when he asked if the girl from *Bridgerton* had gained weight to play me?' She blew her nose. 'That actress wasn't even on *Bridgerton*.'

Meg frowned. This was her sympathy frown, Cherry knew. They'd been working together long enough that Cherry could read all of Meg's microexpressions.

'You know . . .' Meg said, 'you could tell people that you're getting a divorce. There's no shame in it. Three-fourths of the executive team is divorced.' Meg Jones herself had been divorced twice.

Cherry shook her head and pressed her fingers into her eyes, trying to stop the tears at their source. 'No. I don't want them gossiping about me. I don't want *that* to be the thing that gets attached to my name – "*Cherry, that fat lady in Comms who used to be married to the famous artist.*"'

'Hmph,' Meg said. 'More like "*That ferocious badass in Comms who used to be married to some weird nerd.*"'

Cherry rolled her eyes and kept going – '"*I heard her husband left her the second he got famous.*"'

Meg frowned more deeply. Her face barely moved. 'You've got to stop thinking like this, Cherry. You have to keep your head up and set the narrative.'

Cherry looked into Meg's eyes. She couldn't tell if she was getting personal advice or an order from her supervisor. With Meg Jones, there was never much distinction.

Cherry nodded. 'I'm sorry. I'll do better.'

Meg sighed again and dug into her bag, pulling out a silk scarf. 'Stop apologizing. This is the first time I've seen you cry about Tom.'

'I usually do it in my office with the door closed.'

'That's what offices are for.' Meg buttoned her coat. 'Did *you* watch the trailer?'

'No,' Cherry said. 'I'm not going to.'

'Good mental hygiene, Cherry. There's nothing for you there.

There's nothing for anyone – that actress has doll eyes and a face full of fillers. She can hardly blink.'

Cherry smiled. From Meg Jones, this was practically maternal. (Meg's age was undeterminable; she was *possibly* old enough to be Cherry's mother.)

Meg wrapped the scarf around her neck and tucked it into her collar. 'You should sleep with someone else, you know. You won't move on until you do.'

That caught Cherry off guard. Was it more career advice? They'd never talked about sex before ... But maybe they *could*? Strategically? Meg Jones wasn't a prude, and Cherry was still dying to say this out loud ...

'Actually,' she said, sitting up a bit. 'I did.'

Meg stopped adjusting her scarf. 'You *did?*'

Cherry nodded. She found herself smiling.

Meg smiled, too. Like a shark. 'Who?'

'An acquaintance. Someone I saw at a concert.'

'You picked up a man at a concert? Cherry, this is very unlike you.'

Cherry could feel herself blushing. 'I mean – I *have* been married for almost ten years, so I wasn't really in the market ...'

'That wasn't criticism.'

'Okay, well ...'

Meg looked sharp. 'Is this someone you'll see again?'

'Oh ...' Cherry looked down. 'I don't know. Probably not. He took my number, but ... that was Friday night, and he hasn't called. I don't think I'm the sort of person he dates.' When Cherry looked up, Meg's eyes had narrowed. 'I don't even *know* if he dates,' Cherry said. 'He has a kid. It felt very ... in the moment. Like – *a* moment, you know? A night.'

Meg nodded slowly. 'Good.' She pulled the handle of her bag up onto her shoulder. 'You're alive, Cherry. Act like it.'

With that, she opened the door behind her and walked out.

(Meg Jones was never much for 'hello' and 'good-bye.' She started meetings with 'let's get to it.')

Cherry looked back at the table. She picked up her notebook and papers and slid them into her bag. She was still holding a Kleenex, but she realized that she wasn't crying anymore.

She took her phone out of her bag. (She always silenced it during meetings.) She'd gotten the usual deluge of texts from her sisters and her mom, plus two messages from an unknown number:

Three cherry emojis.

Then, *'We should go on a date.'*

Chapter 12

The next weekend, Cherry went on a date with Russ Sutton.

Sort of a date – he invited her to his house for dinner.

He came to the door wearing a blue cardigan and gold khakis, and Cherry laughed when she saw his face because she still couldn't believe he'd walked back into her life, and this time, somehow, directly into her arms.

Russ laughed, too, and hauled Cherry inside by her wrist. 'Get in here.'

His house was small, in an up-and-coming neighborhood. Craftsman-style, with two bedrooms – one for his son, Liam, who lived with Russ not quite half the time. Russ's ex had a bigger house in a better neighborhood. 'Divorce,' Russ said lightly, fussing with some garlic bread and putting it back in the oven. He'd also made pasta and Alison Roman's Bolognese sauce – he had a crush on Alison Roman.

It was more carbs than Cherry would usually have in one meal. Or in one day. (Everyone in Cherry's family had high blood sugar. She tried not to eat anything white.)

They ate at a small kitchen table. Russ used the dining room as a home office. Liam had a desk in there, too, 'for homework and *Minecraft*.' The house was very minimally decorated. There were a few framed concert posters in the living room. And lots of pictures of Liam. (Light brown hair, Russ's deep-set eyes. Apparently very into soccer.) Cherry's mind skated past the possibility of being a stepmother, then quickly skated away.

She and Russ talked like old friends. They *were* old friends. They spun in different circles now, but adjacent circles. They had so many acquaintances in common, it was a shock they'd never run into each other. Cherry's social life was more private than Russ's – dinner parties, family gatherings. Russ liked to go *out*. He went to fundraisers and did charity walks. He volunteered for boards. He was like a kid building his résumé for college applications. 'Are you running for office?' Cherry asked him.

'No,' he said, like she was being silly. And then – 'Not yet, anyway. I'm waiting for my state senator to run for congress.'

She smiled. 'I'll vote for you.'

'You're not in my district.'

'Huh. I can't believe you slept with me for nothing.'

He barked out a laugh. Russ had a great laugh. He really should run for office. He was that rare brand of charming that didn't seem thin or false.

They were done with dinner. Cherry was sitting across from him, winding her cloth napkin around her fingers.

'You look nice tonight,' he said.

'Oh,' Cherry said. 'Thank you.' She was wearing a snug knit fit-and-flare dress, dark purple, with big blousy sleeves. It was the most sweatery outfit she owned. (Cherry would have worn one of her old rockabilly dresses tonight if any of them still fit.) (Maybe she should try one on; she'd lost weight since Tom left. She was solidly a size eighteen at the moment.) She'd worn gray cable-knit tights and calf-length boots, but she'd taken off her boots at the door. She felt like a little kid, in her stocking feet.

'You also look nice,' she said. 'I like your cardigan.'

Russ looked pleased. 'Thanks.'

'You always look nice,' Cherry said. 'I mean ... in my distant experience. I always liked the way you dressed.'

'You did?'

She narrowed her eyes. 'Don't play dumb. You know you're a snazzy dresser.'

He laughed. 'Snazzy.'

'I've always liked your glasses,' Cherry went on. She couldn't help herself – she needed *someone* to talk to about him. 'I'm glad you haven't switched it up.'

'This is going really well,' Russ said.

'What is?'

'Our date.'

She laughed. 'It's going okay . . .'

He shook his head. His eyes didn't leave hers. 'No. I think it's going *really well*.'

Cherry's voice was soft – 'Are you trying to hypnotize me again?'

He shook his head more slowly.

'I should tell you,' she said, still soft, 'that I don't stay over on the first date.'

He raised an eyebrow.

'I know what you're thinking,' Cherry said, 'but that *wasn't* a date.'

'Huh . . .' Russ suddenly dropped from the chair to his knees.

'What are you doing?'

He was knee-walking over to her. 'Well . . .' He put his hands on her hips, pushing between her knees (she opened them). 'If you're not staying over, we better get to it.'

Cherry shook her head, laughing.

'I'm just kidding,' he said, wrapping his arms around Cherry's waist. He craned his neck, lifting his chin up to her.

Cherry leaned over to kiss him.

Russ's kisses were just like the rest of him: Clever. Confident. Surprisingly sweet. He brought one hand down her thigh and then up her skirt. He stroked her tights with his thumb . . .

After a few good minutes of kissing, he pulled away and hopped to his feet. Cherry had to lean back so they didn't hit heads. 'Come here,' he said. 'I want to show you something.'

She stood up. 'Do you want me to put my dish somewhere?'

Russ was on the way to the living room. 'Leave it.'

Cherry followed him.

He walked over to a very crowded bookshelf – if you ever needed to borrow the biography of a Democratic politician, Russ Sutton was your man – and motioned toward the couch. 'Sit down.' She did. 'I went looking for this yesterday,' he said. 'I knew I had it. I save everything.' He grabbed a piece of paper – an eight-by-ten photo – and sat down on the couch right next to Cherry, handing it to her.

It was a black-and-white snapshot of the two of them, dancing at the Galway on the night they first met. Russ was holding Cherry close in the picture – he'd probably just reeled her back into his arms. They were both smiling, but they looked surprised, too, like they were completely in the moment, delighted, unsure what would happen next.

Russ looked young and gorgeous. That hair. Those dark lips. His eyes shining.

And Cherry . . .

She felt slapped in the face by how good she looked in this photo. It was like she was looking at someone else, someone objectively beautiful. Her hair was dark. Her eyes were bright. Her breasts were practically touching her chin. This was a peach of a girl.

'Where did this *come* from?' she asked.

Russ put his arm around her shoulders. 'One of my friends was a photographer for the *Creightonian*. He took his camera everywhere.'

Cherry stared at the picture. 'I can't believe this exists.'

He squeezed her. 'It's kind of magical, right? How often do you have a photo of the moment you met someone?'

'This isn't the moment *we* met . . .'

'Close enough.'

What she meant was, it wasn't *just* the moment they met – it was the moment he met Stacia, too. His friend's camera had been pointed in the wrong direction. Russ himself had been pointed in the wrong direction.

'I remember everything about that dance,' Russ said.

Cherry shook her head, still hardly believing the photo was real. 'We look so young . . .'

'You look exactly the same.' He kissed her neck.

She shook her head again.

Chapter 13

Stacia's son was turning three, and Cherry was invited to the party.

This was when Cherry saw the adults in her life now, when their kids had parties. Between her nieces and nephews and all of her friends' kids, she could eat cake almost every weekend if she wanted.

A three-year-old's birthday party was still mostly for the parents. There were more adults than kids at this one. Stacia and her husband, Jim, were serving wine spritzers.

They'd rented a ball pit with a slide and set it up in their family room. (The family room was *huge*. The whole main floor was open plan.) Jim and a few other dads were standing over the pit like lifeguards.

Cherry was sitting at the bar in the kitchen, eating spinach dip and grain-free tortilla chips. Stacia and Jim didn't do gluten. The party had been spritzing for a couple hours already.

Stacia came to lean on the other side of the counter. She sighed. She was wearing white pants and a cropped white sweatshirt. All her jewelry was gold. 'Sorry I haven't said hello.'

'You said hello,' Cherry said.

Stacia glanced around them. 'I wasn't expecting all these *people* – I don't know why Jim invited his sand volleyball team.'

Cherry smiled. She liked Jim. 'It seems like the perfect amount of people. Everyone's having a good time.'

Stacia was still looking around. 'You know what, I should introduce you to some of these volleyball players ... A few of them are single.'

This was something that Stacia had started in the last couple months – and something she used to do before Tom. She'd make a fuss about how she was going to fix Cherry up. As if anyone in Stacia's circle would date a fat person.

Stacia had grown up beautiful with money, and then married someone beautiful with money. Her kids went to expensive schools, and she worked out at an expensive gym. Her clothes all looked like something Meghan Markle would wear on casual Friday. And most of her friends had a similar vibe.

Cherry had always been the outlier. Cherry had been a scholarship kid at Creighton. She was poor and fat and artsy. She and Stacia might never have become friends if they hadn't been thrown together as roommates freshman year. They lived together all through college.

After Cherry graduated and got a corporate job – and several promotions – her world had moved closer to Stacia's. Cherry worked almost exclusively with Stacia types now, on the top floor of the Western Alliance building, but she still never quite felt like she belonged.

Stacia's other friends had stayed skinny even as they got older and had kids. Actually, none of them seemed to be *getting* older. According to Stacia, they were all on semaglutide and testosterone – so they were skinnier and hornier than ever.

This checked out; Cherry was the only one eating the spinach dip.

Stacia herself was naturally lean and worked hard to stay that way. Her husband frowned on prescription drugs, so there was no Mounjaro in her life. (Stacia wasn't even vaccinated for Covid.)

Cherry got through Stacia's parties the same way she'd gotten through college surrounded by upper-middle-class, thin people – by keeping her chin up and being a good hang. People generally liked Cherry.

But there was no amount of good humor, or wine spritzers, that would make anyone at this party romantically interested in her.

'I'm serious,' Stacia said. 'You should think about it.'

'About dating a sand volleyball player?'

'About dating *someone*. It's been almost a year.'

'Well.' Cherry tipped her head and stuck a chip in the spinach dip. 'Sort of.'

Tom had left a year ago, but they'd only been separated for six months.

'I know you're not ready' – Stacia grabbed a handful of chips – 'but you might never *be* ready. You don't want to wallow away your youth.'

In Stacia's mind, the worst thing Tom had done was waste Cherry's fertile years. (Cherry's sisters would agree.)

'I'm not wallowing,' Cherry said.

'The last time I asked about your weekend, you told me you were making curtains.'

'I've always made curtains. I'm crafty.'

'Yeah, but it was different when you were married. Single women shouldn't be making curtains on weekends. It's getting you nowhere.'

'Where am I supposed to be going?'

'Forward,' Stacia said. 'Into the future.'

'I'm not defying the rules of time and space by making curtains. The future will still happen.'

Stacia dug into the spinach dip, frowning. 'Cherry, you know what I mean. You're treading water.'

'You're supposed to be happy that I didn't drown.'

'I *am*.' Stacia sighed and repeated herself in a nicer voice, looking in Cherry's eyes. 'I am. But I don't want you to end up like' – her voice dropped – '*Elaine*.'

Jim's mother had never gotten over her husband cheating on her with his receptionist. (He was a chiropractor, too.) She'd never remarried or even dated, and now she was too much a part of Jim and Stacia's life. Elaine was never happy. She was sitting in the family room now, probably sighing.

'You've got to get back out there,' Stacia said. 'Before you're ready.'

Cherry had already decided not to tell Stacia about Russ. Not yet. Maybe not ever.

Whatever was happening with Russ Sutton might not even turn into anything real. Cherry had seen him four times so far – including the night they hooked up – and they hadn't had sex again. She wasn't exactly sure why not. Maybe Russ had taken her seriously when she'd said that she didn't usually rush into sex. Or maybe *he* felt like they'd rushed in.

Maybe Russ was trying to figure out whether he actually wanted Cherry. In a regular, ongoing way. During daylight.

She couldn't hold that against him. That was just dating, right?

'I just don't want you to waste any more young, hot years on Tom,' Stacia was saying. 'You gave him plenty.'

'Look,' Cherry said. 'I'm not wallowing. I promise.'

'Cherry –'

'I'm seeing someone.' It came out before Cherry could stop herself. 'I mean, I *have* seen someone. A few times.'

Stacia's eyes got huge. Her mouth dropped open, full of spinach dip. '*What?*' She leaned over the counter to grab Cherry's arm. (Still with that long torso.) 'Who?!'

'It's so new,' Cherry said. 'There's nothing to talk about yet.'

Stacia pinched Cherry's arm. '*Who!*'

'*Ow.* Stacia!'

Stacia let go. 'Cherry, you can't not talk to me about this. I'm your oldest friend.'

Cherry wrinkled her nose. 'Are you? I've known Jena since grade school . . .'

'You never even talk to Jena. She was a bitch to you at your wedding.'

Cherry took a breath. 'I . . . um . . . Okay –'

'Wait,' Stacia said, like she'd just thought of something. 'Is it a guy?'

'*Yes.*' Cherry goggled her eyes. 'Why would you even ask that?'

'I don't know . . .' Stacia shrugged. 'You have a lot of LBGTQIA friends.'

'Do you even know what all those letters stand for?'

'Yes. I did a seminar at the clinic – so, suck it. Now, tell me where you met this guy. Did you join the apps?' She stuck out her bottom lip. 'You told me that you'd let me take pictures for your profile when you joined the apps.'

'I didn't join the apps. It was someone I already knew –'

'Oh god, it's that married guy who always flirts with you during meetings! This is a terrible idea, Cherry.'

'Stacia, no. Stop guessing. It's –' Cherry made a face like she was about to drop a drinking glass on a tile floor. 'It's Russ.'

Stacia didn't react. 'Russ who?'

Cherry sighed. '*Russ*. Russ Sutton.'

Stacia pulled her chin into her neck. '*My* Russ?'

Cherry nodded.

'Oh my god.' Stacia's eyes were big again. 'Really? He works in the mayor's office now.'

'I know.'

'Did you *call* him?' She seemed shocked.

'*No.* We just ran into each other, like, two weeks ago.'

'Cherry, are you *sleeping* with Russ Sutton?'

'*No.*' Cherry grimaced. 'I mean, yes. Yes, but not much.'

'Oh my god,' Stacia said again, looking over Cherry's head. '*Wow.* Wow, wow, wow.'

'Stacia, I'm sorry.'

Her eyes snapped back to Cherry. 'Don't be sorry. It's been fifteen years.'

'Yeah, but there's a code . . . I think. For these things. Hoes before, I don't know – men.'

'Wow.' Stacia picked up another chip and pointed it at Cherry. 'You know what? This isn't surprising.'

'It isn't?'

'No.' Stacia dipped the chip and put it in her mouth. 'I mean...' She chewed. She looked thoughtful. 'Yes, a little. But you guys *always* got along. I could tell he liked you.'

'You thought Russ liked me?'

'Well...' Stacia bobbled her head back and forth. 'Not like *that*. But I knew you were friends. I knew that *you* liked *him*.'

Cherry cringed. 'You *did*?'

Stacia shrugged again. 'Yeah, sort of. I mean...' She nodded. 'Yeah.'

Cherry felt so guilty. And so embarrassed. She couldn't even deny it – she *had* liked Russ. 'Did it bother you?'

'*No.*' Stacia reached across the counter again to touch Cherry's shoulder, reassuring. 'No, no. He was cute. I knew you wouldn't, like, make a pass at him. And I didn't think he'd cheat on me.'

'He didn't. I mean – not with me. There was never anything there.'

Stacia raised her eyebrows and smiled at Cherry. 'Or maybe there *was*...'

'No. Stacia. He *really* liked you. He didn't even talk to me after you dumped him.'

'No, I know that he liked me...' Stacia sighed, like she was remembering something nice. 'That was a good year. I thought I was going to marry Russ Sutton.'

'Oh god. I'm *so* sorry.'

'Cherry, it's okay – I dumped him. I met someone else.'

Cherry was still grimacing. 'I know, but...'

'How did this even *happen*? Where did you run into him?'

'At a concert.'

'And...?'

'We just... hit it off. It was good to see him. He's divorced. We caught up.'

'And he asked you out? Did *you* ask him out?'

'No. We – We left together.'

Stacia gasped. (Only mostly for effect.) '*Cherry*. This is very unlike you.'

'It seemed like a good idea in the moment.'

'*Was* it? Have you seen him since then?'

'A few times. Yeah.' Cherry nodded. 'It's good.' She shook her head. 'I think it's good.'

Stacia smiled. It was a genuine smile.

Cherry felt relief wash through her. 'I like him so much, Stace.'

Stacia laughed. She slapped Cherry's arm. 'Wow! Russ Sutton! I mean, why not?' She looked thoughtful again. 'I don't think there's anything wrong with him ... At least there wasn't in college – he never asked me to do anything weird. He was actually really sweet. His parents were stuck-up. But they'll probably like you – you're an intellectual.'

'I am not.'

'You read ...'

'He has a kid,' Cherry said.

'Have you met the kid?'

'We're nowhere near that.'

Stacia looked far away for a second. 'He was so cute ... Is he still cute?'

Cherry nodded. Guiltily.

'*Cherry*,' Stacia said. 'We're good. You didn't break any code.'

'I think I probably did ...'

'Now, if Jim and I get divorced, *he* is off limits.'

Cherry held up her hands. 'I would never go *near* Jim.'

Stacia looked hurt. 'Don't say it like that! Besides, I know you like Jim ...'

'I like him a normal amount.'

'You guys love to play cards. Always with the spades.'

'I like Jim the way you like your oldest friend's husband. Also, for the record, Jim would never come *near* me.'

Stacia got another chip and crunched into it, frowning at Cherry. 'Hmmmm.'

Cherry stayed at the party until all the skinny ladies and sand volleyball players and toddlers had gone home. Until it was just Stacia and Jim and Jim's mom and Cherry. The four of them played spades and ate the rest of the gluten-free party food while the kids watched *Bluey*.

When Cherry couldn't stop yawning, Stacia walked her to the door.

'Oh my god,' Cherry said, putting on her coat. 'I forgot to tell you – Tom's movie trailer came out.'

Stacia made a sad face. 'I know, I'm sorry.'

'Did you watch it?'

Stacia still looked sad. 'Yeah.'

'I can't believe you didn't mention it. Nobody mentioned it to me all day.'

'I told them not to – I figured you wouldn't want to talk about it.'

Cherry put her hand over her heart, feeling touched. 'I *don't* want to talk about it.'

Stacia nodded sympathetically.

'You're a really good friend,' Cherry said.

'I try.'

Cherry gave her a hug, then walked out onto the sidewalk.

'Tell Russ I said hi!' Stacia called after her.

Cherry looked back, grimacing.

'Or maybe don't,' Stacia said.

'I don't think I will,' Cherry agreed.

Stacia seemed delighted. 'This is going to be so *awkward...*'

'Good night!'

Chapter 14

Confessing to Stacia made Cherry feel a hundred pounds lighter. (Her recommended body weight.) Maybe there was something to Catholicism after all.

She felt almost completely unconflicted about seeing Russ the next day. They were going out to dinner for the first time, to a Thai restaurant near Cherry's place, and she was going to invite him to come back to her house afterwards.

It took most of Saturday afternoon for Cherry to de-Stevie the main floor. (She got out the industrial-strength vacuum.) Then, in a fit of supernatural fortitude, Cherry decided to de-Tom it, too.

She put his boots in the hall closet. She gathered up his sketchbooks and shoved them in a drawer. She tucked half his collection of *Space Ghost* toys inside the TV cabinet and then, when she ran out of space, hid the other half in the kitchen with the canned goods.

She couldn't hide *all* his things . . .

Tom loved *stuff*. He loved little figurines and action figures and vintage bubble bath bottles. He loved mechanical toys that didn't work and cartoon characters that no one recognized. He loved cute things, and clever things, and contraptions.

Cherry had never wanted to make Tom bury the things he loved in boxes – but she also hadn't wanted the house to feel like a junk shop. She'd tried to integrate his magpie collections into her own decorating. She wanted their home to reflect them both.

The house had become the main outlet for Cherry's creative energy after she gave up graphic design – and while she and Tom waited to have kids. She spent all her free time sewing curtains (there were *two dozen* windows) and painting patterns on the wood floors. She watched YouTube videos to learn how to refinish all the old furniture they brought home from estate sales and auctions.

If you took a photo at Cherry's house for Instagram, you didn't have to worry about your angles; the background would always be adorable.

And Tom's stuff was *part* of that. It was intrinsic. That's one reason Cherry hadn't surgically removed it already. Putting Tom's stuff away would leave big gaps in the house that she couldn't just fill in overnight. She'd have to redo every room to make the house feel whole again.

That afternoon, Cherry cleared away the most obvious of Tom's things. She moved quickly, like someone getting paid to clean, without letting her eyes or hands linger.

An hour before Russ was supposed to pick her up, Cherry changed her clothes and put on eyeliner, then walked through the house one more time, looking for anything she wouldn't want to explain to him.

She ended up in the dining room, staring at the photos of Tom with his mom.

She carefully took them off the wall and buried them in a drawer under some table linens.

Then she sat on the couch. To cry.

Stevie heaved herself up onto the cushion next to Cherry and laid her big head against Cherry's chest. Cherry put a hand in the dog's fur and reflexively pushed her fingers through it.

The tears on Cherry's cheeks were fat.

In the months after Tom left – and the months after it became clear that he wasn't coming home – Cherry's tears had changed.

There were days when her eyes felt so full, the tears ran in rivulets. She'd swear that crying had never felt that way before – that before, she'd cried drops, and now, she cried streams. There must be some science to it, one sort of crying for transient pains and another sort for crippling grief.

When Russ rang the doorbell, Cherry was covered in dog hair and thirsty from crying.

The first thing Russ said when she opened the door was, 'Are you okay?'

'Yeah,' Cherry lied. 'I'm fine. Come in.'

It was already less of a lie now that he was there.

Russ was letting Stevie jump on him, scratching her neck and saying things like, 'You are a monster, aren't you? You are a *kaiju*. Did you fight Godzilla and win?'

He looked charming, attractive. Laid-back. He looked easy.

He looked up at Cherry, still scratching Stevie's fur. 'Is she weirdly ... *oily*?'

Cherry laughed. 'Apparently that's natural. I wash my hands constantly.'

Russ looked in the dog's eyes. 'It's like dating a woman who uses a lot of product.'

Stevie dropped to her back so he could rub her belly.

'This'll go on all night if you let it,' Cherry said. 'She'll just keep moving to give you new angles.'

'She has so *many* angles ...'

Cherry got a dental chew out of the pile of treat bags that sat on Stevie's kennel. (Stevie could reach these bags, but never bothered them; she was either very dumb or very well-behaved.) 'Stevie, *come*.' Stevie came. Cherry gave her the bone, and the dog immediately trotted away to gnaw on it in peace.

Russ was trying to brush himself off. 'Here,' Cherry said, handing him a lint roller. She had them stashed all over the house.

He smiled at her and went to work on his sleeves. Russ was wearing a wool sports jacket and cotton chinos. He'd come from a work thing.

He was very bad at lint-rolling. Cherry took the roller back from him and started on his jacket.

'Hi,' he said.

'Hi,' Cherry said, smiling at him.

He kissed her cheek. 'Are you sure you're okay?'

'I am. Just a little undone, sorry. I should go look in a mirror.'

'You look great,' he said. 'Just . . .' He lowered his eyebrows.

'I had a moment. It's already passing.'

He glanced around the room. 'Your house is incredible.'

He was looking at the blue ribbons painted around the front door. Cinderella's mice were hidden near the floorboards. Cherry was a closet Disney adult.

'Did your ex do all this painting?'

'I did it,' she said.

Really? He turned back to Cherry. She was still lint-rolling his sleeve. 'It's fantastic. I missed all this the last time I was here.'

'Yeah, well . . .' She felt herself blush.

Russ grinned and put his arms around her.

She tried to pull back. 'I'm covered in fur. I'll have to lint-roll you again.'

He tugged her close. 'Don't threaten me with a good time.'

Cherry laughed and rested her arms on his shoulders, holding the lint roller away from his head.

Dinner was great. Even though the restaurant owner recognized Cherry – she'd been in before with Tom – and asked her about the *Thursday* movie. Cherry ordered green curry and tried not to eat too much rice. Russ talked to their waiter about the mayor's plan for public transit.

After dinner, they walked back to her house and sat on the couch, kissing. When Russ started unbuttoning her dress, Cherry led him upstairs – to her bedroom, which had also been hastily de-Tommed. (She'd basically swept everything under the bed or into a drawer; anything more thorough would have incapacitated her for days.) They made love in her bed again, using the still-not-expired condoms, and this time was even better. Cherry didn't worry about any of the reveals. She knew she could come with Russ, so she let herself do it. They were still getting to know each other. They were still smiling a lot.

She asked Russ to stay the night, and he said yes. He was out the door before Cherry's alarm went off the next morning.

Chapter 15

When Tom called Cherry, he still came up in her phone as *Emergency Contact*.

She debated whether to answer. She was at work. She could always text him to see what he wanted – she and Tom hadn't really talked on the phone since they'd stopped fighting.

She got up to close the door to her office. 'Hello?'

'Hey. It's me ... It's Tom.'

'Yeah,' Cherry said. 'Hi.'

His voice was tight. 'How are you?'

Cherry's was tighter. 'I'm fine, Tom. How are you?'

'Oh. Fine, I guess. Um ...'

Cherry waited a second, then prompted – 'Tom. Why did you call?'

'Uh ... right.' He exhaled. 'I wanted to give you a heads-up. Or, um, figure out ... I'm coming home next week. Back to Omaha.'

'Oh.' That shouldn't be surprising. Tom had to come back eventually. 'Okay.'

'I was gonna pack up my stuff – whenever that works for you.'

'Right.' Right. This had to happen, too. 'Okay,' Cherry said, 'just ... I guess, tell me when you want to come over. Maybe you could do it while I'm at work?'

'I mean ...' Tom sounded unsure. 'We'll probably have to talk about it, right?'

'No.' Cherry didn't want to talk to Tom about anything. 'Just come get your stuff.'

'Well . . . it's our stuff, most of it.'

'What do you mean – what all do you want to take?'

'I don't know,' he said. 'What if I wanted something from the kitchen?'

The *kitchen*? 'What do you want from the kitchen?'

'I don't *know*, Cherry. I haven't been home for almost a year.'

'And you've done without everything in the kitchen so far.'

'Well, I've been living in a fully furnished Airbnb.'

'Are you moving?'

'Yeah,' he said. 'I'm getting my own apartment.'

'Oh.' *None* of this should be surprising. Tom had to live somewhere; they were getting a divorce. 'Okay,' she said again, trying to ground herself. 'Well . . . you're going to have to buy new stuff. You can't just take our stuff. I'm using it.' She sounded defensive.

'Are you using the juicer?' He sounded exasperated.

'When have I ever used the juicer, Tom?'

He was quiet.

Cherry heard him take a deep breath. 'This is the sort of thing we can talk about when I come home,' he said. 'I'm not going to take anything that you need. But I don't want to just *take* things.'

'Yeah.' She rubbed her forehead. 'Okay.'

'So – is there a day next week that works? It doesn't have to be next week. I'll be home for a while.'

'Where are you staying?'

'With my dad.'

Tom's dad was a difficult person. To put it mildly. 'Is that going to be okay?'

'It'll be fine. It's temporary.'

'You could come over Saturday,' Cherry said. 'After lunch.'

'Great,' he said. 'Thank you. I'll see you then.'

'See you.' Cherry ended the call.

Then she closed her eyes and told herself that she wasn't going to cry.

And then she cried.

And then she went back to work.

Chapter 16

Cherry didn't know how to get ready for seeing her not-quite husband (and not-quite *ex*-husband) for the first time in almost a year.

Was she supposed to clean the house? Was she supposed to look good? As she liked to say to her team at work, '*What's our key message here? What's the takeaway?*'

Cherry didn't have a key message for Tom. Did she want to remind him that he used to love her? Or reinforce his decision to leave?

Her sisters would want her to strike fear in his heart. They wanted Cherry to go hard after Tom's new money and future earnings.

That seemed unnecessary. Cherry had talked to a divorce lawyer; she would almost certainly get half the publishing money. (The entire *Thursday* series had been on the bestseller list for two years.) And she'd get half the movie money, at least for the first movie. The lawyer had been shocked that Tom wasn't moving faster toward divorce, to cut off Cherry's claim on his income.

Cherry had laughed. Tom had never rushed a decision in his life.

It was Cherry who'd decided they should get married. Cherry who'd urged Tom to say yes to the graphic novel editor who wanted to publish *Thursday*. Cherry who told Tom to go to Hollywood and see what came of it.

And Cherry who told him not to come home.

Tom would be here any minute...

What did Cherry want him to feel when he looked at her? *Guilty*.

That wasn't a very noble goal, but it was true.

She ended up in jeans and a T-shirt and an oversized pear-colored cardigan that hung around her hips.

She'd had Stevie groomed that morning. (Cherry definitely wanted Tom to think that *Stevie* was living her best life.) She vacuumed while she waited for him. Her pulse was racing. She thought about calling him and saying that today wouldn't work after all. That no day would work. That she'd pack up his things and ship them to California. That she'd pack up the *entire house* and ship it to him. Money, as her therapist said, was no longer a limiting factor.

Cherry herself was the limiting factor. She didn't have the heart for this.

Tom used the doorbell when he got there. (*Because he doesn't live here*, Cherry told herself. She felt like throwing up.)

Stevie was already at the door, barking. Cherry held her collar to keep her from squeezing through the open door. The dog jumped up onto Tom before he could even walk in.

Cherry stepped back. Let them both do whatever.

Stevie was going *wild* – did she recognize Tom? He squatted down to greet her, and she was all over him. He was grinning and petting her roughly. 'Stevie Nicks, what a good girl. Did you miss me? I missed you, too. What a *good* girl.'

Tom was wearing ratty old green corduroys and a black hoodie. (He was going to be covered in white fur.) His hair was longer than Cherry had ever seen it.

Tom had curly blond hair. Truly blond, even as an adult. His hair was so light that you almost couldn't see the color when it was short – and he'd always kept it short because he didn't like dealing with the curls.

But it was grown out now, just past his ears. Ash-blond curls as thick as Cherry's thumb. He must be using some product to smooth them out.

It was a knife to Cherry's heart that Tom had waited to leave her to grow out his hair. (Probably the first of many knives headed her way that afternoon. She'd have to make room in her chest for them.)

Tom stood up, still petting Stevie. He looked at Cherry. Less excited, less at ease. 'Hi.'

'Hi,' Cherry said.

Tom wasn't quite six feet tall, but he was big, so he seemed taller. He'd played football in high school, but he hadn't been good at anything but standing there and letting people plow into him. At least that's what he'd told her.

Tom had always been heavier than he wanted to be – but he seemed to have lost weight. California, Cherry figured. And no more desk job. And money to spend on protein boxes and sea moss smoothies. (Cherry had also lost weight in the last year, but it was purely from misery and self-neglect.)

His face was changed ... Still handsome. Still thick-boned and rugged. Still just a little bit strange – with his wide-bridged nose and narrow eyes, and high, wide cheekbones that pushed out into his temples. But Cherry had missed a whole year of wear.

'She's gotten so big,' Tom said, rubbing Stevie's flank.

'A hundred and thirty-eight pounds at her last visit. Dr Lewis thinks she's finally done growing.'

Tom scratched Stevie's ears with both hands. 'What a beauty. What a good girl.'

'Did you just get in?' Cherry asked.

'A couple days ago.' He was still scratching Stevie's ears.

'Well ...' Cherry looked around them. 'I didn't know where you'd want to start ...'

'Oh.' Tom looked up again. He was frowning. 'Where do you want me to start?'

'Did you bring boxes?'

'They're in the car.'

'I guess, start with the boxes,' she said.

He nodded. 'Right.'

Cherry took hold of Stevie's collar again so that Tom could get out the door. When he went outside, she put Stevie in the kennel – ostensibly to keep her out of the way, but mostly because watching Tom shower the dog with affection was making Cherry want to howl like a wounded banshee.

Tom thumped back up the porch steps and slowly opened the door. He was carrying a flat pack of brand-new boxes.

They both stood there in the foyer, not looking at each other.

'I could start with my clothes –' Tom said.

Cherry cut him off. *'No.'* She didn't want him in the bedroom.

Maybe he guessed that, because he said, 'I could leave you with some boxes for my clothes.'

'I'm not packing your clothes, Tom.'

He stared at the floor.

'Just start down here,' Cherry said.

'Okay.'

She looked up at him, her composure cracking. 'I know you said we should both be here, but I think I'll just . . . get out of your way for a while.' She walked past him to pick up her purse. 'Let you get the lay of the land.'

'Okay,' he repeated.

'Just start packing,' Cherry said. 'And if we need to talk about something, I'll be back.'

She held her tears until she got out the door, but it was a near thing.

Cherry went to the grocery store. She walked up and down the aisles for an hour, pushing an empty cart. She thought about Tom, back at the house for the first time in a year. Tom in *their* house. Opening their cabinets and sitting on their couch. Petting their dog.

She could tell herself that none of it was Tom's anymore – but it wasn't Cherry's, either.

All of it was theirs together. When Tom left for California, he'd taken the whole point of the house with him – that it was something for them to *share*. Cherry lived there now like a squatter. Like one more thing Tom hadn't needed and left behind.

She remembered the day they'd put in a bid for the house. How happy they'd been when they got the call from the Realtor. They could just barely afford the place, and it wasn't in the best neighborhood – but it was *near* a good neighborhood. And it had three bedrooms. They wanted three bedrooms. For children they weren't quite ready to seriously discuss.

The apartment they'd been living in had always felt temporary. It had been Cherry's apartment first, and they weren't allowed to paint or plant anything. They couldn't even take down the blinds.

But this house would be *theirs*.

They planted fruit trees that first spring. And lilac bushes and perennials. Things that wouldn't bloom for years. Things they could watch grow.

When Tom left for California, Cherry had become the house's keeper. And the dog's keeper. The person who had to pick the fruit and weed the garden and change the filters in the new furnace. The person who opened all the bills.

Tom hadn't just left *her* – he'd left her with their broken life, with all their abandoned plans and dead projects. He'd left her *in* their broken life. The last resident in a ghost town.

Cherry did another full circuit of the grocery store and bought dog food. (She always needed dog food.) And cream, so she could offer Tom coffee. And packaged salad and a rotisserie chicken, so she'd have something to eat when he left.

When she got back to the house, Tom was sitting at the dining room table. He stood up, abruptly, when she walked in the door. Stevie jumped up, too. She'd been sitting at his feet.

Tom didn't look good. He was pale, and his eyes had that hollowed-out look they'd had for so much of the year before he left.

Cherry used to go to him when he looked like this. She'd take his hand, touch his cheek. *'You okay?'*

She didn't go to him now – but she still felt pity for him. She made room in her hard heart for the fact that this was the first time back for Tom, too.

'Do you need help with the groceries?' he asked.

'This is all there is.' Cherry set down the dog food. 'Can I get you a cup of coffee?'

'Um ...' Tom's forehead wrinkled. 'Would it be okay if I came back tomorrow?'

Cherry clenched her jaw. 'I have plans tomorrow.'

'Right,' he said. 'Maybe Monday night?'

She didn't want Tom here at night. It was too grim. She needed the sun to help keep her head up. 'Never mind,' she said. 'Just come back tomorrow.'

'But if you have plans –'

'They're movable.'

'Thanks, Cherry. Sorry.'

Cherry shook her head, like he didn't have to apologize. Tom gave Stevie a few more scratches, and the dog followed him to the door.

Cherry went into the kitchen. She didn't want to see him out.

'I'll text you before I come over,' Tom called.

'Okay,' she said. 'Thanks.'

Cherry set the groceries on the island. When the front door closed, she hung forward over the counter. She took a few deep, intentional breaths, letting a great wave of *something* wash over her.

What was it ... Sadness? Loss?

Whatever it was, it hurt.

She sank to the floor and leaned back against the cabinet under the sink, then stayed there, staring at the baseboards.

Stevie came in to investigate – pushing her wet nose into Cherry's neck and face.

Stevie didn't like it when Cherry was on the floor. Or bending over. Or even lying on the couch. (She wouldn't let Cherry do anything resembling yoga.) Her protective instincts kicked in. She'd bark sharply and nose at Cherry's face. Sometimes she'd rest her teeth around one of Cherry's wrists.

'I'm fine,' Cherry said now, patting Stevie's muzzle.

Stevie seemed mostly satisfied that Cherry was all right. She flopped down heavily on the floor next to Cherry and laid a paw over her leg. This was one of Stevie's more charming habits – the way she'd rest a leg on you, like someone putting a hand on your lap. Cherry mindlessly combed her fingers through the fur on Stevie's neck.

Cherry had always been a furious thinker, the kind of person who could never really turn *off*. It was sort of incredible how grief could clear her head – how Tom could make Cherry go totally still inside. None of her gears spinning. None of her neurons firing. The way the sadness settled inside of her like concrete.

Cherry hadn't told her sisters that Tom was coming over today. They'd make too much of being angry and offering Cherry support. One of them might have shown up to snub him.

She hadn't told Stacia for the same reason.

The only person Cherry had told was Russ – because it seemed like the sort of thing you *should* tell the person you were dating. And also because Russ had asked her if she wanted to get together today.

He'd been very careful when Cherry told him why she couldn't. They were lying in her bed. Undressed. Sexed. Cherry was draped over him, and he was playing with her hair.

'I can't,' she'd said. 'I have plans on Saturday.'

Russ toyed with her bangs. 'What kind?'

'Tom's coming over to pack up his things.'

'Ohhh,' Russ said. (Just like that, with three *h*s.) His eyebrows dropped down, concerned. 'That sounds awful. Do you want to talk about it?'

'To you?' she said, trying to smile. 'Right now? Absolutely not.'

He laughed softly and tugged at her hair. 'Okay.'

Russ had never asked for details about Cherry's divorce. (Probably because he didn't want to talk about his own.) Cherry had given him the highlights: arguing, long-distance arguing, *Rachel*.

All Russ had told Cherry about his ex-wife was, *'I think she always kind of hated me, and I mistook that for "interesting."'*

'Is this the first time he's come back?' Russ asked.

Cherry nodded her head.

'Fuck,' he said. 'I'm sorry.'

Her eyes were burning. She closed them.

'It's going to get easier,' Russ said, running his fingers through her hair. 'Not immediately. Immediately, it's going to be horrible. But it will just keep getting less horrible, and eventually it will be mostly okay.'

Cherry hummed, dubious.

'I never got any distance from my ex,' he said. 'Because of Liam. It was relentless – I'd see her every couple days, and we were constantly texting each other ... I wonder if that made it better or worse.'

'It sounds worse.'

'Yeah, but I built up some immunity. And I got to process my anger and guilt. You haven't had a chance to process anything.'

She lifted her head to look at him. 'I've processed.'

It was Russ's turn to look dubious.

'Why are we talking about this?' Cherry asked. She felt rankled. Poked. Naked in a bad way.

Russ had just shaken his head and smiled, already stroking her shoulder and back. Soothing her. 'We're not talking about it.'

Now, sitting on the kitchen floor – not processing, not thinking, and numb around the edges – Cherry heard her phone chime. She had everyone silenced but work and Russ, and probably still Tom. She took her phone out of her pocket, hoping that it wasn't Tom saying he was on his way back.

It was Russ.

'I was torn about whether to check in with you today or give you some space. I decided to check in. I hope you're doing all right.'

Cherry sat up a little to type. *'I'm fine. He's gone already.'*

'That was fast.'

'We didn't get started. I think he chickened out.'

Russ sent a medium-sad emoji. *'That sucks. I'm sorry.'* Then he sent, *'How are you, really?'*

'On the floor, nearly immobile.'

'There's the truth – I knew I'd find it.'

'You got me,' she sent. *'I can only lie once.'*

'Do you want some company? Or is today a floor day?'

Cherry smiled. She realized that she'd been petting Stevie for so long, there were tracks in the dog's white fur.

Cherry had spent too many days like this. On the floor. On the couch. Sitting on the front steps some nights after work when she couldn't bear to go in.

'I'll take company,' she typed. *'But not here.'*

'Liam's at a birthday party, and I'm free until 8. Come see me.'

Chapter 17

Cherry didn't sleep well that night. (She'd had sex with Russ in the blinds-closed afternoon darkness of his bedroom, then fallen asleep for an ill-advised six-o'clock nap.)

But she woke up Sunday morning in her own bed, determined to handle things better than she had the day before.

Cherry needed to help Tom get this done – to help him out of her life – the same way she'd always helped Tom get things done.

Tom got bogged down. He got overwhelmed by decisions. Cherry thought too much and moved too fast; Tom thought too much and barely moved at all. He broke every decision down into a thousand smaller decisions until all he could manage was to back away, completely discouraged.

And that's how he was about normal things – like what kind of cell phone to buy – not *actually* discouraging situations. Like this one.

Plus, Tom hadn't been living in the reality of their failed marriage for a year. Not like Cherry had. It must have been jarring for him to walk back into the house and have to reckon with their sad ending. It must have been *shocking*.

Cherry could help. Cherry was velocity – she was speed plus direction. And helping Tom would be helping herself. Even if it hurt (even if it was *excruciating*) in the short-term.

On Sunday morning, before Tom got there, Cherry took Stevie for a long walk so she wouldn't be so excitable. Then Cherry came back to the house, opened all the curtains, and turned on a generic

Spotify playlist. 'Sunday Morning Vintage Vibes.' She made a pot of coffee.

Tom had left the pack of moving boxes in the foyer. Cherry opened it and unfolded one, taping up the bottom.

When Tom rang the doorbell, she'd already packed up most of their DVDs and all of the video game cartridges.

Stevie went crazy when Cherry opened the door. (Long walk be damned.) Tom immediately knelt down to give the dog the full treatment. He was wearing pants Cherry had never seen before. Very expensive-looking cargo pants. And bright white Air Jordans. His hair was as cherubic as yesterday. Cherry was still pissed about it.

'I made coffee,' she said. 'Let me get you a cup.'

Tom looked up at her. He was scratching Stevie's ears. 'Uh, sure. Thanks.'

Cherry came back with his coffee – cream, no sugar – in a *Thursday* mug. (From Tom's very first merch drop. Cherry had designed this mug and set everything up with the vendor.)

He stood up to take it from her.

'I got started on the living room.' Cherry walked that way. The main floor of the house was built so that all the rooms connected in a circle: foyer, dining room, living room, kitchen, foyer. Tom followed her.

She gestured at the box of DVDs. 'I kept a few of the boxed sets, but these are all yours.'

He frowned down at the box. 'This looks like everything.'

'It's not. I kept *Pushing Daisies* and *Buffy*. I mean, you can have *Buffy* if you want . . .'

He picked up a DVD. 'You don't want the Disney movies?'

'They're all streaming.'

'They're not all streaming.'

'Well' – Cherry put her hands on her hips – 'I just think you're more likely to watch *Herbie Goes Bananas* than I am.'

Tom looked confused. 'Why would I watch *Herbie Goes Bananas* without you?'

'That's how I feel about that whole box!'

Tom clenched his jaw.

Cherry closed her eyes. A few tears leaked out anyway. This wasn't going well.

She wiped her eyes and took a breath. 'If you don't want something in the box, set it aside. I'll either keep it or give it to Goodwill.'

Tom was still staring at the DVDs. 'Okay.'

'I'm going to do the books in the foyer,' Cherry said.

'Yeah. All right.'

Cherry walked away. Stevie stayed right next to Tom, looking up at him the way she had when she was a puppy. Like she was awaiting instructions.

Cherry got another cup of coffee and built another box. The books were easier to sort than the movies. Either Tom had read them or Cherry had. She filled two boxes in minutes, then called into the living room – 'Do you have more boxes?'

'In the car,' Tom said. He walked into the foyer. 'I'll go get them.'

He came back with two more packs and opened one, starting to build out the boxes. Cherry felt like he was watching her. When she looked over, he was frowning over one of the boxes of books that she'd packed.

'Are these mine or yours?' he asked.

'Yours.'

'Don't give me the Tolkien books. Those are special editions.'

'You love them more than I do.'

Tom let his arms hang. 'You're arguing that I love *The Lord of the Rings* more than you?'

'You reread them every other year.'

'Cherry, you said that if you ever got a tattoo, it would be that Frodo Baggins quote.'

'*I will take the ring,*' Cherry thought, '*though I do not know the way.*'

'Yeah,' she said, 'but I didn't get it.'

Tom took *The Hobbit* out of the box and set it back on a shelf, shaking his head. His curls wobbled.

'Fine,' Cherry said sharply, 'but you're just going to have to buy the whole series the next time you want to read them.'

'Yeah, where am I going to find the *Lord of the Rings* books.' He put *Fellowship of the Ring* back, too. His hand stayed on the shelf. He laughed gruffly. 'I thought we were going to fight over things you *didn't* want me to take.'

Cherry rubbed her face. Her hands were dusty. 'I can't think of anything in the house I'd fight for,' she muttered. 'Can you?'

He looked over at her. His chin was pushed out. 'The exit sign I found on eBay, from the old Country Bear Jamboree at Disneyland.'

Cherry's head jerked up, alarmed. 'You want that?'

'No,' he said. 'But I think you'd fight me for it.'

She would have, five minutes ago. But now . . . 'No. You take it.'

'Cherry, I don't want it.'

'You're the one who found it.'

'It was a *gift*,' Tom said.

It was an anniversary gift. He'd spent five hundred dollars on it, back when five hundred was an awful lot of dollars for them to spend on anything. Cherry was crazy about the Country Bears. The sign had hung inside the front door of their old apartment, and now it was in the kitchen, by the back door. It said, *We Hope That You'll Be Coming Back Again.* Cherry wanted to go into the kitchen right now and take it down.

'Just let me finish sorting the books,' she said. 'I don't want to fight.'

'Yeah,' Tom said. 'Okay.' He walked back to the living room. Cherry stared at the bookshelves for a few minutes, then went outside to sit on the front steps. It was too cold to be out here without a sweatshirt, but she needed some distance.

After a little while, Tom came out.

He stood behind her. She didn't look up at him.

'I think you had the right idea,' he said.

She still didn't turn.

'You can set aside what you want me to take,' he said. 'And I'll go through it and leave what I don't want – or take it to the Goodwill.'

Cherry huffed. 'So I'm supposed to pack up your things?'

'Or I can do it? I can pack what I want, and then you can go through the boxes? I just meant – you were right, we don't have to do this together.'

Cherry wasn't sure why she found that so infuriating. Tom was right – *she* was right. One of their neighbors was out walking his dog. He waved. They both waved back.

'Cherry?' Tom said.

'Yeah,' she said. 'Okay. You can come by when I'm at the office.'

'And you'll look over the boxes before I take them?'

She shook her head. 'I don't have to check your work. I trust you.'

'Ha,' Tom said, sounding genuinely amused. He took his keys out of his pocket.

'Are you leaving now?' she asked.

'Yeah. Fresh start Monday morning. Do you want me to text you before I come?'

'No. You know my hours – I still work from home most Fridays. I'm sure Stevie will be glad to see more of you.'

'Yeah . . .' Tom walked down the steps. His dad's car was parked on the street.

Cherry watched him drive away.

The next day, when Cherry got home from work, the rest of the books from the main floor had been sorted. Tom had labeled the boxes with his name and stuck a yellow Post-it note that said *Cherry* on the shelves with the remaining books.

Cherry glanced at what he'd set aside for himself. He'd left most of their art books but taken all the comics collections. That seemed right.

The DVDs were sorted, too. Tom had unpacked some of her favorite Disney movies and put them back on the shelf. *Sleeping Beauty. The Princess and the Frog.* Again with the Post-it notes: *Tom. Cherry.*

She ended up taking a few more movies from the boxes. She'd write him a note, asking if she could keep them. (She'd been too hasty the day before.)

Tom had taken all the video game equipment and stuck notes on some of the hanging artwork, asking if he could take it. It was all stuff she'd assumed he'd take anyway.

Cherry went and got her own Post-it pad in a different color. Blue. She replied to Tom's notes, and left notes on new things, urging him to take them.

The next day, all of the mutually approved *Tom* boxes were sitting in a corner of the dining room. There were several framed pieces of art leaning neatly against the boxes – posters, *Thursday* prints, Tom's first book cover. (Cherry had chosen all of these frames and cut the mats. She enjoyed doing it.)

There were big empty spaces on the walls now, with nails sticking out. She'd have to patch and repaint. She really was going to have to start over.

Tom had left notes replying to Cherry's notes. And he'd left new notes, with questions.

It was all very courteous. Very civilized. (Tom was always very courteous and very civilized.)

He'd left a note saying that he'd walked the dog.

Chapter 18

Cherry's sister was at the door. Stevie was going ballistic.

'Just a second!' Cherry called. 'House, Stevie. *House.*'

'Call off your hounds!' Honny shouted. None of Cherry's sisters were dog people. They all found Stevie either irritating or terrifying.

Stevie reluctantly went to her kennel. Cherry gave her a treat and locked her in. When Cherry opened the front door, Honny walked past her.

Honny was three years older than Cherry, almost forty. She looked a lot like Cherry. A little fatter. A little more *ethnic*. They were part Sicilian, and Honny actually looked it. She was wearing a puffy pink coat (not puffy and pink in a way Cherry would endorse), and she looked put out. 'Mom says you have her health insurance card.'

Cherry frowned. 'Do I?'

Their mom was only in her mid-sixties, but she'd never been good with paperwork or bills. Cherry and her older sisters had been handling everything since they were teenagers.

'She says you took her to the eye doctor,' Honny said.

'Oh, right.' Cherry remembered now. 'It's probably in my purse. Is Mom with you?'

'She's in the car. She's got a mammogram at one.'

Cherry's purse was in her bedroom. 'Let me look. Just a second.' She ran upstairs.

The card *was* in her purse. 'Found it!' Cherry called, coming down the stairs. 'You're lucky I was working from home.' Honny wasn't in the foyer. 'Honny?'

'*What* is going on here, Cherry?'

Honny was standing in the living room with her hands on her hips. Her face was aghast.

Cherry's living room was a little ... deconstructed.

The entire main floor was.

One whole corner of the dining room was stacked with boxes – and that was the only sign of order. Cabinets were open. Drawers were open. There was stuff spread out on the dining room table. There were Post-it notes everywhere. Long Post-it note *conversations* ...

'Tom came home last week to pack,' Cherry said.

'Tom came home?' Honny looked shocked.

'To Omaha.'

'Why didn't you tell us?' Her eyes narrowed. 'Did you tell everyone but me?'

'No, of course not. There's really nothing to report.'

'Your husband came home for the first time in a year, and that's nothing?'

'He's not actually *home*,' Cherry said. 'He's just packing.'

The front door opened. 'Honny?'

'Mom, I'm *coming*,' Honny said.

'Did you get my insurance card?' Their mom walked into the living room. She looked a lot like Cherry and Honny, but with all the Italian deducted. Her hair – salt and pepper now – was darker than Cherry's, but her skin was pinker and her eyes were bright blue.

'I've got it.' Cherry held up the card.

Their mom was looking around the room. 'Cherry, are you moving?'

'Tom came home,' Honny said.

Their mom's face lit up. 'Tom's here?' She looked at the ceiling and raised her voice. '*Tom?*'

Cherry's mom loved Tom. She loved all her sons-in-law. She thought they were all very long-suffering to put up with her daughters.

'He's not here now,' Cherry said.

'But he came back? He came home?' Her mom was getting tearful.

'No. Just to pack his things.'

'Oh, Cherry …' She touched Cherry's cheek. 'This is a good thing. You have to talk to him.'

'It's not like that, Mom. We don't even see each other – he comes while I'm at work. There's no talking.'

'Looks like there's a bunch of note-writing …' Honny said, picking up a Post-it-plastered DVD.

Cherry took it from her. 'We're trying to sort everything out. It's messy.'

Her mom was still trying to touch Cherry's cheek. 'That's your husband.'

Cherry flinched. 'Ex-husband.'

'Not yet,' her mom argued, petting her cheek. 'And not in the eyes of God. Take this opportunity to talk to Tom. You can still heal, Cherry. Forgiveness is powerful. And it's ongoing.'

'Marriages aren't built on forgiveness,' Honny muttered, looking irritated.

'Sometimes they are!' Their mom was daring them both to argue. She felt very righteous about her own marriage. She was the queen of forgiveness; Cherry's dad had given her ample opportunities. 'I'm sure that Carl forgives *you* sometimes.' Carl was Honny's husband.

'Leave Carl out of this,' Honny said.

'Leave me out of it, too,' Cherry said.

'Cherry' – Honny waved her hand around the room – 'this is disturbing. It looks like a forensics team has come through here.'

'Because it's *complicated*,' Cherry said. 'Untangling two lives is complicated.'

'You're letting Tom make it complicated, I can tell. You're letting him be *Tom* about it.'

'He *is* Tom.'

'Yeah, but he's not your problem anymore, Cherry! Why are you letting him be your problem?'

'He is her *husband*,' their mother said. 'He will *always* be her problem.'

Honny shook her head. 'For Pete's sake, Mom, you're even more disturbing than Cherry.'

Cherry set down the DVD. (It was *Rise of Skywalker*. There were twelve Post-it notes on it – twelve reasons why the other person should *have* to take it.) 'I'm not letting Tom be my problem. And I'm not taking him back.'

Honny looked doubtful. Their mom looked devastated.

'I'm actually seeing someone else,' Cherry said, raising her chin.

Their mouths dropped open in unison, like in a cartoon.

'You're *what*?' Honny said. 'How could you keep that a secret? Did you tell everyone but me?'

'No! I'm telling you now! I'm telling you both! I'm dating someone. I'm *not* getting back together with Tom – who doesn't want to get back together, by the way. He's moving to Los Angeles.'

'Oh, Cherry . . .' There were tears in her mom's eyes. 'You're a married woman.'

Honny was frowning. 'You *are* a married woman.' (Cherry's sisters were anti-Tom, but they were also very legalistic about marital vows.) (This was *why* they were anti-Tom.)

'I'm glad I could find something for the two of you to agree on,' Cherry said. 'I'm an adulteress.'

Her mom closed her eyes. 'Don't tell me this.'

'You're *sleeping* with someone?' Honny's hands were on her hips again. 'Do you even know what diseases are out there? If you don't already have HPV, forget about it. You should get that vaccine they give teenagers.'

'Maybe I will,' Cherry said. She handed Honny the insurance card. 'Go get that mammogram.'

Their mom's eyes were open. She took Cherry's hand in both of hers. 'Cherry, you know I love you very much.'

'I love you, too.'

'And Jesus loves you.'

'Okay.'

'Jesus does love you,' Honny said. 'He can't get enough of sinners.'

'Great, thanks.'

'Come on, Mom,' Honny said, leading her toward the door. She reluctantly let go of Cherry's hand.

Once their mom was out, Honny turned back to Cherry. 'Are you *really* dating someone?'

'Yes.'

Honny frowned. 'We were just waiting for your divorce to be final so we could introduce you to a guy from church.'

'Oh my god, Honny – no.'

'He's an architect, Cherry – and a widower. Do you know how in demand widowers are? At your age, all the men are either divorced or weirdos.'

'Thank you for thinking of me. But I'm honestly seeing someone.'

'Someone nice?'

'Of course someone nice.'

'You never know.'

Cherry shut the door behind Honny and let Stevie out of the kennel. The dog immediately ran to the door to bark. *Come back, come back*, she was saying. *I didn't even get to say hi!*

Cherry gave Stevie some consolation pets. Her fur was soft and clean. Tom must be brushing her after all their walks.

Cherry looked around the house . . .

It did, in fact, look like a forensics team was working in here.

Cherry had, in fact, been letting Tom make things complicated.

She'd hoped that he'd move through the house in a sensible fashion, from room to room – but Tom had never worked that way. He seemed to be wandering around the house, picking things up and setting them down, and leaving long, polite Post-it notes for Cherry.

They were having entire Post-it note *parleys* about things that didn't even matter – the stapler, a jade plant, an electric kettle that was apparently no longer in production. And Tom had started bringing things down from the attic.

Cherry didn't know how to discourage this process, especially if she wasn't here with him in the moment, and she didn't think it would help to drastically disrupt him.

If Cherry were to throw everything into a box with a note that said, *Take all this or throw it out*, Tom would just unpack that box and lay everything out on the dining room table with a dozen new notes.

And if she were to tell him he was being ridiculous, he'd shut down altogether.

Stacia thought that Cherry should give Tom a deadline. Cherry had laughed out loud. If Tom got too frustrated, he'd just walk away. He'd leave the house like this, turned inside out.

'Who cares?' Stacia had said. She and Cherry had lunch together sometimes during the week, over videoconference. 'Then you win. You can just box his shit up and get rid of it.'

'I don't want to *win*,' Cherry had replied.

'I just mean, then you'd have your house back.'

'I don't think I want the house back.' Cherry poked at her chicken salad. 'I think I want to start over.'

'Oh,' Stacia said. She looked sad for a second, and then said, 'Yeah, why not? Start over!'

'In a way,' Cherry said, feeling encouraged, 'Tom's doing me a favor. He's helping me do this big cleanse. If he doesn't want something and the thing makes me sad, I'm throwing it out.'

'Huh …' Stacia looked thoughtful. 'It's like reverse Marie Kondo.'

'*Exactly*. It's like I'm touching everything in the house to see if it sparks misery.'

'I don't know . . .' Stacia frowned again. 'I think you might throw out things that you end up wanting later. *Everything* in that house is going to bring back sad memories right now.'

'I'll just buy new things with Tom's money.'

'Why does it sound so depressing when you say that . . .'

Cherry set down her fork. 'I thought you wanted me to put Tom behind me and let in new energy.'

'I do. I *do*. But your house is so cute.'

Cherry had laughed and raised her eyebrows. 'Yeah, not anymore.'

Her house was a huge mess.

It accurately reflected Cherry's life.

She could influence Tom, but she couldn't change him. Their marriage was going to end the same way it had begun: drawn out and overly complicated, with too much thinking and not enough talking, and Tom forever hung up on small things.

Eventually Cherry would say, *'Enough,'* and they'd move on.

Eventually Cherry would say, *'Enough,'* and Tom would be truly gone.

Chapter 19

Today 3:45 PM

Mom
I just want you girls to know that your sister's husband is back, and they're talking. This would be a good time for us all to pray for Cherry and Tom. I know I don't have to tell any of you how important the marriage vows are, in heaven and on earth!! It's right there in Genesis – 'It is not good that the man should be alone!' Or the woman!! With Jesus's love and light, I know that Cherry can see the power of forgiveness! Just like God gives our bodies the tools to heal, he also gives our hearts the tools to heal!

So please pray for Cherry and Tom. (Tom is still your brother!!!)

And pray for me, too. I had a mammogram today. You know that my Aunt Lou died of breast cancer.

Joy
Mom, Cherry is on this thread.

Honny

Also, Cherry has a boyfriend that she hasn't told any of us about. So please let's pray for her to be more forthcoming with her sisters.

Joy

CHERRY HAS A BOYFRIEND?

Hope

Mom, wasn't Aunt Lou your aunt by marriage?

Faith

Tom's back???

Honny

He came back to pack his things. You should see their HOUSE. Instead of packing, he's left little sticky notes all over everything. He's not going to leave until they've had a drawn out discussion about every paperclip. It's the most Tom has ever Tommed.

Joy

CHERRY HAS A BOYFRIEND???

> **Cherry**
>
> I *am* on this thread. And Tom *is* packing his things. And I don't have a boyfriend, but I'm seeing someone.

Joy

WHO?????

Faith

Oh, Cherry, no! We were going to introduce you to this great guy at church! He's an architect!

Honny

And a widower. A widower without kids – that's like a double unicorn.

Hope

Are you guys talking about Brian Nillson??

Faith

Yes.

Hope

Did Kendra die?

Honny

Yes, of skin cancer.

Faith

Yes. Last year. It was so sad.

Mom

She was a wonderful sister in faith.

Honny

Tell Cherry how cute Brian is.

Hope

I went to church camp with Kendra. She was so young . . .

Joy

I don't mean to be rude, but – CHERRY HAS A BOYFRIEND????

        Cherry

        I'm seeing a guy that I went to college with. He's nice. He's employed. He's not a widower, but we can't have everything in life.

Faith

How is Tom doing?

> **Cherry**
> Fine, I guess. He's getting an apartment in Los Angeles. He grew out his hair.

Joy

He grew out his curls??? Do you have a photo?

Honny

He grew out his curls? I'll bet he looks like Shirley Temple.

Hope

Does he look like Shirley Temple?

Honny

Jinx, buy me a Coke.

Hope

I'll buy you a Shirley Temple.

> **Cherry**
> He looks good. He's lost weight.

Honny

OZEMPIC.

Joy

OZEMPIQUE!

Faith

He's probably taking Ozempic.

Honny

Everybody owes me a Coke.

Mom

I didn't know that Cherry was on this thread, but God's hand is in all things! Cherry, you should know that we all love you and that we're praying for you! And we love Tom, too! He'll always be part of our family!!

Honny

I still can't believe you got yourself a boyfriend, and you didn't tell anybody.

Hope

I can.

Chapter 20

Cherry spent almost the whole weekend with Russ.

She slept over at his house for the first time on Saturday night. Then she came home to spend time with Stevie, and went right back to Russ's and slept over again. She was glad to be away from her house. It was just too *much*.

Stevie didn't run to say hello when Cherry got home from work on Monday night. Tom must have worn her out. It was a relief that he was walking the dog on weekdays. Cherry hated having to walk Stevie in the dark after work.

Cherry kicked off her shoes and took her takeout into the kitchen. Chicken soup, from a homestyle restaurant downtown. She'd ordered enough to have the leftovers tomorrow night. That counted as meal-planning for Cherry. She almost never had food in the fridge.

She'd cooked all the time with Tom, but it never seemed worth cooking – or shopping – just for herself. She was lucky her office building had a nice cafeteria.

Cherry decided to change out of her work clothes before she ate. She headed up the stairs. As she turned the corner, she ran into Tom coming down the other way.

Cherry jumped and yelped.

'Sorry!' Tom held up his hands. 'Sorry, sorry. I didn't realize how late it was.' Stevie was behind him on the stairs. She started barking and getting excited. She knocked into Tom, and he fell forward a little into Cherry.

Cherry stepped back. 'It's okay. You just startled me.'

Stevie squeezed through Tom's legs and tried to squeeze through Cherry's. Cherry wobbled. She pushed Stevie aside. 'I can't believe you got her to come all the way down the stairs . . .'

Normally Stevie would go *up* stairs, but would then be too afraid to come down. Even the two stairs on the front porch were a problem.

'We've been practicing on the basement steps,' Tom said. 'Every time I went down there to work, she'd sit at the top and whine.'

Cherry let Stevie herd her backwards, down to the foyer. 'Look at you, Stevie. I'm impressed.'

'Don't be too impressed,' Tom said. 'She's still afraid of water.'

It was an ongoing joke between them that Stevie's Great Pyrenees and Newfoundland genes canceled each other out – that she'd be a terrible mountain dog *and* a terrible water dog.

Stevie jumped up onto Cherry, and Cherry ruffled the fur at her neck. 'Aw . . . what good are you? You'll never save a toddler drowning in the Seine.'

Stevie kept charging forward. Cherry stumbled back. 'Okay, enough,' Cherry said. 'Down.' She pushed Stevie's paws away. 'Down, Stevie!'

'*Off*,' Tom said in a commanding voice.

Stevie dropped down immediately.

'Wow.' Cherry looked up at him, surprised. 'She really listens to you.'

Tom was dismissive. 'She just doesn't know those other words. I taught her "off."'

'When? Just this week?'

'No. When she was a puppy.'

'So all I need to say is "off"?'

'It helps if you make this gesture.' He shoved both palms forward.

'I didn't know that,' Cherry said. 'What other secret words did you teach her?'

Tom smiled, just with his eyes. Tom's eyes were always lighter than Cherry remembered, even when she had just seen him. She used to hope that their kids would get Tom's pale blue eyes, but her hazel probably would have canceled them out. 'They're not *secrets*,' he said. 'They're basic dog commands that I found in a book.'

'Tell me more.'

'Um ...' He made a fist. *'Sit.'*

Stevie sat.

'Okay,' Cherry said. 'I mostly knew that one ...'

Tom pointed at the floor. *'Lie down.'*

Stevie lay down.

'Right,' Cherry said. 'That makes sense.'

He twirled his hand. *'Roll over.'*

Stevie rolled over.

Cherry gasped. 'I didn't know she could roll over!'

'She's very smart,' he said. 'I was going to teach her to pull a cart.'

'Why, do you need to haul something?'

'Nah.' Stevie had hopped back to her feet. Tom scratched between her ears. 'I just wanted to give her something to do.' He looked a little sad. 'I think she'd be happier with something to do ...'

Cherry knew just what he meant. 'I think about that all the time. The way she follows me around the kitchen, looking up at me like she wants to help ... the way she jumps to attention when I walk into the room ...'

Tom nodded. 'Breed instincts. She wants to work.'

Cherry hummed sympathetically and patted Stevie's flank. 'Poor Stevie. She's like a housewife whose husband won't let her get a job. Stuck at home all day, bored –'

Tom scratched under Stevie's collar. 'Taking Xanax and having an affair with the pool boy.'

Cherry laughed.

Tom was smiling at her. 'You could take her to daycare.'

'I do sometimes. It's expensive.'

He shrugged.

They were standing at the bottom of the stairs still, both of them petting different ends of the dog.

'I should head out,' Tom said.

'Yeah,' Cherry agreed. 'You better get out of here before I start reading all your passive-aggressive Post-it notes.'

He shook his head, just a little. 'My notes aren't passive-aggressive. They're just passive.'

Cherry laughed again. 'Touché.'

Tom gave Stevie a few more scratches, then stood up straight. He reached for his hoodie – it was lying on the kennel – and started putting it on.

'Tom,' Cherry said. Impulsively.

His head popped through the neck of the sweatshirt. 'Yeah?'

'I picked up Aunt Ida's for dinner. Do you want to stay and have some? I ordered too much.'

Tom looked at her for a few seconds, like he was trying to read between her lines. He shook his head again. 'You don't have to do that, Cherry.'

'No,' she said, 'I know. I just – Why don't you stay for dinner, and we can settle some of this stuff face-to-face?' She waved a hand toward the dining room. 'I'm out of blue Post-its.'

Tom was still studying her expression. 'Yeah,' he said finally. 'Okay. If that's what you want.'

Cherry raised her eyebrows. 'I don't know if I want it, but I can definitely get through it.'

'That's what she said,' Tom murmured.

Cherry snorted. They'd once spent a month saying, *'That's what she said'* to make fun of a guy in Tom's office who always said it. They said it so much that for about a year, they couldn't *stop* saying it. And then they spent another six months saying, *'Okay, that was the last one, I promise.'*

'Come on.' Cherry walked into the kitchen. 'It's just soup. I didn't order bread or anything fancy.'

He walked in behind her. 'You think bread is fancy?'

Cherry got out two bowls. There was a new batch of miscellany arranged on the kitchen island, along with several Post-it notes. She ignored it all.

'Sorry about the mess in here,' Tom said. 'I've been bringing things down from the attic – and up from the cellar. There's still a bunch of stuff down there from the previous owners. I was thinking about getting a dumpster ... unless you want me to leave it?'

'A dumpster is fine,' Cherry said, dishing out some chicken and noodles for him. 'I just don't want it to sit out there forever.'

'It won't sit out there forever.'

'Then that's fine. Maybe I could make a salad ...' She opened the fridge. There was a bag of lettuce, but it looked rusty. 'Never mind.'

'I was thinking I'd clear out the garage, too. While I'm here.'

She handed him the bowl. 'That's fine. I haven't been in the garage in years.' Cherry parked her car in the driveway.

'Who's been mowing the lawn?'

'No one lately, but I hired someone.'

'Smart.'

'My therapist said to throw your money at problems,' Cherry said, fixing herself a bowl.

Tom bristled. 'It's not my money.'

She raised her eyebrows but decided not to argue. She got out two spoons.

'You should hire someone to shovel, too.' Tom sounded aggressive. Like he was giving her an order.

'I do.'

'Good.'

'And just, like, whatever, Cherry. Like – you could replace the sink in the bathroom. I know you want to. Just do it. Don't worry about it.'

'Yeah,' she said. 'Maybe I will.' She motioned toward the living room.

Tom walked ahead of her. There were new piles of stuff spread out on the coffee table and stacked on the armchairs. Cherry sat on the couch. Tom stood there for a second at the edge of the room.

'Okay,' he said. 'This is untenable.'

'What is?' Cherry was already eating.

He gestured with his spoon around the room. 'This. There's no place for you to eat.'

Cherry shrugged. 'It's tenable. I'm tenning.'

Tom looked embarrassed. 'I'm kind of seeing it for the first time...'

'Yeah,' she said.

'Sorry. I'll clean everything up tomorrow.'

'You don't have to.'

He stood there, still looking around with his brow furrowed.

'Sit *down*, Tom.'

He looked over at her. Then sat at the other end of the couch.

The soup was bland. Cherry wished she had something better to offer him – so that he would think *she* was better. So that he'd think she was doing just fine.

Tom was eating his soup doggedly, still staring out at the room. Ashamed.

'I haven't watched the *Thursday* trailer,' Cherry said. 'But everyone says it looks great.'

He glanced over at her and then down at his food. He shrugged.

'Are you done with your part?' she asked. Tom had been hired to write the film's script, and he was an executive producer. The last Cherry had heard, he was spending a lot of time on set.

'Mostly,' he said. 'I still have to promote it. They want me to do these daylong junkets where I sit there with the actors and say the same thing over and over. They gave me media training.'

'Is that why you're moving to Los Angeles?'

His forehead was still tense. 'Not exactly. I guess Los Angeles seems as good a place as any. Maybe I'll be inspired to do something new there.'

'*Thursday* in L.A.?'

'Ah.' Tom poked at his soup with his spoon. 'No. No more *Thursday* after this year.'

Cherry frowned. 'No more?'

'Nope.' He stirred his soup.

'You're not serious.'

He looked up at her. 'I am serious.'

'You can't end *Thursday*.'

'I can't?'

'I mean – why would you want to?' Cherry was upset. *Why was she upset?* 'It's always been . . . you know.'

'I know. But . . .' Tom shrugged. 'I think it's run its course.'

'Oh,' Cherry said. She was welling up. *Why* was she welling up? Cherry didn't even read *Thursday*. She kind of hated *Thursday*. 'So you're just ending it.'

He looked confused. 'I didn't think you'd have a strong opinion about this.'

'I don't. I just wasn't expecting . . . So you'll write an ending? Or you'll just stop?'

'I'll write an ending. I've got it all plotted.'

'Oh.' Cherry was crying now. She set down her bowl and covered her face.

'Cherry . . .' She felt Tom move closer to her. 'Hey. What's wrong?'

'Nothing.'

He touched her shoulder. 'Cherry.'

'I just –' She cried a little harder. 'I just –'

He stroked her shoulder. 'What is it, baby . . .'

'I don't want you to –'

'You don't want me to end it?'

'No, I mean – *No*. I just – *Tom*.' The tears were coming in sheets. 'Are you making them get a divorce?'

'Am I . . .?'

'In the *comic*. Baby and The Guy. Are you –'

'Oh,' Tom said, getting it. '*No*. No, I would never.'

'Are they breaking up?'

'No. They're not breaking up.'

'Because I know it's your comic, and you need to express yourself –'

'They're staying together, Cherry. I promise.'

'I just don't think I could –'

'They're okay, come here.' He pulled her into his chest.

She went. 'The *idea* of them –'

'They're still in love.'

'Please don't –'

Tom held her head in his neck. 'It's okay, they're okay. I wouldn't do that.'

'You can if you want to.'

'I don't want to. Don't worry.' He rubbed her back. 'Don't worry about this. It's just going to end. I'm moving on, but they're staying together.'

Cherry nodded. 'Okay,' she choked out. 'Thank you.'

'Please don't worry.'

'Okay,' she said into his chest. Tom was so wide and warm. He smelled so familiar, it made her feel faint. Tom was the only person under sixty who used Irish Spring.

It took a few minutes for Cherry to catch her breath . . . to come back to herself. Her neck stiffened, and she sat up, away from him.

'Okay,' she said again. 'Thank you. I'm sorry.'

'Don't apologize.' Tom's hands fell to his sides.

Cherry wiped her eyes on her sleeve. 'Good for you, Tom. I mean, starting something new. That's – That's great. Do you have an idea?'

'No ...' He was still watching her. Still ready to catch her if she started crying again. 'But ... I didn't have an idea for *Thursday* when I started. I literally named it that because I wanted to commit myself to posting once a week.'

'Yeah, I heard you say that on *The Late Show*.'

'Oh.' He looked embarrassed. 'Sorry. I'm like a talking doll with a string – I only have five anecdotes.'

'No, it's fine. I just meant – I didn't know that before I heard you say it on TV.'

'You didn't?'

She shook her head.

'Huh. Well ...' He'd set his soup down on the table. He picked it up. 'There you go. I don't even know what it's *like* to have an idea.'

'Maybe you could do something like *Thursday*, in a new setting.'

He glanced up at her without lifting his head. 'I'm not sure why you're encouraging me, Cherry.'

'Do you think I should be *dis*couraging you?'

He shrugged. 'Maybe.'

Cherry's eyes welled up. She bit the corner of her lip and waited until she thought she could speak without relapsing into tears. 'I know that we're not in a good place,' she said. 'But I still want you to be happy.'

Tom closed his eyes. He didn't look up. He nodded. 'Okay, well ... thank you.'

They finished their soup in relative silence.

When Cherry was done, she made room for her empty bowl on the coffee table, amongst all the stuff Tom had laid out there. It was an insane assortment: A stainless steel apple peeler. Antique bookends shaped like cartoon bears. A cookie jar that looked like the hot air balloon in *The Wizard of Oz*, still full of odds and ends.

'So,' Cherry said. She wiped her eyes again. She tried to be rational, or at least to look rational. 'Let's talk through this.'

Tom sighed. 'Well... you've read my notes.'

'I have,' she said. 'And you've read my notes.'

'And nothing seems to be moving.'

Cherry rested her elbow on the arm of the couch and her chin in her palm. 'I think what's happening is... we're arguing over who should keep things that *neither* of us really want.'

'Okay,' Tom said, 'but *also*... you don't want to let go of anything.'

She sat up. 'That's not true. I keep telling you to take it all.'

'Yeah, but then if I don't want something and I put it in the Goodwill pile, you take it out.'

'Well, you're putting really good stuff in the Goodwill pile!'

Tom laughed at her. 'It's *all* good stuff, Cherry. All our stuff is good stuff.'

Cherry felt sad. She felt *more* sad. 'Yeah... I guess so.'

'That's because of you,' he said. 'Your rule about everything being either useful or beautiful.'

'That's actually William Morris's rule...'

'William Morris didn't say it to me every time we went to Super-Target.'

Cherry rubbed her face. She felt sad and tired. And older than she'd ever been in her life. 'If I'm being honest,' she said quietly, 'I don't know what I want. I don't want you to take everything, but I also don't want you to leave it all for me to deal with. And when I think about giving it away...' She shook her head. 'No one else will appreciate our stuff like we did.'

They both stared at the coffee table.

Stevie had been napping on the other side of the room, but now she lumbered over to them, shoved past Tom's legs, and launched herself up onto the couch between them. It wasn't graceful – if the couch were an inch higher, she wouldn't be able to make it. She landed halfway onto Cherry's lap, and her tail hit

Tom's face. He pushed it away. 'I thought she wasn't allowed on the couch.'

'I promoted her from pet to roommate,' Cherry said, helping the dog settle.

Tom squinted out at the living room and the dining room beyond. 'We could just box it all up. Everything that you don't want to look at. We'll deal with it later.'

'No.' Cherry scratched Stevie's neck. 'I don't want to "Tell-Tale Heart" it.'

Tom sighed, short and exasperated. 'I know you want me to do my part – but I don't feel like I have the, I don't know, *authority*? And I can't read your mind. Especially if *you* don't know what you want.'

'That's fair,' she whispered.

'If I took everything you told me to take, you'd be living in an empty house. Do you really want that?'

Cherry breathed in deep. And decided to tell Tom the truth: 'I don't think . . . that . . . I *am* going to be living here.'

He whipped his head toward her. 'What do you mean?'

'I don't want to live here. In this house.'

He looked confused. And maybe upset. 'But you love this house – you picked it out.'

'Not for myself.'

'Where do you want to live?'

'I don't know. Not here. Maybe I'll get an apartment downtown, near work.'

'An *apartment*?'

'I don't know, Tom. *I didn't think you'd have a strong opinion about this.*'

He rolled his eyes. 'Okay, well – I *don't*. I'm just surprised. I mean . . .' He looked around. 'You put your *whole heart* into this house. There's so much you can't take with you, all the painting, and the flowers – your lilac bushes.'

'I wasn't putting my heart into *the house*,' she hissed.

Tom took the hit. He looked away.

Cherry took another breath. She looked down at her hand, methodically petting Stevie's fur. 'If you get to start over,' she said. 'Why don't I?'

Tom sat still. After a second, he pushed Stevie's rump off his legs and stood up. He took his bowl and Cherry's into the kitchen and then reappeared in the dining room. 'I think I'll clean out the garage tomorrow,' he said. 'I don't think there's anything out there we need to talk about.'

'Okay,' she agreed.

'And I'll get a dumpster.'

She nodded.

'Thanks for dinner.'

She started petting Stevie again. 'Sure.'

Tom cleared his throat.

Cherry looked up.

'I want you to be happy, too, Cherry.'

Cherry didn't think she could respond to that without screaming or crying, so she didn't.

After a few seconds, Tom let himself out.

Chapter 21

Cherry was twenty-five, and it was the first time she'd worked somewhere that had a big Christmas party...

A big, *mandatory* Christmas party.

Cherry had been at the railroad for ten months or so. She was an entry-level designer in the marketing department, which meant she spent her days resizing help-wanted ads for small-town newspapers and formatting endless brochures for Employee Health. Like – *Naps: Part of Your Safety Toolbox*. And – *Tobacco Cessation: No More 'Butt's*.

It was pretty mind-numbing.

But at least she worked in a cool building – Western Alliance's seventeen-story glass headquarters in downtown Omaha – and the railroad itself was interesting. It felt like Cherry was doing something *real*. Everyone at Western Alliance acted like they were part of a patriotic mission to supply the country with finished goods and raw materials. There were American flags everywhere. The company had a famous TV commercial that was just thirty seconds of trains zooming past the camera, with flags painted on their cars. The commercial played in her building's lobby and cafeteria, and on some of the elevators. Cherry knew the voiceover by heart.

This was not how Cherry had expected to use her art degree – but now she wondered what she'd *ever* planned to do with an art degree, from a Jesuit university, no less. All her classmates had gone on to law school and medical school and PT school. Stacia was going to be a chiropractor.

Cherry's goals when she graduated were modest: make art; get health insurance.

The railroad checked one and a half of those boxes.

It really wasn't so bad ... Cherry was doing well at Western Alliance. Her boss, Doug, trusted her – he sent her to all the meetings he didn't want to go to. And Cherry was *mostly* adjusting to corporate culture.

She was really anxious about this holiday party.

The railroad's vice president of public affairs (Doug's boss's boss) invited all her departments to her house every year. Cherry had gone to a fancy liquor store to buy a hostess gift – which her coworkers said was crucial. She'd spent more on one bottle of wine for this rich VP than she'd ever spent on her own mother. It was ridiculous. And now she had to figure out what to wear ...

Everyone at the railroad was so conservative, and Cherry so *wasn't*. It was the only thing Doug got on her case about. He said that she dressed like the host of a children's television show. The first time he'd said it, Cherry had been wearing an adorable red polka-dot dress, with a navy blue sweater and a yellow kerchief tied around her neck.

'I love this outfit,' she'd said without looking up from her computer.

'It's a good outfit for *Pee-wee's Playhouse*,' Doug said. 'Or maybe, whatchamacallit ...'

'*The Howdy Doody Show*,' Wallace offered. Wallace was the senior designer who sat across from Cherry. He was ancient.

'Exactly,' Doug said. 'I was going to say *Bozo's Circus*.'

Cherry side-eyed him. 'Am I supposed to dress like you guys?' (Doug didn't mind a little sass.)

Cherry was the only woman on their team – everyone else wore khakis with red, blue or black Western Alliance polos.

Doug shrugged. 'Just dress like the girls in the other departments.'

'Like the other *women*,' Wallace corrected.

'Right,' Doug said. 'The women.'

'I'm an artist,' Cherry said. 'This is the art department.'

He rolled his eyes. 'This is the design arm of the marketing department. You're a marketer.'

Cherry turned away from her computer screen to give him the full weight of her distaste. 'Am I actually going to get in trouble for having some *panache*?'

'No. You just won't get promoted.'

She folded her arms. 'If my panache gets me pigeonholed, I'll pass on that promotion, pal.'

Doug smirked. Wallace hooted. (Wallace was an easy mark. Cherry could crack him up at will.)

Doug leaned on the top edge of Cherry's cubicle. His voice dropped, even though Wallace could still hear him. 'You should listen to me, Cherry. Everyone around here likes you – but they don't take you seriously.'

'Because I'm a young woman,' she said.

'Yeah, probably.' Doug was at least honest. 'But also because you dress like a cartoon character. This is a railroad – no one values creativity. You make people nervous. If you want a career here, dress like it.'

Cherry wasn't sure that she did want a *career* at the railroad, but she definitely wanted a raise. So she took the note . . .

Sort of. Cherry was too broke to buy all new clothes. She already had credit card debt, and she'd had to buy a new car when she got this job. She was living close to the bone – she still went to her parents' house most nights for dinner.

The best Cherry could do with her work wardrobe was rein herself in. She started wearing her clothes in the most boring way possible. Sometimes in the elevator on the way to her desk, she'd look in the mirrored doors and take off the accessory she liked most.

Her goal for this Christmas party was to look unobtrusive. The invitation said 'holiday attire.' When Cherry asked Doug what that meant, he said, 'For Christ's sake, don't wear anything that blinks. Nothing too cute. No Santa hats and what have you ... *reindeer*. Everything in Meg Jones's house is a neutral color. Just wear black. Do you have anything black?'

'I have some black,' Cherry said. She thought she might, anyway.

Wallace sat back in his chair so that he could join the conversation. 'It's a wild party. Some of the gals around here get kind of ... *slinky*.'

'Some of the *women*,' Doug corrected.

'Right.' Wallace looked ashamed. 'The women.'

Doug pointed at Cherry. 'Don't you dare wear anything slinky. And don't get drunk, either of you. For Christ's *sake*.'

On the night of the party, Cherry put on a pair of very boring, very plain black jeans and a plain black V-necked sweater. In her normal life, she would never wear these two pieces together. She felt like a theater tech. For jewelry, she wore only her gold heart locket. (She always wore it when she needed some luck – it was a gift from her mother with her sisters' baby pictures inside. It folded out into a four-leaf clover.)

The only interesting part of Cherry's outfit was a pair of black leather, calf-length boots with *perfect* heels – three and a half inches, not quite stiletto but definitely not stacked, with the sexiest little curve. They made Cherry feel like a cartoon character in a *good* way. Like Jessica Rabbit from the ankles down. (This line of thinking was the reason Cherry had credit card debt.)

The vice president of public affairs – Meg Jones – lived in one of the wealthiest parts of town, a suburb where the houses looked actually built, not 3D-printed. The house had a two-lane circular driveway, like a hotel. Cherry parked her used Hyundai at the end of a long line of black SUVs. (Railroad execs drove the same cars as rappers.)

She was late. She hadn't wanted to be one of the first people here. Meg Jones was nice, but very intimidating. Cherry couldn't tell how old she was. She wore Michael Kors suits and looked like she had her hair highlighted strand by strand. Her face didn't have a single line.

Cherry hiked up to the double-sized front door and then couldn't decide what to do next. Did you knock at a big party? She didn't think she should just walk in. There was Christmas music playing inside. She decided to ring the doorbell. A minute later, the vice president herself opened the door.

That's when Cherry realized her mistake.

Meg Jones was wearing a long, sparkly red dress. Like a prom dress. Even fancier – like a ball gown.

Cherry's mouth fell open, and she couldn't close it.

'Cherish!' Meg Jones said. (It said *Cherish* on all of Cherry's work documents.) 'Thank you for coming.'

She opened the door, and Cherry stepped inside. Just past the entryway was a huge room with a cathedral ceiling. It was decorated with real greenery and tiny white lights, and it was wall-to-wall rich people in fancy clothes. Men in suits. Women in red-carpet-worthy dresses.

'Thank you for inviting me.' Cherry mechanically held out the bottle of wine.

'You didn't have to do that,' Meg Jones said, taking the wine. 'Thank you. Do you have a coat?'

Cherry shook her head.

'Let me introduce you to my husband. I just saw him . . .'

'Would you mind if I used the restroom first?'

'Oh, of course.' The vice president motioned toward an archway across the big room. 'There's one down that hall. And one off the kitchen. And if those are both occupied, there's one out the patio door, by the pool.'

'Thank you.' Cherry made herself smile. She didn't need to use the bathroom, but she did need to *get away*, as quickly as possible. She thought about walking back to her car, but Meg Jones was standing in front of the door.

Cherry walked swiftly toward the hallway bathroom, along the wall. She could feel people looking at her. She could *see* people looking at her. A waiter strode past her, wearing all black. Cherry hoped everyone would think she was on staff.

She slipped through the archway and stood in a wide, off-white hallway, catching her breath.

Why hadn't anyone told her this was a formal party? She'd asked for guidance! What was she supposed to do now?

On the one hand, Cherry should make sure that Doug knew she was here. (Attendance was mandatory.) On the other hand, she didn't want him to see her dressed like this – and she couldn't bear to walk through that room again! Maybe the bathroom had a window big enough for her to crawl through ...

Or maybe she was overreacting.

Was she overreacting? Was every single person at this party *really* dressed to the nines?

She crept back to the archway and peeked out. *Shit.* Some of them were dressed to the *tens.* Cherry didn't even know where you bought dresses like that.

Fortunately no one was paying attention to her at the moment. They were all drinking and laughing. She scanned the crowd for familiar faces ...

Oh. Fuck. Someone *was* looking at her – a man standing at the edge of another big archway, under a truly *resplendent* garland of greenery. He was watching Cherry.

She froze.

The man lifted his hand in a very minimal wave.

Did Cherry know this guy? Did she work with him? She lifted her hand to wave back.

He stood there staring at her for a second, possibly smiling; it was hard to tell. Cherry let her hand drop.

That seemed to settle something. The guy started walking toward her.

He was big – broad like a football player – and wearing what she could tell from across the room was an ill-fitting suit. No, it wasn't even a suit – it was dark pants and a suit jacket. He was in his twenties. Kind of cute. Cherry definitely didn't know him.

He walked right up to her. He was looking at her the way people look at you when they think you're lost – frowning in a nice way. He had squinty blue eyes and very short, light brown hair.

He stood between Cherry and the room.

'Hi,' he said. His voice was soft.

'Hi,' Cherry said.

He grimaced a little more. 'Nobody told you that this is a debutante ball for rich people.'

She shook her head. 'They did not.'

He smiled, but just with his eyes, and cocked his head. 'Do you want me to help you leave? Or do you want me to help you stay?'

'I'm not sure,' Cherry said. 'I feel like – if I don't move, maybe no one will see me.'

He nodded. 'You're *tharn*. Like in *Watership Down*. Have you read *Watership Down*?'

She shook her head again.

'Well ...' He sighed and glanced behind him, like he was contemplating the situation. He looked even more pained for a second. 'I think you should stay. The food here is really great, and in an hour or two, everyone will be so drunk, they won't remember you.'

Cherry stared up at him. He was getting cuter by the second. He had bristly blond eyebrows and full pink lips. She liked the way his mouth never quite resolved itself into a smile. She liked his diamond-checked necktie.

'Are you still tharn?' he asked gently. 'I've got to tell you, you're not invisible.'

'I'll stay,' Cherry said.

He grinned. Sort of. He kind of clamped it down midway. 'Yeah?'

'Yeah,' she said.

'All right.' He nodded again. 'Good.'

'But I need to get out of this room.'

'I can help you with that.' He stood taller and nodded toward the archway where she'd first spotted him. 'There's a back room over there where all the reprobates hang out.'

'That sounds perfect.'

'Walk with me. I'll cover you.'

Cherry let him walk between her and the party. He was very good at looming without actually crowding her.

'I have to say . . .' she said. 'You don't seem like a reprobate.'

'I'm worse,' he said. 'I'm an artist.'

Cherry laughed. 'I'm an artist, too.'

He smiled down at her. 'Yeah?'

'Yeah. Well. I work in marketing.'

They turned a corner into a smaller room. It was just as crowded in here – and just as cream-colored – but the faces were younger and the suits were cheaper. A few people looked twice at Cherry when she walked in, but their judgment felt less consequential. And she felt shielded by the big guy. The *artist*.

'Here,' he said. 'Stand behind this couch. You're very presentable from the waist up.'

'Every girl's dream.'

He blushed. He had a very visible blush. 'That's not what I meant.'

She smiled at him. 'I know.'

'Let me get you something to drink. And some of the little sandwiches – that's what I was looking for when I found you. How do you feel about canapés, generally speaking?'

'I feel really, really good about them,' Cherry said. She resisted saying, *I mean, look at me.*

'I'm going to bring you a whole tray.'

'And a Coke,' she said.

He nodded. 'Got it.' He was looking down between them and

peering up at her. 'Don't go anywhere. I don't want to find you standing in the hallway again, glassy-eyed.'

'I know that it's about rabbits,' Cherry said. 'Your book.'

'It's a great book. You should read it.'

'Maybe I will.'

'Coke,' he said, pointing at her.

'And little sandwiches.'

'I'll be right back.'

She caught his wrist. 'Wait.'

He stopped.

'I'm Cherry,' she said.

'Cherry?' He emphasized the *ch*.

She nodded.

'Hi, Cherry. I'm Tom.'

That first night with Tom . . .

Cherry was dazzled by him.

By his narrow blue eyes and wide-bridged nose. He looked like a lion. Especially when he laughed. He laughed with his brow furrowed, like he felt sorry about something.

Tom was a designer. Like Cherry.

But not like Cherry. He'd gone to a school with a real graphic arts program, and his job was much more interesting. He actually *designed* things.

Everyone in this room worked for Coates & Branch, the outside ad agency that did all the railroad's advertising and branding. C&B was famous for being the best in Nebraska – and famously stuck-up about it. Cherry could never have gotten hired there. She didn't have the portfolio.

It felt like a different party back here. A sloppier one. With shaggy creative types and leggy account managers. It was like everyone in the room thought they were a character from *Mad Men*. (But also like everyone in the room really *was* a character from *Mad*

Men.) People were sprawled out on the expensive suede couches. They were all holding two drinks – '*Because the goddamn waiters take their goddamn time with refills*' – and Tom wasn't the only one who had heaped a pile of hors d'oeuvres onto a napkin.

'Do you have lots of clients?' Cherry asked him. 'Or just the railroad?'

'Me, personally?' He was eating a tiny chocolate orange tart. He'd brought Cherry two. 'Mostly the railroad. I've only been at C&B a year.'

'Maybe I'd recognize your work . . .'

'I'm not sure you'd *remember* it.'

'Try me.'

He furrowed his brow. 'Okay. I'm the guy behind the signs in your new cafeteria. Heady stuff – "*Place dishes on belt.*" "*Dispose of paper goods.*"'

Cherry smiled. 'Don't sell yourself short. Those are some beautiful signs. Very tasteful.'

'The brief called for "calming."'

'Mission accomplished,' she said, nodding. 'I actually really love the *"You are where you eat"* campaign you guys did for the dining hall, especially the ads that run in our elevators – you know, with the animated cutlery? I want to meet the person who wrote those. Are *they* here?'

Tom was smiling again with his eyes. They were the color of cartoon ice. 'This might be a letdown for you . . .'

'*No.*' Cherry elbowed him excitedly. Her hands were full of canapés. '*You* wrote those ads? Gosh, if you could tap dance, you'd be a triple threat.'

Tom was still not-quite-smiling. 'How do you know I can't tap dance?'

Cherry gazed up at him. Smiling, admiring, possibly expecting him to *start*.

He shook his head. 'I can't tap dance.'

She elbowed him again. 'Yeah, but you can *write*.'

'That's not writing. It's barely even thinking.'

'Hey ...' She made a face. 'I love those ads. I love the talking fork who crosses his tines because he really hopes it's pizza day.'

'It's always pizza day,' Tom said. 'The Western Alliance dining area has an organically supplied pizza station.'

'A fact that the ad effectively communicates.'

His lips quirked up. He looked a little embarrassed. 'You're easily impressed.'

Cherry's voice was faint: 'I'm really not.'

Tom didn't leave Cherry's side all night long. (Except to get her another drink and more canapés.) He hardly looked away from her. His head was tilted down for three hours, and Cherry's was tilted up. She laughed at everything he said, and he smiled at everything she said.

Tom was drinking beer, but he switched to Coke.

Tom was from Omaha. He was a year younger than Cherry. He'd gone to art school because he loved Donald Duck comics. He read a lot of books that Cherry had never heard of and was very into 'sequential art.'

Tom didn't care about music. He didn't recognize any of the pop songs playing over the speakers. (Meg Jones's house had a built-in sound system.) He'd never even heard an Adele song – he'd never heard of *Adele* – but he kept making Cherry sing them all the way through. 'Just a little bit more. I think I might know this one ... No, I guess not. Hit me with another one.'

Tom was *funny*.

Funny in a way Cherry wasn't used to. He dropped his voice every time he made a joke, like he was telling them to himself. (The boys she knew made sure you caught every punchline – sometimes they repeated them.) Cherry kept leaning in to hear him. Cherry just kept leaning *in*.

Everyone thought that the two of them must have come to the party together.

'Who's your friend, Tom?'

'Tom didn't tell us he was bringing a date.'

'What the fuck, Tom – why didn't you tell this poor girl what to wear?'

'It's okay,' Tom kept repeating in his soft voice. 'Nobody really cares what you're wearing.'

'I hope I don't get fired,' Cherry said.

'Do you really think you'd get fired for wearing jeans?'

She gritted her teeth and made a consternated noise in the back of her throat. 'No. But it's a pattern of behavior – I'm never wearing the right thing. My boss wants me to look more corporate. He says I dress like Theresa the Channel 42 Kids Club lady.'

Tom winced. He laughed. His eyes sparkled. '*Do* you?'

Cherry looked offended. 'No!'

'Hmm . . . I might need to judge this for myself.'

Cherry grinned, and Tom looked away. He was smiling. Blushing visibly. Closing one eye and peeking back at her. Scratching the back of his neck.

Tom had wide, ruddy hands. He had a wide face and a square jaw. He moved like someone who didn't want to bump into anyone or knock anything over. Up close, under about a thousand white Christmas lights, his hair was ashy blond, not brown, and you could tell that he hadn't shaved. Cherry kept finding new things to like about him.

Fortunately Cherry's boss didn't spot her until he was two and a half sheets to the wind. Doug came to talk to the agency people and saw her hiding in the corner. 'For Christ's sake, Cherry, what are you wearing? Are those *jeans*?'

'This is your fault!' she shouted over the music. 'You didn't tell me it was formal – you told me to wear black!'

Doug started laughing – *hard*. 'Wallace has gotta see this . . .' He went to find him.

Cherry introduced herself to Doug's wife. Who was wearing a *very* slinky dress.

Cherry ate savory cream puffs and sugared fruits. She ate miniature quiches and cakes. Every time the cater-waiters walked past the back room, the agency people mobbed them.

Doug brought Wallace back to laugh at Cherry, but Wallace sincerely felt bad when he saw her. 'I should have told you to wear a dress, Cherry. I just assumed you'd wear a dress – you have a lot of dresses.'

You could tell that Wallace didn't like the ad agency people. He drifted back to the main room. Doug stayed and drank with some of the older guys, the younger Baby Boomers.

The agency people decided to leave the party all at once, like a flock of birds changing direction. Cherry found herself swept up in their exit, standing at the back of the crowd as they thanked the hostess and waved good-bye.

When they all spilled out onto the front walk, Tom and Cherry hung back. He looked down at her. (He still hadn't *stopped* looking down at her.) 'Can I walk you to your car?'

'Yeah,' she said. 'Thank you.'

Half the black SUVs were gone. Cherry's heels clicked with every step down the driveway. She'd been standing all night. Her feet were killing her.

'This is me,' she said, when they got to her Hyundai.

Tom stopped. He looked up, past Cherry, and ran a hand through his hair. It stayed ruffled.

'Thanks again for extricating me,' she said.

He glanced behind him. 'Anytime. Just call me when you're in an uncomfortable situation, and I'll come in with a helicopter.'

'Maybe I'll see you at work?'

He frowned, squinting out into the street. 'Probably not. Our CEO doesn't trust us in your building.'

'That's too bad. We have a really nice cafeteria.'

'So I've heard.'

'I could probably get you in.'

Tom nodded. He'd turned his whole head away from her. His shoulders were turning, too.

Cherry wasn't sure what was happening. Had some spell broken when they walked away from the house? She'd thought that Tom was as dazzled as she was. (Even if he was only *half* as dazzled as Cherry was, he wouldn't want to turn away.)

'Well . . . have a good night,' he said.

'You, too,' Cherry said, leaning in the direction he was turning. 'It was nice to meet you.'

'It was nice to meet you. Cherry.' He backed up a step, then pivoted fully away from her and started walking.

Cherry stared after him. 'Tom?'

He looked back. 'Yeah?'

He was already a car length away.

'Can I give you my phone number?'

Tom winced. His forehead wrinkled. 'Do you want to?'

'Do I . . .' Cherry repeated in a confused voice. '*Yeah*. I mean – not if you don't want to take it.'

'No, I do. I want your phone number.'

'Okay.'

Tom stayed where he was.

Cherry walked to him. His head slowly tipped down, tracking her, as she came closer. It took him a second to reach for his phone.

She said her number out loud while he typed it in. It was embarrassing – Cherry had never forced her phone number on a man before. She'd never even offered it. But she'd never had a night like *this*. A night that had gone as *right* as this. Cherry had never liked someone so immediately. And so completely. Her attention still felt tethered to Tom, like he would drag her behind him if he walked away.

Tom slipped his phone back in his pocket.

'You don't have to call me,' Cherry said, trying to be brave. 'But . . . this was such a great night. And I'd love to see you again.'

'Really?'

She laughed, still embarrassed. 'Yes, really. Why are you acting like I'm being weird?'

Was this about her weight? Tom was bigger, too. Not as big as Cherry, proportionally. He hadn't seemed to mind her weight when they were inside, even in front of all his coworkers. Sometimes bigger guys only dated wraithlike women. Maybe it was one thing to talk to a fat girl at a party and another thing to call her.

'Do you have nights like tonight all the time?' Cherry asked. She didn't want to give up. 'Do you click with everyone like this?'

Tom shook his head. 'No,' he said softly. His eyes drifted down from her eyes to her mouth ... and maybe to her breasts. Back to her mouth.

Cherry lifted up her chin, just in case.

They stood parallel to each other. Looking up and looking down. If Cherry were to draw them, she'd draw their bodies in an arch.

She felt Tom's attention on her like vibrating light.

'So call me,' she said after a few seconds.

Tom nodded. 'I will.'

He did.

Chapter 22

On their first date, Tom took Cherry to a tiny pizza place near his house called Abbie's Road. 'The pizza's fine,' he said, 'but the theming's extraordinary.'

The restaurant was crammed into an acute angle where two roads converged. There were only seven or eight tables inside, and the whole place was Beatles-themed – and also, for some reason, ocean-themed?

'Because of "Octopus's Garden," I think,' Tom said. He was sitting under a net filled with plastic fish.

Tom and Cherry shared one of the house combos – 'Lucy in the Pie with Onions' – and also their life stories, greatly abridged.

Tom grew up on the north side of town. Cherry grew up on the south side. Neither of them grew up with much money.

Tom's dad worked in building maintenance at the state medical center – it meant Tom got free tuition in college. Cherry's dad hardly worked. She went to school on scholarship – she was the only one in her family who'd gone to college so far.

Tom had one sibling, an older sister. Cherry told him about her own four sisters. He didn't laugh at their names, but you could tell that he wanted to – his forehead crumpled, and he shook his head like he couldn't take it all in. 'Who started calling you Cherry?'

'I don't know – it's the only thing I've ever been called. Even my mom doesn't call me Cherish.'

Tom's mom died when he was eight. He told Cherry this

incidentally: 'We moved over here when I was eight, after my mom died. I think this used to be a doughnut place.'

Cherry had to roll the conversation back. 'Your mom died when you were eight?'

'Yeah. Breast cancer. Then lung cancer.'

'Oh my god.' Cherry sat back a little. 'I'm so sorry.'

He smiled gently. 'Thanks. It's okay.'

'It *couldn't* have been okay . . .'

Tom shrugged and raised his eyebrows like, *Well, you know.*

Cherry felt suddenly tearful. She shook her head and looked down at her pizza. Her chin was wobbling. *Eight.*

Tom reached out and covered her hand with his – was that the first time he'd touched her? 'Hey,' he whispered. 'It's okay.'

'It's just . . .' A few tears spilled onto her cheeks. '. . . eight is really *young*.'

'I know,' he said.

Cherry wiped her eyes with her other hand and glanced up at him. 'Sorry. I shouldn't be . . . doing what I'm doing.'

Tom's eyes were glossy. He squeezed her hand. 'You're okay.'

She laughed, embarrassed, and he pulled his hand away. He was still smiling.

Their second date was at the Western Alliance Railroad Museum. It was Cherry's idea – neither of them had ever been. (It didn't seem like *anyone* had been to the museum since the early '70s. Even the volunteer docent needed dusting.)

Afterwards they got coffee and talked about how they'd change the museum if they could. Tom would change everything. He sketched out a new logo on the back of a napkin, and it was so brilliant, it made Cherry lightheaded. Tom acted like it was nothing – he shoved the napkin into his coffee cup when they were done, and Cherry had to rescue it.

By their third date, Cherry wondered if they were actually dates at all.

Tom still hadn't kissed her. If she thought about it, he hadn't ever asked her out. He'd only called her when she'd told him to call.

He was very polite to her and very attentive – his eyes followed Cherry everywhere – and he seemed gently amused by everything she said . . .

Tom laughed at Cherry's jokes with his eyes and the very corners of his mouth. (Was that as good as a real laugh? Was it maybe better?)

There was something cool about him – like he was watching Cherry from a distance. Observing her. But observing her *carefully*. There were moments when she felt like there must be something in her teeth or on her lips. (She'd turn away from him to wipe her mouth.) And there were moments when she felt magnetic. Bewitching. It made her dizzy to be paid attention to like that. It turned her on.

Hope said that Tom was keeping Cherry in the friend zone – that even a church boy would move faster than this. (Hope was Cherry's least judgmental sister and the only one she could talk to about boys.) (Hope was still *very* judgmental.) 'You can't make a relationship happen by force of will, Cherry.'

'Maybe I can,' Cherry countered. 'I'm very willful.'

She invited Tom over for Christmas Eve. He didn't have plans, and Cherry canceled hers. She made the only fancy thing she knew how to make – lasagna – and they sat on her living room floor, on either side of her coffee table because Cherry didn't have any chairs.

She sat on her knees mostly, craning over the table toward him.

'Is this cottage cheese?' Tom asked, taking a bite of lasagna.

'Yeah,' she said. 'My Italian grandmother made it like this. She probably couldn't afford ricotta.'

He tipped his head and covered his mouth. 'You're Italian?'

She shrugged. 'A little. I'm all of western Europe. I'm Ellis Island, incorporated.'

He smiled. 'And you're Catholic, right?'

'No, I just went to a Catholic school because I got a full ride. My church growing up was like, I don't know – stand-alone Lutheran.'

'What does that mean?'

'It means it was unaffiliated with the larger church, so it could be as conservative as it wanted. My sisters still go. And my mom.'

'But not you?'

Cherry shook her head. 'I feel like I went to church enough as a kid to cover me for the rest of my life. What about you, are you religious?'

'Not really,' Tom said. 'I wasn't raised anything. But there's a Catholic cathedral near my house, and I go sometimes.'

'Are you trying it on for size?'

He smiled again. Gently. 'Possibly. I just like the vibe – it's tranquil. And I like all the stained glass.'

Cherry hummed. 'Maybe I would have liked church better if there was something to look at. Our church looks like a hotel conference center.'

She kept bouncing on her knees as she talked. Gesturing too much. She was too excited about Tom being here. Too excited about him, generally speaking. She wished she'd engineered it so they could sit on the same side of the table.

The truth was, Cherry was ready to do whatever Tom wanted that night – he'd kept getting more attractive to her, every minute she was with him. If you charted Tom's attractiveness to Cherry over those first few weeks, it would have looked like runaway inflation.

She liked the wide planes of his face. The way his cheeks propped up his eyes and pushed them closed. She liked how *pink* he was. Pink cheeks, pink lips. The way the back of his neck flushed red. Cherry liked all Tom's colors – she liked his changeable hair. In her brightly lit kitchen, Tom's close-cropped hair was as blond as a toddler's. In her dimly lit living room, it was sandy brown.

She liked his clothes, even though he didn't seem to care about them. Tom had worn almost the same thing on all their dates: brown moc-toe boots with gold laces, cargo pants with holes worn along the pockets, and a T-shirt under a plaid shirt. She wondered if he could tell any of his clothes apart.

Cherry had dressed carefully – sexily – every time she saw him. In low-cut sweaters and jeans that were three percent elastic.

'When am I going to see your Channel 42 Kids Club clothes?' Tom had asked her.

When I'm not trying to seduce you, she'd thought.

She'd bought a pint of ice cream for dessert, and they passed it back and forth between them. (Cherry had spoons but no bowls.) Tom looked uncomfortable sitting on the floor, with his legs stiff and to the side. He reminded her of a Ken doll with limited articulation.

'I wish I could offer you a chair,' Cherry said, for the sixth or seventh time. 'Or even a box.'

'I'm fine,' Tom said, like he'd been saying all night. He glanced around the room, taking in the big windows and high ceilings. 'This is a nice apartment – you don't have a roommate?'

'No. If I had a roommate, maybe I could afford a couch.'

'I could help you find a couch.' He seemed serious.

Cherry smiled. 'Do you have a couch guy?'

He shook his head. 'No. I . . .' He lowered an eyebrow. 'I go to a lot of estate sales.' He said it like he knew it was weird.

'Your apartment must be very well appointed,' she said.

'Actually . . .' He looked down. 'I still live at home.'

'Like, in your old room?'

Tom shrugged, glancing up at her. 'It isn't really my old room if I still live there.'

'I guess that's true . . .' Cherry didn't want to offend him – he already seemed embarrassed – but she couldn't *imagine* having moved back home after college. She'd gotten her own place before she could even manage the rent. 'You don't want to move out?'

'I don't know ...' He looked down again. 'I think I'd still have to take care of my dad, even if I left. May as well stay and save on rent.'

'Is your dad sick?'

Tom didn't reply right away. He tapped his spoon against the table, then set it inside the empty ice cream carton. When he looked back up at Cherry, his lips were pursed like he was thinking. 'He's a heavy drinker.'

'Mine, too,' Cherry said quickly, without thinking at all.

Tom looked like she'd told him something much sadder than what he'd told her. 'Your dad?'

She nodded.

'Is that why you don't drink?'

She nodded again. 'Why risk it?'

Tom's mouth was so gentle ... that almost-smile that hung on his lips. He looked down at the kitchen towel he was holding. (Cherry didn't have napkins.) 'I brought you a present.'

She clicked her tongue in surprise. 'You don't have to give me a present. This is only – Well, we've barely met.'

Tom laughed for real. 'It's Christmas Eve. I wasn't *not* going to bring a present.' He took something out of his pants pocket – a small package, wrapped in striped paper.

'I didn't get you anything,' she murmured.

'You made lasagna.' He held out the package. 'I've never had homemade lasagna.'

She smiled at him and took the present. She was still on her knees while she unwrapped it.

It was a very old ballpoint pen with an articulated, plastic cartoon bird on the end.

Cherry laughed. 'This is adorable – where did you find it?'

'I've had it for a while.' Tom tapped the bird's head, and it wobbled. 'The beak moves when you use it, like it's singing.'

She looked up at him. 'Wait, are you giving me your *own* pen?'

'It's your pen now. I wanted to give you something that I knew was good.'

They were both leaning over the table, both smiling. If she were to draw them now, she could do it with one line.

Tom was looking at Cherry like she had his full attention. No one had ever looked at her like that before – like their eyes couldn't get enough of her.

Cherry tipped forward, making her chin available, if Tom wanted it . . .

Then making it unavoidable.

She pressed a kiss into his full, pink mouth.

Tom sat back, away from her, and let Cherry fall forward on the table.

A fat girl can't wait for boys to pluck her like a flower or find her on the beach like a seashell.

Cherry had never been Cinderella. She'd always been the prince – chasing down what she wanted. (She'd been a witch, enchanting apples.) She'd had to reach for things. For love. For attention.

She'd reached for Tom . . .

She'd reached too far.

She'd fallen into the Ben & Jerry's container, and there was chocolate ice cream smeared on her chest.

Tom apologized.

And Cherry apologized.

And they got up and started walking toward the door – like it was clear to both of them that the situation had become unbearable. Tom wouldn't even look at Cherry. (Thank god.)

He left, holding his coat.

And Cherry stood by the door, crying.

She'd brought this on herself. Cherry brought everything on herself – she was a real go-getter. But she was usually a bit more strategic than this. She could usually read the room.

She wondered if there had ever been a moment, since they met, when Tom would have kissed her back...

There was a knock at the door, and Cherry jumped.

She saw Tom through the peephole and considered ignoring him. She didn't need to hear any more *I'm sorry*'s.

When Cherry opened the door, Tom stepped in and immediately reached for her chin. He wrapped his hand around her jaw and kissed her so hard, she shifted back onto her heels.

She closed her eyes and let her neck go slack. Tom kissed her in one long press.

Cherry couldn't make any sense of it. She couldn't read him at all – she could usually *read* people.

She felt suspended from the kiss. From his hand on her jaw. If Tom let go of her, Cherry would fall boneless from a great height.

Tom didn't let go. But he pulled his mouth away an inch to take a breath. 'I'm sorry,' he said urgently. 'I just needed a minute to get my head on straight.'

'You needed a minute,' Cherry parroted.

'Yeah,' he said. 'I'm sorry.' He lifted her chin, his eyes avid on her cheeks and mouth. 'Can I kiss you again?'

'Do you want to?' she whispered.

'Yes,' Tom whispered back. 'I really want to.'

Cherry nodded and let him kiss her. Over and over. In long presses and short bursts.

'I really want to,' Tom said between kisses. 'I really want you, Cherry.'

Chapter 23

Cherry wasn't sure she was going to pull this off... Her back already hurt, and her patent leather heels were pinching across the top. She teetered up Russ Sutton's front steps, holding on to the handrail.

She was meeting him here so they could drive together to dinner and come back to his house after.

Russ was being a very good sport about Cherry always coming back to his place. She couldn't let him see the state of her house right now – and she didn't want to see Russ himself there, surrounded by Tom's chaos and handwriting.

Tom was at the house now every night when Cherry got home from work. They'd talk for a few minutes, sometimes longer, before he left. He was cleaning out the garage. There was a dumpster in the driveway. Cherry had to park in the street.

Tom seemed to have forgotten the 'untenable' mess in the living room, which was typical, but Cherry didn't have the fortitude to bring it up. Which was also typical. The house, the mess, Tom ... it all felt familiar to her. Familiar and sticky and sad.

Cherry felt less single than she had a month ago. When she'd first reconnected with Russ, she'd felt totally available. *Utterly* single. Alone.

Now Tom was back in her life every day – not in a way that brought her companionship or comfort, but in a way that reminded her how *entangled* she still was with him. Legally. Practically. (Emotionally.) She and Tom were still baked in the same pie.

Russ knew that Cherry was entangled. He was being respectful. He didn't dig.

He and Cherry were still seeing each other. And still sleeping together. They followed each other on social media now. And they'd met up a few times for lunch. Cherry was high on his pretty face and his flirty text messages. All the parts of her life with Russ in them felt wonderful.

Tonight was Friday. Russ's son was with his ex (Cherry still hadn't met Liam). And Tom had asked if he could walk Stevie Saturday morning – so Cherry didn't have any reason to get up and rush home. For the next eighteen hours, she didn't have to think about anything that had ever happened in that house. Cherry wanted to feel free. She wanted to feel like someone with a future, not just a past.

She rang Russ's doorbell. She waited. It was chilly, but Cherry wasn't wearing a coat over her baby blue angora cardigan. It would spoil the effect.

Russ opened the door. He was already halfway into his canvas jacket. His eyes got wide when he saw her, and his arms dropped. 'Cherry.'

'Hi,' she whispered.

Russ let his coat slip to the ground. He stuck his tongue in his cheek. 'What do you think you're doing?'

Cherry's face felt hot. 'Going out on a date with you.'

Russ hooked his arm around her waist and pulled her into the house. She tripped into him. 'You're not going anywhere,' he said. 'Are you fucking kidding me with this?'

Cherry laughed.

He reached up and touched her neckline. The embroidered lariat. The horseshoes. 'I can't believe you still have this dress . . .'

'It doesn't fit,' Cherry said. She'd had to pull the dress over her head, and then over her chest one tit at a time, without unzipping it, because it never would have zipped back up once it was on. Her breasts were smashed flat and ballooning from the top, and the waistline was severing Cherry in half.

'It fits fine,' Russ said in a low voice. He loosened his hold on Cherry to walk her back through the living room and down the hall.

'I thought we were going to dinner . . .' she said.

'Pfft.' He kicked his bedroom door open. 'You'll be lucky if you get breakfast.'

Cherry laughed. He led her into his room by the hand, then gave her a spin. Her skirt and petticoat swung out around her.

'I can't believe this,' Russ said again. 'It's like I've traveled back in time.'

He put his other hand on Cherry's waist and stepped close to her. 'We need to go dancing.'

'Okay.' She was still whispering.

'And you can wear this dress.'

'I'll wear a dress I can breathe in.'

Russ was already slow-dancing, gently guiding Cherry's hips. He held her hand close to his mouth and kissed it. Then he shook his head, like he was thinking something.

'What,' Cherry whispered.

When he looked up at her, his eyes were glistening. 'You,' he said hoarsely. 'Finally.'

Cherry was caught off guard.

She hadn't expected him to act like this – she'd thought the dress would land like lingerie, not a pressed flower. Her own eyes welled up.

Russ was only a little bit taller than her when she was in heels – he said he was five-nine, which meant he was probably five-eight. He leaned forward and kissed her. Softly.

Cherry kissed him back.

When he pulled away, he kept their faces together and rubbed his nose against hers. They were still swaying. Cherry's breath was shallow.

She hadn't expected this moment to be about feelings, but that was okay. Cherry *had* feelings. Plenty of them. And they predated

Tom. Cherry's feelings for Russ were planted in an untainted part of her heart. They were an antidote, almost, to the tar-like grief that stuck to her.

Russ was something good, and Cherry wanted to lean into him. She wanted every part of him that was on offer.

Russ had moved his lips to her cheek, which was nice. And her neck, which was even nicer. Her eyes stayed closed. She took a deep breath –

Actually, Cherry *couldn't* get a deep breath in this dress. She'd only been able to breathe into the very top of her lungs, even before Russ raised her temperature. Her chest was heaving now. She was feeling a little lightheaded. She looped her arms around his neck for balance.

Russ was touching Cherry everywhere that he could reach, exploring the dress as much as her body. Running his fingertips along the seams. Cherry made herself tall – to be thinner, but also to better feel his hands on her. She was like Stevie, rolling over to expose her stomach. She lifted a foot off the ground and arched her back.

Russ caught her around the waist and hugged her close. His face fell into her cleavage with a groan. Cherry kissed the top of his head.

'All right, you fantasy,' he said, standing upright again. 'Onto the bed.'

Cherry felt unsteady. She waited for him to move her to the edge of the bed and push her backwards. She landed on her palms and elbows. Her feet kicked off the floor.

Russ stood between her legs. He was wearing jeans – he didn't, usually – and an untucked white button-down. He was undoing his belt. Cherry felt her eyes get wide and lose focus.

He shook his head, like he had before. 'Do you even realize what you're giving me with this dress?'

Her lips were parted. She rested her tongue on her front teeth.

'I get to go back and have what I wanted,' he said. He picked up one of her ankles and lifted it high enough to kiss it. Cherry was wearing back-seamed hose. (She'd pulled out all the stops.) Russ rubbed his face into her calf and ran his hand up her thigh.

She closed her eyes again. She tried to breathe past her fourth rib. The dress was even *tighter* now that she was lying down – she felt like she might rip out a seam just trying to inhale.

Russ's hand moved between her legs. Cherry wasn't wearing underwear. She was wet. (Pulling out all the stops – even the autonomic ones.) Russ groaned again and rubbed his knuckles into her pussy. Cherry groaned with him.

His head was suddenly under the skirt and between her thighs – she shrieked. He was sucking and biting at her through the hose. She spread her knees and lifted her feet, gasping.

Russ popped his head out of her skirts. 'How is this going to work?'

Cherry looked in his eyes. 'What?'

'How am I going to fuck you,' he said, 'without taking off your clothes?'

Cherry's elbows gave out. She fell back, laughing.

Russ jerked one shoe off her foot. He tucked it under his chin. He pulled off the other shoe and tucked it under his arm. Then he reached under Cherry's dress, looking for the waist of her pantyhose. She helped him push them down. He got the hose off and tossed them behind him – then tried sliding her foot back into a shoe. The shoes were too pinchy for that. Cherry sat up to help. She was still laughing. Between them, they got both her red heels back on. Russ kissed her ankle again. 'These shoes make your feet look so tiny.'

She wrinkled her nose, smiling. 'Is that a thing?'

'Everything about you is a thing.' He kissed her other ankle and walked away from her, leaning over the side of the bed. Russ kept condoms there, in a drawer. He tore one off and dropped the rest of the strip on the comforter.

Cherry watched him put the condom on. It didn't make Russ self-conscious when she watched. Cherry liked the smell of the latex – it was like a bell ringing. Russ rolled the condom up, and stroked himself once. He was watching her, too. They'd both stopped smiling.

Russ came back to stand between her legs. 'Like this, the first time,' he said softly. 'Okay?'

Cherry nodded.

He maneuvered her knees and felt out the path with his fingers before he pushed his cock in. Cherry arched her neck and looked down at him over her cheeks.

Russ was still dressed. Still standing. Still wearing his glasses. Still young, really. Even at thirty-eight. Russ Sutton would always be young. He just had one of those faces.

'You haven't changed,' he said, maybe reading her mind. His hands were outside her dress, anchoring her hips. 'I'll never forget how beautiful you looked the night we met.' He closed his eyes. 'So sexy. I couldn't keep my hands off you.'

He rocked into her. Cherry shifted her hips, so he'd rub against her clit. She breathed hard through her nose.

'God, Cherry.'

'Russ,' she panted.

Russ pushed harder. He leaned over Cherry, lifting her legs by the ankles, then gripping the backs of her knees, folding her up, so he could sink deeper. Her skirt and petticoat were between them. The lace edges were tickling her nose. Cherry couldn't breathe at all like this, not even a little bit.

Russ was looking into her eyes. 'Do you feel good?'

She grunted. 'Yeah.'

'Are you close?'

'I can't –'

'Cherry, I'm –'

'Unzip me,' Cherry choked out.

'What?'

She tried to pull herself up by his shoulders. *'Unzip me.'*

Russ looked alarmed – he reached behind her, under her sweater. The zipper wasn't hard to find, and it only got stuck twice on the way down. Russ unzipped it all the way, past her waist. Cherry collapsed onto her back. The dress immediately fell open around her shoulders and breasts. She was taking deep, gulping breaths. She was wearing a red push-up bra.

'*Fuck*,' Russ said. He was still inside her. He checked the condom and started pushing again. Cherry inhaled down to her navel. Russ was coming, and Cherry was almost coming – the oxygen rushed to her head.

She watched Russ finish – his hair was in his eyes, he bit his lip. She loved it. She wanted to eat it with a spoon.

When his face cleared, he grinned down at her. He held the condom with his left hand while he pulled out, and immediately slid his right hand into her. He rubbed her clit with his palm, then swept two fingers around it. Cherry always got the feeling that Russ had a repertoire, a few moves he'd try until something worked. She liked it. '*Like that,*' she'd say. She said it now, closing her eyes.

Russ laughed, he sounded happy.

'Like that,' she said again.

'Yeah,' he said. 'Like that, Cherry, come on.'

Cherry squeezed her eyes shut. She dug her heels into the bed – she'd forgotten she was wearing shoes.

'Like that,' Russ said as she came.

They were lying in Russ's bed. The top of Cherry's dress was down, but she was still wearing her bra and cardigan and one high-heeled pump.

They'd made love again. It was too soon for Russ to come, but he'd rubbed Cherry until her clit felt fat and tender and she was squeezing her thighs closed around his forearm. Until her orgasms had started to hurt.

His fingers were still inside her vagina, lazily petting, and his head was resting on her shoulder. She was playing with his hair. They'd both been quiet for a while. She wondered if he was falling asleep. Cherry was too hungry to fall asleep.

Russ sighed. 'I can't believe I didn't have you ride me in your cowgirl dress ...'

She giggled.

He pulled his hand out of her pussy and lifted his head to kiss her, then dropped back down to her shoulder, wrapping his arm around her waist.

Cherry stroked his hair. She felt good. Tired. Hungry. Happy. Far away from the worst of her problems.

There was just *one* thing ... a question scratching at the back of Cherry's throat ...

She tried to swallow it.

It wasn't a productive question. Or a useful one.

It had been scratching there for weeks, and she'd always managed to swallow it so far. It wasn't, as Meg Jones would say, a *progress*-oriented question. (Meg loved people who sped things up and loathed people who slowed things down. All of Cherry's promotions were tied to how well she moved shit forward.)

Cherry cleared her throat.

Russ kissed her shoulder.

The question started to tumble out of her mouth, with momentum all its own – 'Russ?'

'Hmm.'

'When you said earlier ...' Cherry spun a lock of his hair around her index finger. 'I mean, when you've said before ...'

He kissed the top of her breast.

'... that you fell for me the night we met ...'

He rubbed his face into her.

'I just...' Her chin was already trembling. She tried to still it. 'Well, it makes me wonder why you didn't... make a play for me.'

Russ was slow to lift his head. When he did, he looked serious.

Cherry pressed her lips together. She tipped her head to one side and winced, like she was asking him to spare her feelings. (But if she wanted to be spared, she wouldn't have raised this issue.)

Russ shook his head – and then said, 'Because I was immature.'

Her chin wobbled. 'Immature, how?'

He looked pained. 'That was so long ago, I don't want to talk about it.'

'But you *do* want to talk about it,' Cherry said. 'You *keep* talking about it. You keep telling me how much you liked me back then.'

'I *did* like you.'

'But you didn't, Russ.' Her voice broke. 'You didn't ask me out. You didn't date me. You dated my best friend instead.'

'Cherry...'

'*Why?*' There. That was the question.

'Because I was twenty-three and half drunk,' he said, 'and I took the path of least resistance.'

'I wasn't resisting you.'

'No, I know. I –'

Cherry smiled at him. 'Just say it. Just say you didn't want to hit on a fat girl.'

He lowered his eyebrows. 'That's not true.'

She laughed. She was crying. 'It *is* true. Don't lie to me on top of everything else.'

'You weren't even fat, Cherry.'

Cherry held her hands up by her head, palms out. 'Okay. Let me up.'

'Cherry –'

She was already getting up. Russ moved off of her. She held up the front of her dress and kicked off her shoe.

'Cherry, *please*,' Russ said. 'Don't go.'

Cherry didn't have anywhere to go – she was in no shape to walk out – so she went to his bathroom.

She closed the door and locked it. She turned on the faucet. She pulled up her skirts and sat on the toilet and peed.

Her head fell forward. Her shoulders started to shake.

Up rose all the feelings she'd been shoving down every time Russ talked about the past. (Cherry *had* feelings.) Every time he reminisced about how beautiful she was and how much he'd wanted to touch her.

Those were cuts not compliments. *Why didn't you touch me, Russ? Why didn't you choose me?*

Cherry knew why! Because she was too fat!

She was too fat for every boy who looked and acted like Russ Sutton.

The only way Russ was different from the others was that he'd *considered* Cherry. He'd toyed with the idea of her for a few minutes. He'd toyed with *her*.

She wiped herself and flushed the toilet, then got up to wash her hands. She left the faucet running. She sat on the edge of the tub. There was a hamper in here, and a pile of clothes on the floor. A child's dirty soccer uniform. Cherry was sobbing.

She took off her cardigan and pulled up the top of her dress, putting her arms through the straps. She didn't bother with the zipper.

'Cherry?' Russ sounded like he was standing right on the other side of the door. 'Are you okay?'

She wiped her nose on the back of her hand. She was covered in snot. She reached for some toilet paper and blew her nose.

'Cherry, the night we met . . .'

She blew her nose again.

'. . . I thought you were gorgeous.'

She rolled her eyes, ignoring him.

'No, okay –' Russ sounded closer. He sounded miserable. 'You know what? I didn't think that.'

Cherry looked up at the door.

'Because I was young and stupid, and I thought "gorgeous" meant something really specific.'

The door creaked, like he'd leaned against it.

'I thought I was supposed to be with a certain kind of girl,' he said, 'the kind of girl that all of my friends and my older brother would agree was hot . . .

'That felt like success to me.

'That felt like a medal I got to wear all the time.'

Fresh, hot tears spilled down Cherry's cheeks.

Russ huffed out a loud breath. 'When I was in junior high, my brother told me that if I was going to fall in love, I may as well fall in love with someone hot. And I thought that was *wisdom*. I repeated it to my friends like I was the one who'd thought of it!'

Maybe Cherry hadn't actually wanted Russ to be honest – he was making her sick.

He kept going:

'All the girls I dated in high school and college kind of looked alike. They didn't look like you – I didn't know what to make of you. I *liked* you. I liked seeing you. I used to watch you in class, and then you showed up at the Galway, and I was half drunk . . .

'I don't know, I was *into* you, Cherry. Then we started talking, and it got worse. All that really mattered in that moment was getting closer. We were sparking, you know?'

Cherry pressed her palms into her eyes.

'But then, I don't know. Stacia was there. And she was flirting with me. And you were playing kind of hard to get – am I remembering this right? And all my friends were there, drooling over Stacia. She probably wasn't wearing a bra. She never wore a bra . . .

'And I wasn't really *deciding* anything, Cherry. I was drinking, and she was there. And you disappeared, I think? And . . .'

Something hard knocked against the door. Cherry jumped.

'And you were chubby,' Russ said. He sounded beaten.

Something knocked against the door again.

'I knew my friends would make fun of me for hooking up with you.'

Cherry sobbed silently into her hands.

'Even though their girlfriends weren't all hot! Corey was with a marshmallow girl – she puffed up as soon as they got married!

'Which is ... not the point. I just, um ...

'I made a mistake, Cherry. And it haunted me as long as I dated Stacia ... every time the three of us were together. I was *not* a good boyfriend. I would have been all over you if you'd ever given me even a hint of encouragement. I was crazy about you ...' His voice trailed off.

Something bumped softly against the door.

Cherry waited.

'I made a *mistake*,' Russ said. 'And I kept making mistakes. I married the wrong person, and part of that – a big part of it – was that I thought we'd look good together. Like, I could see it, perfect pictures of us in my head ...'

His voice was strained:

'I do things because I think I'm supposed to, and I'm not proud of it. It hasn't made me happy. I don't want to be that person anymore – I don't want my *son* to be that sort of person.'

Cherry wiped her nose hard on her palm.

'Cherry?'

She didn't answer.

Russ didn't say anything for a minute.

Then he said:

'When I saw you at the Goldenrod concert, I felt exactly like I always had. Like I needed to be close to you. You're so gorgeous, Cherry – and I get it now! I know what to call it.

'You're *not* like the other girls I dated, but none of them were right for me. None of them made me feel like I *feel* with you.

'Please forgive me?

'Please give me a second chance.

'We're so good together. *You're* so good.'

He thumped against the door again. His voice dropped: 'Also, you're the sexiest woman alive.'

Cherry wiped her nose.

She stood up. And turned off the faucet. She threw her scrunched-up toilet paper into the wastebasket.

She opened the bathroom door.

Russ was leaning against it – he jumped back. He looked like he'd been crying.

'Your brother sounds like a douchebag,' Cherry said.

'He is a douchebag,' Russ agreed. 'He's also my best friend.'

She looked up into his eyes. 'I *knew*,' she said, with new tears in her eyes. 'That night, at the Galway, I knew.'

Russ winced, but he didn't look away. 'I'm sorry.'

'I am never losing weight,' Cherry said.

'Okay.'

'I'm probably going to *gain* weight because I've been too depressed to eat for a year – and now I'm not depressed, because you make me feel alive again, and living people eat.'

He smiled a little. 'I make you happy?'

'Not tonight.'

His smile fell. He nodded his head.

She folded her arms. 'I just need you to know that I'm always going to be fat.'

'Cherry, you're not –'

'Don't say it. I swear to god.'

'Okay. Sorry.'

'When you say I'm not fat, what you mean is, I'm not ugly. But I know I'm not ugly.'

He closed his mouth. He nodded.

'Also, I might want to have a baby,' she said. 'Someday. So, you should know that. You should take that under advisement. That will make me even fatter.'

Russ nodded. His eyes were shining.

'I just have a lot of issues with my weight,' she said. 'And I don't want you to make them worse. I'm in therapy – that's also for the record.'

'I'm in therapy, too,' he said. 'For the record.'

Cherry nodded.

Russ cleared his throat. 'You should know that Liam has ADHD. And some ... learning challenges. And he's still really struggling with the divorce.'

Cherry cocked her head sympathetically. For Liam.

'And I never want to leave Nebraska,' Russ said. 'I want to be governor someday.'

Cherry laughed. 'Okay.'

'Be advised.'

'I've been advised.'

'Also, I have a receding hairline.'

'No, you don't,' she said softly.

'I do.' He held his hair off his forehead. 'It's receding at the corners.'

She stepped closer to look. 'It looks the same as it always has.'

He let his hair fall. 'It's gradual.'

Cherry brushed his hair off his forehead. 'You're very vain.'

He nodded. 'I know.'

She stroked his hair. 'What about your perfect girl for your perfect pictures? For all your campaign ads ...'

'Are you kidding me?' He touched Cherry's cheek. 'We look *fantastic* together.'

Chapter 24

On Monday evening, as Cherry was walking up her steps, Tom walked out the front door. He had Stevie.

'Oh,' Cherry said. She smiled at them. 'Hi. I didn't see your dad's car.'

'I rode my bike over.' Tom nodded toward the garage. 'I found it in the garage last week.'

'Right,' she said. 'That's nice.'

'We're just going for a walk.'

Cherry looked around. 'It's a beautiful night.'

'Do you want to come with?'

'Um …' She looked down at her wide-legged pants. She was wearing ballet flats. 'Sure. I've been sitting at a desk all day.' Stevie was sniffing at Cherry, trying to get her attention. Cherry petted her. 'You've taken over my only source of exercise.'

Tom clicked his tongue at Stevie, and she followed him down onto the sidewalk. 'You aren't going to yoga in the health center?'

'Nah.' Cherry walked with him, on the other side of Stevie. 'There's a new teacher who gets on my nerves – we're constantly standing up as soon as we've sat down, and she wears those Kim Kardashian clothes that are just tan underwear.'

'Your bike's in the garage, too, if you want it. I dug it out and filled up the tires.'

'Thanks,' Cherry said. 'I'll get right on that.'

The last time they'd gone bike-riding together, Cherry had ended up lying in the grass, saying she felt like she was being '*jackhammered in the crotch.*' Tom had to walk both of their bikes back to the car.

'How's the garage going?' she asked.

'Good. I took a bunch of stuff to Goodwill last week. And I set some speakers aside for Henry.' Henry was one of Cherry's nephews. 'I stuck a note on them.'

'I'll tell Hope.' They'd stopped to let Stevie sniff at some bushes. 'You guys are late with your walk today.'

Tom tugged Stevie back from a patch of mud. 'This is our second walk.'

'Lucky Stevie.'

'They're more for me than her,' he said. 'They clear my head.'

Cherry looked up at him. She realized that at this moment – like *right* now, this very second – she didn't feel angry with him. Maybe for the first time in two years. Cherry felt light today. Hopeful. Decidedly un-doomed. 'How is your head?' she asked.

Tom lowered an eyebrow, like that was a surprising question. Fair. It had been at least a year since Cherry had asked how he was doing – instead of some version of '*What the hell are you thinking?*'

'My head's okay,' he said.

Cherry smiled a little. Sincerely. 'Good.'

On Tuesday, Cherry went to Russ's house after work. They made dinner together. Cobb salad. And made love, twice.

On Wednesday when Cherry got home, the garage door was open. She walked up the driveway to peek in.

Tom had cleared out one half of the garage, and he was working in the corner. There were new shelves. Stevie was asleep at his feet.

'Hi there!' she called out.

Stevie lifted her head. Tom looked up, startled. 'Hi.'

'It looks great in here,' Cherry said. The garage had been packed with random junk for years; there'd never been room for their cars.

'Thanks.'

Stevie had run up to Cherry and was rubbing her face on Cherry's pin-striped suit pants.

Tom clicked his tongue. 'Hey. Get off. You're messing up her nice clothes.'

'I'm used to it.' Cherry patted Stevie's flank. The dog had already turned back to Tom.

'You're wearing heels,' he said, making a curious face at Cherry.

'Yeah, I felt like being tall today.'

'They don't hurt your back?'

'Not when I'm sitting. Are those new shelves?'

He looked up at them. 'Yeah, I got the gardening stuff all sorted. It should be easier for you to find things.'

'Oh, I forgot about this . . .' Cherry pointed at a huge blue willow vase on one of the top shelves. They'd bought it at a garage sale.

'We never figured out where to put it,' Tom said.

'Well, it's so big . . .'

'Cool, though,' he said.

'It is.'

Tom looked over at her. 'You're in a good mood this week.'

Cherry laughed and shook her head. 'Am I?'

'Yeah.'

'Huh. I guess things are going my way.'

'I'm glad,' Tom said.

'Thanks.'

Russ had Liam for the weekend, so he and Cherry crammed in one more night together on Thursday, even though Russ had some complicated problem to manage for the mayor. He was on the phone for hours. Cherry waited on his couch and tried to read a book on her phone, but ended up writing work emails and scrolling through Instagram and Pinterest.

When Russ was finally done, he crawled to Cherry on his knees to apologize. She laughed. She told him not to be offended but that next time she was bringing over her embroidery hoop.

He crawled between her knees and up her skirt.

Tom wasn't at the house when Cherry got home on Friday, but neither was Stevie. They were probably on a walk.

Cherry kicked off her shoes. Then she noticed the blue willow vase sitting in a corner of the foyer – holding a huge arrangement of dried flowers and grasses, probably from the yard. Pampas grass. Panicle hydrangea. Some sort of branch with red berries. Tom had always been good at arranging flowers. (Tom could make anything look good.) This was striking.

It didn't escape Cherry's notice that he was supposed to be moving things *out* of the house, not in. But she took the arrangement for what she guessed it was – a peace offering.

She texted him. *'Nice flowers.'*

He texted back, ';)'

'Are you guys on your way out or on your way back?'

'Just at the park.'

'If I order Indian,' she asked, *'will you pick it up?'*

'Yep.'

'Do you want me to order something for you? Lamb vindaloo?'

Tom didn't reply right away. Cherry called the order in. She got naan. And samosas. And mulligatawny soup. She was hungry. She set her phone down and went into the dining room to clear some space ... Maybe she could make some headway in the house over the weekend, while Russ was busy. Maybe Cherry didn't have to be so *rigorous* about everything. Maybe Stacia was right – Cherry could just start boxing things up to deal with after she got a new place, when the memories would be less sharp.

The moving pieces in her life were *already* feeling less sharp. That was all Russ, Cherry knew that. It made her feel very unevolved as a person that she couldn't get over one man until she'd snagged another. There was no complete and confident version of Cherry that had emerged from the separation and *then* fallen for Russ. Cherry hadn't bloomed until Russ shined on her. It was pathetic …

… but it was working.

Cherry focused on some vacation souvenirs (snow globes, salt and pepper shakers, figurines) that had been sitting on the table for weeks because neither she nor Tom could decide what to do with them. She peeled off the Post-it notes and set all the knickknacks in a box. She'd wrap them in bubble wrap later.

She checked her phone to see what time it was. Tom had texted back – *'That's okay. Thanks.'* She shrugged. He could take the vindaloo home.

Cherry was making real progress on the dining room table, so she kept going. There was a complete set of china that they'd found at an estate sale. The pattern along the border was lime green with red rosebuds. They were beautiful dishes – Cherry would keep them. She'd use them. She carried them into the kitchen and put them in a cabinet that Tom had emptied.

When she walked out of the kitchen, with a damp washcloth, Tom and Stevie were coming in the door. He hadn't knocked or rung the bell.

'Hey,' Cherry said. 'I didn't get your message in time. You can just take the food with you.'

'Sorry,' Tom said. 'Thanks.' He unclipped Stevie's leash with one hand.

Cherry started wiping off the table.

Tom walked into the dining room with the takeout bag. 'Did you decide to make a clean sweep and give it all away?'

'Nope. I'm keeping it all.' She glanced at him. 'Unless there was something you wanted?'

Tom looked surprised. 'No.' He rested the bag on the table. 'You're keeping the snow globes?'

'Yep. For now. I'll see how I feel when I unpack them.'

'After you move.'

'Yeah, I guess.' It felt good to see the table again. Cherry just felt *good*, in general. She turned back to Tom. 'You sure you don't want to eat before you go? It'll be better hot.'

Tom looked like he was still processing the situation. It made Cherry smile. Tom was forever processing. He'd probably still be trying to make sense of their wedding by the time they were divorced.

She took the bag from him. 'Yeah?'

He nodded. 'Okay, yeah.'

'You get the dishes and forks.'

Cherry opened up the plastic containers of meat and rice. She laid out the bread and popped open the cups of raita and mint chutney. She could hear Tom washing his hands. 'Do you want something to drink?' he called.

'I'll take a Coke Zero.'

'It's kind of late . . .' He knew the caffeine would keep her up.

'It's Friday night.'

'Time to get wild,' Tom said, coming back into the room with dishes and a can of pop. He stopped when he saw the food. 'This looks great. I haven't had Jaipur in forever.'

Probably not since the last time they'd ordered it together. 'Sit down,' Cherry said.

Tom handed her an empty plate. They sat on neighboring sides of the table, in the opposite corner from where they used to sit.

'Speaking of the weekend,' he said, 'I'm headed back to Los Angeles tomorrow.'

'Oh, yeah?' Cherry was serving herself some food. She'd ordered chicken saag.

Tom reached out and gave her a scoop of his lamb. 'Yeah, just for a few days.'

'Do you have movie stuff?'

He was making a grim face, getting some rice. 'Yeah.'

'You don't seem excited.'

He raised his eyebrows, like that was an understatement. 'Media,' he said.

'Like, interviews?'

He nodded. He didn't seem to want to talk about it. Cherry tore off a small piece of naan and handed him the rest. (Tom's blood sugar was fine.) He took a samosa, then dropped the other one onto her plate. 'Is it okay if the dumpster sits out there while I'm gone?'

'Yeah.'

'They'll come and empty it, but I paid for the whole month.'

'That's fine.' Cherry was eating.

Tom took a bite. He covered his mouth. 'This is so good.'

'I'm sure they have great Indian food in Los Angeles,' she said.

He raised his eyebrows again – again like there was more to say, but he didn't want to say it. 'So what's happening at work?' he asked.

'What do you mean?'

'You said the other night that things were going your way.'

'Oh ...' Cherry hadn't meant at work. 'Yeah, things are good. We're, um, prepping for the grand reopening of the railroad museum – finally.' It was a massive project. Tom had worked on the early stages, before he quit. He'd designed all the signs; they were fantastic.

'Oh, geez, that took long enough.'

'You know how Meg is. Everything had to be perfect.'

'I do not miss Meg Jones,' he said.

Cherry laughed. 'That's not saying anything – you don't miss anyone.'

Tom had never been a great fit at the ad agency. Too independent. Too introverted. Too talented for his own good. By the time he quit, he'd hated his job so much, even his best work relationships were strained. *Thursday* had become a hit in the nick of time – Cherry had worried that he'd just walk out of the office someday. Or that he'd get fired.

Tom was smiling down at his food. 'That's not true.'

'Matt brags about you now to new clients.' Matt was Tom's old boss.

'He *brags* about me?'

'Oh, yeah. "*That logo was designed by the creator of* Thursday. *Do you know* Thursday? *They're making a movie out of it.*"'

'He's a *character* in *Thursday*,' Tom said in disbelief. 'He's Jake That Shitbird.'

'*I* know that.' Cherry was laughing again. 'I don't think *Matt* knows that.'

'I swear people don't see themselves in the comic because they can't actually *see* themselves ... I could quote Matt and draw an uncanny caricature of him, and he'd still think I was writing about some other asshole.'

'I doubt that Matt has read *Thursday* ...'

'I want to say that he can't read,' Tom said, 'but I've seen him read his profile in *Communication Arts* magazine, out loud, several times to several people.'

Cherry laughed through her nose. She had a mouthful of saag. Cherry got along fine with Matt. Better now that Tom was gone. After her last promotion, Cherry had started managing the relationship between the railroad and Tom's agency. Everyone on both sides was painfully aware that her husband was the most valuable and the most difficult person on the team. Cherry's job got *much* simpler when Tom quit. Even though the work suffered.

'I've got pictures of the museum setup,' she said. 'Do you want to see?'

He looked interested. 'Yeah.' He wiped his mouth with a cloth napkin. Tom always dug out the cloth napkins.

Cherry got out her phone and found the photos. She handed it over to him. 'Scroll to the right.'

Tom looked at a few pictures. 'This is nice,' he said.

'Thanks.'

'Who did the printing?'

'Garza.'

'It looks great.' He stopped on a photo and zoomed in with his fingertips. 'I think this is the wrong red.'

'Where?'

He handed the phone back to her. He'd zoomed in on the Western Alliance logo on one of the signs. The railroad had its own trademarked shade of red. Whenever they printed anything in four-color ink, the printer had to mix an additional red, just for the logo.

Cherry flipped between a few photos. 'You're right. *Fuck*. I can't believe I missed that.'

'Check the purchase order,' he said. 'I'll bet it was a printer error. Have them make you a new sign.'

'I can't believe I *missed* that.'

'No one will notice.'

'*You* did,' she said.

'The only person who will notice, noticed – and he doesn't care.'

Cherry sighed.

'I shouldn't have mentioned it,' Tom said. 'The exhibits look really great.'

'Thanks,' she said. 'Damn your eyes!'

'You should have sent me the proofs. I would have looked them over.'

Cherry raised her eyebrows, like there was something to say there, but she wasn't going to say it.

'Okay,' Tom said, 'but you really could send me stuff if you wanted. It's not like I'm busy. I'm unemployed.'

She raised her eyebrows again and laughed. 'You're unemployed like Barack Obama is unemployed – you just don't have to work.'

'Neither do you,' Tom said softly.

Cherry's voice dropped, too. 'I like to work.'

'I know.'

She set down her phone and used a piece of naan to pinch up a bite of chicken. 'You said you're going back to L.A. for interviews – is the movie premiere soon?'

'Not for a couple months . . . I think they just want me *out there* all the time. Doing press. So people can't forget about the project.'

'It's because you're good at it,' Cherry said.

Tom scoffed. 'I'm not good at it. I'm awkward and grumpy.'

'It comes off charming. You're very meme-able.'

'It's always so *stressful*.' Tom's face was getting red. 'I don't have anything new to say about the comic, and there's nothing I *want* to say about the movie.'

'Have you seen it?' Cherry asked.

'Parts of it.'

'Is it that bad?'

Tom shrugged. He looked miserable. 'I don't know. I can't tell. When I'm watching it, all I can think about is how hellish the process was . . . How many times I had to rewrite a scene . . . How many meetings I had to sit through – when the number of meetings I *wanted* to sit through was *zero*. Zero meetings. Zero Zooms. Zero calls with the producers while they were going through security at the Salt Lake City airport.'

'That's very specific,' Cherry said.

Tom scoffed again. He stuck his fork in his rice, and the tines hit the plate. 'The conversations I've had . . .' He shook his head. 'Maybe they'll be funny someday.'

'Like what?'

He looked up at her. 'They wanted to give The Guy a name because they said it would confuse audiences.'

'Audiences already know The Guy. He's the main character of an insanely popular series of books.'

'I guess even an insanely popular book is nothing compared to a movie audience. Nobody reads.'

'So, did you give him a name?'

Tom jerked his head back. 'Fuck no. Oh – also, they wanted to take out the cursing.'

'There's so much cursing.'

'I know. Jake That Shitbird was going to be Jake That Jerk.'

Cherry laughed.

'And they wanted to add all these characters . . .'

'There are already a lot of characters.'

'Apparently none of them are likable.'

'People *love* the books.'

'See previous note,' Tom said. 'And, oh god – Baby was the worst.'

Cherry's smile froze. 'Baby?'

Tom made another miserable face. 'I'm sorry, Cherry. I know . . .'

Cherry didn't want to hear whatever he was about to say. 'I heard,' she said in a light voice, 'that they fired the first actress for losing weight on semaglutide.'

'The *meetings* . . .' Tom said. 'The *tortured conversations* . . .'

He tilted his head and adjusted a pair of imaginary glasses. '*"Does she still read as . . . buxom? You know, in the American imagination?"*

'*"Could we accomplish it with camera angles, like in* Lord of the Rings?*"*

'*"Are her . . . assets . . . central to our understanding of the character? I mean, are they* really?*"*'

Cherry was laughing again.

Tom dropped the impression. 'One producer said we couldn't cast a white actress, because the character's butt was appropriation.'

'Yeah, you appropriated it from *me*! I should charge you a licensing fee.'

'Last I checked, you were getting fifty percent.'

Cherry snorted. Then remembered something – 'Oh my god, Tom.' She set down her fork. 'Do you know who's on Ozempic?'

'Everyone who makes more than a hundred thousand dollars a year?'

'Hope.'

'Your sister Hope?'

'*Yes*. It's a whole thing. Honny and Joy are freezing her out, like she's a traitor to the cause.'

'How's she doing on it?'

'I don't know,' Cherry said. 'She's skinny, so I guess it's working? She looks like a different person.'

'She must have really good insurance.'

'Dan probably does.'

Tom nodded. 'Firefighters union.'

'I think Joy's jealous, underneath it all. But Honny feels judged.'

'I get it,' he said.

'I get it, too! If Hope doesn't like the way *she* looks, she doesn't like the way *any* of us look – and she always seemed so confident! She was our role model for what it meant to be fat and beautiful and happy.'

Tom's smile had gone gentle. After a second, he looked down at his food.

Cherry looked down, too. 'Anyway,' she said, 'you must still be excited about the premiere. It's a big deal.'

'I'm not going.'

'What?' She looked back up at him. 'You have to go.'

He cocked his head, peering up at her from the top of his eyes. 'Contractually, I do not. I've checked.'

'*Tom* . . .'

'I just want it to be over, so I can get back to my life. Or you know – *a* life. Whatever my life is now, I don't want it to be all this Hollywood shit.'

'Then maybe you shouldn't move to *Los Angeles*,' Cherry said.

Tom laughed, defeated. 'Maybe *not*. I don't know . . .' He shrugged. 'I like the weather. I like the ocean. Good comic book stores. Plus, it's very, very far from my dad.'

Tom and Cherry had talked about moving to the West Coast. Before Cherry had been promoted.

She took another bite of saag. It was getting cold. It was still good. 'I think you should go,' Cherry said. 'To the premiere. It's a once-in-a-lifetime thing. Even if it all sucks.'

'Pfft.' Tom had gone back to eating, too. 'Who would I even go with?'

The saag got stuck at the back of her throat.

Tom shook his head. 'Yeah ... no thanks.'

Cherry wiped her hands on a napkin and started packaging up the leftovers. Tom seemed to take her cue. He stood up and gathered their dirty dishes. They took things into the kitchen together. The dishwasher was full and clean, so Tom started to unload it. Cherry helped.

He opened a cabinet and saw the stack of china there. 'Oh,' he said, 'I'm glad you're keeping these.'

'They're so pretty,' she said. 'We got them at an estate sale, right?'

'Yeah, don't you remember? That was the "dimples and freckles" guy!'

Cherry laughed. 'That was for these dishes?' There'd been an older guy running the estate sale, and he'd given them half off because he liked Cherry's face.

'"*Dimples* and *freckles?*"' Tom quoted, grinning down at Cherry. '"*That shouldn't be legal.*"'

Tom had said it to her for *years* after that – she'd almost forgotten the joke's origin story. She beamed up at him now, remembering.

Tom was looking in her eyes. He dipped his head down ...

To *kiss* her.

And Cherry – so used to his mouth, so used to his hand on her jaw – kissed him back.

For a second.

For maybe a minute.

Maybe longer?

Then she pulled away, covering her mouth. 'Tom, I –' She shook her head. Her face pinched up in apology. 'I'm seeing someone.'

Tom stood up. And away. 'Oh.' He took a step back and nearly fell over the open dishwasher. 'I'm sorry. I'm sorry regardless. I shouldn't have –'

'*Tom* . . .'

He held up his hand. His eyes were closed. 'Please, Cherry, I – I'm gonna leave.'

He squeezed between Cherry and the dishwasher and out of the kitchen. She let him go.

Chapter 25

Tom had told Cherry about *Thursday* the first night that they met.

They were talking about what they liked to do when they weren't working, and Tom said that he had a webcomic. Cherry hadn't known what a webcomic was, exactly.

Later, when they were dating, he mentioned it again and gave her slightly more detail: 'It's a stupid comic strip that I write, that lives online.' She asked if she could read it, and Tom made a face like she'd asked to read his diary. 'Nobody reads it,' he said.

'How would someone find it if they wanted to read it?'

'They wouldn't. Nobody wants to read webcomics except for other people who write webcomics. And even then . . .'

'I want to read it.'

'Trust me. You don't.'

It felt like what he was really saying was that *he* didn't want her to read it.

So Cherry didn't go looking for *Thursday*. She figured he'd let her see it someday . . . In the meantime, they were falling in love.

Tom spent most nights at Cherry's apartment. He'd come over after he made dinner for his dad. Sometimes he'd bring dinner for Cherry, too.

They went for walks. They watched TV. They got up early on weekends and went to estate sales – they found a hundred-year-old couch for $650. Tom paid for half.

They talked about work – a lot. They didn't work together directly, but they worked with some of the same people. Cherry did funny impressions of all their managers. It was the only thing that ever made Tom laugh out loud.

They slept in Cherry's room, on her mattress on the floor, and had started having clumsy, eager sex. Cherry was pretty sure that Tom had never done it before, but she didn't feel like she could ask him directly. She never wanted to embarrass him or scare him back into his shell. She liked him so much – too much, probably.

Tom was so smart.

He was so funny.

He was an effortless artist. A good thinker. She'd quickly realized that Tom had a hand in all the best pieces of the railroad's more recent advertising.

He liked to solve problems and fix things. When Cherry's car radiator was leaking, Tom bought a repair manual on eBay and, after a few tries, patched it up.

He was *so* handsome...

She wasn't sure whether other people thought so. Tom was heavier. His hair was too short. His head was a block.

Cherry kind of hoped that no one *could* see him like she did. She'd never be able to keep him if other women caught on to how hot he was. Tom was all shoulders. He was all thighs. He was a minotaur. Cherry liked to hold her hand up to his, to see how short her fingers were in comparison. She was constantly rubbing up against him like a cat, just to feel how solid he was. Just to get his attention.

Now, when Cherry got Tom's attention, he kissed her. It didn't really matter where they were or what they were doing – it was like he was making up for that first, failed kiss. It made Cherry insatiable.

It made her rash. She told him that she loved him after just a couple of weeks together. Cherry was like a drinking glass sitting under a faucet – she'd said 'I love you' as soon as she'd felt full, and then she kept saying it, as her feelings slopped over the edges.

Tom had looked startled the first time. And concerned the second time. And then he'd started kissing Cherry every time she said it – tenderly – which was just incentive for her to say it more.

Cherry's sisters knew she was dating someone, but she was nervous about bringing Tom to a family event. Her sisters were a lot. Her mom was a lot. Cherry was afraid that Tom would realize that Cherry herself was a lot if he saw her in that context.

At Easter dinner, when her sisters were badgering her about meeting her boyfriend, Cherry googled Tom from Honny's desktop computer, trying to find a photo to show them. (He covered his face whenever Cherry tried to take his picture.) Tom wasn't on Facebook, but he had a distinct last name – Valentine.

She found his photo on the ad agency's website.

'He looks young,' Honny said.

'He's twenty-four,' Cherry said.

'Oooh,' Joy said. 'You're robbing the cradle.'

Cherry was only twenty-five. 'Coates & Branch almost never hires people right out of college, but they hired him because he's so talented.'

She backed out of the page to look at the other Google results. There was a MySpace page. She clicked on it, thinking there might be photos of Tom from college. (She'd love to see those.)

There were no photos – but there was a section for his comic strip. *Thursday*.

'Go back to his photo,' Joy said. 'Make it bigger.'

Cherry quickly, guiltily, clicked back.

Tom wasn't smiling in his work photo. His face looked flat. He never looked like that with Cherry – when Tom looked at Cherry, there was always a smile hiding out in the corners of his eyes and the corners of his lips.

'I guess he's cute . . .' Joy said.

'His hair's too short,' Honny said.

'Oh my god,' Cherry said, closing the browser window. 'I'm never introducing him to you people.'

Tom was staying at his dad's house that night because Cherry hadn't been sure how late she'd be. She got home a little after midnight and went straight to bed, already missing him. She lay awake awhile, listening to the radiator turn off and on ...

Thinking about Tom.

And how diligent he was about his webcomic.

On Wednesday nights, Tom wouldn't come over until he'd finished *Thursday*. (It posted once a week.)

Cherry stared up at the popcorn ceiling.

She chewed on her lip.

She got out of bed and went to get her laptop, settling on the mattress with her legs crossed.

Tom had apparently launched *Thursday* on MySpace during college and then moved it to a webcomics site. You could read the entire run of *Thursday* there, starting with Tom's very first post.

Thursday was usually five panels long. At the beginning, the subject matter was all over the place. Campus life. Absurdities. Politics. There weren't any recurring characters.

After a few dozen strips, a main character emerged. It was Tom, obviously. He drew himself square and hulking. Always wearing the same hooded sweatshirt. And almost completely silent. The character didn't have a name.

The strips fell into more of a groove over time. The guy who was clearly Tom went through his life silently observing things and experiencing things. Meeting people. Finding himself in complicated, uncomfortable situations. None of the strips were funny on their own – but they built on each other. And sometimes they snuck up on you and made you laugh out loud. Once, Cherry found herself crying.

It would be hard to explain to someone why *Thursday* was great ...

There was no plot. There weren't any traditional jokes or sight gags. And Tom's art was deceptively simple. Cherry knew he could draw realistically, but his comic lines were loose and cartoonish. There was a *Bloom County* quality. And some early Disney vibes. (Like – what if Berkeley Breathed had worked on *Snow White*?) *Thursday* was sweet. It was funny. It was sharp.

It was *great*, undeniably. Ineffably. Cherry was falling deeper in love with Tom, panel by panel. She stayed up for hours, paging through his old strips . . . Tom's main character graduated from college. He got a job. He started working for a railroad.

Cherry's stomach started to tense as she got closer to the present. How autobiographical *was* this comic?

She got to December.

Just before Christmas, Tom had posted an unprecedented extra-wide, single-panel strip. On the left side, he'd drawn a woman.

A very fat woman.

Wearing black jeans and a low-cut black sweater. Black high-heeled boots. A heart-shaped pendant around her neck.

Her breasts were extremely large.

Her hips and thighs were comical.

There was a curved line giving her a double chin and another curved line giving her a belly.

She had long dark hair and bangs, with slashes on her cheeks for dimples and three freckles on either side of her nose.

She was smiling with one side of her mouth.

She didn't say anything.

Tom's character was facing the woman, so the reader couldn't see his face. There was a rare thought bubble hanging over his head:

'I just met the most beautiful girl.'

Chapter 26

'I just met the most beautiful girl.'

Cherry closed her laptop.

She lay on her back.

She realized she was crying when the tears ran into her ears and tickled.

Was it a joke?

Tom's comics were usually driving toward a joke, though sometimes it took a while to get there. The main character's thought bubbles were always sardonic when they appeared.

Was that how Tom saw Cherry? Like someone put lipstick on the Michelin Man?

Was that how he saw her the first night they met? Like someone had taken a regular girl and inflated her to the point of popping?

Had he looked at her and seen someone who was already a caricature? An easy punchline?

(Did Tom's friends read his comic? Had they laughed?)

A few other girls had appeared in the comic strip over the years. They were all busty. All a little Tex Avery. But not like this – not like Cherry.

That was *Cherry*.

That cartoon.

A man had drawn a picture of her as a joke and posted it online. And Cherry had *pursued* him. She'd *chased* him. Was that what the next week's strip would be about? That crazy-looking fat girl following Tom's avatar around?

'I just met the most beautiful girl.'

Cherry knew what she looked like. She knew that no one would ever describe her that way, even generously.

But she wasn't a *joke*. She wasn't pathetic.

She didn't deserve this.

Chapter 27

She fell asleep just before dawn, the laptop under the covers with her – and woke up a few hours later when Tom climbed into bed behind her, his bare arms moving around her waist. Cold hands slid up the front of Cherry's shirt. He slotted into her, tucked his knees behind her thighs, and sighed.

Cherry didn't respond. She didn't even open her eyes.

Tom moved her hair off her neck and kissed it. He tugged the collar of her pajamas open so he could kiss her shoulder. 'You're so warm,' he said. Cherry let him kiss her. He was much looser than when they first started seeing each other. Much easier with his affection. 'Sleepy girl,' he whispered.

Cherry didn't respond.

After a minute, Tom tried to roll her around to face him. She went along, limply.

'Hey,' he said, when he could see her face. He lifted her chin. 'What's wrong?'

Cherry shook her head. 'Nothing.'

He ran his thumb along her cheek. 'Your eyes are swollen.'

She shook her head again. She felt her eyes start to swim. 'It's nothing.'

Tom's face was serious. 'Did something happen?'

'No.' Tears spilled onto Cherry's nose and into her hair. 'Nothing happened.'

Tom's whole hand cupped her cheek. 'Do you promise that nothing happened?'

She nodded, crying a little harder.

'Baby, baby ...' Tom said, working an arm underneath her to hold her against him. 'What's wrong?'

'I'm just ... sad, about something. I don't want to talk about it.'

'Okay,' Tom said, hugging her.

She cried even harder.

He stroked her cheek. He smoothed back her hair and kissed her forehead. 'Baby ...' he whispered.

Cherry keened softly.

'What can I do for you?' he asked.

She shook her head.

He'd pulled her completely against him. He was soothing her with both hands and kissing her hair every few seconds. 'Cherry, baby ...'

He lifted his head up to kiss her wet cheeks. To try and look in her eyes. 'It's okay if you need to cry ... Would you like to cry over a bagel?'

Cherry smiled, sort of, but shook her head.

'Okay,' Tom said, 'but they're from Bagel Bin. And they're still warm.'

She sniffed. 'You went all the way out to Bagel Bin?'

He nodded. 'And I got you two sesame bagels ...'

Cherry tried to hide her face in his neck.

'... one with lox cream cheese,' he said, 'and one with green olive, so you don't have to choose.'

Cherry laughed. It triggered more tears.

'Why don't you have a bagel, and then you can cry on me all morning?'

She didn't respond.

'I got coffee, too,' he whispered.

Cherry looked up at him. There was a furrow between his eyebrows, and his sky blue eyes were open and searching. This must be what Tom looked like when he was *actually* concerned about her, and not just generically concerned about everything.

'Okay,' Cherry said, giving in.

Tom smiled. 'Okay.' He moved away from her. 'Let's get you sat up.'

She pushed herself up. She was wearing gray flannel pajamas with a tipsy pink-elephant pattern. The elephants were dressed in evening wear and drinking champagne. Tom liked these pajamas. Tom liked anything whimsical. Once she'd unleashed her wardrobe on him, he'd been wholly appreciative.

He sat up next to her, in a T-shirt and boxer shorts. He handed her the coffee cup first. Then he reached into the paper Bagel Bin bag and set two bagels in Cherry's lap. He tucked her hair behind her ear. 'Here,' he said, 'do you want to blow your nose?' He got a napkin out of the bag and gave it to her.

Cherry blew her nose. She took a sip of coffee. 'Thanks.'

She set the coffee on the floor next to the mattress and unwrapped her bagel. It *was* still warm. She took a bite.

Tom was watching her. He had a bagel, too. He leaned over and kissed her cheek.

After a few bites, Cherry felt better – because food always made her feel better. Because she was a fat girl inside and out. Tom had got her right in that comic. She was a caricature.

Tom kissed her cheek again. He moved his lips to her ear. 'I know I said you could cry on me all day' – his voice was softly urgent – 'and you *can*. But I'd move heaven and earth to never see you cry again, Cherry. I love you so much, you know?'

Cherry was taken aback.

She *didn't* know.

She looked up at him, her eyes wide and welling with more tears.

He kissed her mouth quickly, twice. 'Tell me you know.'

'I . . .' Her voice broke.

'Oh, baby, no.' Tom huffed out a breath, like he felt helpless. 'That's not supposed to make you cry. What am I doing wrong?'

Cherry set her bagel on the bed and leaned into his chest.

He stroked her hair and let her cry – he couldn't do anything to stop her.

'If this is what happens when we spend a night apart,' Tom said, 'I'm done with all that.'

Cherry laughed. She felt ridiculous. She felt aimless. Like she really didn't know how she was supposed to feel and what she was supposed to want. She knew what she *did* want – Tom. As desperately as ever. 'Promise?' Cherry said.

Tom squeezed her tight, probably grateful for a sign of life. 'I promise. I couldn't sleep, anyway.'

'I missed you,' she said. If Tom had been here, Cherry's mind never would have gone a-wandering.

'I missed your cute pajamas,' he said.

'I love you, Tom.' Cherry's voice broke saying it.

'I love you, too,' Tom said very quietly. He squeezed her. 'Do you know?'

Cherry nodded her head.

Chapter 28

Cherry wasn't much of an artist.

But she was *enough* of an artist to know, even at twenty-five, that you couldn't put a bridle on someone else's creative expression. Art came out of people and it came out in messy shapes. Like dreams.

Cherry could separate it. (She thought she could.) Artist from art. Tom from that hulking figure with the scornful thoughts.

It really was like she'd read his diary.

Like she'd eavesdropped on his thoughts.

Tom didn't make *Thursday* for other people to see it – she believed that. He didn't promote it. Cherry wasn't sure why he even posted it... But why did anyone put anything online? Why did Cherry complain about work on Twitter?

Tom didn't want people to read *Thursday*, and nobody *did* read it. Cherry's sisters would never see it.

What was Cherry supposed to say to him now – '*You can't put me in your comic*'?

She knew already, after reading two years of his comic strips, that that would be like asking him not to think of her at all.

Tom was clearly using the comic to process his thoughts. *Thursday* was his RAM. It was his REM. Cherry couldn't just crash into his life and tell him to stop. And she couldn't hold herself back from his art without holding herself back from Tom himself...

Could she?

It would mean talking to Tom about *Thursday*...

It would mean admitting that she'd read it. (Behind his back, against his wishes.) Admitting that she'd seen herself through his eyes ...

It would mean parading that parody of a fat girl out in front of them, between them, and acknowledging her.

How could Cherry ever face Tom, if he knew that she knew?

Chapter 29

You'd think that, over the years, it would have gotten harder for Cherry to make peace with Tom's comic strip . . .

After people were actually reading it.

After that fat character got a name and strangers started to use it on Cherry.

But literally everything gets easier over time.

Cherry got used to *Thursday*.

She knew that Tom was always working on it. He told her so. Sometimes he'd ask for her help with a joke.

And he told her when he started to get more readers. The webcomics site that hosted him was acquired by a larger blog site, and *Thursday* was featured on its front page.

Tom was unsettled by the attention. Flattered, possibly. But any attention at all made Tom uncomfortable, in every circumstance.

When a graphic novel editor reached out, Tom ignored the email.

Cherry was the one who pushed him to reply.

Maybe that was crazy . . . *Why would Cherry want more people to see Tom's version of her?*

But by that time, they were married. By that time, Cherry knew Tom's whole story. She knew how much he hated his job. She knew how beaten down he felt, generally – how hard it was for him to feel good about the world and his place in it. And she just loved him so much. She was so attached to him. She was living with him under his skin.

Tom was her husband; Baby was just a drawing.

What happened in the comic wasn't important. What was important was what the comic did for Tom. It was the corner of his life where he got to make every decision. Where he felt the most free.

And Cherry knew that *Thursday* was excellent. She didn't have to keep reading it (she had *not* kept reading it) to know that.

'You deserve every good thing that comes your way,' Cherry told him, the night before he called the editor. They were sitting on their couch, and she was holding his face in her hands. '*Thursday* deserves it.'

Baby came up between them only once. Explicitly. After Tom had made a deal with the publisher.

His first advance was small, but it felt like money for nothing. The work was already done.

'Ophelia wants to start the actual book a couple years into the series,' Tom said. Ophelia was his editor in New York. 'She says that's when *Thursday* found its groove.'

Tom and Cherry were out in the driveway. Cherry was refinishing a big oak wardrobe that they'd bought at an auction. Tom was helping her paint an art deco border on the sides; he could freehand a right angle.

'That makes sense,' Cherry said. She was crouched down, painting a scene on the wardrobe's doors – two talking hats from an obscure Disney cartoon. Cherry had tried to make Tom draw the characters, but he said they'd be cuter if Cherry drew them, even if she was out of practice. Cherry was working as a manager by then. Not an artist.

'So,' Tom said, 'that's about the point where ... The Guy meets ... Baby.'

Cherry's tongue was sticking out. She was painting a really finicky part. 'Uh-huh.'

'I just – Well, I don't know if you . . .' Tom's voice trailed off.

Cherry glanced up at him. He'd stopped painting, and he was looking down at her. Helpless. There were two lines between his eyebrows.

'It's okay,' Cherry said.

Tom looked in her eyes. 'It's just, um . . .'

'It's *okay*,' she repeated.

They'd been together almost seven years, and it really *was* okay, all of it. But Cherry still didn't like talking about the details. If she was going to keep Tom's art separate from their life, she needed it to *stay* separate. She didn't even like hearing Tom mention Baby by name.

But there Baby was. Standing there with them in the driveway. With her big butt and her belly and both of her chins.

Cherry ignored her.

'It's always going to be okay,' she said to Tom. 'This is your story.'

He set the paint can aside and pulled Cherry up to hug him. She was still holding her brush. She got baby blue paint in his hair.

Chapter 30

Russ Sutton was always campaigning, even though he wasn't running for office.

Russ couldn't just go out to dinner. He had to go somewhere where he had a connection or where he wanted to make a connection. There was always some business for the mayor's office, or business for one of the boards Russ was on. Russ knew everyone, everywhere. And he needed everyone to like him.

Cherry was surprised how little this bothered her.

There was something very sincere about Russ. When they were together, Cherry felt like he really wanted to be with her. And when he stopped to talk to someone – or to press some agenda – that seemed sincere, too.

Russ took her to a spaghetti dinner in a Catholic rec center across town and introduced her to an entire neighborhood. Cherry sat across from him at a long cafeteria table eating meatballs and hot-dog-bun garlic bread, and never once felt like he'd forgotten about her as he worked the room.

Going out with Russ meant meeting *dozens* of new people and making *so much* small talk. That was okay. Cherry was good at small talk.

Going out with Russ also meant meeting single women who clearly had their sights set on him – and who were frankly shocked to see him with someone like Cherry. That was okay, too. Russ was very obviously *with* her.

He stood with his arm around her. He held her hand. He

introduced her as 'my friend Cherry,' but he made it clear that she was his date.

It made Cherry feel seen. And . . . *prized*. Like Russ had chosen her, and then he'd chosen to introduce her to the entire city. And she knew she was getting ahead of herself, because she still hadn't met his kid or his ex-wife or his parents or any of his siblings – but still, it felt good.

Only one person at the spaghetti dinner connected Cherry to *Thursday*. 'Cherry . . .' he said. 'Are you the Omaha Cherry who's married to the *Thursday* artist?'

'Yes,' she said, and then, 'I was.'

The guy was embarrassed. 'Oh. Sorry. I'm a fan.'

'It's fine,' she said. 'I'm a fan, too.'

That was two lies:

First, Cherry was very legally *still* married to Tom, and second, Cherry hadn't intentionally read a *Thursday* comic in years.

But it was the first time she'd told someone outside her inner circle that she wasn't with Tom anymore. (Well, technically the first person she'd told was *Russ*.) Cherry wondered if this guy was the sort of fan who would tell the internet that she and Tom had broken up. Probably not. Most of the people on r/tomvalentine were women.

Someone would tell the internet. Eventually.

There was some relief to be had there. Cherry was eager to be yesterday's news.

After they left, Russ told her that they'd gone to the spaghetti dinner because he was trying to press a city councilman on a vote. It worked, he said, and Cherry got most of the credit, because the city councilman's wife had loved her.

'Which one was the city councilman's wife?'

'The little Polish lady with the jewelry.'

'She had sixty-four charms on three Pandora bracelets,' Cherry said. 'She is *living*.'

'She loved you,' Russ said. 'She said you're much prettier than my old girlfriend and have better energy.'

'Who's your old girlfriend?'

'A homely girl with bad vibes, apparently.'

Russ was so good at networking and making the most of every interaction that Cherry asked him if he was dating her because he needed something from Western Alliance. 'I'm dating you because you're sexy,' he said, 'but I don't mind having a friend at North America's largest railroad.'

'My *old* girlfriend,' he'd said. As if Cherry was his new one.

Russ and Cherry were going to see a movie. Which meant they were going to the pretentious nonprofit arthouse theater where Russ knew the executive director. There was a snooty cafe in the lobby and arty plaques hanging up with the names of wealthy donors. Cherry teased Russ while they waited in line for tickets. They were holding hands. (Tom had been back in Los Angeles for two weeks. That errant kiss felt small and far away now.) 'When was the last time you went to a real cineplex, Mr Shop Local?'

Russ smiled at her. 'I'm an everyman, Cherry.'

'Have you seen a single Marvel movie?'

'I have an eight-year-old son.'

Cherry laughed and leaned into him. 'You're so good at this. You haven't answered a single one of my questions. *Mr President, have you had sexual relations with that woman?*'

'The night is young.'

Russ recognized the tattooed lady selling tickets. He introduced her to Cherry, and the woman looked at her funny, but Cherry ignored it.

The theater had two screening rooms. Cherry and Russ ended up in a tiny room with maybe twenty-five seats. They were seeing some Finnish movie – '*A darkly comic romance.*' Russ knew the people sitting behind them and started chatting.

'I'm going to get popcorn,' Cherry said, excusing herself. (Carbs didn't count at movie theaters.)

'I'll get it,' he said.

But Cherry was already up. 'You stay and talk. I'm gonna use the bathroom, too.'

She went to the bathroom, then stood in line for popcorn. It took a while. The same woman who was selling tickets was also handling concessions, and she was moving at a very nonprofit pace.

When Cherry walked back into the theater, the trailers had started.

Jesse Plemons was onscreen, wearing a dark blue hoodie and looking anxious. He was facing a British actress in tight black jeans and a black V-neck – who was almost definitely wearing a fat suit.

Cherry had never reversed course so quickly in her life. She practically flew back to the lobby, like a cartoon character leaving a trail of popcorn hanging in the air behind her. *Yoink.*

Her heart was thundering in her chest. The woman at the concessions stand was watching her. Cherry walked back into the bathroom (even though she was holding popcorn and that was gross).

She stared at herself in the bathroom mirror ...

Cherry was wearing a very cute red plaid shirtwaist dress with a flared skirt, and a tulip-yellow cardigan. (Russ had really brought back her cardigan habit.) She had on dark green tights and black Mary Poppins boots. Her mulberry lipstick was perfect. Her emerald-green eyeliner was perfect. Her hair was cut to frame her round face. Her cheeks were flushed red. Her hands were trembling. She wanted to run away. She thought about calling an Uber, but she'd left her phone in her handbag on her seat.

If she went back to the theater now, Baby would be there with her. Baby *was* there! With Russ, crashing Cherry's date. Crashing Cherry's whole life, at every turn. There was nowhere to hide from her.

Cherry was breathing heavy. Maybe she was hyperventilating. She thought about splashing her face with water, like on TV, but she didn't want to ruin her makeup. Instead she ate some popcorn. She watched herself eat popcorn. She drank some Diet Coke.

She had to go back.

There was no real escape from all this. Cherry just had to keep moving through it.

She walked back to the theater, still breathing too hard. The Finnish movie had started. (It was black-and-white; that was a real choice in 2024.) Cherry sat down next to Russ without looking at him.

He immediately put his arm around her. He squeezed her shoulders. She glanced over at him, a stiff smile pasted on her face.

Russ smiled for real. Was he trying to make a point? *Look at me smiling at you in this extremely weird situation.* Yes, probably.

'Can I have some popcorn?' he asked.

Cherry held the bag out to him. He took some. He smiled at her again. He squeezed her shoulders a little harder.

Cherry turned to the screen and concentrated on acting normal. She couldn't concentrate on anything else – certainly not subtitles. She had no idea what this movie was about. There was a lot of drinking. No one looked happy.

Russ shifted after a while and moved his arm away from her, but he settled with his hand on Cherry's leg. He rubbed her thigh idly, tugging her skirt up so he could stroke her knee.

When she finally looked over at him again, he smiled back at her. Just for a second. He seemed invested in the movie.

Maybe everything was going to be okay.

When the lights came up, Cherry didn't want to make eye contact with anyone else in the theater. What if they recognized her? Cherry had avoided wearing black for a decade – she'd destroyed that black sweater – but sometimes people *did* recognize her, out of the blue. Tom was a master of caricature.

She and Russ had planned to have dinner in the little cafe in the lobby. It had a bakery that made fresh bread and pastries every morning. Russ had been talking it up.

But when they got to the hostess stand, he said, 'Why don't we go somewhere else?'

'I thought you liked this place.'

He shrugged. 'I don't feel like waiting.'

They were second in line. 'It'll take us just as long to drive somewhere.'

Russ wasn't looking at Cherry. He hadn't looked at her for a few minutes. He was squinting out toward the windows.

'What's wrong?' Cherry asked, sotto voce. 'Is there someone here?' She looked around, not sure who or what she was looking for.

She saw the poster.

There were *Coming Attractions* posters all along this wall, and Cherry was standing right in front of a *Thursday* poster. It was Jesse Plemons again, in the sweatshirt, but the world around him was sketched. He wasn't facing the British actress. He was facing Baby. The *cartoon*.

Cherry felt sliced across the middle. Like, in a movie, where a character gets hit with a sword, and they smile at the camera before the top half of their body falls off.

'I guess I didn't realize . . .' Russ said.

She looked back at him. He was staring at the poster. He looked fucking *dismayed*.

If Baby were a real person, and Cherry were a person with a gun, Cherry would have murdered her right here. In cold blood. Right between the eyes.

If Tom were here, too, Cherry might shoot him next.

'. . . that you were a *character*,' Russ finished.

'I'm not a character,' Cherry said. She clenched her teeth. Her chin was up.

Russ looked at her, confused. Like Cherry was denying what was right in front of them.

She wasn't denying it.

She was *decrying* it.

She was denouncing the whole endeavor.

'I...' Russ said.

'It wasn't a secret,' Cherry hissed.

'No, I know,' he said. He looked up at the poster again.

Cherry looked at it through his eyes:

If you were dating a fat woman, and it was already difficult for you... Like, if you were already struggling a little with the way it looked to other people, and what it might say about you...

Did people think you couldn't get a hot girl? Did people think you were settling? That you were gay? Did they see you as less hot now? Less attractive, less virile? Less valuable on the open market?

If you were that guy, who always dated objectively, conventionally attractive women, and now you were dating an objectively fat woman, and you *liked* her – you liked talking to her, you liked fucking her – but you still couldn't quite set aside her weight, or look past it...

If it was *really* important to you to look past it...

What would it be like to get confirmation – from Hollywood, no less – that your girl was *super fat*? That everyone saw her that way? That even a Hollywood-fat actress had to wear a fake butt to portray her? That if you boiled this girl down to her essential lines, they were all rolls and bulges – and *literally everyone* could see it?

The headline for this girl, this woman you were with, was that she was fat. And you were never going to trick the world into seeing her any other way.

'I think you should take me home,' Cherry said.

She started walking toward the door. The tattooed girl at the concessions stand was staring at her again.

'What?' Russ was right behind her. 'Cherry, no.'

She kept walking.

He followed her out the door, then grabbed her arm. 'Wait.'

Cherry turned to face him. Her mouth was open, and her jaw was cocked to the side, ready to fight.

Russ ran his other hand through his hair. 'Give me a second, okay? I'm just surprised.'

'How is any of this a surprise? You knew about the movie!'

'I didn't know you were *in* it.'

'I'm *not* in it!'

'Okay!' He took hold of her other arm, too. 'I'm sorry! I didn't know – I guess I didn't know what *Thursday* was about.'

'It's a global phenomenon,' Cherry said.

'It's a comic book,' he said. 'I don't read comic books.'

She rolled her eyes painfully. 'It's actually a collection of weekly strips.'

Russ looked overwhelmed. '*Okay*. I didn't know that. Did you want me to know that? Did you want me to read it?'

'No!'

'Then what *do* you want from me, Cherry?'

'I want you to not be freaked out!'

'I'm not freaked out,' he said.

She frowned at him. She'd been frowning at him this whole time.

Russ closed his eyes. 'Okay, I'm a *little* freaked out.' He opened them. 'Just give me a second.'

Cherry was breathing at the top of her chest, even though her dress fit fine.

Russ loosened his grip. He rubbed her arms. 'Give me a second, okay?'

She looked down.

He brushed his fingers over her bangs. 'It's a global phenomenon, huh?'

Cherry's anger finally ebbed, and her eyes filled with tears.

'Hey, hey, hey,' Russ said, leaning close to her. 'Look at me – I'm not freaked out. I'm just surprised.'

Cherry looked up at him without lifting her head. She was biting her bottom lip.

'I'm just acclimating,' he said. 'I feel stupid. Apparently I'm the only person in Omaha who hadn't seen this trailer. My mom said something to me about it, and I didn't get it – I get it now.'

'Your mom's a *Thursday* fan?'

'No, she just knows I'm seeing you.'

'She does?'

'Yeah.' Russ smiled a little. He touched her cheek. 'Everybody knows.'

Cherry exhaled. She felt herself softening. Tilting her head toward his hand. He stroked her cheek.

'This must really suck for you,' he said. 'I hadn't realized . . .'

Cherry blinked up at him, feeling new tears. 'I hate it,' she whispered.

'I'm sorry,' Russ whispered back. 'Fuck that guy. *Fuck* Jesse Plemons.'

Cherry laughed. A few tears fell. 'I love Jesse Plemons.'

'He was so good in *The Power of the Dog*,' Russ said.

'Do you *only* see black-and-white movies?'

'That was in color.'

'It *felt* black-and-white.'

Russ kissed her. 'Let's go to my place.'

'What about dinner?'

'I ate all that popcorn.'

'No, *I* ate all that popcorn,' Cherry said, 'and I'm still hungry.'

'Do you want to eat here?'

'In the shadow of my ex? No.'

'I'll take you anywhere you want,' Russ said.

She made him take her to the Cheesecake Factory. He didn't know anyone there.

Chapter 31

Thursday turned into something else – before the first book was even published.

The webcomic caught fire in certain corners of the internet. There were Tumblr fan blogs and Twitter memes. A reference in a Kanye lyric.

Tom stayed away from it all. He wasn't on social media.

Cherry watched it from a distance. She set up a Google alert.

Her more culturally plugged-in friends were the first to become aware of Tom's comic. Another designer at work mentioned it, and then a few people from college posted about it on Facebook . . .

But whatever was happening still wasn't happening in the real world. Tom had never monetized *Thursday*. Nothing in their life changed. The *New York Times* wrote a small piece about the comic, but nobody in Cherry and Tom's circles read the *New York Times*.

The first *Thursday* collection – at that time, the only planned collection – debuted on three bestseller lists. Ophelia, Tom's editor, said this was unheard of for an adult graphic novel.

Everything about publishing was unheard of for Tom and Cherry, so the impact didn't really sink in.

They still lived in the same house and drove the same car. They still went to work every day for the railroad, and Tom still hated it.

Cherry had been promoted again. They were talking about getting pregnant. They were talking about getting a dog.

Tom had gotten twenty thousand dollars for the first *Thursday* book, and they'd used it to pay off their credit cards. There'd be royalties eventually, but not for six months, and even then the royalties would be held back against returns. Tom didn't know what that meant. Tom didn't know how many books had sold exactly or how much he got from each sale.

Cherry's sisters all bought the book. Or said they did. Cherry told them that she didn't want to talk about it. She was sure they started a new group thread without her.

Some of their Western Alliance coworkers bought the book, but it didn't seem like they were actually reading it.

The local library wanted Tom to give a speech. He said no.

His publisher wanted him to go on a promotional tour. He said no.

But then Charlie, his agent – Tom had an agent now – said that he was contractually obligated to promote the book, within reason. No one could say what 'within reason' meant.

Tom really, *really* hated his job at the ad agency. Cherry encouraged him to take a month off and go on tour.

Tom didn't want to. 'What will I even talk about?'

'The comic. The characters.'

'There's nothing to say – everything I had to say is already *in* the book.'

'Talk about your process.'

'I sit at a computer.'

'Just be handsome and funny and sign books.'

'So now you're asking me to become a different person . . .'

'You're very handsome and very funny, Tom.'

'To you. Maybe.'

'To me, definitely.'

'I don't want to do this, Cherry.'

'How do you know? You've never done anything like this. Let them pay for you to see the country. Stay in nice hotels. Try regional takes on eggs Benedict. Visit comic book stores.'

'You're making it sound like a vacation.'

'It *is*.'

'If it was a vacation, you'd come with me.'

Tom's bookstore events sold out, so they moved him into bigger venues. Into theaters and community centers. He did readings from *Thursday*; they were apparently hilarious. *Vox* did a piece on him, but Tom wouldn't comment. Then *The Atlantic* called, and Charlie the agent and Ophelia the editor and Rachel the publicist – she was new – *made* him comment.

A production company wanted to option the first three volumes of *Thursday* for film.

(Tom's publisher had decided to release *six* volumes, one every six months. They were already rereleasing the first book in hardcover. Tom was doing new art for a boxed set.)

This production company was top of the heap, according to Andrea, Tom's new film agent. It was the kind of place that cranked out Oscar bait. Though Tom could also make a deal directly with Amazon or Netflix . . .

Every time that Andrea called, Tom would leave his cell phone in the house and go for a bike ride. Or out to the yard. Or to walk their new puppy.

Cherry finally took Andrea's call.

Andrea was going to get Tom everything: An executive producer credit. A piece of the backend. First run at the screenplay.

Tom quit his job, and it was the first *real* thing that happened because of his success – and the first unalloyed good thing. He got to walk away. (And Cherry didn't have to be a party to firing him.)

They went out to dinner to celebrate. They called it their sixth anniversary celebration, too, because Tom was going to miss the actual date of their anniversary – his publisher was sending him to a librarians' conference in Cincinnati. Rachel, the publicist, said that librarians loved him.

There were so many conferences. And award ceremonies. And book festivals.

The production company wanted Tom to come out to Los Angeles to collaborate with an experienced screenwriter on the movie script. And then they wanted him to come back to L.A. to meet with the director.

Tom's suitcase sat in the foyer when he was home. He never unpacked it; he did laundry on the road. 'Hotels will wash your pants for fifteen dollars,' he told Cherry, 'and your underwear for seven.'

His first big royalty check hit their bank account with a thunderclap. Tom wasn't home enough for them to talk about how to spend it. When he was home, his head was somewhere else. He was always on deadline. He was struggling to keep up with posting new comic strips. He actually *missed* two *Thursday*s in a row, for the first time ever. The *Washington Post* ran a story about it.

Rachel booked his first TV appearance.

The Cut ran a column about how he was '*your new grumpy Midwestern crush.*'

The second royalty check landed with a sonic boom. Tom was huge in France and the Philippines. Tom went to a book festival in Brazil.

Cherry had to come home for lunch every day to walk Stevie Nicks.

Tom sent her photos of high-speed train cabins and room-service cheese plates. His publicist took photos of him for the *Thursday* Instagram account. Cherry followed the account because Tom never sent her selfies.

Cherry went along on one promotional trip with him, fairly early on – to Japan. They were going to go to Tokyo Disney when he was done with his book events. They were going to fly first class. Her nephew came to stay with Stevie.

The flight was long, and Rachel kept coming up from coach to go over business stuff with Tom. She was in her mid-twenties with messy red hair, and she was very, very sharp. She reminded Cherry of Natasha Lyonne.

When they got to Tokyo, Cherry was exhausted and perpetually in the way. She went to a giant bookstore signing – it was the first time she'd gone to one of Tom's events – and one of his readers called her 'Baby' and asked for a photo.

She skipped the rest of Tom's Japanese appearances. She had so much work, and she was fourteen hours ahead of the Western Alliance team in Omaha. (Or ten hours behind.)

Tokyo Disney was wonderful. A rare charmed day with Tom. Followed by a rare charmed night in his arms. Both of them still jet-lagged. Cherry only mostly sure she wasn't ovulating.

Tom was going on to Sydney after that.

He tried to talk Cherry into going with him, but she had to get back to work. And to the dog. And what would she do in Sydney, anyway – sit in Tom's expensive hotel room and feel unnecessary?

She was melancholy and upside down. She cried on the plane on the way home.

She just wanted to get back to Nebraska.

Chapter 32

Today 8:10 PM

Faith
Cherry, Mom says you're bringing your new boyfriend to Thanksgiving.

Cherry
I don't know what she's talking about.

Joy
Why aren't you bringing him??? I thought you really liked him!!

Honny
Yeah, you rejected an architect for him.

Cherry
We've only been dating a few months.

Joy
I got engaged to Jeff after three months.

Cherry
You were 18 years old and very eager to have post-marital sex.

Joy
We were in love!!

Faith

It's going to be so weird having Thanksgiving without Tom.

Joy

Seriously!! The last time I saw Tom was LAST Thanksgiving.

Honny

The last time I saw Tom was on 60 Minutes.

Joy

Who's going to eat my brocco-slaw salad at family gatherings if Tom isn't there???

                Cherry

                Literally no one, Joy.

Honny

I don't think Cherry should bring a new man to Thanksgiving until she's divorced.

When are you getting divorced, Cherry? Have you even started?

Joy

Divorces take forever. I want to meet this new guy SOON!

Chapter 33

Cherry hadn't planned to invite Russ to Thanksgiving.

They were walking Stevie in the dark. They'd gone to a fundraiser right after work, and Cherry had pushed Russ to leave early – she kept thinking of Stevie at home, pacing the foyer and watching the door, possibly chewing up paper products.

Stevie missed Tom.

'Having a dog is worse than having a kid,' Russ said, 'because a kid will eventually walk themselves.' Russ was shivering. He was wearing a thin topcoat over a wool suit. He was dressed for commuting.

Cherry knew he was cold – she was cold, too – but she didn't want to rush Stevie. Cherry felt bad about how often the dog was alone lately. They stood in front of someone's house while Stevie sniffed an evergreen bush.

'Your ex didn't want kids?' Russ asked.

Cherry was surprised by the question – Russ didn't usually mention Tom outright. Maybe he felt like he needed to know more about him, in the wake of the *Thursday* revelation.

Or maybe Russ had been thinking about what Cherry had said, about wanting a baby . . .

'I think he did, actually,' she said.

Russ's head was down. Very focused on the ground. 'Was there a problem?'

'Several,' Cherry said. 'But mostly we just couldn't agree on when to try.'

He looked up at her. 'You never tried?'

She shook her head.

Russ looked thoughtful, like he was doing the math. Cherry was thirty-six, and she'd been with Tom for more than a decade. The ideal time to try for a baby had definitely come and gone.

At first it had been Cherry who wanted to wait. She and Tom didn't make any money when they met. Daycare would have been crippling. And having a kid would have slowed Cherry down; she might never have been promoted. Plus it felt like they should spend some time *being* together, just the two of them.

Once Cherry was promoted, it was even harder to think about slowing down. She had new responsibilities, new ambitions – and by then it was clear that she needed to be the one with a stable salary. Tom was constantly on the verge of quitting his job at the ad agency. She wanted to be in a place where he could quit or take a pay cut, and their family would still be okay.

When they got to that place, and Cherry told Tom she was finally ready to have a baby, or to try – he wasn't ready anymore.

Maybe Tom never would have been ready, whenever Cherry had called his bluff.

He said he wanted to talk about it more. But Tom didn't actually want to talk about anything, ever.

He said they should see how they did with a dog. But once they had a dog, he said it was hard to imagine taking care of a new person on top of Stevie. He'd already started traveling for *Thursday*. It was the beginning of the end.

Cherry should have gotten pregnant when they met. She should have stopped handing him condoms. She should never have started taking her temperature and carefully tracking her menstrual cycle.

Now she had nothing *but* financial stability. Literally. Nothing.

Stevie tugged on her leash.

'I didn't mean to bring up a sore subject,' Russ said.

Cherry huffed out a sad laugh. She let Stevie pull her forward. 'Didn't you?'

'I guess I did . . .'

Cherry looked over at Russ. His face was kind. He looked like he liked her and was trying to figure her out.

She forced herself to shake off some of her bitterness; none of it was about Russ. 'It's okay,' she said. 'I think this is probably a better-sooner-than-later conversation. What about you? Did you plan on only having one kid?'

Russ shook his head. 'No, but … by the time Liam was old enough for us to try again, it was clear that our marriage was on thin ice.'

'I'm sorry,' Cherry said.

'*Ope*,' Russ said, motioning at Stevie. 'There she goes.'

Cherry looked at Stevie and sighed. She pulled a plastic baggie out of her pocket. 'I can't believe this is my job.'

He laughed. 'For someone whose life revolves around a dog, you are the most reluctant dog owner.'

Cherry was crouching over. 'My life doesn't revolve around a dog!'

'Then why is my nose going numb? Why am I out here, instead of in a warm bed with my warm girlfriend?'

She couldn't help but laugh. 'Because my husband wanted a dog instead of a baby!'

Russ barked out a laugh. 'Sorry,' he said. 'That's really sad.'

Cherry was standing up again. 'I know.'

He kissed her cheek. 'You're cute when you're pitiful.'

'I must be so adorable, all the time.'

He cocked his head. 'Actually you're unnervingly confident and self-assured most of the time. This is a rare moment.'

She narrowed her eyes.

'Fortunately, you're *sexy* when you're confident. So it's a win–win situation for me.'

'Oh, okay.' Cherry laughed. She wished she wasn't holding a bag of warm shit. She clicked her tongue and tugged at Stevie's leash, turning her toward home.

Russ followed them. He bumped his shoulder against Cherry's. 'I'd have another kid,' he said quietly. 'Just for the record.'

Cherry was surprised again. She looked over at him.

He glanced at her, but kept walking. 'I didn't say anything before, when you first brought it up, because I needed to think about it. Liam's a lot. And he's always going to be a lot, I think. But . . . I like being a dad. So. Yeah. I would have another kid. If I was in a relationship I believed in.'

Cherry felt suddenly tearful. 'With someone who liked you this time?'

He smiled at her. 'Those are the table stakes.'

She watched their feet hit the pavement. She bumped her shoulder into his arm.

An hour or two later, after Cherry had taken a shower, and then Russ had taken a shower, and they'd climbed into her bed, and Russ had teased her about wearing a peekaboo bra to bed when he was *so fucking tired*, and Cherry had crawled under the blanket to suck and kiss and feel glad of him, and Russ had pulled her up to lick her mouth and call her a vixen, and Russ had looked at her the way men looked at her right before they said '*I love you*' – Cherry said, 'Do you want to spend Thanksgiving with my family?'

Chapter 34

The kitchen was very empty without Tom.

Cherry stayed up late the night before Thanksgiving, making all their usual recipes by herself.

This was her first Thanksgiving without him.

Even last year, when the connection between them was stretched and strange and ready to snap, Tom had flown home for Thanksgiving and then again for Christmas.

Tom had always spent holidays with Cherry's family. His family didn't get into them.

Cherry's family did holidays to the max. They took them way too seriously – they went overboard. And Cherry, famously among them, went the most overboard. With Tom's help, she went *way, way* too far.

Their first Thanksgiving together, Tom had helped Cherry make cheese straws, Sicilian meat pies, squash casserole, and cupcakes that looked like turkeys.

They both liked to cook, and they didn't have kids, and – that first year, especially – they were high on what they could accomplish together, two artists with lots of free time and a limited budget.

Their whole life was a project back then. They'd filled Cherry's apartment with secondhand furniture. Tom had built bookshelves for her and a TV stand. They cooked dinner together most nights and brought the leftovers to work for lunch the next day. Everything they touched was beautiful. They were living charmed nights and Chelsea mornings.

Their holiday cooking had only gotten more elaborate over the years. Her whole family teased them about it – but also expected it. There were several dishes that Cherry and Tom brought every year...

It all took twice as long without Tom's help. Cherry didn't have enough hands, and she was weighed down by déjà vu. The first batch of cheese straws was brittle and too salty.

Russ had been frank with Cherry about Thanksgiving: He wasn't ready for her to meet Liam. He wouldn't be ready for her to meet Liam *'until we're past all the chicken exits.'*

So Russ was going to have Thanksgiving lunch with his parents and his siblings – *'Who you can meet anytime; tomorrow if you want'* – and Liam, and then he was going to come over to Honny's house later that day to meet Cherry's entire nosy family.

On Thursday afternoon, Cherry loaded the back of her Subaru Forester with pans and platters. She put the broken-glass Jell-O ring on the passenger seat, where she could hold on to it. This was a Tom special, and Cherry didn't want to give anyone in her family a chance to miss it. It had taken *hours* to make all the different colors of gelatin for the 'shards' and then to suspend them in the creamy white base. It had come out perfect.

Honny's split-level house in the suburbs was only a little bigger than Cherry's. Hope's house was bigger. Honny got to host Thanksgiving because she was the bossiest – and because she owned the most card tables and folding chairs. When Cherry walked into the house, everyone in the living room – her sisters' husbands and kids – called out her name.

'Is that Cherry?' Joy rushed into the living room from the kitchen. Her face fell. 'Where is he?'

'He's coming later,' Cherry said. 'Take this plate.'

'Aunt Cherry' – one of her nieces took the plate of cookies – 'it's okay if you didn't bring the Jell-O with the beautiful jewels in it. We understand.'

'Mallory, honey, I brought it. It's out in the car.'

Mallory was eleven. She was Faith's oldest and sweetest kid. 'You did? Did you also bring the pastieri?'

'They're in the car, too. Put your shoes on and help me.'

Joy had her hands on her hips. Of all Cherry's sisters, Joy looked the most like their dad. Olive skin. Dimples. Dramatic eyebrows. 'How'd you manage all that? Were you up all night?'

'It's just Jell-O.' Cherry had only slept from four a.m. to eight. She was wearing concealer under her eyes, and fake eyelashes.

'Where is he?' Honny walked out of the kitchen, already making a suspicious face.

'Aw.' Faith – the shortest and roundest of them – was right behind her. 'Did he back out?'

'He's coming later,' Cherry said.

Her mom walked out of the kitchen, looking elated and holding a big spoon. 'Tom's coming?'

'No,' Joy said. 'Her new boyfriend.'

Cherry's mom was crestfallen. 'Oh.'

'Look –' Honny stepped closer to Cherry. 'Be careful how you talk about this guy in front of the kids. I don't want them to know you're having an extramarital affair.'

'I'm *not*.'

Honny waved her off. 'Don't start an argument you can't win. Just call him your friend, okay?'

'Mom, I can't mash the potatoes *and* baste the turkey.' Hope was standing in the doorway to the kitchen. It was still jarring to see her.

Hope was *half* her old size. Her face was different, her posture was different. She was wearing a beautiful tailored shirt tucked into waisted pants. She looked great – she looked thin. She looked ten years older.

She didn't really look like Hope at all.

'Oh, hey, Cherry,' she said. 'I thought you were bringing your boyfriend?'

Honny frowned. 'They're just friends.'

'He's coming later,' Cherry said. She looked at her niece. 'You ready to help?'

It took the two of them two more trips to empty Cherry's hatchback.

'Aunt Cherry,' Mallory said, 'I know you might need some help setting the table ...' Cherry and Tom usually decorated the tables and arranged everything just so. Tom always took extra care with the kids' table. 'I can help you.'

Mallory had clearly been briefed on the Tom situation. They'd probably all been briefed. Cherry had the only broken marriage in the family; she was a parable now. 'I'd love your help,' she said.

There were too many people in their family to sit together at one table for holiday dinners. The nieces and nephews – some of whom were six feet tall now – sat at folding tables in the living room. Honny used card tables to extend her dining room table, and the adults crammed in there, elbow to elbow.

It was Cherry and Tom's job to make everything look festive. They'd bring over a big box of tablecloths and cloth napkins and vintage napkin rings. Tom would cover the kids' table with kraft paper and draw an entire holiday scene, using the kids themselves as characters.

They loved it.

Honny always tried to save Tom's holiday drawings, even though they'd be torn and covered in gravy by the end of the meal ...

Cherry was tired.

She was having a hard time staying in the present.

Fortunately there was twice as much work as usual to keep her busy. And fortunately there were too many people buzzing around for anyone to home in too closely on Cherry.

Her family was loud – well, her sisters were loud. And their kids were loud. Their husbands tended to be mild-mannered, quiet guys who didn't get too fussed about anything. They sat in the living room, not saying much to each other. Or they ran out to the car (or down to the basement, or out to the garage) to fetch things.

It had been a joke between her and Tom – that Cherry's sisters had a type. Cherry's sisters *were* a type. They were variations on a theme.

Cherry was the quietest, but she wasn't quiet. She was the most ambitious, but they were all ambitious in their own ways. They all looked enough alike that Cherry's teachers would look at her on the first day of class and say, *'Another Bonacci.'*

Growing up, they'd looked like matryoshka dolls. One round girl after another, with pretty long hair and pretty pink cheeks. Everything about them overlapped.

The table was set. Cherry had remembered the box of Thanksgiving decorations. She was just fiddling with an antique cornucopia. (Tom loved a cornucopia . . .)

Faith brought a pitcher of water out to the table. 'Should we wait for your friend to start dinner?'

'No,' Cherry said. 'I don't know when he'll get here. And he's having a late lunch.'

'He's not going to eat?' Joy was bringing out the gravy boat. She looked shattered. 'I made an extra pumpkin pie!'

Cherry took the gravy boat. 'You made an extra pie for one person?'

'I didn't want to not have enough.'

Honny set some rolls on the table. 'It's the same number of people, Joy. Minus Tom, plus this guy. No net gain.'

'Tom doesn't like my pie.'

'He just doesn't like pumpkin,' Cherry said. 'It's not personal.'

'Who doesn't like *pumpkin?*' Honny made a face. 'Good riddance.'

'Don't talk about Tom like that,' Faith said.

They started dinner without Russ – and without Tom – though everyone made sure there was an empty seat next to Cherry.

The food was all good, and there was way too much of it. Every holiday meal with Cherry's family was one long lament about how sad it was that you could only really have one bite of everything before you got too full.

Hope sat on the other side of the empty seat, and Cherry couldn't stop herself from noticing what Hope put on her plate and how little of it she ate.

Cherry should mind her own business ... (Her sisters would break down every bite Hope took on the group chat anyway.) But the point of holidays – the point of family – was to mind everyone's business.

The conversation around the table got louder as the meal went on. Everyone talked over each other. They raced each other to punchlines. They laughed at the top of their voices.

By dessert, Cherry was laughing so much, she thought she might be crying off one of her eyelashes.

She had a mouth full of Joy's pumpkin pie when she saw Russ standing at the end of the table.

His mouth was hanging open. He looked a little dazzled. *Tharn*. Well ... here it was, the final reveal.

It was *one thing* to see Cherry on her own ... a singular fat lady.

It was another to see her at a table full of fat people. In a house full of fat people. All of them eating pie and acting jolly.

Cherry's mom was there to show Russ what Cherry would look like in thirty years. And her sisters were there to show him what she'd look like after she had kids.

Cherry wasn't just fat; she was from the *land* of fat, in the *kingdom* of fat. Her ancestors had been fat even before video games and high-fructose corn syrup and sedentary lifestyles. There was a black-and-white photo of Cherry's grandmother and her sisters at a holiday party in the '50s – they were all hips and heavy bosoms. Cherry could fit in their dresses.

'You must be Cherry's friend,' Honny said.

Russ snapped out of it. He smiled. 'I am.'

Cherry was already up, squeezing past one of her brothers-in-law. 'This is Russ. Russ, this is ... Well, they can introduce themselves. Are you hungry?'

'Absolutely,' Russ said, like someone whose job it was to win hearts and minds.

Cherry's mom was up, too. 'I'll make you a plate, honey. You sit down.'

'This is my mom,' Cherry said. 'Nancy.'

'It's so nice to meet you,' Russ said, holding out his hand.

Cherry took his coat. She was so nervous, her heart was in her mouth. 'Do you want a Coke?' she asked. 'There's Coke. And sparkling cider. Water.'

'A Coke's fine.'

'I'll get it,' Faith said. 'You sit down.'

They sat down. Everyone at the table looked a little dazzled now. Russ was dazzling. He was different. He was a little too dressed up – he always was. His hair looked like it took some effort. He was one of the only men she knew who was always clean-shaven. He was thin. 'Handsome' still wasn't the right word for him ... But he looked like the kind of guy movie stars dated when they were experimenting with normies.

'Did you find the house okay?' Cherry asked him.

'I did. I brought a pie, but a small child took it from me.'

'Scallywags,' she said. 'It's a real problem in this neighborhood.'

'I'm Hope.' Hope was smiling at him. 'I'm the oldest. And this is my husband, Dan.' Hope introduced the whole table.

'Cherry's the middle child,' Faith said.

'That's why she's so agreeable and retiring,' Honny said.

'Here you go, sweetie.' Cherry's mom was back with a *heaping* plate of food.

'Oh ...' Russ said, looking slightly alarmed. 'Thank you.'

'I gave you a little of everything.'

'Just a little,' Cherry said.

Russ turned to Cherry. 'Did you make any of this?'

'She made the best things,' Hope said.

He smiled at Cherry. 'Really?'

'Hasn't Cherry cooked for you?' Faith asked.

'Are you sure she even *likes* you?' Joy asked.

'I thought I was,' Russ said.

'Cherry always makes the Sicilian meat pies and the squash casserole,' Faith's husband said. Kevin was a straight-talker who got tired of all the high jinks. 'And the tiramisu.'

'I love tiramisu,' Russ said.

He very gamely tried to get through his plate while Cherry's sisters took turns asking him questions and making fun of him. (They eventually went back to making fun of each other.) When it was time to play cards, he helped clear the table.

Chapter 35

'I can't believe you told Joy that you didn't like her pie.'

'I said that I don't like *pumpkin*.'

'You should have just said that you were allergic!'

'Is *anyone* allergic to pumpkin?'

'Joy took it personally. They *all* take *everything* personally.'

'Joy's the oldest, right?'

'No, Joy's the fourth, right after me.'

'And Honny's the first?'

'Honny's the second. She just *acts* like she's the oldest. When Hope got married young, Honny usurped her.'

'It would help me if only one of your sisters had an H-name...'

'I'll see if one of them is open to changing.'

'I appreciate that, thank you. So *Honny's* the first –'

'No, I just told you – Hope's the first, Honny's the second.'

'Then Joy.'

'No – then *me*. Joy's the fourth. And Faith's the fifth.'

'You sound like you're listing queens. Honny the First. Hope the Second.'

'Tom. *Hope* is first.'

'And who's on second?'

'Ha, ha.'

'It would also help if all your sisters didn't look like the same person...'

'Next time I'll wear a name tag.'

'I don't need a name tag to identify the cutest.'

'Pfft. Everyone knows that Joy's the cutest.'

'Who is this "everyone"?'

'Your cupcakes were a big hit.'

'They were your cupcakes, Cherry. I just did the finish art. Next year I'm making fancy Jell-O; I promised your nephew . . . What are you smiling at?'

'Nothing.'

'You should be smiling at the road.'

'My mom said you're invited to Christmas, too – but I told her you'd probably want to spend it with your own family.'

'My family doesn't do holidays.'

'What do you mean – what do you guys do?'

'Nothing. My dad doesn't think they're worth the effort.'

'What about your sister?'

'She spends them with her girlfriend's family, in Des Moines.'

'You and your dad could come to Christmas with us?'

'That's sweet of you. Am I invited to come without him?'

'Tom. Of course.'

'Does your family go all-out for Christmas, too?'

'What counts as "all-out"?'

'Turkey. A tree.'

'A tree isn't all-out. That's the bare minimum. Your family doesn't have a Christmas tree?'

'I told you, my dad doesn't do holidays.'

'Not even when you were a kid?'

'Sometimes when I was a kid. But nothing like today. Thank you for inviting me.'

'You're invited next year, too.'

'I'll be there.'

'You're invited all the years, Tom.'

'Eyes on the road, baby.'

Chapter 36

'You're being quiet.'

'Am I? I'm just tired. And cold. Get under the blankets with me.'

'Thank you for coming tonight.'

'Thank you for inviting me. Thank your sister Honny for me.'

'You already thanked her. It was nice of you to bring pumpkin pie.'

'I didn't know there would be four *hundred* pies.'

'Joy made one especially for you.'

'Oh, she told me. I ate two pieces.'

'I know it was a lot . . .'

'It was good pie.'

'No, I mean – I know that my sisters are a lot . . .'

'What's up with your older sister?'

'Which one?'

'Hope.'

'I can't believe you remember all their names.'

'I use mnemonics.'

'Like what?'

'Like . . . Honny looks like a honey bear. And Faith wears a George Michael cross, so "Faith."'

'Honny doesn't look like a honey bear.'

'She doesn't *not* look like a honey bear.'

'How do you remember *my* name, Russ?'

'I met you before I needed mnemonics, but I can think of a few good ones . . .'

'Men love to sexualize my name.'

'I like to sexualize your everything, Cherry.'
'What were you asking, about Hope?'
'Did she do something terrible? No one was talking to her.'
'You were talking to her.'
'Your sisters kept talking over her.'
'It's complicated. She's taking Ozempic, but she won't admit it.'
'Ahhh.'
'What does "ahhh" mean?'
'It just means "ah." So you guys aren't talking to her because she's on Ozempic?'
'Because she won't *tell us* she's taking it.'
'It sounds like you all already know.'
'She told my mom she was watching her carbs.'
'Maybe she is.'
'No one loses a hundred pounds watching their carbs!'
'Holy shit, did she lose a hundred pounds? That's impressive.'
'You aren't getting it.'
'I guess not.'
'If Hope loses a bunch of weight "watching her carbs," it implies that all any of us have to do is watch our carbs.'
'But you do watch your carbs.'
'Exactly! And it's pointless!'
'Then why do you do it?'
'Because I like myself better when I'm trying.'
'I didn't realize Ozempic was so effective . . .'
'It isn't for everyone. And there are risks.'
'Huh . . .'
'I'm not mad at Hope. Honny and Joy are. Really it's just Honny . . . You haven't said anything about how we all look alike.'
'Well, you are sisters.'
'People have a hard time telling us apart.'
'I was more struck by how their husbands all look alike. How does that work?'

'They don't look alike. They're just a type.'

'I don't think any of your sisters' husbands liked me – were they attached to your ex?'

'To Tom? I don't think so. I mean . . . they liked him well enough, but he didn't really fit in.'

'He wasn't the strong, silent type?'

'No, I guess he was – but he wasn't a churchgoer.'

'I don't think I got any credit for my Catholicism.'

'They probably didn't like the idea of someone bringing a shiny new man to Thanksgiving. Maybe it made them feel replaceable . . . Don't worry about them. My sisters all liked you, and their husbands think whatever my sisters tell them to.'

'Is that so?'

'No, I'm just kidding.'

'Huh . . .'

Chapter 37

Cherry was going as Russ's date to the mayor's holiday party the next week, and she knew just what to wear.

She had a flowy green dress with a high ruffled neck and puffed sleeves. Silk chiffon. Deep forest green. It looked like something Loretta Lynn would have worn to accept a country music award in 1972. Cherry was going to wear her hair up, with some tendrils hanging around her face. And she was going to wear metallic gold pumps with four-inch heels, even if it made her back hurt for weeks.

She wore extra sparkly makeup that night. Gold eyeliner. A very pink shade of cream blush.

She put Stevie in her kennel before she even started to get ready – Stacia had agreed to come by later and take her out – and stashed a mini lint roller in her evening bag. (Beaded. Black. With a wine-red-rose pattern.)

Cherry met Russ out on her porch, so that he wouldn't get dog hair on his suit. He ran up the steps to get to her, then held out his arms. 'You . . . look . . . *marvelous*.'

He took her hand and spun her slowly around. Cherry laughed breathily.

'Look at this dress . . .' Russ kissed her cheek. 'I was a little worried you were going to wear something goofy.'

'When do I look goofy?'

He grinned. '*You*, darling? Never.'

'I don't like your tone.'

'You *did* tell me that you loved Bjork's swan dress . . .'

'If I had that dress, I'd wear it every day.'

'Guess I have to spend the rest of my life seeking to destroy it.' He kissed her again. 'Where's your coat?'

'I don't have the right coat for this. I'll be okay.'

Cherry didn't get to see Russ's outfit until they got to the party and he took off his own coat. She wasn't really surprised that he owned a black velvet dinner jacket. If they stayed together, Russ was never going to relinquish his side of the closet.

'You look very distinguished,' Cherry said, petting his collar.

Russ straightened his jacket. 'Why would you bring up my hairline at a time like this?'

She laughed and brushed his hair off his forehead. 'You're not losing your hair. And even if you were, you'd still be the best-looking guy here.'

'You haven't even met anyone here.'

Cherry shook her head. She was wearing rhinestone chandelier earrings, and they danced against her neck. 'I don't have to.'

Russ slid his arm around her waist and leaned in close. 'Let's skip to the part of the night where we go back to my house.'

'Don't you want people to see you in your fancy suit?'

'Right now I just want to see you take off your fancy dress.'

'I can't believe you say things like that with a straight face.'

He kissed the skin behind her ear. 'I work in politics, Cherry.'

The party was in a big house in an expensive neighborhood. Typical C-suite party. The mayor was the heir to a mail-order-steak fortune. Russ kept his arm around Cherry as they walked into the living room. 'You haven't briefed me,' Cherry whispered. 'How should I be with your boss?'

'Be yourself,' he said. 'You'll like Mark. His wife, Molly, pours it on a little thick. Just smile and be noncommittal.' He glanced over at her. 'You'll be fine. You're great at this.'

Cherry caught his glance and held it. Russ's color was high. Pink from the cold. It made his eyes look so blue. Cherry loved his sharp, smooth cheeks and the hint of a cleft in his chin. She could get used to this face ...

Maybe.

Maybe she'd never get used to how good Russ Sutton looked.

'You were right,' she said, feeling warm, feeling stirred down the center. 'Let's skip to the good part.'

'Too late now, sweetheart – they've already seen us.'

A handsome older couple was heading toward them.

'Molly!' Russ said. 'Mr Mayor!'

The mayor was in his fifties and prematurely silver. 'Russell,' he said warmly, 'is this the girl you've been keeping from us?'

'This is Cherry. Cherry – Mark and Molly Brooks.'

Cherry held out her hand. The mayor's wife grabbed it with both of hers. 'Oh my gosh – *look at you*. Mark, look. It's Baby!'

'It's Cherry,' Cherry said.

'No, I know – but it's like you walked right off the page!' She squeezed Cherry's hand and shook it with each syllable: 'We are *such* fans of *Thursday*.'

'We are,' the mayor agreed. 'You know, we've tried to get your husband on the phone. The Chamber has an idea for him.'

Molly let go of Cherry's hand, so she could clap. 'It's "The Guy in Omaha"! That's the idea!'

Cherry was confused. 'I think The Guy already lives in Omaha ...'

'Right,' the mayor said, 'but what if your husband did a special comic book highlighting that *Thursday* takes place in Omaha – for the Chamber?'

'The chamber ... orchestra?'

'The Chamber of Commerce,' Russ said flatly.

'Baby could be in it, too!' Molly said.

'We think it would be impactful,' the mayor said. 'People need to see that Omaha is a vibrant, affordable city for the creative class.'

'*Everyone wants the creative class,*' his wife said in a pretend whisper. 'You should see the metrics.'

Cherry smiled and nodded. 'Mmm.'

'You have to link us up with your husband,' the mayor said.

'Have him call me,' Molly said. 'People can't say no to me.'

'I'm afraid,' Cherry said lightly, glancing at Russ, 'that I don't have as much sway with him these days.'

'Oh, that's right.' The mayor's wife laughed. 'Well, lucky Russ, right? I'm going to have Russ give you my personal number to pass along to your husband. I'm telling you – people can't say no to me.'

'I'll pass it along,' Cherry said.

'It can't hurt, right?'

Cherry shook her head. 'It cannot hurt.'

Molly put her hand on Russ's arm. 'Russ, get this woman a drink. Oh my goodness, I'm just seeing you.' She slapped his arm. 'You're such a dish.' She looked at Cherry and loud-whispered again – '*Isn't he a dish?*'

Her husband rolled his eyes. 'Don't me-too my staff, Molly.'

'I'm not me-tooing anyone! I'm being honest!'

Russ was smiling warmly. Everyone was smiling warmly. The mayor smiled warmly at Cherry. 'It's a real honor to meet you, Cherry. We feel like we know you already.'

'We really do,' his wife agreed.

Russ was leading Cherry away. 'Come on, I've been ordered to get my lovely date a drink.'

'The bar's that way.' The mayor pointed.

'*There's* a question he can always answer,' his wife cracked.

'It was so nice to meet you,' Cherry said.

Russ was tugging at her waist. She followed him to the bar. He ordered a Coke Zero for Cherry and a scotch and soda for himself, and immediately took a long drink.

Cherry held on to her Coke Zero. It was poured into a highball glass.

Russ wasn't looking at her. Or anyone. The corners of his eyes were tense.

Cherry leaned into his gaze. She made her eyes big like, *That was crazy.*

Russ smiled. He goggled his eyes, too. He leaned over to whisper. 'I had no idea they were going to do that.'

Cherry laughed. 'It's okay.'

He put his arm back around her. 'Let me introduce you to a few more people. How do you feel about wealthy Republicans?'

'Some of my best employers are wealthy Republicans.'

'See, we have that in common.'

Cherry met the rest of the mayor's staff and several city supervisors. Cherry already knew a few of them from her work in public affairs.

Meg Jones herself was there – which made sense now that Cherry thought about it – and she didn't blink when Cherry introduced Russ as her date. Meg was extremely good at not blinking; Cherry had learned it from her.

Thursday kept coming up. (That fucking movie trailer ...)

'*Oh, right,*' a county commissioner said. 'My daughter loves your books.'

'I haven't written any books,' Cherry said.

'The books you're in,' he said. 'She can't wait for the movie.'

'*Oh my gosh,*' one of the mayor's aides said. 'Are you the Cherry from *Thursday*?'

'I, um ...'

The woman was flustered. 'Sorry, it's just – I know your name from the dedication.'

'Ah ...'

'And I wasn't expecting you to look so much like the character!'

'Well ...'

'I'm so sorry, it's just – it's my favorite book. This is so embarrassing.'

'*What the fuck,*' a drunken lawyer said. 'That's Baby! You are so fucking *Baby!*'

'What the *fuck*, Joe,' Russ said, shoving the guy's shoulder.

'Sorry, Russ,' the guy said. 'Sorry, miss.' He started laughing again and elbowed Russ. 'But you're dating Baby! From the meme!'

'From the comic,' said another lawyer, standing next to him. This one seemed more high than drunk.

'That's like dating a celebrity!' the first one said. 'Not a celebrity, a *concept*. That's like dating *Lisa Simpson*.'

The other one frowned. 'It's more like dating Garfield . . .'

'What the actual fuck,' Russ said. 'Ignore them, Cherry. They're drunk and bad at their jobs.'

'Or like . . .' the high one said, '. . . Lois Lane.'

'What's it like to be a *concept*?' the first one asked Cherry. 'You're immortal. You're one of the faces on Mount Rushmore.'

Chapter 38

There *was* a meme.

There were several memes.

Most people who saw them probably didn't even know where they came from.

Sometimes they were about fat women ... Like, somebody would take a panel of Baby and stretch it wide, and the line would be, *When the bio says she got curves.*

The most popular memes were just silly. There was one with Baby frowning and holding up a sign. You could change the sign to say anything you wanted to complain about. Like, *I was told there would be cake.* Or, *The Spurs are overrated.* (For some reason, it was used a lot by NBA fans.)

'Who cares about memes?' Stacia had texted Cherry, after Cherry sent her yet another new and terrible Baby meme. *'Memes are ephemeral. I can't understand half the stuff I posted on Facebook ten years ago.'*

Cherry took the NBA meme and typed, *The internet is forever* on Baby's sign. She sent it to Stacia.

Stacia changed the sign to say, *My ex-husband made me into a cartoon, and all I got was a million dollars and this chip on my shoulder.*

Chapter 39

Russ drank too much at the Christmas party to drive home.

He probably wasn't *properly* drunk. Cherry wasn't a good judge of drunkenness because she never drank, and she was never around inebriated people anymore – except for her dad, who drank so much, he *never* seemed drunk. It was easier to tell when her dad was sober. He snapped at everyone.

Cherry drove them home in Russ's car. It was a Polestar. Electric. She'd never even heard of that car before she met him. Cherry's heels were too high to drive. She had to take off her right shoe to feel the pedal.

Russ was uncharacteristically quiet on the way to his house.

Maybe he got quiet these days when he drank. There was still that tension from earlier in the night around his eyes.

'I'm sorry,' Cherry said softly.

He looked over at her. 'What? Why are *you* sorry? *I'm* sorry.'

'Don't be sorry, Russ. I had a nice time.'

He laughed, bitterly.

'There were a few awkward moments,' she said, 'but everyone was nice.'

Russ shook his head. 'Was that *normal* for you?'

'It was on the intense end of normal ...' She shook her head, too. 'This movie's changed everything. I'm kind of just waiting for people to forget about it.'

'That could be a long wait. Isn't there a sequel coming?'

Cherry's heart caught in her chest. '*What?* Is there a sequel? Is that confirmed?'

Russ looked startled. 'I don't know – Molly said there was a whole series.'

'Oh,' Cherry said. 'Well, it's a series of books. I don't know if there'll be a movie sequel. I guess I should want that, from a financial standpoint.'

'Do you get money from all this?'

She glanced over at him, to see if he was kidding. He wasn't. 'Yeah,' she said. 'I mean, it's Tom's money, but yeah.'

Russ was nodding. He looked far away. When he used to get drunk in college, he'd get silly. Affectionate. Not like this. 'That makes sense, I guess.'

'Here I thought you were a gold digger,' Cherry said.

'Huh,' he said, still far away. 'Yeah.'

'I keep expecting you to know more about all this. I thought you'd have googled it by now.'

'I figured you'd tell me what you wanted me to know...' Russ said.

If Cherry weren't driving, she would have kissed him for that.

He pushed both hands into his hair. '... but you never tell me anything.'

'What?' She looked over at him. 'What do you expect me to say? I mean – it's not really my story. *Thursday* isn't mine.'

Russ laughed. His voice got high: 'It *is*, Cherry. It follows you around. Actually – it arrives before you do.'

'Well, I can't help that.'

'I'm not saying you can. But you could have prepared me for it.'

'Prepared you how? Was I supposed to make you read a Wikipedia page at the Goldenrod concert?'

'We've been together for months now! I'm serious about you!'

'I still don't know what I was supposed to say, Russ. Was I supposed to *warn* you?'

'I don't know, maybe.' He clenched a hand in his hair. 'Doesn't it bother you? All of it?'

'Yes, it bothers me. I'm getting a divorce.'

'You're not getting a divorce,' he muttered.

'What?'

'You *told* me you were getting a divorce. But you're not. Have you even talked to a lawyer?'

'I've talked to a lawyer – I have a lawyer.'

'Then why aren't you getting a divorce, Cherry?'

'Why are you picking a fight with me?'

'I'm not,' he said. 'I'm talking to you.'

'You're angry.'

'I'm unhappy, not angry.'

'What did I do wrong tonight, Russ? You invited me to a party and I went. I can't help that people look at me and see . . . a *character*!'

'You could help it.'

'*How?*'

'I don't know, do you have to look so much like her?'

Cherry laughed. 'Yes! Literally, yes!'

He waved his hand around his face. 'I just mean the necklace. And the hair.'

'I'm not even wearing my hair like that tonight. I thought you liked my hair?'

'I do! I like your everything! It's just . . .'

Cherry gripped the steering wheel. 'It's just that I look like a cartoon character – who was drawn to look exactly like me. I can't change my entire appearance!'

'Your sister did!'

Cherry sat back against the seat . . .

Like a five-thousand-pound wrecking ball had just swung through the windshield and hit her in the chest.

'Cherry,' Russ said. 'I didn't mean that.'

She ignored him. She'd been driving north on Saddle Creek Road. She got into the left lane and made a U-turn.

'Where are you going?'

'I'm taking myself home.'

He covered his face with his hand. 'Cherry, I'm *sorry*.'

She ignored him.

'I didn't mean it.'

She ignored him; it wasn't hard.

They weren't far from her house. After a few minutes, she parked behind the dumpster in her driveway, blocking the sidewalk.

Russ had turned in the passenger seat to face her. 'Please don't get out of the car, Cherry.'

Cherry put on her right shoe and got out of the car.

Russ scrambled out, too.

'Go home,' she said.

'I can't drive.'

'Take an Uber.' She was walking up her sidewalk.

'Cherry, wait!'

She didn't wait. She went in the house and let Stevie out of her kennel.

Stevie followed Cherry upstairs, and Cherry let her. She let her sleep on the bed.

Chapter 40

When Cherry was a girl – when she was eight, when she was twelve, when she was sixteen – she figured that she'd lose weight someday.

That she would reach some point, and there would be a transformation.

That was the story arc of every fat girl in fiction – of every good girl who was ever overlooked. There was *before* and *after*. At some point, you changed. You blossomed. (Or tightened into a bud.) You assumed your true form.

Cherry believed in herself. And she believed in hard work. And she really believed that someday she would flip a switch and she'd master her weight. She'd put it behind her. Her face and body would sharpen into focus, and she would step into her *after*.

She came to her senses earlier than most women.

The evidence around her was stark, and Cherry wasn't prone to magical thinking.

There was no *after*.

No switch.

No amount of hard work or self-control or even self-abuse that would change her.

This was her true form.

This was the body that would carry her through the world. This was her only vehicle for pleasure.

Cherry refused to dream skinny dreams.

For anyone.

Chapter 41

When Cherry woke up the next morning, she had three texts from Russ, which she didn't open, and one from Tom:

'Hi, Cherry, I was wondering if I could walk Stevie today. And maybe finish up the garage.'

Cherry felt a surge of anger. (Everything bad she was feeling was Tom's fault. The last twenty-four hours were Tom's fault. The last year. The last decade.)

The anger was pointless.

'Sure,' she texted. *'Did you just get back?'*

'I've been back a few days. Sorry I haven't been working on the house.'

'Don't worry about it.'

Stevie was still lying on the bed. She looked up at Cherry like she expected to get kicked off. Cherry got up and put a sweater on over her pajamas so she wouldn't have to put on a bra, and went down to the kitchen to make coffee. Stevie followed close behind – she didn't even hesitate on the stairs.

While Cherry waited for the coffee to brew, Stevie tried to shove between her thighs. Cherry leaned against the counter so that she wouldn't fall over, and absently reached back – half patting Stevie, and half pushing her away. Cherry felt empty, hollowed out from her fingertips to her toes.

Tom knocked on the door when he got there.

Stevie went crazy, barking and jumping on the front door. It was like she knew it was him.

Cherry opened the door and stepped back to let Stevie have at him.

'Who's my good girl?' Tom said, petting Stevie with both hands and letting her jump up on him. They were of a height. 'I missed you, too.'

Cherry put her hand on Stevie's kennel, still feeling numb and off-balance.

Tom didn't come into the house. Or look up at Cherry. 'I think I can finish the garage today. Maybe tomorrow.'

'Whatever works best for you.'

He wasn't wearing a coat – just a hooded sweatshirt and a knit cap. His face was flushed from the cold. 'Do you have her leash?'

'I'll get it,' she said. 'Don't you need a coat?'

'I think my coats are still here.'

'I can get you one.'

He shrugged.

Cherry went to the hall closet and got out his wool peacoat. She brought him the coat and the leash.

'Thanks.' Tom still didn't look up. He clipped the lead to Stevie's collar. 'We'll be back in an hour or so.'

'Long walk,' Cherry said.

'It's a good day for one.' He clicked his tongue. 'Come on, Stevie.'

Stevie followed him eagerly out the door and down the walk.

Cherry watched them for a minute. Until she started to cry. She closed the front door and leaned against it, rubbing the space between her eyes with her free hand. She was still holding her coffee. She took it to the couch and cried some more. She missed Stevie – it had been a long time since Cherry had cried alone. She kept rubbing her forehead.

She thought about texting someone, but there came a point when you'd been so sad for so long, and so repeatedly, that you couldn't actually bear telling people anymore. When it felt like you were retelling the same story.

Russ was just a new wrinkle.

Her sisters would feel sorry for her if she told them what he'd said. And Stacia would, too. But Cherry didn't actually want them to feel sorry for her. She was tired of being the recipient of so much pity.

When Tom came back – after more than an hour – he knocked on the door again. Cherry was upstairs, wrestling with her laundry. She walked to the top of the stairs and shouted, 'Come in!'

He didn't come in. After a few minutes, he knocked again.

For Christ's sake. Was Cherry going to have to tell her ex-husband that it was okay that he'd tried to kiss her? That they could still be civil? That she had other, more lacerating problems at the moment? 'Just come in!' she shouted.

When he knocked *again*, Cherry grabbed her basket of clothes and started down the stairs. She held the basket on her hip and opened the door. 'You can just let yourself in. It's fine.'

Russ looked confused. 'The door was locked.'

'Russ . . .' Cherry breathed out. 'What are you doing here?'

'I came to get my car,' he said. 'I tried to call.'

She'd ignored his calls.

'Okay.' Cherry glanced past him. The Polestar was in her driveway. 'Take your car.'

'Can we talk, please?'

She shook her head. 'I don't want to talk.'

Russ looked clean and fresh. He was wearing a canvas coat with a corduroy collar. She could smell his aftershave. He looked worried. 'When do you think you *will* want to talk?'

Cherry shook her head again. 'I don't think that I will.'

He put his hand on the doorframe. 'Cherry, come on. Please let me apologize.'

She shook her head. 'No.'

His eyes got big. 'I was not in my right mind last night. I was angry, and I'd had too much to drink.'

She took a step forward. 'You shouldn't have been angry at *me*.'

He took a step back. 'I wasn't.'

'You were!'

'I was angry at the situation.'

'Well, you're no longer in that situation.'

'*Cherry.*'

'Stop saying my name!'

'Are you serious?' He spread his arms in disbelief. 'You don't want to see me anymore?'

She did want to see him. She loved seeing him. 'It doesn't seem like a very good idea,' she said.

'That's it? I say one stupid thing, and we're done?'

'Some things are nonnegotiable.'

'What are you talking about?'

Cherry held on to the laundry basket. 'My body is nonnegotiable. I never want it on the table.'

'I wasn't trying to –'

'You *were.*'

'Cherry, I'm *sorry*,' he begged. 'I wasn't thinking. It just came out.'

'I don't have to make myself *available* to your stray thoughts about my body.'

'Stop talking about your body!'

'*You* stop talking about my body!'

'*Fuck.*' Russ's hands were in his hair. He turned around and faced the street. 'This isn't about *your body*. I know you think that I have a problem with your weight, but that's not what bothers me – I swear, it isn't.'

Cherry stared at his back.

'It's that you're already part of someone else's story . . .' he said quietly. 'You've already got your Camelot.' Russ put one hand on his hip and scrubbed at his hair with the other. When he turned back to Cherry, his face was red. 'When I go out with you, people don't even see me. They see your husband, and I fucking hate it. I *hate* it.'

'I can't help that,' Cherry said.

'I know. I swear, I know.' Russ's eyes were wide and bright.

She shook her head. 'I don't want to feel how I felt last night.'

'I won't make you feel that way again.'

'No,' Cherry said. 'What I mean is' – her voice broke – 'I don't even want to *risk* feeling that way. I can't be with you anymore.'

'Cherry,' Russ said in a low voice. 'Please don't do this. I'm in love with you.'

Stevie started barking. Cherry looked up. Tom had just turned the corner onto their street.

Russ followed Cherry's attention – to Tom, in his hooded sweatshirt and peacoat, hunched against the cold. She saw the recognition land on Russ's face. He looked back at Cherry.

Cherry wasn't sure what to say. What was worth saying.

Russ nodded and turned to walk down the steps.

Tom stopped, still a house away. Stevie was barking and pulling at her leash, the way she did when she wanted to get closer and say hello.

Russ got in his car and pulled out. Safely and sensibly. He waved at Tom as he drove past.

Tom lifted his hand to wave back.

Cherry went inside. She went upstairs. She left the front door open.

Chapter 42

Now that Tom was back in town, he was coming by the house almost every day after Cherry left for the office.

And leaving before she got home.

One day Cherry came home, and there wasn't a single Post-it note left on the main floor. There were two new boxes labeled *Tom* sitting on the dining room table, and everything else was back on the shelves or in the cupboards.

It looked like Tom had dusted, too, and vacuumed. The house still looked patchy and sad, with Tom's toys gone and Tom's pictures off the wall. But it didn't look turned inside out.

Cherry skimmed through the new boxes. There was nothing in there that she'd contest. Tom had taken some vintage drinking glasses and mugs – the ones he'd always used when he was home. She was glad to see him staking a claim on something. He'd set aside a teapot he'd always liked. If he were staying in Omaha, or if they were both still broke, maybe he would have taken more of the practical things – a few plates, some of the furniture. But Tom could buy anything he needed. So could Cherry. They could both start over fresh. He was only taking things with sentimental value . . . He was only taking things that tugged at her.

Cherry left a Post-it note on the boxes – *Thumbs up, thanks.*

The next day, the boxes were gone. All of Tom's boxes were gone.

She wondered where he was keeping them.

*

Cherry went to the Western Alliance Christmas party at Meg Jones's house. She wore an off-the-shoulder gold brocade dress with a floral pattern – red roses and green leaves. The dress pinched in at her waist and fell to the floor. It was the fanciest thing Cherry had ever owned. She'd bought it from a dressmaker on Etsy after she got her last bonus. It was prettier than her wedding dress.

She wore her hair pinned up on one side, falling like water down her back. She looked like a fat Disney princess. She took a photo in the mirror to send to her mom.

When Cherry got to the Christmas party, she avoided the back room, where the agency people hung out. Doug and Wallace were at the party; she said hello and gave them a hard time. Wallace was retired now. Cherry was Doug's boss.

Everyone asked her about Tom – except for Meg Jones, who asked about Russ.

'He's been in Los Angeles,' Cherry told everyone, 'working on the movie.'

'He couldn't make it,' she told Meg.

If Tom were at this party, he'd be on his best behavior, pretending not to hate everyone for Cherry's sake. Keeping his mouth full, so he didn't have to talk.

If Russ were here, he'd be introducing himself and making connections. Thriving.

They'd both ask Cherry if she needed anything. They'd both keep an arm around her.

Cherry was a tricksy kind of unlovable . . .

Men *could* love her. Men *would*. They'd touch her. Listen to her. Maybe even marry her. But they didn't love her in a durable way. Not in a way she could trust. That would hold her weight.

(Cherry had trusted Tom. She'd taken him for granted – she'd thought that she was supposed to. She'd believed they were a settled question.)

Cherry worked the party. She said hello to everyone and their wives and husbands. She ate canapés. She gave Meg Jones a box of expensive candy from Budapest.

Tom had been walking Stevie every weekday. He told Cherry that she could assume Stevie was walked, unless he told her otherwise. He never told her otherwise.

Stevie's coat was always brushed. She had a new collar and a new leash.

'You're very beautiful,' Cherry told the dog while they watched TV together on the couch. Stevie looked up at Cherry with big brown eyes. 'You look like a woman in love.'

Cherry went to Stacia's Christmas party.

The house was full of beautiful people. Cherry wore a very cute corduroy jumpsuit – striped pink and green and ice blue. It wasn't very slimming, but it made her butt look big in a nice way. She plaited her hair and twisted the braids into a crown, then wove in tiny jingle bells. She wore pink lipstick.

She was the only person at the party who wasn't wearing black or white – except for Stacia's daughters, who were wearing matching red plaid dresses.

Cherry talked to Stacia's dour mother-in-law and her reed-thin mom friends. She talked to Stacia's husband about a red-light therapy that reduced inflammation. 'It stimulates your mitochondria.'

Stacia finally cornered Cherry by the platter of almond flour crackers and cheese. 'I was hoping you'd bring him . . .'

Cherry stacked some cheese on a dessert plate. 'There's no more him.'

Stacia's face fell. 'Really? Why not?'

Cherry shrugged. 'It just wasn't a good fit.'

'That's not an answer.'

Cherry looked up at her. 'We got into a fight.'

'About what?'

'My weight.'

Stacia's outrage was immediate. '*What?* What did he *say?*'

Cherry looked down again. The bells in her hair tinkled. 'I don't want to talk about it.'

'Why would Russ Sutton even ask you out if he had a problem with your weight?'

'He *didn't* ask me out,' Cherry said pointedly. 'That's not how this started. We just slept together.'

Stacia *hmph*ed. 'I'm really disappointed in him.'

'Don't be.'

'I *am*. I didn't think he was so *shallow*.'

Cherry huffed out a laugh, looking back up at her. Stacia was wearing a white jersey dress with a gold chain belt. She looked slender and expensive. '*Didn't* you?' Cherry said. 'He's only ever dated beautiful women.'

Stacia looked fierce. '*You're* a beautiful woman.'

'Right,' Cherry said.

'You *are*.'

Cherry shrugged again. 'I'm very pretty for a fat girl. It's like being very pretty for someone with three eyes or no nose. Or very pretty for a malamute.'

'What's a malamute?'

'It's a dog.'

Stacia's eyes got big. 'You're not a *dog*, Cherry.'

Cherry glanced away. 'That's not what I'm saying.'

'Have you been *drinking?*'

'Of course not.'

Stacia was shaking her head. 'I hate that he made you feel this way. You're normally so confident.'

'This is how I always feel, Stacia.' Cherry's voice was flat. 'I just don't bother you with it.'

'You always feel like a *dog?*'

Cherry rolled her eyes. 'No, I always feel like –' Her voice came out shrill. The bells were ringing over her ears. 'I mean, I *know* that I'm fat. I always know what that means. It's not shocking that Russ cheated on me – it's shocking that he went out with me in the first place!'

Stacia pulled her chin back. 'Wait, did he cheat on you?'

'*No*. That's not what I meant.' What *did* Cherry mean? Why was she letting herself get so upset? 'I meant . . . it's not shocking that he doesn't want to be with me.'

'Did Russ *say* that?'

Cherry set down her plate. Her head jingled. She reached up to take out the bells. 'No, he said I should lose weight. And you know what?' The bells were tangled in her hair. She left them. 'He's not even wrong! I'm sure that's what everyone thinks.'

'I don't think that.'

Cherry shook her head. The bells rang. She tried again to take them out. 'Come *on*, Stacia.'

'Cherry, I never even think about your weight!'

It was Cherry's turn to be outraged. 'That's a *lie*.' She waved a hand at Stacia, the hand that wasn't in her hair. 'We talk about *your* weight constantly!'

'Well, that's mine!'

'So you're haunted by the tiny amount of flesh on your stomach, but you never notice the eighty extra pounds that I'm carrying?'

'You're not eighty pounds overweight, Cherry.'

'I am. Actually. Depending on the actuarial table.'

'Why are we even talking about this?'

'I don't know!' Cherry could feel herself tearing out hair along with the bells. 'Because you asked why I broke up with Russ Sutton!'

'Did *you* break up with *him*?'

'It doesn't matter!'

'I thought you really liked him.'

'I did . . . but I can't . . . I just can't.' Cherry felt tearful. One of her braids had come unpinned.

'Here.' Stacia took the braid from Cherry and pinned it back in place. 'Do you want the bells in or out?'

Cherry dropped her arms. 'Out.'

'You should leave them in. They look cute.'

'Maybe I'm tired of looking cute.'

Stacia pulled the bells free. Some of Cherry's hair came with them.

'I'm going to head home,' Cherry said.

'I wish you wouldn't,' Stacia said. 'Stay and play spades.'

'I don't think I can be good company.'

Tom had finished cleaning out the garage. And possibly the cellar. The dumpster was gone from the driveway.

Cherry came home from work early on a snowy, slushy day, and Tom was standing in the foyer, rubbing Stevie with a towel. He was still wearing his coat and boots.

He looked up when Cherry walked in the front door. 'Sorry. I was just drying her off. I'll get out of your hair.'

'You're not in my hair.' Cherry stomped her feet and leaned over to unlace her snow boots. Stevie broke away from Tom to sniff at Cherry's legs and headbutt her cheeks. 'Hi,' Cherry said to her. 'I know. You're always so concerned.' Stevie nosed at her face. 'You don't like it when I'm upside down, do you?'

Tom laid the towel over the kennel.

'The garage looks great,' Cherry said.

He nodded. 'All that's really left is the closets and, uh ... the bedroom.'

'Oh.' Cherry stood up. The blood rushed from her head.

Tom's face was tense. Unreadable. 'You can just pack my things if you want.'

'No. Just ... give me a few days to straighten up.'

'Sure.' Tom was moving past Cherry toward the door.

'How was Los Angeles?'

'Fine,' he said. 'I'll just get out of your hair.' He was halfway out already. 'See ya.'

'See ya.' Cherry stepped out of her boots.

There was no way to clean or straighten or prepare their bedroom for Tom to walk back into it.

Like, Cherry couldn't put enough of her*self* away.

It made her skin crawl to imagine Tom in here, seeing her jewelry and face creams. Looking at their bed. Maybe she *should* just pack his things . . . and get it over with.

She opened the top drawer of Tom's dresser. She'd never looked through his drawers, even when they were together. He kept socks in here. Boxer shorts. Ties he never wore. A little Mickey Mouse watch that his mother had given him, stored in an acrylic box.

Cherry felt sick and tried to slam the drawer shut. It got stuck. She rammed it closed, catching her little finger, and yelped.

A minute or two later, while Cherry was sniffling and still rubbing her hand, Stevie shuffled into the room. The baby gate was open all the time now that Stevie could manage the stairs – and now that she was allowed to sleep in the bed. Cherry had surrendered to having dog hair all over every inch of the house.

Stevie sniffed at Cherry's stomach and headbutted her thighs. Cherry held on to the dresser so the dog could shove through her legs. 'Are you here to rescue me?'

Stevie didn't like it when Cherry shouted or cried out. (She used to bark from downstairs if Cherry was being too noisy during sex.) Cherry tried to think of a situation where Stevie's gentle mauling might actually rescue her . . . Maybe if she fell asleep in the bath, Stevie could rouse her.

Cherry leaned over to rub the dog's flank. 'You're not very helpful, but you're very sincere.'

Stevie looked up into Cherry's eyes, as intent and person-like as ever. Like someone in a fairy tale trapped in an animal's body.

Cherry sighed. 'God, Stevie, I feel like you're going to spend your whole life trying to tell me something, and I'm never going to know what.'

The cold settled in. Cherry went to get her goose-down coat out of the hall closet and realized that all Tom's coats and boots were gone, and all of his scarves and wool hats. Would he need them in California?

He'd left the umbrellas.

Russ called. Not all the time. Three times over as many weeks. He texted Cherry: *'I'd really like to talk to you. I'd really like to see you.'*

'Not yet,' Cherry texted back.

She missed him. She was still angry with him. But those feelings had soaked into Cherry's larger feelings of loneliness and anger. They didn't feel specific to Russ at the moment. When she thought about him, she sat up taller, like she was trying to pull herself tight.

'Are you mad at me?' Stacia texted.

'No.'

'Do you want to talk about Russ?'

'Definitely no.'

'I've decided that, if something happens to me, I'd WANT you to hit on Jim.'

'That is weird and gross, but I think you're saying it from a place of love.'

'I am.'

'I love you, too.'

Winter had arrived. With freezing temperatures and afternoon flurries. Every time it snowed, everyone who worked in Western Alliance's seventeen-story glass office building would stand at the walls and look down at the street to see if it was sticking.

Meg Jones stopped in Cherry's office around three one day, on her way out the door. There was a blizzard coming. It was a few days till Christmas. Cherry was standing at her window, looking out into the whirling white.

'You should get out of here,' Meg said. 'Beat the traffic.'

Cherry hated driving in the snow, even though she was fine at it. 'Maybe I'll wait for everyone else to plow a path down Dodge.'

'You'll be here till midnight. I heard they're closing the interstate to Lincoln.'

Meg left, and Cherry left right after her. The office was already empty.

Cherry's fifteen-minute drive took an hour and a half. Bumper to barely visible bumper. She lived at the top of a hill, and tonight she had to rev her engine at the bottom to power up the unplowed street to her house. The car rolled back the first time she tried it.

It was a relief to finally pull into her driveway just as the sun was setting. Cherry had forgotten her snow boots at work, and her dress shoes – very cute tasseled oxfords – were full of snow by the time she got to the porch.

There were fresh paw prints in the yard . . . It looked like Stevie had been rolling around. Stevie *loved* snow.

Cherry trudged up the front steps and inside the warm house, finally letting herself relax. Stevie didn't come running. She and Tom must still be on their walk. Stevie was lucky that Tom was around – Cherry never would have taken the dog for a walk in this weather. Stevie was too hard to manage when it was icy. She'd drag Cherry down the block like a sled.

Cherry took off her wet shoes and flipped the light switch. The lights didn't come on. She tried it again. Then walked into the kitchen and tried that light, too. Was the power out? It could just be a fuse . . . The house was old and glitchy.

The fuse box was out in the garage. Cherry glanced out the window. Maybe she could just wait for Tom to take care of it . . .

No.

She could do this.

She'd done it before.

She didn't have extra snow boots, so she put on rubber rain boots and carefully made her way back down the front steps. The boots were slippery, but they kept her feet from getting even wetter.

When she got to the garage door – not the big door, the side door – it was already open.

She peeked in.

Tom was standing in the shadows holding a snow shovel. He was looking down at his phone.

'Oh, hey,' Cherry said. 'I thought you guys were still on your walk.'

'We just got back.' He tucked his phone in his pocket. 'I was going to shovel the front sidewalk before I go.'

'You don't have to do that.'

'It won't take long,' he said.

'But it's just going to keep snowing.'

'It'll make a dent.'

Cherry shrugged.

Tom frowned at her. 'Were you coming in here for the shovel?'

'No. I came out to check the fuse box.'

'Is the power out?'

'Maybe. At least on the main floor.'

Tom set the shovel down and tried the garage light. It was dead. He opened the fuse box. Cherry stood behind him. 'I think the power must be out,' he said. 'Probably ice on the lines.'

'Hopefully it won't be out all night.'

He lowered his eyebrows at her. 'Is your phone charged? There's a camping battery in the basement.'

'It's charged. I'll be okay. You should get home – see if your dad has power.'

'Yeah, maybe I will.' He shut the fuse box.

'You won't miss blizzards in California, huh? Though I guess they have earthquakes . . .'

'And wildfires.'

'And landslides, right?'

Tom was giving her a serious, squinty look, like he was still worried about something. 'Cherry, I'm . . .'

Cherry waited.

'I signed a lease,' he said. 'In Pasadena.'

'Oh.' She nodded. She reminded herself (*again*) that this wasn't a surprise. She knew that Tom was moving away for good; it was the only reason he came home. 'I thought you were looking in Los Angeles.'

'It's a suburb. Basically.'

'Oh. An apartment?'

'No. A house. I wanted a yard for Stevie. If I like it there, maybe I'll buy something.'

Cherry furrowed her brow. 'For . . . like, for when Stevie visits? Do you want Stevie to visit?'

Tom narrowed his eyes further. He looked confused. 'No, I mean – I can take her now. When I go. I got a place that allows dogs.'

Cherry clenched her teeth. She felt her nostrils flare. 'Tom. You can't take Stevie.'

He shook his head. 'What?'

'You can't just *take* Stevie.'

He shook his head some more. 'Cherry, you were mad that I *didn't* take her before.'

'No, I was mad that you *left* me with her!'

'It's the same difference.'

'It is not!'

Tom tried to run his fingers through his hair. He was wearing a wool hat. 'You told me that she was too much to manage on your own. You said that you hadn't even *wanted* a dog – you said that a dog isn't a baby.'

'A dog *isn't* a baby!' Cherry half shouted.

'You said you were glad that I was back to walk her every day – you act like she's a huge hassle!'

'Tom, she *is* a huge hassle!'

He threw his hands up. 'So, why are we even arguing?'

She pointed at him. 'Because you can't just take her away from me! You don't get to *take* everything!'

Tom leaned toward her with his big barrel chest. His arms were still out. 'I didn't take *anything*! I've been living out of a suitcase for a year!'

'You took everything!' Cherry was shouting. Maybe she was screaming. 'You took *everything!*'

Tom looked speechless. He took a step back.

Cherry's lungs were heaving. She tried to catch her breath. 'You don't get to take her,' she said. '*Stevie!*' Cherry looked around. 'Where is she?'

'She's inside,' Tom snapped.

'She's not inside. She's – Oh my god.' Cherry ran for the garage door. She slid when she stepped out into the snow.

Tom was right behind her. 'What's wrong?'

'I left the front door open.'

'Cherry, slow down.'

'I left the door open!'

There were new paw prints on the front steps. New snow angels in the yard.

'Tom, she got out!' Stevie was a runner.

'Let's check the house.'

'I thought she was with *you.*'

Tom passed Cherry on the steps. The front door was still open – Cherry had thought she was only stepping outside for a minute. She hadn't wanted to grab her keys.

Tom raised his voice – '*Stevie!*' He was already inside the house. Cherry followed him. '*Stevie?*'

Tom clomped up the stairs to the bedrooms. Cherry checked the main floor. The cellar door was closed.

'*Stevie!*' she heard Tom call.

Cherry went to the bottom of the staircase. 'Tom, she's not here! Didn't you see the tracks in the yard?'

He was coming down the stairs. 'I'll go look for her.'

'I'm coming, too.'

'No. You stay here.'

'I'm coming.'

'Cherry, you're wearing a dress.'

'I'm wearing wool tights.'

He shook his head and raised his hands again, this time like Cherry wasn't his problem. She wasn't.

She followed him out onto the porch. 'Should I leave the door open in case she comes home? Or is that crazy?'

'That's crazy,' he said. He cupped his palms around his mouth. '*Stevie!*'

'*Stevie!*' Cherry shouted.

They both waited. If you'd asked Cherry what Stevie sounded like, she wouldn't have been able to tell you. But now she was straining to hear the dog's tags jangling and her heavy pant.

'We'll find her,' Tom said. 'She left a trail.'

They followed Stevie's paw prints down the sidewalk. Down the block. Out into the street, where they disappeared under tire tracks.

'I think she went this way,' Tom called from the other side of the road.

Cherry followed him. There were several dog prints over here. The snow was falling so fast, it was filling everything in. 'Do these seem small?' Cherry asked.

'Yeah ...' Tom said. 'Maybe.' He went looking in the other direction.

One of their neighbors was out shoveling his walk. Why couldn't people just let the snow finish falling?

'Have you seen our dog?' Tom asked him.

'The big white one?'

'Yeah.'

'Not today. Boy, she'll be hard to spot in all this.'

'Thanks.' Tom was walking back to Cherry. She could tell he was irritated. 'She has a black head,' he muttered. He took his keys out of his pocket. 'Let's go back for a car. We'll cover more ground.'

'Will we?' Cherry said. 'The roads are a mess.'

'The sidewalks aren't great shakes, either. And you're freezing.'

'I'm fine.'

He motioned at her. 'At least button your coat.'

Cherry buttoned one button. She was shuffling back toward their house, trying not to slip. *'Stevie!'*

Tom's dad's car was parked out on the street. An old Volkswagen Jetta.

'Let's take the Forester,' Cherry said. It had all-wheel drive. She unlocked the doors, then, after a second, handed the keys to Tom.

He took them.

Cherry got in the passenger seat. She watched Tom get behind the wheel and push back the seat. She wanted to scream again. She turned toward the window and buckled her seat belt. 'You should follow the path that you guys usually walk.'

'We mix it up,' he said.

'She always tries to pull me toward the park.'

'That's a good place to start.'

Tom drove slow.

They both rolled down their windows and shouted Stevie's name.

You couldn't get to the park without driving downhill. Tom took the hill cautiously, riding the brakes. It was a controlled slide. Cherry held her breath. They spun slowly sideways when they got to the bottom.

It took a minute or two for Tom to work the car back in the right direction.

'*Stevie!*' Cherry called out the window. She was crying again. 'I can't believe I left the door open. I never leave the door open.'

'You thought she was with me.'

'Because she didn't come to the door when I walked in. She always comes to the door.'

'She was probably upstairs. She goes straight up to look for you as soon as I let her off the leash. If the baby gate is open.'

'*Stevie!*' Cherry called.

Tom pulled up next to the park. 'Should we get out and look?'

'Yeah,' Cherry said. She opened her door. '*Stevie?*'

'*Stevie!*'

'She might have gone the other way,' Cherry said, stumbling over the curb. 'She likes the Dalmatian's house.'

'She might have,' Tom said, pulling gloves out of his pockets. '*Stevie!*'

It was a sprawling park, with pathways that wound through tall fir trees. There were picnic tables and a playground at one end, and a basketball court at the other. Everything was blanketed in three days of snow, and no one had shoveled the trails. Snow was coming in over the tops of Cherry's rain boots.

'Jesus,' Tom said.

Cherry looked up. Another car was coming down the hill – in a much less controlled slide. It careened toward Cherry's Subaru, then spun and jumped the curb.

Tom broke away from Cherry, jogging toward the car.

The driver was already trying to back up. His front wheels were spinning in the snow. Tom ran to the front of the car and leaned over to push, throwing his weight against it. His boots slid back. The tires whistled. Cherry thought of John Henry and locomotives. She wondered if she should try to help.

The car finally lurched backwards. Tom followed it, still pushing. Then he stood up and watched the driver steer back onto the road. The man waved at Tom.

Tom raised his hand.

He looked back at Cherry and called out, 'Button your coat!'

Cherry buttoned another button. Her fingers were so cold that she could hardly feel the hole.

Tom was walking back to her.

'What if Stevie got hit by a car?' she said when he was close enough to hear her. 'They wouldn't even be able to see her.'

'She has a black head,' he said again. 'And remember, she doesn't have any trouble getting around in this weather. She was made for it.'

Cherry nodded.

Tom was standing next to her now. He took off his hat and held it out to Cherry.

She took it and wrung it between her fingers.

He motioned at her head.

She put on the hat. It was still warm from Tom's head.

Tom turned away from her. *'Stevie!'*

'Stevie!' Cherry shouted.

They walked deeper into the park.

'Stevie?'

'Stevie!'

There were fading dog tracks in the snow. And fading people tracks.

Cherry was crying. Her face was numb. She took a wrong step in her rubber boots and started to go down – Tom caught her arm. 'I think we should go back,' he said.

'We have to keep looking for her.'

'I think we should go back, and you should stay home, in case she shows up.'

'I don't think she knows the way home. She's very dumb for such a smart dog.'

'I still think we should go back.'

Cherry tried to wipe her eyes. She couldn't feel her fingers or her face. 'This is my fault. If anything happens to her, it's my fault.'

'It's not your fault, Cherry.'
'Then whose fault is it?'
'Does it have to be someone's fault?'
'No,' Cherry said, wiping her face. 'Unless it's mine.'

Tom pulled one of his gloves off and reached for her hand. 'Jesus,' he said, squeezing it. 'You're freezing.'

He tucked his other hand under his arm to pull off his glove. It dropped to the ground. He took both Cherry's hands between his and chafed them. His skin was cool and dry. 'We're going back home now.'

'We can't give up on Stevie.'

'We're not giving up on her.'

Cherry's face crumpled. Her head tipped forward.

'Hey ...' Tom hauled her closer. He wrapped an arm around her. Cherry fell against his chest. 'Stevie's built like a polar bear,' he said, 'and she loves everyone. She'll play until she gets tired, then she'll walk up to someone's house and bark until they let her in. She might already be in one of these houses, eating beef stew and drinking warm milk.'

Cherry could see it. She was still crying. 'They'll probably try to keep her.'

'That'll solve *one* of our problems ...'

Cherry laughed a little.

Then Tom laughed a little. His chest hitched. 'Let me take you home,' he said.

Cherry cried a bit more. She felt cold everywhere. Her feet were wet. She might have frostbite. How would she get to the hospital in this weather if she had frostbite? 'Okay,' she said tearfully.

Something thumped against the back of Cherry's thigh. For a second, she thought it was another slow-moving car. She looked down. It was Stevie.

'*Stevie!*'

Stevie jumped up on Cherry. Then jumped off.

'Stevie Nicks!' Tom shouted.

'Steven!' Cherry cried out.

Stevie was already running away from them. She had a special galloping run for moments like this, when she was playing and wanted to be caught.

She ran toward Tom, then bolted away when he reached for her – looking back at him, absolutely grinning.

'You terrible dog!' Cherry yelled.

'See?' Tom said. 'She's fine. She's having the time of her life.'

'Stevie!'

'Stevie, come.' Tom made a fist and drew it toward him.

Stevie stopped galloping and looked at him.

'Come.'

She trotted back his way.

Tom stood very still, to show he wasn't playing.

As soon as Stevie got close, he held out his fist. *'Sit.'*

She sat.

Tom leaned over and hooked his fingers around her collar. He looked up at Cherry. 'Grab my gloves?'

Chapter 43

Stevie tried to get away from Tom all the way to the car. She still wanted to play.

Tom opened the hatchback, and Stevie made him lift her up into the car. She kept trying to turn and spring herself back over his shoulder.

'You're being really awful, Stevie,' Cherry said.

'Get in the car,' Tom said to Cherry. 'Turn on the heat.'

Cherry did. She held her hands in front of the vents, even though they were still blowing cold air.

Tom got in the car. His ears were bright red. His hair was curling over them.

He drove a long, circuitous route on the way home to avoid the steep hill. Stevie climbed into the back seat. Normally they'd clip her into the cargo space with her leash.

'Don't let her up here,' Tom said.

Cherry petted Stevie's panting head and pushed her back. 'Come on, Stevie. Calm down. *Off.*' Cherry's fingers stung. 'I'm not sure I've ever seen her this happy.'

Tom sighed. When they got home, he wrangled Stevie back into the house. The electricity was still out. Cherry turned on the flashlight on her phone.

The heat wouldn't run without power, but it was still much warmer inside the house than out.

'Come on,' Tom said to Stevie, 'let's get dry.' He grabbed the towel they kept on her kennel.

Cherry took off her rain boots and stripped out of her wet tights.

She caught a flash of Tom's eyes in the dark. His face. He was glaring at her legs.

He reached out and grabbed Cherry's ankle. She stood stock-still. He was feeling her toes. He pulled his hand away. 'Go upstairs and take a warm bath. While there's still hot water.'

Cherry wanted to argue. 'Is that safe? For frostbite?'

'I don't think you have frostbite. But google it. I'll find the camping battery.'

'Be careful on the stairs,' she said.

'You, too.'

Cherry googled frostbite. You were supposed to take a warm bath.

Her feet burned when she lowered herself into the bathtub. In all the places Tom had touched. She left her phone lit and sitting on the toilet.

She stayed in the bath until she felt warmer than the water. Then she got dressed carefully in the dark. In her elephant pajama pants. Thick socks. A bra and sweater. She grabbed a pair of clean socks for Tom before she headed downstairs.

She found him in the kitchen. He'd lit a jar candle that smelled like sugar cookies. 'The camping battery's dead,' he said.

'Sorry.'

'I'll charge it tomorrow.'

Stevie was sniffing at Cherry's legs. She was always very intrigued by the smell of soap. Cherry petted her head and scratched her back.

'Was there hot water?' Tom asked.

'Yeah,' Cherry said. 'Thanks. There might be some left.'

'I'm fine.'

'I brought you dry socks,' she said, and set them on the island counter.

'I'll just move out one pair at a time.'

Cherry didn't laugh.

'Well,' Tom said. 'I'll get out of your hair.'

'*Tom.* You can't drive home in this.'

'I'll be fine. I'll go slow.'

'But there's no *reason* for it. Don't risk your life and limb just to spite me.'

'I'm not –' He stopped himself. He exhaled. 'When have I ever done anything just to spite you?'

'I don't know,' Cherry said, looking down at the dog. 'Don't start now.'

Tom didn't say anything.

Neither did Cherry for a while.

'I was going to have leftover pizza for dinner,' she said. 'It'll be just as good cold.'

Tom nodded.

Cherry brought the pizza out to the living room.

Tom brought the candle. He lit another one – bergamot and cedar – and set them on the coffee table. 'Do we have any candles that aren't scented?'

'I don't think so.'

'I'm going to order an emergency kit on Amazon. With candles and more flashlights.'

'Okay.' Cherry sat at one end of the couch and opened the pizza box. She'd ordered it for herself the night before. Fuck her blood sugar.

Tom sat at the other end of the couch. Stevie hauled herself up between them – Tom dove forward to keep her tail from swishing into the candles. Cherry handed him a piece of pizza wrapped in a paper towel.

Stevie tried to sniff it.

'No,' Tom said. 'You don't get people food.' He looked at Cherry. 'Does she?'

'No, you said it would ruin her manners.'

Stevie settled with her chin on Tom's leg, already giving up on the pizza.

Tom was looking at Cherry. He was frowning again. 'I didn't know that you wanted to keep Stevie.'

'I can't talk about this right now,' Cherry said. 'It's too much.'

'But I –'

'Tom, please.' Cherry was tearing up. She was so tired of tearing up; she'd have her tear ducts sealed if she could. *'Please.'*

He didn't argue or answer. Which she appreciated. Cherry was exhausted. She was getting cold again. She tried to chew her pizza.

Tom rubbed Stevie's head while he ate.

Cherry sniffed back tears.

She chewed.

She sniffed again.

'Sometimes . . .' she said softly, 'when we'd be sitting on the couch, or at a red light – just being quiet, not looking at each other . . . I'd feel like we were in a panel from *Thursday*.'

Tom looked over at her.

'Like . . .' Cherry went on, 'one of those *Thursday* strips that doesn't seem to be about anything – until you really think about it, or until there's some payoff a month later . . .' She sniffed. 'Sometimes I could see us. Just as we'd be in the comic.'

Tom was watching her. Listening. He looked sad.

Cherry laughed – like she knew she was being pathetic. She shook her head.

'Sometimes,' Tom said, 'when we were sitting on the couch, or in the car, or at the hospital when my dad was sick . . . I was drawing panels in my head.'

Cherry nodded. She reached for another piece of pizza. 'Why didn't The Guy and Baby ever get a dog?'

Tom looked down at Stevie and scratched her ears. One side of his mouth quirked up. 'By that time I was famous. It didn't seem fair to make her famous.'

They both stared at Stevie for a while. They used to do this when she was a puppy – just sit and watch her while they talked. Or didn't talk.

'I didn't think you were reading *Thursday* . . .' Tom said.

'I wasn't,' Cherry said. 'Not regularly. Not for a long time.'

He nodded. He was still looking at Stevie. He looked weighed down. Heavy-hearted.

'It wasn't that I didn't like it,' Cherry said. 'I *do* like it. I thought I was giving you space.'

'I think I knew that.'

'Did you *want* me to read *Thursday*?'

Tom glanced up at her. He smiled a little. It was still sad. 'Not really.'

Cherry nodded. She wiped her eyes with the back of her hand and then with the paper towel. 'Maybe I gave you too much space.'

Tom set his half-eaten pizza on the table.

He rubbed Stevie's head with both hands. She rolled onto her back. He rubbed her neck and her belly.

Cherry patted Stevie's rump. 'Are there scenes like that in the movie?'

'Like what?'

'Like the quiet panels that don't seem to have a point.'

Tom made a noise like '*huh*' that was almost a laugh. 'Yeah. I guess those are my signature.' He looked over at her again. 'Are you going to watch it?'

'Do you want me to?'

He shook his head. 'No.'

Cherry bit her lips together and shook her head, holding back another wave of tears. After it passed, she said, 'Then I won't.'

The lights came on then. All of them, all over the house.

Cherry jumped. And Stevie jumped. And Tom dove forward to keep Stevie's tail from flicking into the candles. Cherry blew them both out. 'That was fast,' she said.

Tom was standing. 'Yeah ...' He brushed himself off. 'Well. That's good. That's my cue, I guess. I better ...'

'What do you mean? The roads are still terrible.'

'I'll drive slow.'

'Tom –'

Tom looked in her eyes. He looked anguished. He looked like Stevie – like he desperately wanted Cherry to read his mind.

She could.

He was miserable here. In this house. With her.

He'd rather die in a snowstorm. He'd rather get hit by a plow or go sliding into traffic than spend another moment in their dead house, with their dead memories.

'Will you text me when you get home safe?' she asked.

He nodded.

Cherry nodded, too.

Tom put on his coat and said good-bye to Stevie and was out the door so fast.

Cherry waited up for him to text and tried to be reassured by how long it was taking. He was driving slow, like he said he would.

Eventually her phone lit up.

'Home safe.'

Chapter 44

'I wouldn't get it, anyway,' Cherry said. 'Meg Jones doesn't know my name.'

Tom frowned. 'Meg Jones knows your name.'

They were on the way home from work. Tom had moved into Cherry's apartment, so it made sense for them to ride together. Their offices were only a few blocks apart.

Cherry always drove. She kept her car cleaner, and it got around better in the snow. It was snowing that evening. The windshield wipers were on high.

Cherry shook her head. 'The last time I presented at a meeting with Meg Jones, the only feedback she gave Doug was – "*What was that girl wearing?*"'

'What *were* you wearing?'

'My snail vest.' A wool sweater vest with a snail knit over the chest. The snail was wearing glasses and reading a book.

Tom smiled. 'Cute.'

'With a blazer,' Cherry said.

'Keeping it profesh.'

'I don't know why it matters what I wear!' she said.

'It doesn't matter – hey, give that guy some space.'

'What guy?'

Tom motioned at the car ahead of them.

'I'm giving him space.'

'I know,' Tom said. 'Just . . .'

'I'm not going to apply,' she said. 'I'll never get it.'

'You may as well apply – you're already running the department.'

Cherry grimaced. 'That's not fair to Doug . . .'

'Doug would be the first person to say so.'

'Yeah, but –'

The car ahead of her slammed on the brakes, so Cherry slammed on the brakes. Tom put his hand on the dashboard. Her car slid a few feet.

Cherry waited for the traffic to start moving again. It was snowing so hard. 'I don't even know if I *want* to work for the railroad,' she said.

'You already work for the railroad.'

'I don't know if I want to *stay*.'

'You don't have to stay.'

'It's not *art*. I'm not *making* anything.'

'Hey.' Tom was giving her a concerned look. 'That's not true.'

'You would never want my job.' She had to slam to a stop again. The anti-lock brakes kicked in and crunched.

After a second, Tom said, 'I couldn't *do* your job. No one in your department can do your job. The place falls apart when you take a vacation day.'

'Well, I just really like making things work.' Cherry had started crying. It was embarrassing. Railroad execs didn't cry. Assistant department heads didn't cry.

'Baby, I know . . . You're allowed to like it.' Tom was giving her a soft look. When their eyes met, he nodded toward the road.

Cherry looked back at the car in front of her. 'They'll never give me a promotion.'

His voice was stern: 'If they don't give it to you, you can leave.'

Hers was strained: 'Tom, I don't want to leave!'

'You don't have to! But you're already doing the work. Get the title and the money and the bigger office. No one there –' She hit the brakes again. 'Okay,' Tom said quietly, 'I'm gonna need you to pull over.'

She was wiping her eyes on her coat sleeve. 'What? Why?'

'Because . . .' His brow was furrowed. 'I just . . . need to drive.'

'I can drive.'

'I know. But . . . I need to.'

'Tom, it's not my fault that it's snowing.'

'I know.'

'I'm doing fine. Am I not doing fine?' The anti-lock brakes engaged again, loudly. 'They're supposed to sound that way!'

Tom had both hands on the dash. 'Cherry, I love you, but –'

'You love me, *but*?'

'– I'm a better driver than you!'

'*Tom*. That's so sexist!'

He laughed. He was stressed. 'It's not sexist – it's *true*. Let me drive, and you can talk, and we'll get home in one piece.'

There was a gas station coming up. Cherry turned into the driveway. The car slid. She put it in park, got out, and left her door open. Tom got out, too. She didn't look at him when they passed each other.

Tom got in and adjusted her seat. He'd never driven her car before. It took him a second to shift it out of park. Cherry didn't say anything.

He moved them back onto the road.

The streets were as bad as Cherry had ever seen them. She felt smug when Tom had to hit the brakes. Then less smug when the car didn't skid.

'You can talk,' he said without looking at her.

'I don't have anything to say,' she said.

Tom didn't push her.

Cherry watched the headlights in front of them. She watched an SUV slide right through a red light. Her teeth had been clenched in anger . . . She clenched them in fear.

The street in front of their apartment was the most treacherous. They got stuck for a few minutes. Tom kept rolling the car back and forth, and it finally broke free.

He parked the car outside their building, pulled the keys out of the ignition, then held them out to her. She took them.

'I'm sorry,' he said.

Cherry didn't answer.

'You're not a bad driver.'

'No,' she snipped. 'You're just better.'

'Cherry...'

'It's true. You're better.'

Tom had turned toward her in the seat. 'I would follow you anywhere.'

His voice sounded different. Raw.

Cherry had argued so much with her college boyfriend... She almost never fought with Tom. Tom got quiet, not angry.

She didn't look at him.

'I mean it,' he said. 'I would put you in charge of... everything.'

'Except the car.'

'Cherry...'

She looked at him. She felt tearful again. 'I wasn't trying to *endanger* you, Tom.'

He brought his hand to her jaw. 'Hey. I'm sorry.'

'Don't be sorry.' She waved her hand. 'You got us home in one piece. You're a better driver – it's fine.'

He was looking in her eyes. His face was open. More open than Cherry was used to. Like he was struggling with something. 'You can drive... everywhere else, okay?'

'When it's not snowing?'

Tom closed one eye. 'No – I always want to drive the car, in all weather. From now on. But you can drive, you know, when we're *not* in the car.'

Cherry shook her head. 'What are you even...'

He wrapped his thumb around her chin. 'I mean' – his voice dropped even lower – 'I'm at your service.'

Cherry shook her head again.

'You just tell me where to go.'

It was hard to talk to Tom about some things.

Personal things.

His family. Work. *Thursday*. Sex. The future.

(That was a lot of things.)

It was like he kept everything important deep, deep inside of him ... Like he had to hike three days through the wilderness to reach his feelings, and then hike three days back to share them with Cherry.

(Had he buried his feelings there? Or was that where they were naturally located?)

Tom would *do* anything for Cherry.

He liked to do it before she even asked. He liked to anticipate her wants. To show up with lunch. To fix something before she'd thought to complain about it. To discover something she'd never heard of that would make her smile.

In Tom's perfect world, maybe they never spoke at all. Or maybe *he* never spoke. (In *Thursday*, The Guy went months without a dialogue balloon.) Tom was foundationally, maybe fundamentally, reticent. And Cherry didn't want to pull feelings and memories out of him like teeth.

She still didn't know whether Tom had dated anyone before her – she'd never asked him. It felt ... *intrusive* to ask Tom questions like that. (It felt heretical, to mention anyone who came before.)

The first time they'd had sex, Tom had been so hesitant ... Cherry had to undress herself. She had to take his hand and put it on her breast.

He had been so *reverent*. He made Cherry feel like she was something rare and brand-new. A first edition.

But she didn't *know* that it was his first time. Even now.

Stacia couldn't believe that Cherry didn't just *talk* to Tom about things. Cherry was normally so forthright.

'I just ... can't,' Cherry would say.

'What's he going to do? Yell at you?'

'Of course not.'

'Snap at you?'

'No. I can just tell that it makes him uncomfortable.'

'Oh, *"uncomfortable."* Perish the thought.'

'You don't understand. Making Tom uncomfortable is like ... making a mountain uncomfortable. Or a volcano.'

'Like, he's going to erupt?'

'No.' Tom never erupted. 'More like he's going to get bigger and stonier and change the entire landscape in a way that affects weather patterns for years to come.'

'Cherry, that doesn't make any sense.'

'Not to you.'

Stacia wasn't married to the kind of guy whose moods affected the weather.

That wasn't a useful memory.

That didn't get Tom right.

That was leaving out the *lightness*.

The everyday magic of living with Tom – of Cherry and Tom, together.

'Just get them.'

'What are we going to do with a full set of china?'

'Eat off of it. They're just dishes.'

'We already have dishes.'

'Cherry, we don't go to estate sales because we need things. We go to estate sales because we *like* things.'

She picked up a dinner plate and watched the gilt flash in the light. 'They're so pretty, with the roses, and the absinthe green ...'

Tom had heard enough. 'We're getting them.'

'They want three hundred dollars for the set.'

'Yeah,' he said, 'and I want a pony.'

Cherry laughed. 'You do want a pony. Every dog you show me is the size of a small horse.'

'I see you eyeing that china …' One of the people running the sale had wandered over – a guy in his seventies who looked like he was playing an antiquarian in a movie. Waistcoat. Rosy cheeks. Glasses at the end of his nose. 'It's a complete set.'

'I think it's missing a gravy boat …' Tom became a different person at estate sales. Ridiculously gruff and stubborn. (Maybe this was who he was with his coworkers.)

'Made in England,' the man said. 'Hardly used.'

'Well, who has any use for china?' Tom said. 'It just sits in your cabinet until your own inevitable estate sale.'

'Exactly,' Cherry said.

Tom frowned at her over the man's shoulder.

She picked up a footed platter. It was beautiful.

'That's a very rare pattern,' the man said, then leaned toward Tom as if he was confiding in him. 'Your lovely wife has a good eye.'

Cherry wasn't Tom's wife. She was his girlfriend.

She glanced up at Tom. He wasn't smiling, but his eyes were bright. 'I mean,' he said, 'I can't argue with you there.'

Cherry smiled.

The man put his hand over his heart, theatrically. 'Madame, put that smile away. I wasn't prepared for it.'

She laughed and rolled her eyes.

'You should let her do the wheeling and dealing,' the man said to Tom.

'They're beautiful dishes,' Cherry said, 'but we can't afford them.'

'I'd be prepared to let them go for one hundred dollars,' he said.

'Seventy-five,' Tom said.

The man looked at Cherry. She smiled.

'Sold,' he said, 'to the lovely young lady who won't let these dishes die in a cabinet.'

Tom paid in cash. The man seemed reluctant to let the china go. He looked up at Cherry and shook his head. 'Dimples *and* freckles, that shouldn't be legal.'

As they were walking away, Tom said, 'He doesn't know the half of it.'

Cherry was made assistant department head. Then department head. Then put in charge of several departments.

Tom was unwavering in his support – even though he disliked her coworkers and felt indifferent at best about the railroad. He listened to her talk. He helped her strategize. He never let her feel alone in her frustrations. (Western Alliance got so much free expertise out of Tom over their dinner table.)

Early evening, a weeknight, the year that Tom quit:

They'd stopped at the grocery store on the way home from work, and they were both tired and hungry, and Tom was putting away groceries while Cherry started dinner, and Tom was complaining about one of the account managers.

'She's so *literal*,' he said. 'We don't have to use the word "jobs" in every recruitment headline. If someone doesn't understand that the ad is about jobs, they're not smart enough to work on trains anyway. I asked her if she needed restaurants to hang a sign that said "food" in the window...'

Cherry had been slicing cucumbers. She turned away from the cutting board.

Tom glanced over at her. 'What's wrong? Did you cut yourself?'

'That was my note,' Cherry said. 'On the recruiting ad.'

Tom let the refrigerator door swing closed. 'Oh.' He looked like he was thinking. 'Okay.'

'They're billboards,' she said. 'We need them to be obvious.'

He smiled a little. His shoulders had dropped. 'You're right. I'll change it.'

She frowned. 'You can argue with me . . .'

'I'm not going to argue with you. You're the boss.'

Cherry shook her head. 'Tom. I don't want you to agree with me just because I'm the client.'

Tom walked over to her and rested his hand on her hip. 'I'm not. That's not what I meant.'

'You called me the boss . . .'

He shrugged. He looked in her eyes. 'You are the boss.'

She frowned.

He was standing in front of her. He bumped his hip against hers. 'I trust your judgment.'

'If you thought the note was idiotic when Katie gave it –'

'Katie's an idiot.'

'– and then when *I* say it –'

'You're not.'

'Tom, I want you to be *honest* with me.'

He wrapped his hand around her chin. 'Cherry, I am being honest with you.'

'You can't just do whatever I say at work because I'm your wife.'

He tilted his head. 'Wouldn't that make your life easier?'

'I don't want my life to be *easy*. I want it to be good.'

Tom was smiling with his eyes. He kissed her.

She kissed him back half-heartedly. 'I want you to argue with me,' she said.

'I don't like arguing with you,' he murmured. 'If I'm arguing with you, it usually means I'm wrong.' He pulled back to look in her eyes –

Then dropped gently to his knees in front of her.

Cherry was surprised. *'Tom.'*

He lifted up his chin. 'Baby . . .' he whispered.

She shook her head.

'You're the boss,' he said.

Cherry couldn't tell if he was teasing. His eyes were light, but he wasn't laughing. She shook her head some more. She ran a hand through his hair, tugging on it. Tom let his head fall back and brought his hands up to her thighs. 'I don't want to be *the boss*,' Cherry said quietly.

He was just barely smiling. '*Don't* you?'

His scalp was warm under her fingertips. 'Not with you.'

He smiled a little more. Like she was full of shit.

'*Tom*,' Cherry said insistently. She wasn't sure what she was insisting on. She tugged his head farther back.

Tom let her. His eyes were still light. 'I want your life to be easy *and* good.'

Chapter 45

Today 2:08 PM

Joy
Just a heads up, Jeff and I are GLUTEN-FREE now, so everything I'm bringing for Christmas will be gluten-free!!

Honny
Gross.

Cherry
Thanks for the warning.

Joy
That isn't very supportive!!

Honny
It wasn't meant to be.

Cherry
What do you want, Joy, a cookie?

Faith
My sweet potato casserole doesn't have gluten, I don't think. Is there gluten in marshmallows?

Cherry

That was a gluten joke. About the cookie.

Honny

I laughed, Cherry.

Joy

This is serious – Jeff has inflammation!!!

Faith

Where?

Joy

Generally, I guess??

Honny

Joy, do you really want to be gluten-free on Christmas? It's just one day.

Joy

They say it stays in your system.

Cherry

I promise not to peer-pressure you into eating gluten.

Honny

Cherry, is your boyfriend coming? I bought him a gift.

Cherry

I hope you saved the receipt.

Joy

What does that mean??

Cherry

It means I don't have a boyfriend.

Faith

Like, you don't call Russ your boyfriend?

Cherry

I don't call him at all. We're not seeing each other anymore.

Faith

Oh no! What happened?

Cherry

It wasn't a good fit.

Faith

He was so nice!

Honny

He was nice.

Cherry

He's still nice.

Joy

He's really not coming?? Who's going to eat my pumpkin pie?!?

Honny

NO ONE.

Cherry

Your gluten-free pumpkin pie? No one.

Honny

Jinx! Cherry, you owe me a Coke.

Chapter 46

Stevie was three months old when they brought her home – they drove five hours to get her from a breeder in Missouri – and she was already as big as a full-grown schnauzer.

She was a roly-poly sausage. Fluffy and white, with a bandit mask and a comically long tongue that rolled out like a lizard's every time she yawned.

'She looks more like a Gene Simmons than a Stevie Nicks,' Cherry said.

Tom carried the puppy into the house like a baby. 'You look like a Stevie Nicks – don't you, Stevie Nicks?'

'I didn't think I'd feel threatened by a dog, but then you named it after your dream girl.'

'You're my dream girl,' Tom said, swatting Cherry's bottom. He was in a good mood.

He wanted this, and Cherry had made it happen.

He'd been circling the idea of a dog for months. Hinting. Sending Cherry links to breeders when they were sitting right next to each other on the couch. Sending her photos of puppies.

'You really want to do this?' she'd ask.

And he'd say, 'I don't know. It's a big commitment. And I'm traveling so much . . .'

Those were the same reasons Tom didn't want to have a baby.

That had felt like a mean trick. A real switcheroo.

In the beginning of their relationship, it was Cherry who didn't want to have kids. She'd grown up in a big family in a small house, and she was done with kids by the time she was done being one.

Cherry wanted to work. And travel. And she wanted to love Tom with her eyes open.

You know how parents say they blinked one day, and their kid jumped from kindergarten to college? Cherry didn't want that. She wanted her years with Tom to go slow. She wanted to savor them.

It was Tom who'd said, 'It'd be nice to have a family, don't you think? Someday?' Back when they were first dating.

It was Tom who said, 'I don't know. There's a lot of life to be lived as a parent.' After they got engaged.

And then, on their honeymoon – 'It doesn't seem like people usually regret having kids.'

It planted a seed in Cherry.

Maybe it *would* be nice, she thought passively. Maybe kids would make their life richer. Maybe parenthood would be another thing she and Tom could share.

She didn't immediately say so. But she softened. And started to assume they were headed that way.

She started to make plans. Cherry couldn't *not* make plans. Everything in her life was on a timeline. (Women are born with clocks in their hips and calendars in their bellies, and Cherry's brain never stopped ticking.)

It was a shock – the first time she said out loud, 'Maybe we should start thinking about getting pregnant,' and she realized that Tom *hadn't* been making plans.

His face dropped. 'I thought you didn't want to.'

'Well, I wasn't sure. I thought you *did* want to.'

'I wasn't sure, either.'

'If we're going to,' she said, 'we should do it soon.'

'Yeah . . .'

The next time she brought it up, Tom's face clouded over. He got quiet. His knee bounced.

Cherry pushed him to explain himself.

He said it had gotten harder to imagine making a choice that would change their lives that much. And harder to imagine taking on that much responsibility.

'So ...' she said. 'No kids?' She felt empty saying it. Like the horizon ahead of her was the flat line of an old TV turning off.

'I'm not saying that,' Tom said. 'I just don't want to mess up a decision this big.'

That was *exactly* what he'd said when they'd found their house. They'd had six hours to make a bid, and Tom had been so angry about the deadline that he didn't even want to talk about it. He *couldn't*, really.

Cherry had been the one to pull the trigger. If she hadn't, they'd never have gotten out of their apartment.

But she couldn't just *pull the trigger* on a baby.

She wouldn't.

There was another way to tell this story: that Cherry said no; then she said nothing; then she said she wanted to wait; and then, when Tom was at his most overwhelmed, she pushed it onto his plate.

Her timing could have been better.

Tom had only seemed interested in giant dogs – dogs who could guard the underworld or welcome the Darling kids home from Neverland.

'Every dog you show me looks like a mythical creature,' Cherry said.

They were sitting on the couch, and he was showing her a picture of a Saint Bernard. 'I like big dogs,' he said. 'They seem more alive to me.' He laughed. 'Is that a terrible thing to say?'

Cherry laughed, too. And kissed his shoulder. 'Maybe. Honny told me that when she had Maddox' – Honny's second kid – 'the doctor came in one night to check on the baby, and he was just standing there smiling down at him. And he told Honny that doctors like fat babies best, because they know they're going to be okay. Like, they have a firmer hold on life.'

'There you go,' Tom said.

And Cherry didn't say, '*Let me give you a fat baby.*'

Instead she called a NewfiePyr breeder in Missouri and put down an eight-hundred-dollar deposit.

All the way there, Tom worried that they'd made a mistake. And all the way home, he *glowed*. He was so happy.

He was pretty sure Stevie Nicks was the cutest dog he'd ever seen. And Cherry couldn't argue with him – Stevie was very cute.

She was smart, too.

Tom had her house-trained in a few weeks. He taught her to ring a bell by the door. It was adorable.

He used to send Cherry photos of the puppy while she was at work. (Tom had quit his job by then.)

And Cherry would send him photos of the puppy when he was on the road.

The dog was a lot for Cherry when Tom was traveling. Stevie chewed on everything at first. You couldn't look away from her. She chewed the corner off an antique Persian rug. She chewed up a pair of Rachel Antonoff penny loafers. Cherry had to go home at lunch to take the puppy out, and then again right after work. And she felt guilty going anywhere at night and leaving Stevie in her kennel. It was like having a baby she'd never wanted.

Tom doted on Stevie when he was home, especially as things got bad – when they were going unmanageably well – with *Thursday*.

He took longer and longer walks with her.

He took to sitting on the floor with her while he drew on his tablet.

Tom couldn't sleep the night before he left for his first big trip to California to work on the movie.

'I feel bad leaving you with Stevie for this long.'

'It's just a month,' Cherry said. They were lying next to each other in bed. Cherry had rolled onto her side, facing away from him.

'It's at least a month,' he said glumly. 'If you want, I could hire someone to walk her.'

'You don't trust me to walk her?'

'I trust you. I don't want to burden you.'

'It's not a burden,' she said.

'You don't mean that.'

'It's a small burden.'

'You don't mean that, either.'

'It's only a month, Tom.'

Tom slung an arm over her waist, his hand on her stomach. 'I could do all this over Zoom.'

'You hate Zoom.'

'Do you *want* me to go?'

Cherry had to think about that . . .

She didn't want Tom to go. She hated sleeping without him.

But he was so unhappy, so much of the time. And he always seemed angry lately. Not with Cherry – with the *world*. With everyone who was asking too much of him. (Any amount of asking seemed like too much. Cherry couldn't imagine a question that wouldn't snag at Tom and needle him.)

She'd thought Tom would feel better when he quit his job, but in a way this was worse. Now Tom had *several* jobs. He answered to people in New York and Los Angeles. He answered to the entire internet. To late-night talk show hosts and those assholes at *Saturday Night Live*. He always got so much email. He always got so much *mail*. He got up early to take phone calls from reporters in other time zones.

Tom had to be *on* all the time and smart all the time. He had to be creative and productive and game. And he couldn't seem to be all those things *and* be happy. He couldn't seem to be all those things and be the person Cherry had fallen in love with.

She still loved him.

She loved him.

She couldn't sleep without him.

But it was like living with a shadow – like living with someone who never smiled at you and never looked forward to anything. (It was kind of like living with her dad.)

Did she want him to go?

What Cherry wanted was irrelevant.

She'd already decided that she was never going to be the reason that Tom said no to something. She never wanted him to have a smaller life because of her. She would support him at every step, even if it meant spending her whole life carrying his water. And watching his dog.

'I want you to do as well as you can on this movie,' she said. 'I want it to be a good experience for you. And I think it will be better if you really invest yourself in it.'

Tom rubbed her stomach. Cherry didn't have to roll over to know that he was frowning. She could scent his unhappiness in the air now. (Like her dad's.)

He sighed. 'Yeah, all right,' he said. 'I'll go.'

Chapter 47

'Okay, I know. I know – I'm sitting on the floor, and you don't like it . . .

'Stevie.

'*Stevie*.

'Hey. Calm down.

'Calm down.

'Okay, sniff me. Yep. See, I'm okay. I'm just trying to talk to you . . .

'Stevie, down. Down. *Off.*

'You don't listen when I say it, do you?

'Do you want a treat? Steven, sit. *Sit.*

'Good girl. That's better. Yeah, that's better. Look at you. So pretty. So nice.

'Just let me say this, okay?

'Yeah, eat your treat. There you go.

'Here's the thing, Stevie . . . Are you listening?

'Hey, I'm talking to you – listen.

'I want you to know that I love you.

'Do you understand that? I love you.

'But I think Tom will do a better *job* of loving you. I can't just keep you because I want to cry into your fur every day. Do you see what I'm saying?

'No, no more treats. No more, see? Look at my hands. They're empty.

'I don't even think you'll miss me, Stevie. I don't think your memory has much permanence, if I'm being honest – I think you'd go home with the mailman and never look back.

'But I'll miss you. I'll really *miss* you.

'I know, you don't like it when I cry. I know.

'I'm okay. Yep. Look, I'm okay. Look at me. Stevie. This is all I'm good for. Crying on you.

'I don't want to take you for walks. I actually *hate* taking you for walks. And I hate cleaning out your ears – yeah, your floppy ears – even though I know they're prone to yeast infections.

'I know. Yeah, I know. You want me to shake your hand? Okay. We're shaking. Yep. Look at you. You're so civilized. You're so tender.

'You know what else I hate?

'Okay, we can shake again.

'I hate that you're only going to live eight to twelve years. I don't think I can handle watching you fade so soon. What sort of person does that make me?

'That's right, look at me. Are you trying to figure it out?

'You'll be happier with him, Stevie.

'*I* was happier with him.

'I know, I know. You don't like crying. I know. Okay, shake – yep, shake. Good girl. What a good girl.

'I just wanted you to understand my rationale, Stevie. Do you understand?

'Will you miss me?

'No. I know you won't.

'I know, I know.'

Chapter 48

Tom was sitting out on the front steps when Cherry got home from work. Even though it was cold.

It was the day after they'd lost and found Stevie. Cherry had been counting on not seeing him.

She took a deep breath and walked up to the house. He'd shoveled the walk.

She stopped a few feet away from him.

Tom looked tired. He held up a blue Post-it with his name on it. The last time she'd seen that note, it was stuck to Stevie's kennel.

'You caught me off guard,' Cherry said. 'Last night.'

'I didn't mean to.'

Cherry sighed and sat down on the porch next to him. She was tired, too.

'It never occurred to me that you'd want to keep Stevie,' Tom said.

'I don't know if it had occurred to me, either.'

He stuck the Post-it to Cherry's knee. 'We're not deciding it this way.'

'Are you offended that I treated Stevie like a DVD?'

'No.'

'I just didn't want to *talk* about it. I still don't.' Cherry's voice broke. 'I'd rather let you take her than talk about it – which is probably proof that I shouldn't get her.'

Tom clenched his fists between his knees. 'I'm not taking Stevie away from you, away from her home, if you want to keep her.'

'Tom, Stevie doesn't know what home is! You're the closest thing she has to home. I'm just her roommate.'

He shook his head.

Cherry sighed. Again. She folded her arms under her chest and leaned forward. 'I'm so tired.'

When she glanced back at Tom, he was watching her.

'Are you tired?' she asked.

He nodded.

'Let's be done talking about it,' she said. 'I've thought it through, and I'm not going to change my mind. It doesn't make any sense for me to keep Stevie.'

Tom didn't say anything.

Cherry peeled the Post-it off her knee and crumpled it up as she got to her feet.

'You home tomorrow?' Tom asked.

Tomorrow was Christmas Eve.

'Yeah,' she said. 'I'll be home. I can walk Stevie.'

'Do you want me to walk her on Christmas?'

'That'd be great.' Cherry turned for the door. 'Thank you.'

'Merry Christmas, Cherry.'

'Merry Christmas.'

Chapter 49

As tired as she was, Cherry didn't sleep much that night.

Tom was leaving Omaha.

Her marriage was over.

She'd thought that she'd already understood that – that she'd been living with it for a year.

But, really, she'd been living in a perfectly preserved diorama of her married life, with only one piece missing – the husband – and it hadn't seemed like he was gone for good.

For a year, if you'd walked into Cherry's house, you might have thought that Tom had just stepped out.

Well, not anymore.

Tom was leaving, and he was taking everything he loved with him.

What was *Cherry* supposed to take?

From this house? From this marriage?

What was she supposed to do with all her memories? They were mostly happy. Was she supposed to block them out? (Block *him* out?) Recast them as sad-memories-waiting-to-happen? Like the scenes before things go to shit in a horror movie?

Tom had been Cherry's whole life. She'd given him her whole heart. (Maybe she'd forced it on him, but he'd taken it.) Tom and Cherry had been something whole, together. That was the goal, wasn't it? That was the assignment? Wasn't she *supposed* to love him this much?

*

Cherry got up early on Christmas Eve, determined to manage things better than she had on Thanksgiving. She wrote down a plan of attack for everything she needed to make that day:

Sicilian meat pies called pastieri – Cherry made these for every holiday, they were her specialty.

Two kinds of cheese spread.

Two kinds of cookies.

Tom's broken-glass Jell-O salad again.

Squash casserole again.

And a relish tray.

She should have enough time for everything. She should have enough baking sheets.

She set out the butter and cream cheese to soften. She made four different colors of Jell-O and stacked the dishes in the fridge to cool.

She made the filling for the meat pies. It was her grandmother's recipe. (Cherry doubled the garlic and the parsley.)

Her back hurt by lunchtime. Russ Sutton may be gone, but all those high-heeled dates were still with her. Cherry ate some of the parsley-and-hamburger filling with crackers, and kept going.

She'd decided to make the pastieri gluten-free. The dough felt a little gummy in her hands, but she figured it was supposed to be that way. The first two pans went into the oven, and Cherry went looking for the Christmas Jell-O mold. It was shaped like a wreath. She couldn't find it.

She made more pies. She took the first batch out to cool. She walked Stevie in a rush. Her lower back was killing her.

When she got back, she ate a meat pie off the cooling rack. It was hard as a rock. They were all hard as rocks. Fuck. Cherry should have tested the dough – she didn't have enough parsley to start over. *Fuck.* She dumped the whole rack into the trash.

It was already midafternoon, and Cherry hadn't finished anything – she hadn't even started the cookies. Cherry and Tom always brought gingerbread cookies to Christmas. Those were non-negotiable. Also, Cherry had a new recipe she wanted to try, for rolled tuile cookies. She wanted to bring something that she'd never made with Tom – something spectacular.

Tuiles weren't complicated, but you had to be precise: You spread the batter in very thin circles, baked for just a few minutes, then rolled the resulting wafers into a cigar shape while they were still hot. Cherry had an idea to pipe little red and green flowers onto the cookies before she put them in the oven, so the design would bake in.

Piping the tiny flowers calmed her down a little. Working with her hands always did.

Stevie bumped into her legs, wanting attention. Cherry ignored her. Red flowers. Green dots. Maybe she should dip some of the tuiles in chocolate after they cooled ...

She got the first two pans into the oven – and immediately felt stressed again. The kitchen was a disaster. Cherry hadn't cleaned anything up or put anything away, and she'd gotten red cookie batter all over her hands and then all over everything else.

Cherry got messy whenever she went into the creative side of her brain. When she painted something, she used her fingers as much as the brush. (Tom could paint the Sistine Chapel without getting anything on his clothes.) (Tom could probably paint the Sistine Chapel.)

Cherry made messes while she worked, but then she couldn't *think* inside of them. She should clear some space. She should clear her head.

She looked in the cupboard over the sink for the Jell-O wreath. Maybe she should get a ladder. Stevie was barking at something outside. Cherry ignored her. Her back was *killing* her.

When the doorbell rang, Cherry thought about ignoring that, too. She walked into the foyer and peeked out the window ...

It was Michelangelo himself. (It was Tom.)

Cherry pushed Stevie out of the way. She got cookie batter in the dog's white fur. She got cookie batter on the doorknob. She probably got it on her face when she pushed her bangs out of her eyes.

'Hey,' Tom said. 'Sorry. You weren't answering your texts.'

'Sorry,' Cherry said.

He hooked his thumb toward the driveway. 'I just wanted to give you a heads-up that I'll be in the garage.'

She rubbed her nose with the back of her wrist. 'That's fine.'

'Are you okay?'

'I'm fine. Just, you know – Christmas. Hey, do you know where the Jell-O wreath is? The mold?'

'Yeah, it's in a box in the attic.'

'Cripes, I never would have looked there.'

'You want me to bring it down?'

'That'd be great, thanks.'

Tom brought the whole box down. 'I thought you might need the cookie cutters, too.' He stopped in the doorway to the kitchen.

Cherry had just taken a pan of tuile cookies out of the oven, but she didn't have anywhere to set it. She was using the sleeve of her sweater as an oven mitt.

Tom dropped the box on the floor and grabbed a kitchen towel from the fridge handle. 'Here.'

Cherry let him take the pan. 'They've got to be rolled while they're hot,' she said. She felt tearful.

'I've got it.' He glanced at the oven. 'Are there more?'

'Yeah.'

'I've got these.' He moved a plant off the window ledge and set the pan down. 'Should I use a dowel or something?'

She handed him a wooden spoon and set the second pan over the sink. She rolled the wafers into tubes. *Fuck, fuck, fuck.* They were so *hot.*

Stevie had picked up on the excitement and was pushing

between Cherry's legs. Cherry shoved the dog back with her thigh. 'Not now, Stevie.'

'I didn't wash my hands,' Tom said.

'These cookies are going to burn off your fingerprints, I don't think it matters.'

'Did you pipe these flowers?'

She nodded. 'Yeah.'

'They look great.'

Cherry's pan was already cooling off. A wafer cracked under her fingers. She exhaled heavily. 'I shouldn't have made so many at once – I don't know what I was thinking.'

'Sorry. I took you off your game.'

She stood up and arched her back. 'I was already off my game.' She looked over at Tom. 'How many did you get rolled?'

He held up a pan of perfect tuile cigars.

'Nobody likes you, Tom.'

He smiled.

'Maybe I should scrap this idea,' she said. 'I'm so far behind already.'

'What do you have left to do?'

Cherry laughed. 'What don't I have left?' She looked at the list on the refrigerator. 'The cheese balls are half done. The Jell-O's half done. I wasted all morning trying to make gluten-free pastieri, and they taste like hardtack . . .'

'Are you gluten-free?'

'Joy is. And Jeff. Or at least they were last week.'

'You're not making gingerbread this year?'

'No. I am. I just haven't really started.'

Tom set his pan of cookies on top of a dirty mixing bowl on the island. 'I can help you whip through the rest of these butter cookies. You already have the batter, and they're so pretty.'

Cherry shook her head. 'You don't have to do that. It's Christmas Eve.' What she meant was, *You don't have to do that. We're not married anymore.*

The corner of Tom's mouth quirked up. 'My Christmas Eve plans were to clean up the oil stain on the floor of the garage. My dad's driving me crazy.' He tipped his chin up, like he was pointing at her. 'Let me help.'

Cherry looked in his eyes.

She shouldn't say yes just because she missed him . . . because it had been torture all morning doing this without him. (Any given day without Tom was torture, but *Christmas* without Tom . . . Dante could never.)

Cherry was taking too long to answer. Tom looked away from her, like she'd already said no. Or maybe like he'd realized that he shouldn't have offered. He looked like he was about to apologize.

'Okay,' Cherry said. 'Thank you. I'd love some help.'

Tom turned back to her, surprised. He smiled and looked away again. 'Okay. Good.'

He shuffled out of his coat and hung it over a chair. He was wearing a T-shirt underneath. (Because Cherry was still holding all his long sleeves hostage.) 'You want me to clean off the island and give you some room?'

Cherry laughed out a breath, feeling tearful again. 'Yeah. Thank you.'

He scooped all the dishes off the island and quickly wiped it down. Cherry moved the finished cookies to a cooling rack.

'There you go,' Tom said. 'Clean slate.'

Cherry laid out fresh sheets of parchment paper and started spooning out the tuile batter. 'How many wafers do you think I should make at once?'

Tom hummed. 'Eight per sheet if you don't want to break any. Twelve if you want a challenge.'

'I already feel pretty challenged.'

He pointed at the red and green piping bags. 'Is that just regular batter with food coloring?'

She nodded.

'Did you see that on Pinterest or something?'

'I saw somebody do it with chocolate . . .'

'You should do chocolate, too,' he said. 'You could make tartan.'

'Why do my plans get more complicated as soon as you walk into the room?'

'You mean, why do your plans get more *awesome*?'

'I should let you do the piping,' Cherry said. 'It'll look cleaner.'

'Hush, you're doing great.'

Stevie was trying to squeeze between Cherry's hips and the island. 'Stevie,' Cherry said. 'Not now.'

'Stevie,' Tom said. 'Time to go to your house. Come on.'

The dog followed him out of the kitchen.

Tom came back and added chocolate to some of Cherry's batter. He cleaned out the sink and started the dishwasher. Then he stood behind Cherry, watching her pipe. 'You said the Jell-O is half done?'

'More like a third done. I made the colors this morning.'

'I'll work on that.'

Cherry piped cookies on the island, and Tom stood behind her at the counter. Every eight minutes, they rolled tuiles. Tom didn't break a single one.

When Cherry ran out of batter, she grabbed a few cookie fragments and leaned against the counter to watch Tom. He was stirring a can of condensed milk into a saucepan on the stove, making the white base for the broken-glass Jell-O ring.

'Did you have this growing up?' Cherry had never thought to ask before.

'Yeah,' he said. 'My mom always made it for holidays. I thought it was magic. My dad called it Midwestern slop.' Tom's dad was from the East Coast.

'They don't eat Jell-O in Baltimore?'

'As far as I can tell, they drink every meal with a splash of tonic.'

'Hmm.' Cherry bit off the end of a cracked tuile cookie. It tasted fairy-light and buttery. 'Oh, these are good. I'm glad I broke a few.

Try one.' She held out a cookie, and Tom looked over, but he had lifted the saucepan off the stove and was stirring.

Cherry paused for a second, then held the cookie up to his mouth. Tom paused for a second, too, then took it. His lip brushed her thumb. They were looking in each other's eyes. Tom smiled while he chewed. 'Really nice.'

Cherry wished she had an excuse to feed him another one.

'What's next?' he asked. He put the pan of Jell-O aside. It had to cool down, but not set.

'The last batch of tuiles is in the oven.'

Tom rubbed his chin with his wrist. 'Want to take another crack at the meat pies? With the regular crust?'

Cherry groaned. 'I don't have enough filling to make a full batch, and I ran out of parsley.'

'I can go get parsley.'

She almost told him that he didn't have to – but he already knew he didn't have to. 'Okay,' she said.

He smiled.

While Tom was gone, Cherry started again on the pastry dough, with regular flour, the way she usually made it. She started cooking more ground beef. She checked on Stevie and gave her a chewy bone, but left the dog in her kennel.

On the way back to the kitchen, Cherry hooked her phone up to the house speakers – Tom had installed house speakers – and started her Christmas playlist. She couldn't believe she'd been making Christmas cookies in silence all day.

Tom came back triumphant. He'd found premade gluten-free pie crust at the grocery store.

'But pastieri crust isn't supposed to taste like pie crust,' Cherry said.

'Gluten-free beggars can't be choosers.' He'd also bought a packaged charcuterie plate. He cracked it open.

'You went to the fancy grocery store,' she said.

'It was the only one open.'

Tom took over the parsley filling. He'd helped Cherry make pastieri a thousand times before.

Cherry ate cheese and crackers while she rolled out the dough. Then Tom helped her cut out circles. She used a teacup as a pattern. He did it freehand.

They filled the circles with meat and pinched them into boats. Tom arranged the boats in neat rows on the baking sheets.

It went twice as fast as it had that morning. And it was more than twice as nice. They were standing next to each other at the island.

'Have you made the gingerbread dough?' he asked.

'Last night.'

'Look at you.'

'I still have to make the icing.'

'What's the theme this year?'

Cherry's nieces and nephews always voted on a gingerbread theme at Thanksgiving. Over the years, Cherry and Tom had done *The Hobbit*, Harry Potter... One year, they did the Hall of Presidents.

'Disney cats,' Cherry said.

Tom smiled a little. 'Great theme. Once we get the pastieri going, I'll roll out the gingerbread.'

'Okay,' she yawned.

He elbowed her. 'No sleep till Brooklyn, baby – do you want me to make you some tea?'

She yawned again and laughed. 'Yeah.'

Tom made tea. Tom rolled out the gingerbread dough. Tom sang along to 'The Holly and the Ivy.' He looked big and cherubic. With his curly blond hair and rosy cheeks. Happier than she'd seen him in so long. He asked her if she wanted him to cut out the cat shapes, and she said yes.

'This'll be a good game,' he said. 'You'll have to guess the character from the shape – even though they're all gonna be shaped like cats.'

'Don't forget Marie,' she said. 'That's Lily's favorite.'

'Pfft. Like I was gonna forget Marie.' He picked up a knife and squinted down at the gingerbread dough.

'Or Berlioz,' she said.

'I'm not gonna forget Berlioz.'

'Or . . .'

Tom looked up at her. His eyes were sparkling. 'Who forgot Toulouse?'

Cherry laughed. She yawned again. 'I was going to say, "Or any of the other Aristocats."'

Cherry moved meat pies in and out of the oven. She made six special gluten-free pies for Joy and Jeff. She made royal icing. She watched Tom work, and picked all her favorite things off the charcuterie plate – the Marcona almonds and the honeycomb and the Brie. She leaned against the sink and tried to take the weight off her back. She tried not to get sleepy while they waited for the first pan of gingerbread cookies to bake and cool.

'What can I be doing?' Tom asked.

'You can take a breath.'

'I was breathing all day before I got here.'

She let him finish up the cheese balls and roll them in walnuts. There was no space in the kitchen, so he did it at the dining room table.

'You should decorate the cookies out here, Cherry, so you can sit down. And there's more space.'

That was a good idea. Cherry took the icing out to the dining room. She'd start with a big bowl of white icing and mix the colors as she needed them.

The gingerbread was still cooling. Cherry stood at the dining room table and leaned forward on it, pillowing her head on her arms. 'I'm getting too old for this.'

'You're not old,' Tom said. 'You just bite off more than you can chew.'

'I like a challenge,' she said sleepily. 'It keeps me sharp.'

He poked her side and sang, *'The old gray mare, she ain't what she used to be.'* He poked her hip. *'Ain't what she used to be.'*

Cherry laughed into her forearms.

'Ain't what she used to be.'

Tom rested his hand for just a second on her lower back, right where it hurt. Right where he knew it hurt. Then he walked back into the kitchen.

Cherry must have dozed off for a few minutes. On her feet.

When she opened her eyes, Tom had some cookies spread out on the table, and he was mixing some icing in primary colors. He made eye contact with her. 'You okay?'

She nodded.

He pointed at a chair with his chin. 'Take a load off.'

Cherry nodded again. She stood, resting one knee on the chair, and took a long drink of tea. Tom must have freshened her cup.

She squinted at the spread of cookies in front of her. There was no way she was going to be able to guess these cats. Tom made her try anyway.

Cherry held up a cookie. 'This is ... the Golden Gate Bridge. Or maybe a bat?'

'That's Rufus from *The Rescuers.*'

'Awww ... Rufus.'

Cherry used her phone for reference. She iced the cookies with a plastic knife, her index finger, and a round-tipped tool made for nail art.

Tom let Stevie out of her kennel. She lumbered under the dining room table and promptly fell asleep.

Cherry didn't know what time it was. Probably late. 'I'm not icing all of these myself,' she said.

Tom hummed. He was eating Manchego and fig jam. They were listening to 'Silver Bells' – the Stevie Wonder version. 'Maybe you are.'

'*Tommm,*' Cherry whined.

He laughed and ate another piece of cheese. 'They'll be so much cuter if you do them, Cherry.' They had this argument every year.

The kitchen timer went off, and Tom went to pull more cookies out of the oven. He took too long. 'What are you doing?' Cherry called.

'Finishing the Jell-O. There's yellow squash in the fridge. Are you making casserole?'

'I was,' she said, 'but forget it. We're the only people who eat it anyway.'

'I'll get it ready. It's quick.'

'Come help me decorate cookies!'

Cherry had iced Rufus. And Figaro from *Pinocchio*. And she was working on Dinah from *Alice in Wonderland*, with a wreath of daisies.

She felt more awake. She felt more calm.

Christmas Eve was her favorite day of the year. She liked it even better than Christmas.

(Christmas Eve was her favorite day of the year because she always spent it with Tom. Listening to Christmas carols. Staining her hands pink and green. Working too hard on work that was their own. Tom brought out the best in Cherry – more often than he brought out the worst.)

When he came out to the dining room with the last batch of cookies, Cherry was staring at a gingerbread shape. 'Who's this?'

'Tigger.'

She frowned. 'Tigger isn't a cat.'

'He's a tiger. There aren't enough Disney house cats for all of the kids to get a cookie.'

'All right.' Cherry set the cookie down. 'Tigger it is.'

'I made two Maries, so Lily and Samantha can both have one.'

'That was smart.'

Tom was looking at the platter of finished cookies, smiling softly. 'You should have been the professional cartoonist.'

'Ha,' Cherry said. 'I don't have a burning story to tell.'

'Well, me neither. The *Guardian* called my last book *"predictable torpor."*'

'They're just being contrary,' she said. 'The only interesting thing left to say about *Thursday* is *"I don't understand the appeal."* You're the *Paddington 2* of comic artists.'

Tom hummed. He'd picked out a blank cookie and was scrutinizing it.

Cherry worked on Tigger's eyebrows. She needed to make more black icing. 'I don't think I'd enjoy this as much if I was getting paid for it,' she said.

'That is certainly and universally true,' Tom agreed.

She glanced up at him. 'Did you stop enjoying *Thursday* once you were getting paid?'

'Not immediately,' he said, icing the cookie. 'For a while, working on new comics was like an escape from the old comics, the ones that everyone was reading . . .'

'And then?'

'And then I couldn't ignore the fact that everyone was reading *all* of them. That nothing was mine anymore.'

'It's still yours,' she said.

'Huh,' Tom laughed. It sounded hollow. Cold.

Cherry didn't want to hear more of it. 'Did you remember to make Oliver, from *Oliver & Company*?'

'Yeah.'

'What about Mochi?'

Tom frowned. 'Who's Mochi?'

'From *Big Hero 6*.'

He groaned. 'Right. Mochi. Okay . . .' He picked up another cookie and squinted at it. 'This is Mochi now.'

'Who was that before?'

'That cat girl from *Treasure Planet*.'

Cherry laughed. 'Deep cut.'

He smiled at her. 'You're wide awake.'

'I got my second wind.'

He kept smiling. Tom had a gorgeous smile, and almost no one got to see all of it. He only smiled wide like this when his guard was completely down. Never at work or in big groups – or on television.

It had been a while since Cherry had seen the complete expanse of Tom's smile. It made his chin sharp and pushed his cheeks into his eyes.

Tom's face was so easy to draw ... Flat, slightly tipped eyes. Square forehead. Thick eyebrows, wide jaw. Full lips.

Cherry would draw him happier and more handsome than he drew himself. Tom always drew himself slouching – but he almost never slouched in real life. Tom had lovely broad shoulders. They were one of his nicest features.

He looked good in just a T-shirt ... His arms were nice, too. Thick and capable. Maybe Cherry only thought so because she knew that they *were* capable. That Tom could do almost anything with his hands. And he could carry almost anything a man might be asked to carry.

Cherry had always felt so lucky to be with Tom. Like, on his team. If you were planning an expedition, Tom would be the first person you'd choose. Someone who could figure anything out, and fix anything that broke, and fight off anything that threatened you – with his bare hands, if it came to that.

Cherry was feeling a little unsteady ...

Here, after midnight on Christmas Eve, standing across the table from the man she'd promised to love through hell and high water. (A promise she'd kept so far, appearances notwithstanding.)

Tom held up a perfectly iced Mochi cookie.

'You remembered his bell,' Cherry said.

'Once I remembered him, I remembered him completely.'

They finished the last of the cookies together. The caffeine had worn off. Cherry was exhausted, and her lower back really was unbearable. She kept twisting her shoulders, looking for relief.

'Why don't you sit down?' Tom said. 'I'll put these away.'

'Aren't you tired, too?'

'I'm all right.'

Cherry walked into the living room and sank down into the couch. 'Oh god,' she said. 'I'm probably never getting up.' Her legs *ached* from standing.

She watched Tom take the cookies into the kitchen. She watched him clean off the dining room table.

He came back through the kitchen and sat down on the couch. Right next to Cherry. He groaned.

'You are tired,' she said.

'I'm good-tired,' Tom said.

The Christmas music was still playing. 'This Christmas' by Donny Hathaway.

'Thank you,' Cherry said. 'I'm not sure I would have finished anything without you.'

'I'm sure you would have finished everything. You just wouldn't have been able to walk tomorrow.'

'Well. Thank you for your help.'

'Thank you for letting me help,' he said quietly. 'For giving me a little Christmas.'

Cherry turned to him – you could say *'suddenly,'* but she'd been on the verge of this all night – and said, 'Come with me tomorrow.'

Tom made a face. Like she was being absurd. 'What? To your sister's?'

'Yes. Come.'

'Cherry.' He shook his head, still like she was being absurd. 'I can't do that.'

'Yes, you can. Everyone will be so happy to see you.'

'No.' He shook his head again. 'No . . . You don't want your sisters to think –'

'I don't care what they think. And I'm telling you, everyone will love to see you. Tom, just because you and I . . . broke down, doesn't mean you're not part of the family.'

He raised an eyebrow. 'I think it does mean that,' he said. 'I can't just keep coming every year.'

Cherry was insistent: 'Maybe not every year, but you could come tomorrow. You *should* come tomorrow. You already put in all the work.'

'I wasn't angling for an invite.'

'I know that.'

'Cherry . . .' Tom's forehead was lined. The corners of his eyes were pinched. 'It's hard for me to believe that you'd want me there, considering . . . everything.'

'I *do* want you there. I'll feel better if you're there. I mean, if you want to come.' She put her hand on his arm. 'Just come, Tom. It'll only be weird at the start.'

He laughed out a breath. Less hollow than before. Much less cold. 'Okay.' He laughed again, shaking his head. 'Yeah, all right.'

'You're coming?'

'Yeah. Yeah. I'll come. You know . . .' He squinted at her. 'Unless you change your mind. Just tell me if you wake up tomorrow morning and can't believe you invited me.'

'That's not going to happen – that's like inverted Scrooge. Don't *you* change *your* mind. Don't have second thoughts.'

'Well . . .' Tom stood up.

'Are you getting out of my hair?'

He glanced back at her. Their eyes met.

'That's what you say every time you leave,' Cherry said.

Tom's eyebrows twitched down, but he didn't say anything – just went to get his coat from the kitchen.

Cherry got up, too.

Stevie hauled herself up off the dining room floor to follow them. When they got to the foyer, the dog started walking up the stairs. Tom watched her go.

'She puts herself to bed these days,' Cherry explained.

'You're letting her sleep with you?'

Cherry shrugged. 'All her bad habits are your problem now. I'm going to start letting her eat bacon directly off my plate.'

Tom snorted. 'Great, thanks.'

She smiled up at him.

'Are we driving together tomorrow?' he asked.

'In for an inch.'

'I'll come early and walk Stevie.'

'Eleven?'

'Sounds good.' He opened the door and looked back at her, over his arm. 'Good night, Cherry.'

'Good night, Tom.'

Chapter 50

Yesterday, 9:15 PM

Russ Sutton
Merry Christmas, Cherry.

Russ Sutton
I think about you. A lot. Often. And I'd love a chance to talk to you again.

Russ Sutton
Please let me say I'm sorry, Cherry.

Chapter 51

Today, 8:16 AM

Cherry
Hey, I need you to do me a favor.

Hope
Let's hear it.

Cherry
I need you to tell everybody that Tom's coming today, and I need you to tell them not to make a big deal out of it.

Hope
WHY IS TOM COMING?

Cherry
Because he doesn't have anywhere else to go.

Hope
You know that it's no longer your job to take care of him, right?

Especially after everything he's done.

Cherry
I'm not sure that's true.

>Everything is hard enough. I don't want to be angry with him anymore.

Hope
I guess that's your prerogative.

>**Cherry**
>Will you tell everyone not to be weird? Or rude? Tell them to be good Christians.

Hope
I can try.

Chapter 52

Cherry was still getting ready when Tom showed up at eleven.

She was wearing an expensive cherry-pink batwing sweater with wide-legged jeans and ridiculously twee high-heeled oxfords. The shoes were patent leather – juniper green and candy pink – and the jeans were *just* short enough to reveal an inch of pink fishnet stockings.

She'd braided her hair into a crown and was taking time with her cherry-red lipstick and silver eyeshadow.

Cherry hadn't slept well, but she looked bright-eyed and Christmassy.

Tom rang the doorbell, then let himself in. 'Cherry?' he called up the stairs. 'I'm going to take Stevie for a walk!'

'All right!' she called back.

The squash casserole was in the oven. The cookies were on platters on the kitchen island. Cherry had decided to wait and flip the Jell-O out of its mold at Honny's house, so it wouldn't slide around in the car.

She was still wrapping a gift for one of her nieces when Tom and Stevie got back. 'That was a short walk!' she shouted from upstairs.

'I didn't want to make you late!'

'I'll be right down – I'm wrapping a present!'

'Did you bring down the tablecloths?'

'Yeah! On the dining room table!'

'I'll start loading up the car!'

She heard him coming and going. She finished the gift. When she went downstairs, Tom was just coming in the door.

She saw his eyes widen when he saw her. She stopped on the staircase.

The corners of his mouth turned up. 'You look... like the girl on the front of Target's holiday sale circular.'

Cherry put her hand over her heart, pretending to feign delight. 'That's the nicest compliment you've ever given me.'

Tom laughed, softly. 'Sorry,' he said, glancing down at himself. He was wearing another T-shirt and cargo pants. 'I didn't have time to shop.'

Cherry's smile faded. 'You could...' She glanced upstairs.

'No.' Tom shook his head. 'A T-shirt's fine, right?'

'Yeah,' Cherry said, 'it's fine.'

'Can you see if there's still some kraft paper in the upstairs closet? With the wrapping paper?'

'Yeah.'

'Is that casserole ready to go?'

'Yep – the carrier's in the drawer by the sink. And I made coffee.'

Tom nodded and headed for the kitchen. 'My second choice after "girl on the Target circular" was "Santa Claus's high school sweetheart."'

Cherry smiled. 'That also would have been good.'

She went upstairs to get the kraft paper. Then into her room, and to Tom's dresser. She opened the bottom drawer and took out a navy fair-isle sweater with a bright geometric pattern banded across the shoulders.

When she came downstairs, he was in the kitchen. Drinking coffee and looking out the window above the sink.

He glanced over his shoulder at Cherry, then turned around.

She held out the sweater.

Tom looked down at her hands, like he wasn't sure he was going to take it.

It was silly. This wasn't a gift; it was his own sweater. If it wouldn't have been a huge scene, Cherry would have brought all his clothes down. It was embarrassing now that she hadn't given them to him.

'Thanks,' Tom said.

He set down the coffee and took off his coat. She watched him pull the sweater over his wide chest.

'It's beginning to look a lot like Christmas,' Cherry said.

Tom smiled a little. 'Okay ... Gingerbread, butter cookies, cheese balls ...'

'I'm waiting to do the Jell-O after we get there.'

'Pastieri ... tablecloths ... Do you have your presents?'

'I'll grab the rest.'

'And I've got the squash casserole.'

'We're ready,' Cherry said.

Tom huffed out a dry laugh. 'Are we?'

He picked up the casserole dish in its handmade quilted carrier, and Cherry went for her coat and the laundry basket of gifts. She always bought gifts for her mom, one of her sisters, and two of her nieces and nephews. (They drew names at Thanksgiving.)

When they got out on the porch, Tom took the basket and said, 'Wait here. I'll help you down the steps.'

'I'm fine.'

'Your shoes are reckless.'

'My shoes are really cute,' Cherry said, waiting on the top step. 'I have boots in the car if I need them.'

Tom came back for her, his hand on her elbow as she walked down the steps, and hovering near her elbow as she walked to the car. He opened the passenger door for her. She hadn't even told him he could drive.

They were both quiet on the way to Honny's. 'White Christmas,' Cherry said unnecessarily, looking out the window.

Tom only hummed.

When they were almost there, he asked, 'Do they know I'm coming?'

'Yeah,' Cherry said.

He looked pale. His lips were tense. 'Did you tell them we're not ... that it doesn't mean ...'

Cherry clenched her teeth. She swallowed. 'Yeah, of course. I told them that I invited you. And that we're not fighting.'

He threw her a concerned look. 'I guess that's true.'

'Yeah,' she said. 'Go figure.'

Tom dropped Cherry off right in front of the house. 'Could you wait for me?' he asked.

'Tom, I'm fine. I'll walk like a penguin.'

'No, I just ...' He squinted one eye. 'Could you wait for me? To walk in?'

'Oh,' she said. 'Yeah.'

She did wait. Holding on to the hood of someone's SUV. Tom parked the car and grabbed as much as he could carry in one arm. Cherry hadn't taken anything – because she really might need both hands to get up to the house, these shoes were idiotic – and because she was already taking Tom's arms for granted. Tom's endless, unspoken willingness to be helpful.

He took her elbow as she climbed the stairs from the driveway, and then again when she stepped up to the porch.

She glanced up at him when they got to the door. He looked like he was at his own arraignment.

'Let's just have a nice Christmas,' Cherry said. 'We both deserve a nice Christmas.'

Tom looked in her eyes. His brow was furrowed. He nodded.

When they walked in, everyone shouted, 'Cherry!' And then, louder, 'Tom!' The younger kids called out, 'Uncle Tom!' and ran to grab on to his legs. (A childless uncle was a precious commodity; was anyone ever more fun?)

'Hey, hey,' Tom said, patting their heads and hugging them.

Cherry took the squash casserole from him, feeling suddenly

uncertain. Did Tom actually want one more day with these people? Knowing it would be his last?

'Who's going to help carry in the cookies?' Tom was saying. He drafted a few of the older kids and told them to put on their coats.

Honny and Joy were standing outside the kitchen, mutely watching.

Cherry walked past them, holding the squash casserole in both hands.

'You look cute, Cherry,' Joy said, following her.

'Yeah, you look really *cute*, Cherry,' Honny said, like it was an accusation. As soon as they rounded the corner into the kitchen and out of sight, she said, 'What in *tarnation*?'

'We are *not* doing this,' Cherry hissed under her breath. 'We're being normal.'

'We *are* being normal,' Joy said. 'You're the one who brought your ex-husband to Christmas!'

'They're still married,' Honny said. 'The weird part for me is that she brought a *different* guy to Thanksgiving.'

Faith came into the kitchen, still wearing her coat, and rushed over to Cherry, slapping her arm. 'Oh my *god*,' Faith whispered. 'Are you and Tom back together?'

'*No*,' Cherry said. 'We're just ... getting along. He's moving to California next month, and he was going to be alone on Christmas, so I invited him.'

'You look really cute,' Faith said, like she was just noticing.

Honny's arms were folded. '*Doesn't* she.'

'This casserole should stay warm in the carrier,' Cherry said. 'It's insulated.'

'Oooh, did you make squash casserole?' Joy asked.

'Yeah,' Cherry said. 'Sorry, it has Ritz crackers.'

'Pfft' – Joy waved a hand – 'I'm taking the day off from worrying about gluten.'

'You're *what*?' Honny said.

'Are you serious, Joy?' Faith said. 'I made gluten-free potica.'

'I made gluten-free pastieri,' Cherry said.

'I made gluten-free chocolate cake,' Honny said.

Cherry frowned at Honny. 'Did it turn out?'

'No!'

'Well . . .' Joy was pouting. 'You all told me I was being stupid.'

'You *were* being stupid,' Honny said.

A line of kids was coming into the kitchen, carrying Cherry's dishes.

'Here.' Cherry took a plate of cookies from one of her nephews. 'Let's set everything on the counter for now.'

Tom came in at the end, carrying the box of table decorations.

'Tom!' Faith said, reaching up to hug him.

Tom shifted the box to one hip to hug her back. 'Hey, Faith.'

Joy was right behind her. 'Merry Christmas, Tom.'

Honny waved from the other end of the kitchen. 'Hey, Tom.'

'Hey, Honny. Did you guys redo that retaining wall?'

'Yeah, in the spring.'

'It looks great.'

'Cost us an arm and a leg.'

'I'll bet.' Tom looked at Cherry. His eyes were a little too bright. 'You want me to set up the tables? I was going to have the kids help me with the paper tablecloth.'

'Go ahead,' she said. 'I'll do the adult table. Mallory will help me.'

He nodded and waved at the room at large before he headed out. Cherry waited for her sisters to start haranguing her again. But when she looked around, everyone just looked awkward and sad.

Normally Tom spent a few days illustrating the paper tablecloth for the kids' table. Obviously, this year, he hadn't had a chance.

Instead he rolled the kraft paper out on the folding table and quickly drew a long mantel, like the top of a fireplace, with black marker. Then he drew stockings with each kid's name. He gave them all crayons to decorate their stockings, and he moved around the table, drawing gifts peeking out of the stockings and adding details to the mantel. He drew candlesticks and a clock. He called Cherry over to draw a Santa mouse peeking out from behind the clock.

He helped the toddlers. He joked with the teenagers.

Hope came into the house with Cherry's parents.

Cherry's mom had clearly been briefed about Tom – but it didn't stop her from being weird.

She put her hand over her heart when she saw him. Then she came and took both of his hands in hers. He was still holding a Sharpie.

'Tom,' she said. 'It's so good to see you.'

'It's great to see you, Nancy.' Some of the brothers-in-law called Cherry's mom Mom. Tom called her Nancy.

'You look good,' she said. 'Have you lost weight?'

'Um . . .'

'Everyone's losing weight. Have you seen Hope? She lost a whole person! I never thought I'd have a skinny daughter.'

Tom glanced up, reflexively. Hope had just walked over, wearing a jersey wrap dress that showed off her narrow shoulders and slim arms. His eyes widened, also reflexively – then he caught himself. 'Hey, Hope. Merry Christmas.'

'Merry Christmas, Tom.'

'And look at your hair,' Cherry's mom said, smiling up at him. 'It suits you.'

'California must suit you,' Hope said.

Being single must suit him, Cherry thought.

Her mom was still holding Tom's hands. Her dad had settled onto the couch – where he wouldn't move for the rest of the day. 'It's so good to see you,' her mom said again, squeezing Tom's hands. 'You're my son, you know that?' She was tearing up. 'You'll always be my son.'

'Thank you,' Tom said, letting her squeeze him.

Cherry should intercede, but if she came any closer, her mom might grab Cherry's hands, too. She'd handfast them back together, right there in Honny's living room.

'Mom!' Honny called from the dining room. 'Come on in – we've been waiting for you to start eating. Did you bring the mashed potatoes?'

'Well, Danny has them.'

Hope's husband, Danny, had stalled out in front of the football game. He was carrying a big soup pot.

'I'll grab them,' Tom said, pulling his hands away from Cherry's mom. 'Hey there, Danny.'

'Oh, hey, Tom – Merry Christmas.'

The tables were ready. The buffet was ready. Honny had one of the kids turn down the volume on the football game. She made her husband, Carl, stand up to say grace.

Cherry's brothers-in-law took turns saying prayer on holidays. (They'd offered it to Tom one year, and he'd declined.) It was Carl's turn today. Carl was a sturdily built Mexican American guy. He and Honny spent every other Christmas with his family out in Grand Island. He put an arm around Honny, and Joy's and Faith's husbands followed suit. They all looked round and rosy and comfortably in love.

Cherry was standing next to Tom. She gave him a smile, just to make it less awkward, and he smiled back, tight-lipped, making the best of things. They bowed their heads.

Carl encouraged them all to be thankful. He encouraged them to remember God, who gave His only son for them and watched Him die on the cross – which struck Cherry as more of an Easter sentiment – but Carl brought it back around to generosity. To family. To kids growing older. To families getting bigger. 'How fortunate we are to be here together,' Carl said. 'How fortunate we are to have this day.'

'Amen,' Cherry and Tom agreed, with everyone else in the room.

'Oh, Carl, you made me cry with that one,' Cherry's mom said.
'Amen,' Faith said.

The nieces and nephews went through the buffet line first. Honny spotted the kids' paper tablecloth, and said, 'Oh my god, Tom – are you kidding me? No! We are *not* letting that get ruined. Everybody lift up your plates!' Honny pulled the paper out from under them, and Cherry helped her spread it out against the actual fireplace (which wasn't lit). 'We have to hang this up after dinner,' Honny said. 'Tom has outdone himself this time.'

Honny was probably thinking that this was the last of the Tom tablecloths – and her last chance to hold on to one. (Tom really had outdone himself.)

Cherry made her dad a plate. There was no alcohol at Honny's house, so he'd probably filled himself to the brim before he got there. Their father was an accomplished drunk. He could plan his work and work his plan, around all his daughters' machinations. Cherry wasn't sure she'd *ever* seen him sober. Imagine having that sort of stick-to-itiveness for forty years.

Right now, he was topped up and sullen. He might mellow into chatty and loudly bemused, or he might just get nervy and short-tempered. It was hard to get their father to family gatherings. He didn't like to feel trapped.

'Hey, Dad,' Cherry said. 'I brought you some lunch.'

He didn't look up from the game. 'Thanks, honey.'

Her dad was a heavyset guy with wavy hair and deep, craggy dimples. He'd been handsome once. Roguish. He looked a lot older than Cherry's mom, even though they were the same age.

Cherry set down the plate. 'You want to come sit with us, in the dining room?'

'Nah, I'm all right. I'm watching the game.'

He wouldn't want to move around much. He wouldn't want any of the grandkids to bother him. Just like he hadn't wanted any of his own kids to bother him.

Cherry's mom had always gone overboard on holidays. They never had much money for presents, but her mom would cook for days. They'd decorate the whole house with paper chains and popcorn garlands. They'd make pomanders out of oranges and cloves.

Hope said their mom was always dancing in double time to cover for their dad, to distract from him. *'All of those frantically wonderful Christmases.'*

They really had been wonderful . . .

Cherry made her own plate, carefully taking tiny portions so she could try everything.

Honny had brined the turkey and stuffed the skin with sage and butter. Hope had made the bread-crumb dressing with celery and chestnuts. The green bean casserole was Joy's – plus the brussels sprouts with maple syrup and bacon. Faith had baked yeasty yellow rolls and spent a whole day making homemade noodles in chicken gravy. Everyone brought dessert. Pumpkin pie, apple potica. Red velvet cake, a Swiss roll. There were plates and plates of cookies and homemade candy. Peppermint bark and Christmas crack.

Cherry and Tom ended up together at the table, sitting just where she'd sat with Russ – with Hope in the same place, too, sitting next to Tom and looking like she'd shown up at the wrong family dinner. Tom's plate was so full, he'd had to stack his roll and pastieri on top of everything else. He was being just as polite as Russ had been. But softer, more hesitant.

Maybe Tom was thinking about how everyone at this table knew his marriage was over. And how everyone at this table knew he'd been unfaithful.

But Tom had *always* been soft-spoken and hesitant, so it was hard to say what he was thinking.

Her sisters had already forgotten to be strange with him. They'd shifted into their holiday selves, loud and happy. Their husbands had *not* forgotten. They were being even more taciturn than usual. They must not appreciate Cherry dragging all these marital nightmares to the table, the ghosts of Christmas past and future. Hope's husband, Danny – usually warm and quietly witty – wouldn't look at Cherry, even when she asked him a direct question.

After dinner, they played cards. Tom wasn't a games person. At least not like this, with everyone shouting and getting competitive. He let one of the nieces take his spot at the table and went into the living room to sit on the couch next to Cherry's dad, forever willing to take one for the team. Cherry drifted away from the card game to go sit with them. She and Tom ended up playing Uno with some of the younger kids – and then having great seats to watch everyone open presents. Cherry drank afternoon coffee and ate cookies. (All bets were off on Christmas.)

Her family always took time with the presents, opening them one by one. They took photos. They made it a whole production. The television was still on, because their dad wouldn't let anyone turn it off, and it was driving all of his daughters crazy, including Cherry.

He'd sobered up enough to start talking Tom's ear off about Nebraska football and what the coaches needed to do. Tom didn't care about Nebraska football, but her dad seemed to have internalized that Tom had played football once and was a good target for this sort of monologue. Tom was being a good sport about it. Cherry caught herself patting his thigh, like *thank you* and *I'm sorry*. At least he'd never have to do this again.

Cherry wondered whether her dad even knew about her and Tom . . . Probably not. He hadn't been at Thanksgiving.

When it was Cherry's turn to open a present, someone handed her an envelope. Joy had drawn Cherry's name and bought her an individual membership to the botanical gardens – which was as good as saying, '*I'm sorry to hear about your divorce.*'

'Thank you,' Cherry said. 'I've never been.'

The nieces and nephews wanted to eat the gingerbread cookies, and the older ones had prepared an argument that the younger ones shouldn't get to pick first *every* year.

Cherry and Tom heard them out, and decided they were right. Cherry let the middle kids pick first. Everyone told Tom how great the cookies looked, and Tom told everyone that Cherry had made them. And Joy said, 'Cherry, sometimes I forget you can draw.'

Tom got Cherry another cup of coffee, and one for himself, and a poinsettia-shaped napkin piled with tuile cookies for them to share.

One of her nieces wanted to sit next to Cherry, so Cherry scooted closer to Tom. He put his arm on the back of the couch behind her, to make room.

The little kids were playing with their toys on the floor. And Cherry's sisters were playing cards again. And Tom was so solid. So warm. The sun was starting to set. The neighbors' Christmas lights came on.

'I think I'm going to run your dad home,' Tom said.

Cherry leaned forward to look at her dad. 'You're not staying, Dad?'

His eyes were red. His eyebrows were disordered. 'I'm ready for an early night.'

Cherry's mom was in the other room, playing cards. There was some back-and-forth about whether she should leave with him. He told her to stay – he was just going straight to bed.

Cherry and her sisters all knew that if anything, he was going straight to the bar. But they didn't get involved. It was pointless. Faith finally said, 'Mom, stay. Let's finish our game.'

'I'll be back,' Tom said.

'I'll save your seat,' Cherry said.

'Save my cookies.'

As soon as their dad put on his coat, Honny turned off the TV.

Joy's four-year-old daughter immediately claimed Tom's seat and his cookies. Cherry played with her for a while, then got up to gather napkins, crumpled-up gift wrap, and dirty dishes. She went into Honny's kitchen. Honny's husband was in there, emptying the dishwasher. 'I've got this,' Cherry said. 'Take a load off, Carl.'

She got another batch of dishes going. She put the kettle on. She leaned over the sink, trying to stretch her back.

Tom found her like that.

When Cherry looked up, he was standing in the kitchen doorway. One of Cherry's nephews squeezed past him to get a spoon and then squeezed out again.

Tom walked over to stand by Cherry at the sink. He rested his hand on her back. 'How're you holding up?'

'I'm up,' she said.

He rubbed her back for just a second. 'You're supposed to be saving our prime seats on the couch.'

'Thanks for taking my dad home.'

'It was fine. He wasn't in the mood to talk.'

'Do you want to leave soon?' she asked.

'No, I'm fine. I stopped by the house and let Stevie out.'

'That was smart. Well . . . just tell me when you're ready.'

'Cherry, I'm *fine*. It's been nice, thank you.'

Another hip-high nephew was running into the kitchen.

'Slow down,' Cherry said.

'Uncle Tom, will you play Taco Cat Goat Cheese Pizza with us?'

'What's Taco . . . What was it again, Taco Goat Pizza?'

The kid cracked up. 'It's a game.'

'Uncle Tom's been playing with you all day,' Cherry said. 'He might need a break.'

Tom smiled at her. 'I don't mind.'

Tom had known all these kids since they were babies. He'd sat in the hospital waiting room when they were born. If you asked the little ones, they wouldn't be able to tell you that Cherry was their aunt by blood and Tom was their uncle by situation.

This was his last Christmas with them. He wouldn't go to any more birthday parties. He'd miss their graduations and weddings.

Cherry followed him into the family room to play Taco Cat Goat Cheese Pizza. (Which was a very silly card game.)

They stayed at Honny's house long enough to have a second plate of turkey. And to hear Cherry's mom tell the story (for the thousandth time) of going into labor with Faith on Christmas Eve. How Hope and Honny had cried because Santa didn't come, and how Cherry told everyone at church that Santa had brought the baby, and everyone thought it was so cute, they didn't correct her.

They stayed at Honny's long enough that everything hard fell away. They sat at the dining room table, and Tom's arm hung off the back of Cherry's chair. Tom cracked open almonds and pecans, and Cherry and Hope stole them. Tom didn't say much, but he never did. He laughed. And when everyone was trying to get Cherry to do her impression of Joy's husband that time Joy wrecked their Prius, it was Tom who nudged her over the edge. (You had to know Joy and her husband, and to have seen the Prius, to get it.)

Hope left first, with their mom. Who hugged Tom too hard and looked too long in his eyes.

After another hour of making fun of their mom and gossiping about Hope – *who'd hardly eaten, even Dan hadn't eaten, was Dan on Ozempic now too, did Tom know lots of people on Ozempic out in Hollywood, Joy's gynecologist was skinny now, and so was Faith's pediatrician, plus Whoopi Goldberg, have you seen her, she looks great, they all look great, not Joy's gynecologist, she looks gaunt* – everyone stood up from the table and stretched.

Tom went to get the car while Cherry rounded up her pans and platters. All her cookies had been eaten, and all the meat pies, too, and Honny said she'd keep the leftover cheese spread. Faith stood by Cherry at the kitchen sink and squeezed her arm. 'You okay, Cherish Anne?'

Cherry smiled. 'I'm good.'

(That was a lie. If Cherry had been good – essentially, fundamentally, in a core and abiding way – she would probably still be married. She hadn't been the one to *break* things, but she suspected that she was the one who'd worn them down and made them fragile.

The person who had put pressure on their relationship's weakest points. The points of wear and past damage.) (It was also a lie in the more immediate sense: Cherry wasn't good or all right or fine or holding up or keeping her head above water.)

Tom left the car running in the driveway and came back to the house to help Cherry out. He held on to her elbow all the way to the car.

It was cold – 'bitter cold,' her mom called this weather. Cherry got into the car and sat on her hands. The roads were clear, but she was still glad Tom was the one driving. He turned on the radio. 'You sick of Christmas carols?'

'Never,' Cherry said.

'I wasn't prepared for Hope,' he said.

'Every time I see her, she's lost more weight. Her eyes look *huge*. I wonder if my eyes would look that big if I lost weight . . .'

He glanced over at her. 'Would you want them to?'

'I don't think so. She looks like someone drew a picture of her from memory and got the eyes and mouth wrong.'

'Honny's being vicious about it.'

'Yeah.' Cherry sighed. 'What else is new.'

Tom glanced over at her. 'You look tired.'

'I am.'

'Me, too.'

When they got to the house, Tom parked the car in the driveway. 'You could start using the garage now if you wanted. There's room.'

'Meh,' Cherry said. 'Seems like an extra step.'

Tom carried the Christmas stuff, and Cherry took his arm on the steps. They both stopped outside the door. Stevie had already spotted them. She was barking at the front window.

Tom was squinting up, almost like he was looking through the porch ceiling at the sky. His chin stayed tilted, but his eyes found Cherry's. 'Could I come in for a second?'

'Yeah.' She nodded so hard, she felt her cheeks wobble. 'Of course.'

They both waited.

'You have my keys,' she said.

'Oh.' Tom shook his head. 'Right.'

He got her keys out of his pocket and unlocked the door, pushing it open so she could walk in first.

Stevie ran up to Cherry, snuffling at her legs, then switched to Tom, who petted her and scratched behind her ears. 'Hey there, Stevie Nicks, did you have a long, lonely Christmas?'

Cherry took off her coat and hugged it against her waist. She was watching Tom. Watching his big hands in Stevie's fur. Watching the curls bounce on the top of his head.

'Okay,' Tom said. 'Okay, good girl. Why don't you go rest. Here –' He grabbed a chewy treat from Stevie's kennel and gave it to her. 'There you go. You go rest.' Stevie dropped to the floor, preoccupied with the treat.

Tom looked back at Cherry, his eyes narrow and concerned, and the bridge of his nose creased. 'I have something for you.'

'Like ...' She took a step back. 'Like what?'

His face fell. 'Like a present.'

'Oh.' For a second there, she'd really thought he was going to whip divorce papers out of his jacket. In the most dramatic way possible. 'You didn't have to get me a present.'

'It's Christmas,' Tom said, pained. 'I wasn't *not* going to bring you a present ...'

Cherry didn't say anything.

'Can I ...' Tom asked.

She nodded.

He reached into his coat pocket and took out a long pink velvet jewelry box. It was tied with dark green ribbon. He held it out to her.

Cherry took it. It looked old. She untied the ribbon and pried the hinge open. Inside was an antique charm bracelet with sterling silver Disney charms. Fancy ones, with moving parts. With levers and beads. Snow White holding an enameled red apple. Cinderella's coach with wheels that spun.

Cherry clicked her tongue.

'It's one person's collection,' Tom said. 'I got it at an estate sale, in Pasadena.'

She looked away from the bracelet. 'You've been going to estate sales?'

'Cherry, I'm a red-blooded man in my prime. What do you expect from me?'

She laughed and went back to the bracelet. There was a Dumbo charm with ears that flapped.

'I hated to think of someone selling it for parts,' Tom said. 'I polished it, to the extent that I could.'

'I love it.' Cherry looked up into his eyes. 'I love it.'

Tom smiled a little and glanced away. Pleased.

'I didn't get you anything,' she said.

He lowered his eyebrows. 'You gave me today,' he said softly.

'More like I took it from you,' Cherry whispered. There were tears in her eyes. 'I wanted it.'

Tom met her gaze. His face was serious. The corners of his eyes were very, very tense.

Cherry felt the loss of him so keenly in that moment. As if the final stitch between them was popping. As if he'd been carved out of her for a year, but someone was finally pulling the meat of him away.

The list of ways that Cherry's life would be unrecognizable without Tom was too long for her to fathom. It was an uncountable number. It wasn't just Christmas. It wasn't just sleep and sex. Every night that she wouldn't spend with Tom counted individually – every one was a loss.

Why did she feel so awful? Why now?

Tom had been gone *a year*. Cherry had already passed through several stages of grief. Was this the end? Was the final stage 'exquisite pain'? And if she survived it, would she be free?

Tom shook his head. 'Cherry,' he said, as if her name meant '*no.*' He shook his head again. He looked sad and sorry. 'I . . .'

Cherry should let him off the hook. Send him on his way. She should reach inside her ribs and finish scooping out the last bits of him.

Tom shook his head one more time, and then his head lurched down toward her.

Cherry's head pulled back – reflexively, the way you'd move your head if there was a baseball flying toward your face.

Tom stopped himself.

Cherry stopped herself.

'Sorry,' they said at the same time. All of this happened in a second, and Tom was already pulling away.

Cherry reached up and grabbed the neck of his sweater. His head caught. He looked in her eyes.

'Tom,' Cherry said. It meant '*yes.*' It meant '*Tom.*' It meant '*I'd do anything, anything.*'

Tom lurched again. His hand caught her jaw, beneath her chin, and Cherry's weight nearly gave out. She pictured herself hanging from his grip, her feet swinging.

His mouth hit hers too hard, and she made a noise at the very top of her throat – a sob, maybe. Yes, probably. Her eyes were burning. Her mouth felt wet. She was kissing Tom back clumsily, her jaw was working too hard. She pulled on his sweater. She sobbed again when his arm locked tight around her waist. 'Tom,' she said into his mouth.

Tom moved his other hand from her chin to the back of her head. He was holding her waist so tight that he was doing all the work of holding her up. She was swaying on the balls of her feet.

Tom's mouth was as clumsy as hers. Kissing and kissing. Missing her lips. Humming from his sternum. Cherry was still holding on to the charm bracelet. She wrapped both arms around his neck. If Cherry were magic, she'd grow six more arms to hold him.

He kept kissing her. He kept holding her. Cherry's feet hurt. Her back hurt. Her pussy felt like a hand, grasping. Her heart felt like a wind tunnel. Her head had stopped working.

Tom pulled away and pressed his face into her cheek. 'Tell me what to do, Cherry.'

'Stay,' she breathed out. 'Tom, stay.'

He nodded. His face was still in her cheek. Cherry hugged him as tightly as she could.

Tom started kissing her cheek and neck. He stepped back, toward the stairs, and Cherry stumbled forward – there wasn't enough weight in her feet to walk. Tom loosened his grip and her heels hit the floor. He'd stopped at the bottom of the staircase. His expression was helpless.

Cherry stepped away from him, grabbed one of his hands, and pulled him up the stairs. She led him to their bedroom like he didn't know the way. She was glad she couldn't see his face when she pulled him over the threshold.

The bed wasn't made. Cherry had left her nightshirt lying out. There was a pile of laundry by the door.

Tom started walking more quickly, pushing Cherry, grabbing at her waist. She turned to face him, and he pushed her onto the bed, crawling on top of her, kissing her again. Cherry put her arms around him. She wrapped her legs around him. She was still wearing shoes. His kisses were softer now – he wasn't missing her mouth – but he still seemed desperate. Cherry's hands scrabbled at the back of his sweater. She was holding the jewelry box – she dropped it on the bed. She tried to kick at her heels to take off her shoes, but Tom's whole body was in the way. Tom's heavy body. He was so much thicker than Russ. He was exactly the right size. His skin was exactly the right temperature. She pulled the back of his sweater up, and the back of his shirt. She touched the broad spread of his ribs.

Open. Cherry was wide open to him. He could take what he wanted, even if he never brought it back.

He was holding himself up with his knees and one hand. He was on her. He was kissing her. Cherry was dragging his sweater up over his head.

Tom moved away and pulled his head through the opening of the sweater. He sat up and took his T-shirt off, too. He really had lost weight. He looked different – slightly deflated. Cherry felt herself adjusting to it in real time. Like her eyes were refocusing. Tom was pale. The hair on his chest was darker than the hair on his head. His arms were still thick. His shoulders were still broad. This was still Tom, she still wanted him. He was reaching back to her right foot – he tried to slide the shoe off her heel, but it wouldn't come. He picked the laces open with one hand and pulled it off. The left shoe came off easier.

He crawled onto the bed again, next to Cherry, facing her, pulling her into him. She'd missed her chance to get undressed. They were kissing frantically again, their knees bending between each other's thighs. Tom's hands were on her back. She loved them there. She touched his bare shoulders. She cradled his jaw. She moved her hand up into his hair and groaned. All of those curls. Those *fucking* curls. He'd run away from her and grown out his hair. She fisted both hands in it. She kissed him like a wolf, devouring, a curl wound round every one of her fingers.

Tom shoved her onto her back. He wrenched his mouth away from hers and rubbed his face in her neck. 'Cherry,' he said. She held on to his head. 'Cherry,' he said again.

He kissed her neck. He kissed her throat. He hunched down to kiss her stomach. To push up her sweater and kiss her ribs. She squeezed her eyes closed. She scratched his scalp. He kept pushing up her sweater. Pulling at it. Pulling up her body so he could lift it over her head. She had to let go of his hair. And then he was yanking her jeans down over her hips, taking her lace underwear with them. Without ceremony. (They'd already had the ceremony. They'd exchanged rings.) He kissed her hip. His cheek in her belly. *'Cherry.'*

She was still wearing a red plaid bra.

She was still wearing pink fishnet knee-highs. One of them was sliding down her calf.

'Tom,' she said.

Tom reared up to take off his own pants. To take off his socks. She watched him. He'd lost some weight, but he moved the same. He loomed the same. He looked at her with that same dumbstruck hunger.

Maybe Tom looked that way no matter who he was mounting. Like he wanted it so bad, he couldn't think. Like he wanted it so bad, he'd let go of all his insecurities and inhibitions.

She reached up to him, grasping at air, spreading her legs. Skipping ahead to the part she wanted.

Tom groaned and crawled over her again. Cherry closed her arms around him, kissing what she could reach – first his shoulder, then his neck. Feeling their skin come together, warm everywhere and mostly naked. Feasting her hands on him. (She'd looked at him once and decided to keep him. She'd been his first, and he'd been her only. If something happened to Cherry today, tomorrow, all her worldly possessions would automatically be his.)

Tom held her by the chin – by the throat, the way he liked to – a thumb in her cheek and finger at her jaw. He kissed her less frantically but with no less intent. His body was everywhere, as far as Cherry could stretch. As far as she could reach. She moaned and whimpered beneath him, in a state of constant assent.

Tom pulled away – just enough to reach for the drawer where they'd kept condoms.

Cherry caught his arm. 'It's okay,' she said. 'I'm not . . .'

He looked back at her, confused – then hungry again. His mouth was hanging open. His bottom lip was wet. He kissed her. 'You're not . . . ?'

'Ovulating,' she whispered. She pulled on his arm. 'It's okay.'

Tom was slow to give in. His hand was still reaching for the drawer. He was studying her face. Cherry arched her neck, baring it. Tom went for her throat. She hugged him. She did the math in her head. She was *very probably* not ovulating. (She needed to feel his skin. She needed to feel his come. She needed every part of this. Was parched for it.) (Cherry wasn't always strong.) (Or good.) She closed her eyes while he kissed her.

Tom pushed into her without any more discussion. They didn't talk during sex. They didn't talk *enough*, generally speaking – Cherry knew that. She knew it was a problem. Maybe even a red flag. (Probably their downfall.) But she didn't think she could *change* it. She certainly couldn't change it now, in this moment, at this late hour in their marriage, this early hour in their divorce.

Whenever Cherry and Tom made love, she didn't want to say anything that would slow them down or change the mood. She didn't want him to feel bad about not talking. Or ashamed. Cherry never wanted Tom to have *even a moment* of shame when he was naked in bed with her. She wanted him to feel like he was gorgeous and good.

He was gorgeous and good.

He watched her, always. He was watching her now, as he pulled his hips back and pushed into her again, his eyelids heavy.

Cherry's legs were spread, her knees were up. She felt a little faint from how right this was. How correct. Tom in her body, in her bed, in her house, in her city. Tom at the center of her world.

He lifted up to push deeper, to hold on to her hips. He watched her face. He watched his cock move in and out of her. (Cherry couldn't see it, but she knew it was thick.) 'Cherry,' he said. 'Baby, baby. My baby.'

Cherry nodded. She reached for him, but her fingertips could only brush his chest. He leaned forward to kiss her fingers. To let her cup his cheek. He held her hand to his face and kissed her palm again and again. 'Tom,' she said.

Sex with Tom could go on and on...

It didn't follow Freytag's Pyramid of rising action/climax/denouement. Maybe it had, in the beginning, when he was still figuring it out... (When they were figuring it out, together.)

But it had evolved into something less predictable over the years. He might fuck Cherry for a while and watch her come, then turn her over and fuck her some more, then take a break to touch her, to lick her, to let her come again. She couldn't predict how he'd finish. Tom seemed to like her every which way. Sometimes he *wouldn't* finish – he'd sort of fuck her past his ability to come, like he didn't want to stop as long as she was hungry for more. And then he'd fall asleep half hard. He might wake her up again in the middle of the night, asking with his hips and hands to be let back in. (You could see why she didn't beg for more conversation.) (With a man who never made her beg.)

But tonight Tom was already gritting his teeth, like he was on the edge. Cherry nodded up at him.

He pushed his hand between their bellies – it was always awkward like this – reaching for her clit, giving her two knuckles to rub into. Cherry would take it. She didn't need much. She'd already started to clench inside.

She came in a thundering way. Seizing up from her toes and fingertips. Tom wedged his hips deeper, to take it. He closed his eyes and shook his head. He said her name. He twisted his hand to rub her more directly.

The second orgasm came up from Cherry's stomach. Through her chest. Hung out in her throat and hitched. Cherry sobbed.

'Cherry?' Tom asked. Square-faced. Angel-haired. Sweating.

'Don't stop,' she said through tears.

'Baby...'

'Please don't stop.' She was coming again. Or still. 'Tom, Tom...'

Tom pulled his hand free when she went limp. He lifted himself up again and held her by the hip and the back of her thigh. He was half on his knees.

Cherry was still crying. 'Don't stop,' she chanted. 'I love you, don't stop.'

Tom came with a long groan. With his eyes closed and his mouth open.

After a few panting breaths, he slumped forward, with his head on Cherry's chest. She brought a hand up to his hair.

He kissed the top of her breast. 'My baby.'

Chapter 53

He'd never named the character 'Baby.'
That's just what The Guy called her, in the comic strip.

Chapter 54

Tom didn't try to leave, thank god.

He went to the bathroom and came back wearing his briefs and holding a hot washcloth. Cherry had gotten under the blankets. Tom crawled in next to her and pressed the cloth between her legs. He knew she liked it.

She was still crying, a little. She wasn't sure how she was ever expected to stop. Tom kissed her forehead. He looked rattled, too.

He held the cloth between her legs until it started to cool, then gently wiped the inside of her thighs. He dropped the cloth onto the floor and settled on his back, so that Cherry could rest her head on his chest. (He knew she wanted to.)

She closed her eyes and laid her hand on his stomach.

After a few minutes, Tom unclasped her bra – it took two hands – and then gently scratched under the strap, where it always itched.

'You still want me to stay?' he whispered.

She wrapped her arm around his middle and nodded her head. She felt him relax.

His hand drifted down her back. Less scratching. More rubbing. Cherry whimpered.

'Does your back still hurt?' he asked.

She nodded.

Tom pressed his fingers into the muscles under her ribs and along her spine. 'Why'd you wear those shoes all day?'

She groaned. 'I was trying to seduce you.'

Tom laughed. It made Cherry's body bounce. 'Oh, baby,' he said softly, 'I'm in the bag. No one in the world has ever needed less seducing.'

Chapter 55

They slept like spoons facing one way.

And then Cherry rolled over, and Tom rolled over, and they slept like spoons facing the other way.

They slept with their arms draped over each other. With their knees and ankles crossing.

Even during the months when things had gone very cold and quiet between them, they'd find each other in the middle of the night and nest in each other's bodies.

Tonight they didn't leave space between them for even a stray thought.

Cherry fell asleep thinking that the bed must be so happy to have Tom here. That the whole house must be holding them. That Stevie would defend them from any threat. Cherry alone didn't satisfy Stevie's shepherding instincts. But she and Tom were a flock. A family.

Chapter 56

Cherry woke up alone.

The down comforter was pulled up and tucked around her.

She lay quiet, listening for sounds downstairs or in the bathroom...

Nothing.

She sat up, looking around for some sign that she hadn't slept here alone...

There wasn't any. Tom's clothes weren't lying on the floor. There was no wet washcloth.

A desolate feeling settled in the pit of Cherry's stomach. A loneliness without borders.

Then she heard the front door open.

And Tom's hushed voice.

Stevie running back and forth.

She heard the baby gate clicking open, then closed.

And Tom on the stairs.

How many times in the last twenty-four hours had Cherry wished for time to stop? She wanted to be stuck in this moment, like a fly in amber – naked in bed, with Tom climbing the stairs.

He got to their room. He was wearing his coat and hat, and holding coffee. 'You aren't supposed to be awake.'

Cherry clenched the blanket in front of her chest. 'Where'd you go?'

He sat down on the bed. 'Stevie was at the bottom of the stairs, whining – I think she thought she was being punished. I took her for a walk, so she wouldn't wake you up.' He frowned at Cherry's face. She must still look hurt. 'I'm sorry,' he said softly. He held up the cup. 'I brought you a latte.'

Cherry took it. She smiled.

'And,' Tom said, reaching into a bag she hadn't noticed, 'something called a Christmas scone.'

'What's a Christmas scone?'

'I don't know. The girl at the bakery said it has ham, orange glaze and Madagascan cloves.'

Cherry was taking a sip of her latte. She raised her eyebrows. '*Well.*'

'I know,' he said. 'Our neighborhood has gotten very bougie. There's almost nowhere left to buy vapes.'

She laughed.

Tom reached into the bag. 'I also got an egg wrap with spinach and feta.'

'Like Starbucks.'

'Like Starbucks,' he said, 'but make it bougie.' He held up both paper-wrapped parcels. 'Your choice.'

'I kind of want both.'

'You can have both.'

Cherry just smiled at him. She'd been trying to pretend that everything was normal ... that Tom had gotten up early to walk Stevie and get breakfast, and now he was home, and he was just *home*. But her eyes were getting glossy.

Tom watched her face. He wrinkled his forehead. 'Hi,' he whispered.

'Hi,' Cherry said.

He kissed her cheek, and she closed her eyes. 'Hi,' Tom said in a softer whisper.

'Hi,' Cherry breathed out.

'Can I come back to bed?'

She nodded. 'Yeah.'

Tom stood up and took off his pants. (He'd put on yesterday's clothes, even though there was a dresser full of clean clothes a few feet away.) He left on his T-shirt and underwear, and climbed back under the covers. 'You can drink your coffee,' he said, 'but come here.' He put his arm around her shoulders.

Cherry leaned against him, taking sips of the latte. Tom unwrapped the scone with one hand and broke off a piece for her. She took it. She glanced up at him, and smiled when he smiled.

'You grew out your hair,' she said.

'I didn't want to find a new barber. And every time I did a TV interview, the hair person would tell me my hair was too short ...' He frowned at her. 'Do you hate it?'

'No. You look like the guy from *The Bear*.'

Tom snorted. 'I look more like *a* bear.'

Cherry laughed. He handed her another chunk of scone. It was delicious. 'I like it,' she said, tilting her chin up at him. 'You look nice.'

'"*Nice*,"' Tom said, like it was a dubious compliment.

She pushed her bare shoulder into his chest. 'I liked it before,' she said, 'but I like it now, too.'

Tom picked up the egg wrap and took his arm back so he could peel off the paper with both hands. 'Well, thanks. Here – try this.'

Cherry was still holding the comforter in front of her chest, clamped in her armpits and under her elbows. Still holding the coffee. Tom held the egg wrap up to her, and she leaned in to take a bite. He took a bite, too.

'Not bad,' Cherry said.

'Better than Starbucks,' he said with his mouth full, 'but not *enough* better, you know?'

She nodded. Tom was making her laugh. He was in a good mood. 'I'm glad you're here,' she whispered.

He looked over at her. At her face. In her eyes. 'I'm glad I'm here, too.'

Cherry swallowed.

Tom leaned in to kiss her. He leaned in slowly – she had plenty of time to get away. Cherry lifted up her chin.

It was much gentler than anything they'd tried last night. She smiled.

He moved his head to kiss her from the other angle. She smiled even bigger.

Tom put his hand on her coffee cup, to take it away. Cherry held on to it. She broke the kiss – 'One more drink.'

She took another gulp of latte, then handed it to him. He took a swig, too, before setting it on the table. Then he turned back to Cherry with both arms. She let go of the blanket. Tom got his hands on her and sighed. She kissed him.

'You're still warm,' he said, dragging her down onto the pillows. She went.

'It was so hard not waking you up . . .' he said in a hushed voice. 'I had to leave the building.'

'You could have woken me up.'

'I didn't want you to tell me to go,' he said even more quietly.

Cherry kissed him – because nothing she was thinking could be said out loud. *'I would never tell you to go'* was a lie. *'I never want you to go'* was too true. She didn't want to say anything that would cast them too far into their past or their future. She didn't want Tom to wake up.

'So warm,' Tom said between kisses. He was rubbing her back, her hips, her bottom. He pulled her knee over his hip. With her leg open, Cherry smelled like last night's sex. She knew it wouldn't bother him. She knew that almost nothing like this did.

He reached up between her thighs to touch. 'Are you still wet, or are you wet again?'

She shook her head. 'I don't know.'

Tom pushed his fingers deeper into her. She closed her eyes. He was pushing. Exploring. It felt good. *Good.*

'Wait,' she said. 'Let me go to the bathroom first.'

'Yeah.' He was already breathing heavy. 'Okay.'

Cherry pulled away and sat on the edge of the bed. Tom's hands followed her. She stood up, unsteady at first, and his hands kept following her. She looked over her shoulder. Tom had sat up, too. She took a step away from him.

'Wait, wait, wait,' he said. 'Turn around.'

Cherry did.

Her hair was hanging over both her shoulders, skirting the tops of her breasts. She was naked, mostly – she was still wearing one pink fishnet knee-high.

Tom was motioning for her to come closer.

She took a step toward him.

'Sorry.' His voice had dropped. 'Come back.'

'Tom.'

'Come back.' He had her hands. She let him pull her closer and push her down, so he could climb on top of her. 'You look totally debauched, Cherry.'

'I feel totally debauched.'

He licked her chest. 'You're covered in crumbs.' He licked her again. He rubbed his face between her breasts. His hand was between her legs again. Questing.

She inhaled. 'Tom, I have to pee.'

'That's fine,' he said, pressing his fingers in.

She laughed – it turned into a whine. She *did* have to pee. It felt good like this, and he knew it.

'Touch yourself,' he said, *pressing*.

'Tom . . .'

He pulled away long enough to take off his T-shirt – then bunched it up and shoved it under her bottom. 'There.'

Cherry laughed genuinely, bringing the backs of her hands to fall over her eyes.

'Touch yourself,' Tom said, pushing his fingers into her again.

She reached down and touched.

Tom reached inside and pressed. He watched.

Cherry worked herself over. It was almost immediately too much – she was afraid to come. '*Tom.* I'm going to leak.'

'Cherry, you're so wet, I won't notice.'

She laughed again.

He hooked his fingers. 'Come on, baby.'

She gave in – she let herself fall over the edge. It was disturbingly easy. And felt so good. She did it again. She knew that Tom was watching, even with her eyes closed. Her orgasms felt sharp and dangerous. Overlapping. She cried out. Stevie barked at the bottom of the stairs. Cherry laughed.

'More,' Tom said.

'No more,' Cherry said. She planted her foot on his chest.

He drew his hand away, then leaned over to kiss the inside of her thigh.

Cherry was boneless. Tom gently turned her onto her side and lay down behind her. His hand slid into her again, from behind. She sighed and hitched up her knee. Tom pushed his cock in. He wasn't pressing on her bladder like this. And he was being very gentle. It still felt good. He held on to her hip. It didn't take long.

Neither of them moved when he was done.

'Did I leak?' Cherry whispered.

Tom felt between her legs. 'I don't think so . . . Maybe next time.'

She pushed her elbow back into his chest. He was laughing.

Cherry sat up, away from him, and stood up. 'I might take a shower.'

'Don't take a shower. Come back and be filthy with me awhile longer.'

He looked so happy, she couldn't say no.

But then, once she was in the bathroom, Cherry felt so disgusting that she couldn't *not* get in the shower. She rinsed off quickly. She didn't wash her hair.

When she came back, Tom was lying under the comforter, on his side – and on his side of the bed. He looked perfect like that. The room looked perfect with him in it.

She got under the covers again, lying on her side, facing him.

He wasn't smiling anymore.

'Oh no,' Cherry said. 'Did I give you too much time to think?'

Tom smiled and looked down at the mattress between them. 'Maybe.'

She exhaled. Bracing.

'Cherry . . .' he said. 'I know you're seeing someone.'

'No,' she said, surprised. '*No.* Tom, I'm not.'

He looked up at her, even more surprised. 'But you said you were.'

'I was,' she said. 'I'm not anymore.'

'Oh . . .' he said, processing.

Cherry was processing, too. 'Wait, you thought I was seeing someone? And that didn't give you pause? Last night?'

'It gave me *pause* . . .' he said. 'Not a long pause.'

'Really?'

'You're my *wife*,' Tom said. Half fierce. Half indignant.

Cherry huffed out a laugh. She tried to be offended by it all. She couldn't. She *was* his wife. She had been, all along.

(And that wasn't to say that she agreed with her sisters. Or that she felt guilty about Russ, or believed that she'd done something wrong. It was just to say – she'd never stopped wanting to be married to Tom.)

'You're my wife . . .' Tom said, more brokenly.

Cherry nodded.

'Cherry, I want to come home.'

Chapter 57

'Go to Los Angeles,' Cherry had told Tom. 'Stevie and I will be fine.'

They weren't fine.

Stevie was getting too big to manage, and she didn't listen to Cherry.

'*She will,*' Tom texted. '*She just sees you as her litter mate right now.*'

'Her *litter* mate?'

'*She thinks I'm the pack leader . . . which speaks to her limited cognitive ability.*'

Tom said that Cherry should read one of the books he'd bought on dog training. Cherry didn't *want* to read a book about dog training. She didn't want to train a *dog*.

Stevie had been good for Tom. Indisputably. It was like someone had turned on a small light in his everyday darkness.

But even that got under Cherry's skin – the way Tom walked around dead-faced and sullen, and only came alive for this giant lunkheaded puppy.

Tom was in California for so long, he rented an Airbnb. It wasn't just the movie keeping him away. He was promoting a *Thursday* omnibus. (Called *Every Thursday*.) And he'd launched a streetwear collaboration with Supreme. (Cherry was the one who told him to say yes. Tom told *Hypebeast* that he '*wouldn't wear any of this stuff.*' They loved it.)

His publisher flew his publicist to L.A. to make sure Tom took phone interviews and showed up for photo shoots. Rachel, again. Tom liked her. Probably because she bossed him around and made all his decisions for him. If Cherry asked him what he was having for lunch, he'd say, 'Whatever Rachel orders.'

Tom had been in Los Angeles for three months when he told Cherry he'd signed a first-look deal with HBO because Rachel thought it was a good idea.

'Isn't Rachel your *book* publicist?'

'She's kind of my everything publicist.'

'I'm his consigliere,' Rachel said in the background.

Cherry hadn't known she was there.

Cherry was very good at her job.

It was the sort of job that would take as much as she gave it. Cherry was never *done* with work – she never had to be. There was always something else to propose or review. (Once you'd successfully proposed something, you could then review it.) She spent her days in meetings, selling ideas, then smoothing their progress through the bureaucracy. At night she replied to emails, scheduling them all to send the next morning, so she wouldn't look like she was working as late as she was.

Everything Cherry worked on at the railroad was an 'initiative.' She liked the sound of that. She liked the urgency.

'I can't right now,' she'd said to Tom once, when he wanted her to go ... *somewhere* ... with him. On some *Thursday*-related trip. 'I've got too much on my plate.'

'You don't have anything on your plate that you didn't put there,' Tom argued.

Cherry failed to see his point. Didn't he recognize what a beautiful situation she was in? *She didn't have anything on her plate that she hadn't put there.* And neither did he!

After a while, Cherry got used to being alone with Stevie. She stopped sending Tom frustrated text messages about it. When he was delayed, when he apologized, when he was miserable and caught up and *still* not coming home – Cherry would say, 'It's okay.

Do what you have to do.' And, 'We'll be here.' ('We' because Cherry was a 'we' now with this stupid dog.)

But Cherry didn't *feel* okay . . .

She was lonely. She was resentful. She felt like she'd given Tom everything, and he'd taken it, and then he'd taken it somewhere else.

The less she saw of him, the more she seemed to see of *Thursday*.

Tom's comic was everywhere. It was 'having a moment.'

'*Is Tom Valentine our Charlie Chaplin?*' asked *The Atlantic*. And the *New York Times* wanted to know, '*Is Anything Better Than "Thursday"?*'

Rachel was earning her keep.

'Cherry?'

Tom had called without texting first. He almost never called. (He almost never texted.) '*I'd rather just get through it and come home,*' he'd told her once, when he first started traveling.

'Tom?'

'Hey, can you hear me?'

'I can hear you – is everything okay?' Cherry was walking Stevie. It was already dark.

'What?'

'Tom? Were you in an accident?'

'What – No. No, I'm fine.'

'Oh,' Cherry said, waiting for her heartbeat to slow down. 'Good.'

'I was calling . . .'

She waited. 'Stevie, no,' she said. '*No!*' Their neighbors had a row of winter-dead peonies, and Stevie always tried to dig them up. '*Stop it* . . . Tom? Are you still there?'

'I'm here. I was calling . . . Cherry, why don't you come to L.A. for the weekend? I could show you . . . I don't know. Around.'

'This weekend?'

'Yeah.'

'I can't come this weekend. I've got the shareholder meeting.'

'That's this weekend?'

'Yeah.'

'You've probably got everything ready for it.'

'Well, I have to be on hand anyway.'

'Cherry, come.'

'Why do you need me *this* weekend? Is something happening?' It wasn't their anniversary. Or anyone's birthday. Tom had already missed her birthday.

'No,' he said. 'I just ... miss you.'

'Well, I miss you, too,' Cherry said. It came out defensive. 'I could come ... not next weekend, but maybe next month. Or *you* could home this weekend.' That came out as a challenge.

'I'm supposed to meet some actor ...' Tom said weakly. 'Maybe you could come meet him, too.'

'I've never missed the shareholder meeting,' she said.

'I know.'

'And what would I do with Stevie?'

'You could board her.'

'We've never boarded her. I don't know how she'd do.'

'Only one way to find out.'

'Tom, why are you being like this?' Cherry swung her arm out in frustration. She was holding a bag of shit.

'I don't know,' he said. 'I just thought maybe ... you would come.'

'When you leave,' she said sternly, 'my life keeps going.'

'I know that,' he said. 'I'm sorry.'

'Well, I'm sorry, too,' Cherry said. She didn't sound sorry.

The shareholder meeting went smoothly. And everyone complimented Meg Jones, who graciously gave Cherry most of the credit. Cherry had overseen the signage, the presentation, the music, the venue. She'd approved everything that was served. She'd named the signature cocktail and staged a photo op with a vintage 'Big Fella' locomotive.

It wasn't important work.

But it was *adjacent* to important work.

And Cherry was good at it. She was so *good* at it.

She could probably leave Western Alliance if she wanted. She could be a VP somewhere. If she stayed, she might get Meg Jones's job – Meg had practically said so. Cherry wasn't sure she'd want to move even further away from the creative work . . . Tom would say that what Cherry was doing now was creative work – that making something look and feel great was still *making* something.

She missed Tom. Sincerely.

She was feeling guilty about their phone call. They hadn't talked since. Which wouldn't be that unusual, in a normal week . . . but Cherry didn't like that that spiky conversation was their last interaction.

She got home late from the shareholder meeting, around one a.m. She'd walked Stevie at five, but the dog still acted like she'd been alone for weeks when Cherry walked in.

Cherry took off her fancy, low-heeled boots and went to sit on the couch, still wearing a Western Alliance–red cocktail dress and nude hose.

Stevie brought Cherry an indestructible nylon boomerang, and Cherry played at trying to take it from her.

It was only eleven o'clock in Los Angeles. Tom would probably still be up.

She picked up her phone and pressed his name. *Tom (Emergency Contact)*. At the last second, she decided to make it a video call. Her makeup still looked nice. Her dress showed off her shoulders. She'd had her hair professionally blown out. She and Tom almost never video-called – she'd apologize. She'd look in his eyes. She'd remind herself that she loved him, and hopefully vice versa.

It rang a few times.

Cherry figured Tom wasn't going to pick up . . .

But then he *did* pick up. As if it was a phone call. He held his phone to his face.

Cherry laughed. 'Tom, I'm here. I FaceTimed you.'

'What?' He pulled the phone back and saw her. 'I didn't know you were FaceTiming me.'

'Sorry. I should have texted.'

'No,' he said. 'You don't have to text.' Tom looked . . . off. Maybe he was tired. His hair was longer than usual. And messier. And his face looked flushed. Maybe he'd been in the sun. It was California – he was probably always in the sun.

He seemed agitated.

'Are you . . .' She wasn't sure what to ask.

'The shareholder meeting was today,' he said, like he was just remembering. 'How'd it go?' Tom's eyes cut away from the phone, past the phone, like he was watching television. But she couldn't hear the television. He nodded. Minutely. (This all happened in a second.)

'Is someone there?' Cherry asked.

Tom looked at the phone again. He hesitated. 'Rachel,' he said. 'She was just saying good-bye.'

'Hi, Cherry,' Rachel said in the background.

Maybe . . .

Maybe Cherry would have let it go. On another night.

Tom worked all the time. Tom took late flights. Tom went to awards ceremonies. And charity events. Rachel went with him. There was always a good reason for her to be there.

Maybe.

If Cherry hadn't seen Tom's face.

If Tom hadn't looked terrified.

She hung up on him.

Her hands were shaking. She couldn't catch her breath.

Cherry ignored the next three phone calls.

She climbed into her bed, still dressed.

She finally picked up an hour later. It was two o'clock in Omaha. Midnight in Los Angeles.

She was incoherent with rage.

Tom was incoherent with fear.

She didn't know exactly why she was angry yet, and he struggled to tell her.

Tom said he was sorry.

Cherry said she didn't want to hear it.

All she wanted were the details. Not even the details – the headline. '*Summarize it for me,*' she'd say to one of her direct reports. '*Lead with the red meat.*'

'Tell me that you're having an affair,' she said.

'I'm not having an affair,' Tom said.

But he was, and he had been, and she already *knew*. That he was closer to Rachel than he was to Cherry. That they ate together and traveled together. That Rachel knew where his head was at. That he texted Rachel when he was with Cherry – but he didn't text Cherry when he was with Rachel.

It was about work. Always.

It was all about work.

But work was Tom's whole life.

Rachel had made several appearances in *Thursday*.

Tom said that nothing had happened. And that it had only happened once. He said that Rachel had kissed him.

Cherry wasn't fooled by the passive voice.

She'd kissed Tom once, too, and look how that turned out.

Cherry told Tom that night, that early morning, not to come home.

(What was there to come home to? His life was everywhere else. His heart was so detached from hers that he'd handed it to a twenty-eight-year-old in a denim jumpsuit.)

When he tried to argue, she told him not to *dare*.

'I don't want you to come home,' she said. 'I don't want to see your face.'

She wouldn't take his calls after that. She ignored his texts.

She was *consistent*.

Cherry would have made a great parent; she held the line. Her yes meant yes, and her no meant no.

After three weeks? Tom stopped trying.

He stopped trying.

He was probably on some deadline. He probably had meetings. He was probably jet-lagged.

He was probably sitting in first class with Rachel, planning his next book.

Rachel, Cherry had often thought, looked like the sort of girl a famous artist would be married to. Sexy. Skinny. Interesting. The kind of hot girl who dated fat indie rockers and homely comedians who eventually won the Mark Twain Prize.

Rachel was a trophy.

Cherry was just barely a first wife.

Tom stopped calling after three weeks.

A month later, Cherry told him she wanted a divorce.

Chapter 58

They were lying in bed. They both smelled like sweat and sex. Their hair still smelled like gingerbread.

And Tom wanted to come home.

And Cherry wanted him to come home.

Cherry wanted Tom back more than she'd ever wanted to marry him in the first place. Because now she knew what it was like to have him, and what it was like to lose him.

Cherry loved Tom like a wild beast. Like a hurricane. She loved him boundlessly.

'It's not that easy,' she said.

'Why not?' he whispered. 'It feels so easy, Cherry.'

They were naked. They weren't touching.

'Because you left,' she said.

Tom looked genuinely confused. 'I never left.'

'You *left*,' she said again.

He lowered his eyebrows. Still at sea. 'You told me not to come home.'

'You were long gone by then.'

He shook his head. 'What are you talking about?' He was still whispering. If they whispered, it wasn't a fight. It was barely a conversation.

'I'm talking about how you checked out,' Cherry said. 'And left me here with our entire life. You moved on.'

'I didn't move on,' Tom said, raising his voice an inch. 'I went away for work, and you told me I couldn't come home.'

'There was nothing stopping you from coming home,' Cherry said clearly.

'*You* were stopping me. You literally told me that I couldn't.'

She sat up, away from him. She took the comforter. 'You're a grown man.'

Tom sat up, too. 'Cherry, you wouldn't even talk to me.'

'Because you were with someone else!'

'I was never with her!'

'You were *literally* with her.'

He winced. 'Okay.' His voice dropped. 'I know. I'm sorry – please listen to me.'

'I still don't want to hear your apologies.'

'You don't want to hear me at all.'

'Because there's nothing you can say to make it all right!'

'Will you please just *talk* to me?'

'Talk?' she said incredulously. 'You don't talk, Tom. You sulk. You draw. You go away.'

'That's not fair.'

'*Fair?*' Cherry was shouting.

'We've been together for eleven years!' he shouted back. 'And you cut me off like I was nothing to you! Like our marriage was nothing to you!'

'That's not true.'

'It *is* true. You wouldn't let me explain or apologize – or beg you to forgive me.'

'You didn't beg me for anything!'

'How could I?' Tom yelled. He'd gotten out of bed. Cherry wouldn't look at him – she could hear him getting dressed. 'You wouldn't take my calls!'

Cherry still didn't look up. She shouted at the floor between them. 'You gave up so easily, Tom! Like *I* was nothing. I wanted you to fight for me!'

Tom laughed, like she was being ridiculous. (Like he hated her.

Like he was giving up again.) 'Jesus, Cherry,' he said softly. 'When have I ever fought you and won?'

Cherry sat at the edge of the bed.

Tom was standing across the room, fuming. Breathing heavy. She could hear him. She still hadn't looked up.

'This was a mistake,' Cherry said. 'I want you to leave.'

Tom walked past her. She saw him scoop up his shirt in her peripheral vision. 'Whatever you say.'

She heard him go – he slammed the front door.

He'd left the baby gate open. A few minutes later, Stevie shuffled into the bedroom to nose at Cherry's knees.

'I know,' Cherry said as Stevie sniffed and pushed at her. 'I know.'

Chapter 59

In the eighth grade, Evan Mackie had asked Cherry to go to the Can Dance with him. (To get into the dance, you had to bring a can of food for the food bank. Evan had brought two cans of green beans to cover them both.)

At the dance – at four o'clock in the afternoon, in the school gym – some of the boys had called Evan over, and they'd all stood in a huddle while Cherry waited for him by the bleachers.

Then Evan had walked back to Cherry, while the boys all watched.

'So, yeah,' he said, avoiding her eyes. 'I kinda need to break up with you.'

They weren't dating – though going to the dance together did imply that they were *something*.

'So . . . yeah,' he said, walking away.

When Evan got back to the boys, they all laughed. And Evan laughed. Though he wouldn't make eye contact with them, either.

Evan stayed with the same group for the rest of the dance. Cherry's own friends circled her, outraged on her behalf.

One of them – Leslie – went to talk to her boyfriend, who was in the boy huddle, and he told her that the guys didn't pressure Evan to do it or anything. 'Some of them were just giving Evan shit for being a' – Leslie mouthed the next word – '*whaler.*'

'A what?' Cherry asked.

'It's what they call boys who like plus-size girls,' Leslie said. 'They're so stupid.'

'You're not even plus-sized, Cherry,' another girl said.

'Yes, I am,' Cherry said. It was the eighth grade; she was a size sixteen.

'Well, you're not *fat*.'

Nobody had said she was fat. Explicitly.

'I don't even like Evan,' Cherry said. It was true, though no one would believe that now.

Cherry didn't even think Evan was *cute*. But she'd thought he was nice enough. They sat together in science. (They still would, after this.) Cherry had said yes to Evan because she'd wanted to come to this dance, and because she'd wanted *some* boy to like her.

Evan didn't hang out with the popular boys, usually. He got to hang out with them that day because of what he'd done to Cherry.

Evan was gay.

That was obvious, in retrospect. He was married now. He lived in Colorado.

Cherry still hadn't forgiven him.

Chapter 60

When Cherry was a sophomore at Creighton, she'd had a crush on one of the other art students.

His name was Cam, and he was a few years older than her. He was from Hawaii and studying ceramics.

Cam was so nice to Cherry...

Like, he always sat by her in class. And was always offering to help her or give her advice. If he saw her in the student center, he'd drop down onto the couch next to her. Sometimes he'd stay there for hours.

He always seemed to be making excuses to touch Cherry's hands.

She liked him.

He was handsome. (She thought he was handsome.)

He licked his bottom lip when she talked.

Cherry spent a whole semester feeling like she didn't know the secret word that would make Cam step fully into her reach.

It was confusing.

And upsetting.

Humiliating in a way that was familiar and that she couldn't put words to.

She was only nineteen, and she'd known several Cams.

Chapter 61

The best thing about Cherry's college boyfriend was that, once he'd decided to like her, he'd done so with his whole heart and his whole dick.

It had been a real mess in the end...

But at least she knew that he'd wanted her.

Chapter 62

When Cherry stripped the bed, she found the charm bracelet shoved between the mattress and the headboard. And she found the half-eaten spinach egg wrap in a paper envelope on the floor.

Tom had left one of his notebooks open on the bedside table – he'd been doodling while she was in the shower.

He'd drawn Cherry standing naked by the bed, wearing one stocking with little cross-hatched fishnet. Knee dimples. Belly lines. Round nipples. He always took time on her hair, the way it parted over her eyes and fell around her shoulders . . .

There were a hundred drawings like this. In notebooks all over the house.

Cherry could probably sell them on eBay.

Baby Revealed.

Baby Undone.

Chapter 63

'Are you feeling okay?' Cherry's mom was frowning at her.

'I'm feeling fine. Are you gonna let me in?'

Her mom stepped out of the way and let Cherry into the house. 'I thought this was Hope's Friday.'

'I had the day off,' Cherry said, 'so I seized it. Are you disappointed? You want me to call Hope?'

'Oh, you.' She pinched Cherry's arm.

Cherry and her sisters took turns running errands with their mom on Fridays. Faith made the schedule. Cherry got the fewest shifts because her hours were the least flexible, but she tried to make up for that when she could.

Their mom *could* drive herself around, but their dad always had the car. And it was always better if one of the girls went along on her doctors' appointments; their mom was a selective listener, in every scenario.

Cherry flopped down on the couch. Her parents still lived in the same three-bedroom house she'd grown up in. It had always been run-down, but it was getting truly dilapidated now. Her dad didn't even pretend to work on it.

The house was still comfortable. Cherry's mom had a way of making things comfortable. She sewed and crocheted. The couch was draped in a homemade quilt. The throw pillows had needlepoint covers with yarn tassels. Cherry had made a few of these pillows when she was eleven or twelve. She'd loved a yarn tassel in middle school.

Her mom was frowning down at her, with both hands on her hips. 'Are you sure you're feeling okay?'

'Mom, I'm fine. I'm just not wearing makeup.' Cherry wasn't wearing makeup, and she hadn't run a flat iron through her bangs to make them lie just so, and she was wearing old yoga pants that she'd had since college.

Her mom tutted and headed for the kitchen. 'You girls are so beautiful, you don't need makeup.'

'Apparently *I* do.'

'Are you hungry, Cherry?'

'Not really.'

Her mom was back in the kitchen, leaning over the stove. 'I've got some fried rice, with beans, and I made homemade tortillas.'

'Why'd you make tortillas?'

'Your dad felt like them last night.'

Cherry's mom was a great cook. She could replicate any recipe once she'd watched someone else make it. She liked to stand behind people in their kitchens while they cooked. YouTube had been a game changer for her.

'I'll have some,' Cherry said. 'I can get it.'

'No, I'll get it. You relax. You look tired.'

'I swear to god, Mom – I'm just not wearing mascara.'

'Oh, you don't need mascara.'

Cherry pulled a throw pillow into her lap and sank back into the sofa. 'Where do you need to go today?'

'Just to Hy-Vee.' That was the grocery store. 'And Kohll's.' The drugstore. 'And I need to pick up a zipper at Walmart – I'm making Ella a dress for the dance. Honny can't find anything cute in her size.'

It was a real shame that her mom hadn't found someone to marry other than Cherry's dad. She had so much to offer. She cooked. She sewed. She cranked out babies and didn't seem to suffer for it. (Though she'd never cranked out a son.) She was fat, but she was still pretty. Cherry wouldn't mind if she ended up looking like her mom at sixty-five.

Her mom had never had a chance with other guys; she'd met Cherry's dad right out of high school. Had he known then that she'd make the perfect wife for a philandering alcoholic? Cherry's mom ignored everything that she possibly could, and forgave everything that she couldn't.

Cherry wouldn't be surprised to hear that her mom had never once talked to her dad about his drinking, or asked him to change a single thing about his behavior. Her job was to accommodate him and make him comfortable.

Cherry could see those behaviors in herself, and she hated them. (Even though she *did* want to accommodate Tom. And she *didn't* want him to be uncomfortable.)

Her mom brought out a dinner plate heaped with fried rice and beans, chicken with peppers, and two flour tortillas yellow with butter. *It's no wonder I'm fat,* Cherry thought for the ten-thousandth time. (Though she hadn't gotten any *less* fat since she'd moved out of her parents' house and started eating salads every day for lunch.)

Her mom made a plate for herself, too. She was just sitting down in her easy chair when the front door opened. Cherry braced herself for whatever energy her dad was about to bring into the house.

But it wasn't her dad – it was Hope.

Hope looked confused when she saw Cherry. 'Hey, Cherry ... no work today?'

'I've got the day off, so I'm chauffeuring Mom.'

'Why didn't you tell me?'

'I sent a note on the group thread.' As soon as she said it, Cherry realized that she'd sent the note on the *wrong* group thread.

Hope realized it, too. She clenched her jaw.

'I must have forgotten,' Cherry said. 'Sorry. You can go home –'

'No, you cannot!' their mom objected. 'I get two of my girls this

Friday. What a treat! Hopey, do you want some fried rice? I made tortillas . . .'

Hope stood by the couch. 'No, thank you.'

'You take my plate.' Their mom got up and pushed the food at her. 'I know you're watching your carbs, but . . .'

Hope took the plate. She didn't have a choice.

Cherry set her fork down. There was no way she could sit next to Hope and eat a plate full of actual food.

Hope was wearing jeans today. With a cropped sweater. Everything she wore lately seemed to show off her waist.

Cherry had always loved Hope's clothes.

Hope was the first of them to get a job and start buying her own things. The first to move out. She got married young, then went to community college and went to work as a bookkeeper.

She'd always dressed way more conservatively than Cherry would – but she always looked cool. And beautiful. She wore tops that showed off her breasts and pretty round shoulders. And skirts that showed off her shapely ankles and calves. Hope liked to wear jackets. She liked to wear boots. She liked a puffed sleeve and a Peter Pan collar. She was thirty percent more Laura Ashley than Cherry, and thirty percent less Betsey Johnson.

Cherry used to borrow Hope's clothes in high school. She used to mimic the way Hope wore her hair – long with long bangs.

They both still wore their hair that way.

Since Hope had lost weight, she was wearing all the clothes that Cherry had never been able to wear. Crisp button-down blouses without any stretch. Neatly tailored trousers and pencil skirts. Everything waisted. Everything belted. Everything tucked in. Hope dressed herself without any camouflage, drawing attention to all the parts of her body she used to obscure.

Hope had worn *sailor pants* to Faith's Labor Day picnic – wide-legged white pants with a flat panel and two rows of buttons – and her belly didn't bulge or pouch. Cherry had felt physically ill when she saw those pants. Sick with something worse than jealousy. Something that was anger, plus longing, plus disbelief.

'Cherry, *eat*,' their mom said. 'Both of you, eat. We've got to get to the store.'

Cherry ate one of the tortillas and half of everything else. She tried not to look at Hope's plate.

Hope was going to drive because she had a bigger car. All of Cherry's sisters had huge SUVs. All of Cherry's sisters had kids.

'Mom, let Cherry go home,' Hope said, helping their mom into the front seat. 'She has the day off.'

'You're both here, and you're both coming,' their mom said. 'Do you know how rare it is for me to see my girls at once?'

'You just saw us,' Hope said.

'Oh, great, I get to see my family on Christmas and Easter. Twice a year.'

'And Thanksgiving,' Cherry said. She was already in the car. She knew she wasn't getting off the hook. 'And Labor Day.'

Her mom turned back to smile at Cherry. 'Do you remember how we'd all go grocery shopping together? You two girls were my helpers.'

Honny and Joy were awful at the grocery store. (And at church. And at school.) They'd run around. They'd try to ride on the end of the cart. *'Worse than boys,'* their mom would say.

And Faith was no help; she was forever the baby.

But Hope was always responsible, and always in charge. And Cherry had liked everything about grocery shopping. The lists. The bright packaging. The registers. She also liked being a good girl, like Hope. Not a scoundrel like Honny.

When they got to Hy-Vee, their mom insisted that they both come into the store. 'You might see something you need.'

They found themselves trailing behind her with the cart. Just like when they were kids.

'Can I push?' Cherry asked. 'My back is killing me. I need a walker.'

Hope relinquished the cart without acknowledging her. Their mom was wandering around the produce section, picking up fruit and putting it down, feeling every grapefruit in the display.

Cherry set one foot on the bottom of the cart and leaned over the handle, stretching her back.

Hope was standing at the other end of the cart with her arms folded, looking away. 'I know you have a group thread without me,' she said.

Cherry exhaled heavily and set both feet on the floor. 'You're not missing anything.'

Hope turned around. Her face was blank. 'I wonder if you'd say that if *you* were the one who got taken off the group thread. I went from getting thirty text notifications a day to two a week.' She shook her head. 'And they're always about Mom.'

Cherry wasn't sure how to reply. She'd never expected Hope to bring this up. Hope never diverted from the high road.

Cherry shrugged. 'Honny –'

Hope cut her off with a huff. 'Don't blame Honny.'

Their mom dropped a bag of grapefruit into the cart. 'When you girls were little, everyone was always eating *grapefruit* on diets. And cottage cheese. Why those two foods? Nobody eats grapefruit on diets now. Grapefruit isn't keto, is it? Hope, can you eat grapefruit?'

'I've never really eaten grapefruit.'

'You did when you were a kid! I used to brûlée the sugar for you. When *I* was a kid, everyone owned grapefruit spoons. Can you imagine? Going to Target to buy grapefruit spoons . . .'

They followed her over to the lettuce and celery. Then to the meat section, where she agonized over the bacon. The store had stopped carrying her favorite brand.

Hope's arms were still crossed. 'Imagine *you* lost weight,' she said in a fierce whisper, 'and your sisters cut *you* off.'

'I can't imagine losing weight,' Cherry whispered back.

'Don't be such an asshole, Cherry.'

Their mom dropped a package of bacon into the cart. She needed ground beef next. And Claussen pickles. Flour. Canned olives. Bottled spaghetti sauce.

Hope was fuming.

Cherry was fuming, too. She stopped the cart at the end of the condiment aisle while their mom kept walking. 'I'm not being an asshole,' she hissed. '*I* didn't leave you off the thread. Honny started a *new* thread –'

'I expect this from Honny.' Hope put her back to their mom, facing Cherry. 'She's a gossip. And she can't tell the difference between funny and mean. But I don't expect it from *you*, Cherry.'

'Look. I'm sorry you're feeling left out. I *am*. But, you cut *us* off first. You've been completely dishonest with all of us!'

Hope huffed again in disbelief. 'How have I been dishonest?'

'Hope, you lost a hundred pounds, and you told us you were *watching your carbs.*'

'I *am* watching my carbs.'

'Okay.' Cherry rolled her eyes. 'Well. This is why we have a new group thread.' She started pushing the cart toward their mom.

Hope stayed where she was. 'It's nobody's business how I lost weight.'

Cherry looked back over her shoulder. 'It is when you lie about it!' She was still trying to be quiet. 'It's an indictment of the rest of us!'

'That's paranoid and narcissistic, Cherry.'

'"Narcissistic," huh? Spare me your internet therapy.' Cherry stalked back toward her sister, abandoning the cart. 'If you sit there at Thanksgiving saying that you did this by counting carbs, it makes it seem like everyone *else* just needs to be more disciplined. But it isn't about *discipline* – it's about *GLP-1 agonists.*'

Hope clenched her jaw. And her fists. If this was Honny – or maybe even Faith – Cherry might actually worry about getting punched. 'You want me to be honest,' Hope said, 'is that right? You think that would go well? If I told everyone that I was taking …' She stalled out.

'Ozempic,' Cherry supplied.

'*Mounjaro*, actually … All it would do is make everyone uncomfortable. You'd *all* judge me. And you'd think *I* was judging *you*.'

'Hope! All of those things are already happening!'

'Yeah, on the group thread that I'm not on!'

Cherry threw her hands in the air – right into the shoulder of a man who was trying to get by. 'Sorry,' she said. She looked around for their mom, and found her standing at the end of the aisle, watching them, holding a jar of mayonnaise. Cherry walked back to the cart and pushed it toward their mom. Hope followed her.

Cherry's mom set the mayonnaise in the cart, ignoring their tense jaws and flushed faces. 'I just need a few more things.'

'Lead the way,' Cherry said.

They followed her to the frozen food aisle. Cherry could hear Hope's huffy, angry breathing behind her.

'You can't even look at me,' Hope said. 'I talked to your boyfriend for an hour at Thanksgiving, and you didn't say a word.'

Cherry didn't look at her.

'My therapist says it's jealousy, but it feels like you're all trying to punish me.'

'I'm not trying to *punish* you.'

'Then why can't you look at me, Cherry?'

'I can look at you.' Cherry didn't.

'Do you hate me that much?'

'For fuck's sake, Hope' – Cherry wheeled on her – 'I don't *hate* you. I just – I feel completely betrayed by you.'

'Be-*trayed*?'

'Yes!' Cherry was crying suddenly. (Maybe not suddenly – her cheeks were already wet.) 'Because you've been telling me my whole life that it was okay to be fat. You used to say to me – when I was just a little girl – that I would never be skinny, so I shouldn't worry about that. That I shouldn't starve myself or pin all my dreams on losing weight. I should just worry about being healthy and being the best me I could be.' Cherry wiped her nose on the back of her wrist. 'You'd say, *"I'm never going to be skinny, and I don't care, because my life is better than all my skinny friends".*"'

Hope looked startled. 'That's exactly what Mom used to say to me . . .'

'Well, I *believed* you, Hope. Because you were beautiful. And you had a cute boyfriend. And a good job . . . And I thought that being fat wouldn't be so bad if it meant being like you.' Cherry shook her head miserably. 'So yeah, the fact that you took the miracle skinny drug just as soon as it was available? It fucking *sucks*. It's like we were all on the same team, and you wanted off that team. You don't want to be like us. You were lying when you said that we could be fat and happy.'

'I wasn't lying.' Hope still seemed startled. 'That's not what any of this means.'

'Well, that's the subtext when the text is *"I'm watching my carbs."*'

'This isn't –' Hope was crying now, too. More messily than Cherry. (She must have less practice.) *'God.'* She wiped her eyes. 'This isn't about *you*. Can't you see that? It isn't about Honny. Or Joy. Or Faith. This is about *me*, Cherry. My *body*. My *life*.'

Hope held her hands away from her slim hips, palms out. 'I was diabetic . . . My knees hurt all the time . . . My blood pressure was high, my cholesterol was high, I was constantly out of breath – and I was gaining more weight every year, no matter what I did or ate. I was in *free fall*.'

She brought her fingertips up to her temples. 'And I know that's just the story of every woman in our family. I know that's Grandma. And it's Mom. But what if it doesn't have to be *me*? I have three kids, and I want as many years with them as I can get. I want to meet my grandkids. I want to be able to *walk*.'

Cherry folded her arms. She shifted her weight back. 'I didn't know you were diabetic.'

'I didn't tell anyone. I was ashamed.'

'It's not your fault,' Cherry said softly. 'It's genetic.'

Hope waved a hand like that didn't matter. She took a few breaths. She wiped her eyes again and looked at Cherry. 'I'm still the same person, you know?'

'You are and you aren't...' Cherry said, still being soft, but not quite relenting. 'You walk through the world completely differently now.'

Hope looked like that was the worst thing Cherry had said so far. Her face crumpled. 'You sound like Danny.'

Cherry was taken aback. *'Danny?'*

Hope had already started walking away from her.

Cherry looked back at their mom. She was standing close enough to have heard the whole thing. She looked sad from her head to her feet. 'Go,' she said.

Cherry left the cart and rushed after Hope – who had disappeared into the maze of the supermarket. Cherry walked toward the exit, looking down each aisle, then out to the parking lot, toward Hope's SUV.

Hope was sitting in the front seat, leaning over the wheel with her head in her hands.

Cherry stood for a second outside the car.

Then she opened the passenger door and sat down. Hope didn't look up. She was taking deep, trembling breaths.

Cherry put her hand on Hope's arm.

Hope shrugged it off. 'I don't want to talk about it,' she said.

'Okay,' Cherry whispered.

'And I don't want you to tell *any* of this to Honny and Joy and Faith.'

'I won't,' Cherry promised.

'They'd love that... *"Hope lost weight, and her husband fell out of love with her."'*

'They wouldn't,' Cherry said.

Hope looked up at her, red-faced and snotty. 'That's not what's happening – with Danny. It's not that simple.'

Cherry just nodded. She was crying, too.

'We were already having problems ...' Hope said, 'before ...'

Cherry nodded again.

'We were arguing constantly and constantly frustrated with each other. And there were ...' Hope looked at her lap. (She had a hell of a lap now.) '... other things, too. You get older, and you hardly recognize each other. You hardly recognize yourself.'

Cherry was *really* crying. She kind of hoped Hope wouldn't notice.

'I didn't talk to him about the Mounjaro,' Hope said. 'That was a mistake. I own that. And then ... I wasn't really prepared for how upside down it would make me feel to lose weight. Like a stranger in my own body ...' She glanced over at Cherry. '*Good*. But foreign.' She shook her head. 'Ashamed. Not always good, actually ...' She grabbed a used Starbucks napkin from the cupholder and blew her nose. 'And Danny ... well.' She looked down again. 'There are other things, too.'

'I'm sorry,' Cherry whispered.

Hope looked up at her, intently this time, into Cherry's eyes. (Hope's brown eyes were so big now. Unencumbered by her cheeks.) 'I'd like to say that I'm sorry, too ... but I'm still not convinced that it wouldn't have made things worse if I'd been honest with you.' She let out a loud breath and rolled her eyes at herself. 'Which is also what I said to Danny.'

'I didn't know you were having such a hard time,' Cherry said. 'With your health.'

Hope shook her head, agitated. 'Oh, it wasn't just my health. It's not like I did this' – she gestured at her stomach – 'for wholly *noble* reasons. I was tired of being fat, Cherry. I've had forty years of it, and I'm *tired*. I'm sorry if that disappoints you. Maybe I'm *not* the same person.'

'Maybe not . . .' Cherry said. 'But you're still my sister.'

Hope looked up at her.

Cherry reached for her hand and took it.

Hope didn't shake her off this time. She started crying again. 'I'm such a mess, Cherry.'

Cherry squeezed her hand. 'I can tell.'

Hope laughed. She lifted up her other arm and hid her face in her elbow. 'Oh my god . . . I'm such a *mess*.'

Cherry moved sideways in the seat, turning toward Hope. (The SUV was so *roomy*.)

Hope let her arm drop to her lap. 'Danny and I are . . . I don't know what we are. He's been sleeping on the couch.'

'Have the kids noticed?'

'They think it's because he snores. He *does* snore, but I've never cared. He's staying at the firehouse sometimes.'

'Are you talking to anyone about it?'

She made a face at Cherry. 'You mean, like a marriage counselor?'

'Yeah.'

'No. That would make it real. Did you and Tom see a counselor?'

'No.' Cherry shook her head. 'He was in L.A., and I was . . . done, I guess.'

'Yeah, you seemed so *done* at Christmas . . .'

Cherry sat back. 'We're not talking about me.'

'We *should* be,' Hope said. 'I don't know what's going on with you. I assume it's *insane* . . . You brought a boyfriend to Thanksgiving and your estranged husband to Christmas.'

'Oh god.' Cherry pulled her hand away to cover her face. 'It's . . . yeah. Not sane.'

'Tell me about it.'

Cherry laughed.

'No,' Hope said, 'I'm serious – tell me about it.'

'Okay . . .' Cherry rubbed her eyes. 'Let's see . . . Tom is moving to L.A. And he's taking Stevie.'

'Thank god.'

'No – I want to keep her.'

Hope looked confused. 'You *do*?'

'She's my dog.'

'I thought she was Tom's dog.'

'Well, I guess she is,' Cherry said. 'Because he's taking her with him. He's moving to California.'

'Yeah, you said that. He told me about it at Christmas. He didn't seem enthusiastic. What about Russ?'

'Russ . . .' Cherry said.

'He seemed so great.'

'Yeah, he did seem great.'

Hope frowned. 'What happened?'

Cherry shrugged. 'We broke up. He, um . . . Basically – *Thursday* really bothered him. We went to see a movie, and the trailer started playing . . .'

'Oh no,' Hope said. 'The first one?'

'Yeah. I think so.'

'Oh *no*.'

'Anyway . . . Russ didn't really know much about *Thursday* when we reconnected. And I thought that was a good thing? But . . . he wasn't prepared for . . . you know, *Baby*.'

'Baby,' Hope said sadly.

'Yeah.'

'That must have been such a shock for him – especially if he'd never read the comic. It'd be like finding out that you're dating . . .'

'Garfield,' Cherry supplied.

Hope looked at her. 'I was going to say Juliet.'

Cherry rolled her eyes. 'Anyway . . . it was a layered thing. I don't think Russ was ever going to get over me being fat.'

'I thought *you* were going to be the one to take Ozempic,' Hope said.

Cherry goggled her eyes. '*Me?* Why me?'

'Because you can *afford* it. You've got railroad insurance and Hollywood money. And you're getting a divorce.'

'I don't know how to take that . . .'

Hope poked Cherry's arm. Right in the fatty part, the way their mom always did. 'I was hoping you'd do it first and draw everyone's fire. Then tell me how it went.'

'Sorry to disappoint you,' Cherry said, rubbing her arm.

'*Would* you, though . . . ?'

'Would I what?'

'Would you ever take the meds?'

'Oh . . .' Cherry grimaced. 'I don't know. It feels like . . . Well, no offense, *honestly*, but that would feel like giving up.'

'On losing weight naturally?'

'God, no – I'll never lose weight naturally. I meant . . . giving up on the fight, you know? The good fight to be . . . accepted, I guess. Or to accept myself.'

'Geez, Cherry, you really *are* noble.'

Cherry was still thinking. 'Also, I worry about what the drugs would do to my brain. Like, every time someone says that Ozempic quiets their "food noise"? I shudder. It's not food noise to me – it's food *music*.'

Hope laughed.

'I'm serious,' Cherry said. 'I *like* liking food. I like being hungry. I like wanting things – and yearning. Do you still yearn?'

'I don't know that I've ever noticed my yearning,' Hope said. 'Maybe I'm not a natural yearner.'

'Oh, I am.' Cherry folded her arms and leaned her shoulder into the seat, getting more comfortable. 'I could yearn professionally. I think I kind of *do* – all my success comes from wanting something more or something better.'

'I still like food . . .' Hope said thoughtfully.

'That's good,' Cherry said.

'. . . but I don't think about it very much.'

'That sounds terrible.'

Hope laughed. 'For the first six months on the meds, I was too nauseated to think about anything. And for the last six months ... Well, all I can think about is whether we can afford two mortgages and whether the kids will want to live with me or Dan. Maybe I'm not the best person to ask about Mounjaro brain.' She smiled at Cherry, fondly – a little indulgent. '"*Yearning*" ... I always think you're the most like me. I forget that you're a romantic.'

Cherry wrinkled her nose but didn't argue. She looked down at her own lap. (What there was of it.) 'Tom wants to come home,' she said.

'*What?* Really?'

Cherry nodded.

'Do you want him to come home?'

Cherry shook her head, but she said, 'So bad.'

'So ...'

Cherry felt a new rush of tears. She looked up at Hope. 'I don't know if I can forgive him. I don't know how I can ever believe him when he says that he loves me.'

'*Cherry* ...' Hope tilted her head. Her voice was tender. 'Whatever else is true – Tom loves you. That's always been clear as day.'

Cherry wiped her nose on her hand. 'I could say the same about Danny, you know.'

Hope had opened the compartment in the armrest and dug out another Starbucks napkin for Cherry. 'Please don't.'

Cherry blew her nose.

They both sat there sniffling for a minute or two. Cherry was wondering whether a GLP-1 agonist would make her think less about Tom.

Finally she said – 'What do you think Mom's in there doing?'

'Texting Honny and Joy and Faith, and organizing a prayer circle.'

'Let me text her.' Cherry reached for her phone. 'Hey – how's your blood sugar now?'

'Normal,' Hope said.

'Wow,' Cherry said, instantly jealous again.

'Yeah ... *wow*.'

Chapter 64

'I don't know how I can ever believe him,' Cherry had said, *'when he says that he loves me.'*

That had been a figurative question; Tom almost never said that he loved her. But she'd believed it anyway.

In the beginning, she'd chased him.

She'd worried that he was too polite to turn her down – or too conflict-averse.

She'd read his hesitation as reluctance.

She'd read his hesitation as doubt.

She'd read *Thursday*, and wondered if it was all a farce.

But then Tom had walked through every door that Cherry ever opened.

She was always the one who made the leap – but Tom always caught her. She always put herself out there first, but he always met her more than halfway.

At some point, Cherry had stopped seeing Tom's uncertainty as a problem ...

Maybe Tom fell in love with her because he *needed* someone who chased and pushed and opened. Maybe Tom needed a girl who was a verb. That was Cherry. (That was Cherish.)

Cherry never worried that Tom would cheat on her. Before he did.

Cherry never doubted that Tom wanted her. Before he didn't.

Had he ever truly not?

You sort of stop noticing that someone never says 'I love you' when they make you feel loved.
    When they make you feel *liked*.
    Tom always seemed so happy to come home to her.

All of the above made it worse.
    Every good thing made it worse.
    Every good memory was streaked with blood.

Places where Tom had kissed Cherry:
    In line, at the grocery store.
    In line, at the bank.
    In line, at their polling place.
    At Meg Jones's Christmas party, every year under one of the arches.
    At every family baptism (on the cheek, usually).
    At her grandma's funeral (on the temple).
    In movie theaters, during the movie, if he noticed she was looking at him.
    At restaurants, waiting for their table. (With his arm around her, the kiss landing wherever was easiest – her shoulder, the back of her hand, the top of her head.)
    In the kitchen, whenever he moved past her.
    In bed, before he rolled over and fell asleep.
    In bed, before she got up, before he rolled over and fell back to sleep.
    On the palm, during sex.
    On her chin, when she was eating something messy.
    On her neck, if he wanted to distract her.
    Always, without a thought, in front of her family or his friends.
    On his sister's rollaway when they visited her in Des Moines.

On the sidelines, when Cherry came to his rec-league softball games.

On the nose, when she pouted.

On her belly, when she had cramps.

On her belly, when they were having sex.

On her belly, when he wanted to have sex.

On her belly, if they were in bed, and she was half asleep, and he was wide awake.

On her belly, whenever she was taller than him.

Inside her knees, inside her thighs, on the back of her thighs, under her arms, under her breasts, on the soles of her feet – whenever he felt like it, for no reason at all.

On the forehead, when he thought she was being cute.

On the knuckles, when he thought she needed encouragement.

Full on the mouth once, in the Western Alliance lobby, the day that he'd quit.

Full on the mouth most of the time. Most places. Most days. Like it was nothing. Like it was breathing. Like he got a little hit of something from it. Like Cherry's mouth was for kissing the way a dog's ears were for scratching or buttons were for pushing.

He didn't seem to ever *think* about kissing her, or even realize he was doing it. Sometimes he did it in the middle of a sentence. Sometimes he did it in his sleep.

That's who Cherry had been, in Tom's life and in the world, for years and years – someone who had always recently been kissed. Someone who was about to be kissed. Someone who walked around with her chin slightly raised and lips slightly parted – ready for it.

Chapter 65

'Well, look who's here. I wasn't expecting to see you anytime soon.'

Tom's dad was in the driveway, working on his truck. He was wearing a coat and holding a travel mug. And smiling at Cherry like she was about to say something funny.

'Hey, there,' Cherry said, walking up the drive.

She'd never had much of a relationship with Tom's dad. Tom had never wanted her to.

Tom used to stop by his dad's house several times a week. He'd bring leftovers. Mow the lawn. Go through the mail. If Cherry was with him, he'd have her wait in the car. *'There's no reason for you to have to deal with him, too,'* Tom would say.

'Is he so bad?'

'He's not so good.'

Cherry walked up the driveway. 'Is Tom around?'

His dad shook his head. 'She wants to know if Tom's around … Where else would he be? Oh, I know – Bever-ly Hills. *"Swimming pools,"'* he half sang. *' "Movie stars."'*

Cherry nodded, making herself smile.

Tom's dad was big like Tom. And he was fair like Tom. Heavy. Red-faced. With bushy eyebrows and a scruffy beard. She was pretty sure he was the reason Tom wouldn't try a beard, even though it might look nice on him.

Cherry couldn't get up to the house without squeezing past her father-in-law – or walking into the snowy yard and making a big show of avoiding him.

'I guess I'll have to see that movie of his,' his dad said, standing squarely in front of Cherry. 'That's what they tell me. Even though I'm not in it. I'm not in the comic strips, either. The funny papers, we used to call 'em, you know?'

'That's right,' Cherry said. 'We did.'

She only really knew Tom's dad from sporadic holidays and birthday visits. She'd sat next to him at their wedding rehearsal. She'd never had a real conversation with him. She wondered if anyone ever did. His dad only seemed to ask rhetorical questions.

'I'm not in any of them,' he said. 'I have people who would tell me if I was.'

Cherry nodded.

'But you're in them,' he said, grinning. Cherry might call it a leer if the very idea wasn't so upsetting. 'Baby, Baby, Baby.'

'I don't think it's meant to be a memoir,' she said.

'Ha! She doesn't think it's meant to be a memoir! Maybe I should have been drawing little cartoons – instead of working on boilers. Seems like a pretty good grift, huh.'

Cherry smiled. 'I wouldn't call it a grift . . .'

He took a drink from his mug. 'Well, you're gonna get your share, aren't you? You put your money on the right horse. Who would have guessed?' He started laughing. 'Not me. I thought he was the one who gambled right. I used to tell him, *"Good job, Tommy. That girl will keep the bills paid."*'

'Is Tom inside?' Cherry pointed at the door.

'I don't really read comic books,' his dad said. 'I never have. I tell people that I don't need the pictures, you know? I don't need to *see* Jane run. But people like his stuff. They're always telling me so. I'll bet *you* like it. He made you famous. Baby, Baby.'

Cherry took a step back.

'*"Baby, baby, baby,"*' he sang, '*"where did our love go?"*' He laughed and took another drink.

'Cherry?'

Cherry looked up at the house. Tom was standing in the door.

'Your *wife's* here!' Tom's dad shouted without turning around. 'Wasn't expecting to see her around anytime soon.'

Tom was already walking toward her. Cutting through the snow to avoid his dad. He was wearing his bright white Nikes.

When he got to Cherry, he put his hand on her back and started leading her down the driveway.

'We were just catching up,' his dad called after them.

'Sorry,' Cherry said quietly. 'I'm sorry.'

Tom shook his head and kept them moving.

'I wanted to talk to you,' she said, 'and you didn't pick up.'

'I was in a meeting.'

'Sorry.'

'Don't apologize,' he said. They were already to her car.

'I forgot how he is.'

'Yeah.' Tom was standing between Cherry and his dad. He wouldn't look at either of them.

'Please can we talk?' Cherry whispered.

'Yeah,' Tom said, opening her door. Then he looked over at her and seemed to realize what she'd asked. 'No. Cherry . . . what more is there to say?'

'I think maybe *everything*.' She stepped closer to Tom. Away from the car. 'I can't imagine running out of things I want to say to you.'

He frowned down at her.

'Will you come home with me?' she asked. 'So we can talk?'

Tom shook his head, still frowning. 'No. I can't keep going back there. I can't handle having to leave.'

She grabbed the bottom of his T-shirt – not to yank on it, just to hold on. 'I won't make you leave,' she said.

She *wouldn't*. If things got terrible, Cherry would be the one to leave. She'd leave him the house and the dog. *She'd* move to California.

Tom was staring at her face. Still frowning.

'Please talk to me,' she said. 'Somewhere.'

Tom told her to meet him at a diner down the road. Cherry had never been there before.

When she got to the restaurant, it was closed. They didn't serve dinner.

She waited by the door. Tom pulled in and parked.

'They're closed,' she said, before he got to her.

'Oh.' He looked around, like something else might be open. But this wasn't a business district. There was just this diner, and a car wash, and across the street, Abbie's Road Beatles-themed pizzeria.

Tom looked back at Cherry.

She shrugged.

Abbie's Road was still tiny. And still strange.

Tom held the door for her, and Cherry walked to the far end of the empty dining room, in the opposite corner from 'Octopus's Garden.' She sat down under a mural of Paul McCartney eating pizza with a walrus.

Tom stood by the table. 'What do you want?'

'Whatever you feel like,' she said.

She watched him walk over to the counter. He ruffled the back of his hair.

Cherry needed to see him make that gesture again.

She needed to keep seeing it, as his hair went gray.

Tom came back to the table and set a glass of ice and a can of Coke Zero in front of her.

He took off his peacoat – he must have grabbed it from the house before he left. He was wearing a nice brown pullover sweater underneath. It looked new. And expensive. Pendleton, maybe. Maybe a Christmas gift.

He sat down across from Cherry and sighed a little. Then looked up at her expectantly, like this was her show.

'I . . .' Cherry said.

Tom waited.

'I don't know how to get through this,' she said.

He waited.

'Like –' She gestured between them. 'I don't know how to get through the part where I'm angry and hurt and I don't trust you.'

Tom rested his elbows on the table.

'I *want* to get through it.' She was talking fast. 'I want to be on the other side of it – I think I wanted you to *pull* me through it somehow, with your bare hands. I wanted you to come home and bang down the door.'

Tom looked down at the table.

'But instead . . .' Cherry forced herself to keep talking. 'Well, you acted like you'd been expecting it, Tom – like you were just waiting for me to end everything. Like you were *relieved*.'

He looked up at her. 'I wasn't relieved.'

Cherry's voice broke: 'Why didn't you come home?'

His shoulders twitched. It wasn't even a shrug. 'Because I didn't feel like I deserved to be there. I started to think . . .' He looked in her eyes. 'Maybe I never deserved to be there.'

Cherry shook her head. Her voice dropped to a murmur. 'Don't say that.'

He tilted his head. 'Why? Because it's true?'

She shook her head again. A tear slid down her cheek.

'If you don't believe you deserve good things,' Cherry whispered, 'how can I believe *I'm* a good thing?'

Tom's eyes widened and started to shine. He pushed his jaw to the side, like she'd punched him. Neither of them looked away.

'*Tom!*' someone shouted.

For a second Cherry thought it was someone who recognized him, but it was just the girl at the counter.

Tom stood up. He wiped his eyes on the back of his wrist. A minute later, he came back to the table with a salad for Cherry and sat down.

'You were right,' Cherry said. She had to keep pushing forward. She had a list in her head, an agenda; there were things that she needed to *say*. 'I never let you apologize – because that would have made it real. I would have had to acknowledge what was happening.'

Tom nodded. 'I get that,' he said gruffly.

'Do you still want to apologize?' she asked.

He looked surprised. 'Now?'

'I mean . . .' Cherry lifted a shoulder. 'Yeah?'

Tom studied her face – maybe to see if she meant it. Then he leaned forward on his elbows. 'Cherry, I'm sorry,' he said. 'I was lonely and depressed. And it had been so long since you and I . . . since we'd felt like ourselves. Together.'

Cherry nodded.

'I felt like you were angry with me all the time,' Tom said.

'I was.'

'*Why?*'

'I don't know, for . . . for suddenly having a life without me.' She pressed her lips together, crumbling. 'You weren't supposed to have a *whole life* without me. We were supposed to be in this together.'

'I didn't have a whole anything,' Tom said. 'I didn't even feel like a whole person.'

Cherry clenched her hands in her lap. She was trying not to cry like a little girl. She was crying like a little girl. 'Tom, were you having an affair with Rachel?'

'I don't know,' he said hollowly.

'How can you not *know?*'

He shook his head. Like he didn't know that either.

'Did you sleep with her?'

'Once,' he said. 'After you told me you wanted a divorce.'

Cherry felt like she was dying. (Again.) (Before all this, she hadn't known you could be so sad that your bones ached.)

'It was a mistake,' he said. 'I'd been drinking.'

'Tom, you've been *drinking*?'

'*Now?* No. Then ... yeah. Sometimes. I'd had a few drinks the night you called ... That was the first time we'd ever kissed, for what it's worth.' He shook his head. 'I don't know what it's worth.'

'So you're not ...'

'I'm not ...?'

'Seeing Rachel,' Cherry said.

Tom made a face. '*No.* I wouldn't have – Just, no. We haven't even worked together since then.'

'Did you have to tell Ophelia?' Tom's editor. Rachel's boss.

He looked beaten. 'I didn't have to tell her. No.'

Cherry felt a new wave of humiliation and pain rush through her. She waited for it to pass. It didn't. She crossed her arms on the table and laid her head down.

'I'm sorry,' Tom said somewhere over her head.

'Okay,' she said. 'I hear you.'

'Cherry ...'

'I hear you.' She waited for the pain to settle before she lifted up her head. She looked in his eyes. 'Do you really want to come home?'

'Yes,' Tom said.

'I don't understand why. You could start over.'

'You really think that sounds appealing to me?'

'*Yes,*' Cherry said emphatically. 'You could have something that isn't already fucked up. In a place with no bad memories. The whole world is at your feet, Tom – *literally*. You could have ...' She shook her head. '... anything.'

Tom leaned over the table. Angry. 'Cherry, if you don't believe that you deserve good things, how am I supposed to believe that I'm a good thing?'

'*Tom!*' the girl at the counter called out.

'*Fuck*,' Tom said, sitting back. He shook his head like he was trying to clear it. 'What are we doing here?'

'The pizza's just okay,' Cherry said quietly, 'but the theming's extraordinary.'

He shot her a helpless look. Nothing like a smile. Then stood up.

He came back with a pizza and two plates, and set them off to the side. Like he'd brought the pizza for people sitting at the other end of the table.

Then he sat down right next to Cherry, on the same side of the table. Facing her. He took her hand.

She let him.

Tom hunched forward. 'I don't want the world,' he said. 'I want *you*. You're my lucky day, Cherry. You're the only home I've ever known, and I don't want . . . *something else*. I don't want a fresh start with someone I'll never love half as much. I just want to find my way back to you.' He squeezed her hand. 'Let me come back to you. Let me come home.'

She looked in his eyes. 'Tom . . .'

'I got lost,' he said. 'I've been so lost.'

Cherry let go of his hand. She stood up. Her chair tipped backwards but didn't fall.

'Cherry?'

Cherry, Cherry, Cherry.

Baby, Baby, Baby.

'I'm getting a box for the pizza,' she said. 'We can eat it at home.'

They had to take two cars. Which was awkward.

Tom beat her to the house. He was waiting on the porch for her, holding the pizza box.

He watched her walk up to the door. Stevie was already barking at them.

When Cherry got to the porch, Tom fished his keys out of his pocket. 'Are you sure about this?' he asked.

She nodded.

'If you kick me out again,' he said, 'I'm not leaving.'

Cherry didn't flinch.

'Not right away,' he added.

She laughed. It made her tearful. 'Are you saying that if I kick you out, you're going to leave *really* slowly?'

Tom smiled at her. But not with his eyes – his eyes were scared. 'I'm serious,' he said.

'Okay.'

He pushed his key into the lock.

'Tom, wait –' Cherry put her hand over his wrist. 'There was ... I *was* seeing someone, and we –'

He shook his head. He brought his hand up to her cheek, leaving the keys hanging in the door. 'Shhh, baby, I know. We don't have to – You don't – I mean, unless you need to say it.'

'I don't need to say it,' Cherry said.

Tom held her cheek. 'Can we leave it out here?'

Out here in the snow, Cherry thought. *In this lost year.*

Could it be that easy?

Could Cherry just empty her pockets and shake out the pain and anger? Wipe away thirty-two kinds of tears?

What if she left Rachel out here? With her red hair and jumpsuits.

And Russ, too. With his gorgeous eyes and good intentions. (*Could Cherry really forget Russ?* Maybe not. But she could let him go. She could let him drift.)

Cherry had died so many times since Tom left. And since she told him to stay away.

She'd felt her bone marrow fester.

She'd spent months picking herself up in tiny pieces and painstakingly putting them right.

Could she set those months aside?

Could she hand this man those pieces?

This man who had failed her.

Who'd abandoned her.

Who'd let the winds blow him far, far away?

No.

No.

No.

Yes.

She nodded. 'Tom . . .'

'What is it, baby?'

'I know you said you didn't want a fresh start, but you're getting one anyway.'

Cherry opened the door.

She pulled Tom inside.

Chapter 66

Cherry didn't look cute.

She was still wearing yoga pants. Her hair was still in a limp ponytail.

When they got inside the house, Tom leaned over to say hi to Stevie. He asked if she'd had her walk. She had.

'Let's go to bed,' Tom said.

'It's five o'clock,' Cherry said.

'I want to go upstairs,' he said.

She nodded.

Tom closed the baby gate behind them. He brought the pizza.

When they got to their bedroom, Tom started stripping the bed. Cherry had changed it after he'd stayed over the other night... but she helped him.

He went to the hall closet to get fresh sheets and pillowcases. His hands were shaking.

Cherry was crying. (Flat and shapeless tears that streamed down her face with no surface tension.)

'Can I take a shower?' Tom asked.

Cherry laughed. 'Yeah. You can even clean the shower. You live here.'

He made a noise like a laugh. He walked over to his dresser and got out a T-shirt and pajama pants.

While he was in the shower, Cherry straightened the bedroom. She picked up laundry and closed the closet doors. She arranged the pillows on the bed.

Tom came back to the room dressed for bed. Cherry hadn't seen his long hair wet. It hung in ash-brown curls over his ears and forehead.

He looked like he'd seen a ghost in the bathroom. And a few more on the way to the bedroom. He looked like he could use a minute.

'I think I'll take a shower, too,' Cherry said. She dug out her elephant pajamas.

The shower was still wet. The bar of soap was slick.

When Cherry got back to their room, Tom was sitting on the edge of their bed, leaning on his knees. His feet were bare. Tom's toes were wide with flat nails. Something about them made her want to laugh. Or maybe cry.

He looked up. He held his arms out to her.

Cherry stepped into them.

Tom rested his cheek on her stomach. After a minute, she laid her palm over the crown of his head.

'Tell me I'm home,' he said.

Cherry hushed him. 'You're home, Tom. You're home now.'

They fell asleep too early, both of them wiped out. Both of them incoherent with relief.

Cherry woke up just after midnight. Then Tom woke up. Then they remembered the untouched pizza.

'I've been eating like shit,' Cherry said a few minutes later, licking marinara sauce off her thumb.

'We'll do better tomorrow,' Tom said.

He took the rest of the pizza downstairs to put in the fridge.

They lay awake for a while.

They kissed.

Cherry told Tom that she loved him more than she loved life and the world. That if she were God or emperor, she'd let everything go right to hell for him. (She didn't tell him that. She said, 'I love you' over and over. She let the faucet run.)

'I think I'm ovulating,' Cherry said later. 'And I don't have any condoms.'

'We'll get some,' Tom said.

There wasn't any rush.

When it was very late, and they were only awake because they were both a little afraid of waking up in a new day, Tom said, 'I'm done with comics after *Thursday* ends.'

'I know,' Cherry said.

'No. I mean . . . I don't want to draw anything else. I don't want to make anything new.'

His hand was curved between her belly and her hip. His head was on her shoulder.

Cherry kissed the top of his head. 'You can be done.'

'What will I do?'

'Walk Stevie,' she said. 'Make gingerbread cookies. Let me bring home the bacon.'

Tom snorted. He rubbed his face into her shoulder.

'I don't believe you're done,' Cherry whispered, 'but you can be.'

Chapter 67

Tom had to leave in two weeks.

He had to be back in Los Angeles for the movie premiere, even though he still wasn't planning to go to the premiere itself, and then on to New York City for promo. They'd booked him on *Good Morning America* and *The View*. And they wanted him to do one of those YouTube shows where you eat chicken on camera. He'd told his new publicist – Michelle – that he'd rather eat gravel.

He brought his suitcase home from his dad's house. And a box full of clothes that Cherry didn't trust because she didn't know their provenance. (The Pendleton sweater was a gift from his sister.) He still had things to bring home from Los Angeles. He'd bought a car there. And he had to break his lease in Pasadena.

Tom had phone calls all the time. And Zoom calls. He took them in the living room, with Stevie lying at his feet.

The meetings made his eyes go flat and faraway. Sometimes he still looked that way when Cherry got home from work.

Cherry almost *didn't* go back to work ... She certainly didn't *have* to. And Tom being home made every day feel like a holiday. 'The trains will run without you,' he told her that first Monday morning when her alarm went off.

It was tempting ...

But work had been Cherry's lifeline for the last year. She wasn't letting go now.

Besides, what would Cherry do in the house all day? Watch

Tom work? Make curtains? (She'd already run out of windows.) The thought made her itch.

The truth was – Cherry had spent so long worrying about what she'd do if Tom got fired, she couldn't quite trust the *freight cars* of money he was earning now. She needed to work.

On those nights when she came home and Tom's eyes had gone dead, Cherry would crowd him against the wall or crawl on top of him where he sat, kissing and nosing at him, looking for signs of life. If his wrist had fit into her mouth, she would have held it between her teeth.

Cherry still didn't know how to rescue him, but she wanted him to know she was there.

Also, she still didn't have any pride. She hadn't found any over the last year. Cherry loved Tom too much, and she showed him too much.

And once she'd decided to forgive him, her heart was wide open to him. (Probably this was why she'd held him off for so long.)

They didn't put anything back on the shelves or the walls. Tom didn't bring home the rest of the boxes from his dad's house. They were in an in-between place, and they both knew it. They were both afraid to jinx it. They ignored the empty spaces.

Tom bought new sketchbooks and left them on the coffee table and in the bathroom. Cherry watched him doodle while he talked on the phone.

He drew Stevie mostly. Walking on two legs and wearing clothes. Taking Zoom calls. Applying to college.

Sometimes he drew Baby – doing something that Cherry had been doing, but doing it more comically than Cherry ever would. Cherry dropped half a plate of garbanzo-bean spaghetti, and Tom drew Baby with spaghetti in her hair and on her nose.

Sometimes he drew himself. Underwater. Except for one hand holding up the phone.

They both got antsy when it was time for Tom to pack. Cherry had watched him pack so many times. When he'd first started traveling, she used to help him.

'You should take something to wear to the premiere.' Cherry was sitting on the bed next to his suitcase. 'In case you decide to go.'

'I'm not going.' Tom was standing in front of the suitcase, folding his fancy cargo pants.

'It's a once-in-a-lifetime experience,' she said.

'If I can help it, this whole thing will be a once-in-a-lifetime experience.'

Cherry looked down at the suitcase. 'Do you have clothes for the interviews?'

'I have a stylist.'

She made a disgusted face. 'A *stylist*?'

Tom was smiling at her. 'My personal stylist wasn't answering my calls.'

'I guess you didn't need me . . .' Cherry said sadly. 'You've looked really great in all your interviews.'

'I've looked like I have a stylist,' he corrected. 'She always brings three options –' He tilted his head at Cherry. 'You want me to FaceTime you and let you pick?'

Cherry sat up. Excited despite herself. '*Yeah.*'

Tom smiled at her. Fully. Then a cloud of anxiety moved over his face. 'I know I haven't always called home . . . as much as I should.'

She nodded. She remembered.

He was looking in her eyes. 'It wasn't the same as *being* home, and I always felt like I may as well just wait and see you when I saw you.'

Cherry nodded. 'I know.'

'But then I was gone for so long . . .'

She took his hand. 'So call me.'

'I'm gonna call you,' he said.

She brought his hand to her mouth and kissed it.

Tom frowned. 'Though I don't know what we're going to talk about.'

She rolled her eyes. 'I can't believe you're already talking yourself out of calling home ...'

'I'm talking myself out of *leaving*.'

'Go,' she said, kissing his hand again. 'Do what you have to do.'

Tom caught her chin and turned her face up to him. 'You always say that.'

Cherry nodded. 'Should I say something else?'

He looked troubled. 'I don't like hearing you tell me to go.'

Cherry kissed his thumb. It was right there. 'I was only ever saying it to be encouraging,' she said. 'I *hate* when you go.'

'Say that,' he whispered.

'I hate that you're leaving,' Cherry said, looking up at him. 'I miss you so much when you're gone.'

Tom dropped the socks he was holding into the suitcase and stepped closer to her.

'I miss you the second I wake up,' she said, 'before I even open my eyes. The room sounds wrong without you.'

He brought his other hand to Cherry's face.

'Every room of the house is wrong without you,' she said. 'I work too much, and I listen to podcasts I don't care about. And I talk to Stevie about you. About what you might be doing. And whether you miss us.'

'You talk to Stevie?'

'I tell Stevie everything.'

He laughed.

Cherry tilted her head up farther. She made her neck long. 'I hate when you leave. I hate everything that makes you go. I hate bookstores. And foreign editors. I hate librarians.'

He slid his hand under her jaw, cupping her chin. 'Why haven't you ever said so?'

'I didn't want to make you feel bad.'

'This makes me feel *great*,' Tom said. He lifted her head up a little higher. He kissed her.

Cherry put her arms around his hips.

When Tom pulled away, he kept hold of her jaw. He stroked the top of her cheek with his other hand, with his thumb. 'I know you don't need me,' he murmured. 'You've got it all under control.'

Cherry shook her head. Careful not to shake him off. 'I need you,' she said, 'to *keep* it under control. You're my other half.'

He kissed her.

'You're the half with all the vital systems,' she said. 'Cooling and life support.'

He kissed her.

'I hate it when you leave,' she said.

Tom pushed her back onto the comforter. He held on to her jaw. Cherry kicked his suitcase off the bed – with malice.

'I'll come home early,' he promised, unbuttoning her dress, pulling off her tights.

'Are you going to cancel *The View*?'

'Fuck *The View*. Jesse Plemons can go on *The View*.'

Tom left her bra on. He liked her bras.

'Is he nice?' Cherry asked.

'Who?'

'Jesse Plemons.'

'Yeah, he's nice.' Tom was pulling his T-shirt over his head. It was a little big on him. All his old clothes were a little big on him.

'How'd you get so skinny?' she whispered.

He dropped his shirt on the floor. 'I only lost twelve pounds, Cherry.' He unbuttoned his pants.

'Are you taking a semaglutide?' She was still whispering.

He lowered his eyebrows. 'No. Hey …' He kicked his pants away and got into bed. He pulled Cherry close, scooping her up, jostling her into his arms. 'I'm not keeping secrets from you.'

'A whole year went by,' she said. 'You got a stylist.'

'I was fucking depressed,' he said. 'That's my secret.'

'Me, too.'

'Here ...' Tom rolled her onto her back again. 'Let me cheer you up.'

'I missed you,' she said.

He kissed the top of her breast – then pulled her bra strap down her shoulder and left it just so. He was art-directing her cleavage.

'Like this,' she said. 'I missed you.'

Tom looked up, and their eyes met. 'Cherry, I ...' He raised himself up onto his knees, between her legs. Away from her.

'Where are you going?'

He rested back on his calves. His cock was springing up under his boxer briefs. He was rubbing his face. 'I think I'm trying to say something.'

She lifted up on her elbows, concerned. 'Say what?'

Tom dropped his hands. 'I know we're not ... back. I know we're still kind of broken. I want to keep coming home, Cherry. I want to keep making it better.'

She nodded. There were tears in her eyes. (She wasn't sure which kind yet.)

Tom seemed to be waiting for her to say something. He looked worried. He looked turned on still. He looked like he'd lost *at least* twenty pounds.

Cherry dropped onto her back and reached for him. 'So come home.'

Cherry took Tom to the airport.

Well, he drove.

She could hardly find anything to say in the car, her mouth was so full of dread. She wasn't sure what she was afraid of ...

She didn't think that Tom would cheat on her or change his mind. But they were going through the same motions that had driven them apart. Tom was going to be gone for sixteen days.

'Will you come pick me up when I get back?' he asked. 'If you're not at work?'

'I'll come pick you up no matter what.'

It wasn't a special promise. She'd always taken Tom to the airport. She'd always picked him up. She'd always hugged him tight when she got out of the car to let him drive home. It hadn't protected them.

Chapter 68

Cherry sent a text message to all four of her sisters, telling them that she and Tom were back together; that she was happy about it; and that she wouldn't be taking questions at this time.

'*Thank God!!*' Joy said. '*I didn't trust that other guy. He was too pretty.*'

'*Tom!*' Faith said. '*I was rooting for him all along.*'

'Obviously,' Hope said. '*You were both googly-eyed at Christmas.*'

'*If you can forgive Tom,*' Honny said. '*I can mostly forgive him.*' Also: '*In God's eyes, you were never apart.*'

'The cousins will all be thrilled,' Faith said. '*Tom's their favorite uncle.*'

Cherry took Stevie for long walks. But not as long as Tom did.

Cherry found the photos of Tom with his mom buried in a drawer. She hadn't intentionally been keeping them.

She put them back on the wall in the dining room. She felt less alone.

Tom called. And FaceTimed. He looked tired and well-groomed. One night when he called, he was wearing foundation.

Tom had so much more to talk about than Cherry did. He spent his days with movie stars. He had his photo taken in designer clothes.

But Cherry did most of the talking. She told him all the silly things that Stevie did – not a single one of them was new or surprising – and she told him what she'd eaten for lunch. She told him that the garbage truck had driven through the corner of their yard again.

At the end of every call, Tom would tell Cherry how many days he had left before he was coming home. 'I'll see you in fourteen days,' he said. In eleven, in nine.

Cherry wasn't reading any gossip about *Thursday*, but Stacia told her the buzz was good – everyone said that Tom had done a terrific job on the screenplay.

That didn't surprise Cherry. She'd never seen Tom do a bad job on anything.

'Can I wear my wedding ring in photos?' Tom texted to ask her.

'You can wear your wedding ring wherever you want,' Cherry texted back. *'We're married.'*

'How married are we?' he asked. At another time in their relationship, it might have seemed playful.

'Terminally,' Cherry replied.

Cherry's wedding ring was in the bottom of her jewelry box. It was a plain gold band – she'd never wanted a diamond.

She put it on and looked down at her hands.

She sent Tom a selfie – sitting on the couch with Stevie. *'Okay if I wear my wedding ring in photos?'*

It started to bother her more, that most of Tom's things were gone.

How was it that they were back together, but there was less of him in the house? Less evidence of him.

She missed his books and his posters and his coffee cup.

'Are your boxes at your dad's house?' she asked. They were on the phone. Cherry was in bed. Tom was in his hotel room, eating tacos. He'd worked late.

'Yeah,' he said, 'in the garage.'

'I could go get them, if you want.'

'There's no urgency. I can get them when I come home.'

'I feel bad,' she said. 'You came back for your things, and now they're in exile.'

Tom laughed out a breath. 'Cherry . . .' he said softly. 'I didn't come back for my *stuff*. I came back for you.'

Chapter 69

The railroad museum had its grand opening. Cherry wore a pinstriped denim dress that mimicked engineer's overalls and a pair of very expensive red boots. (Knee-high, no laces, low heel.)

'You look too cute by half,' Meg Jones chided. 'I should send you home.'

'It's a family event,' Cherry said. 'We told people to bring their kids.'

'You're here to represent a Fortune 500 company. I'm grooming you as my replacement.'

'Be glad I didn't wear the matching hat.'

Meg Jones tolerated a little sass. Especially when Cherry knocked it out of the park the way she had with this railroad museum.

Everything looked so good. The exhibits were fun and interesting, and portrayed the company as an American icon. Western Alliance had gotten so much good press from it already, and there were more photographers here today.

There was a real steam engine parked outside, and custom-printed balloons and picnic food.

Cherry liked planning events for kids. Tom would have loved working on this party.

There was a short ceremony to officially reopen the museum. Cherry introduced Meg, and then Meg introduced the CEO.

Cherry was in the middle of her speech when she spotted Russ Sutton in the crowd. He smiled at her – with his lips pressed together, like he was sorry about something.

Cherry didn't miss a beat. She finished introducing Meg, then stepped away from the podium. Russ was still watching her. He was with his son – Liam. (She recognized him from the pictures.) Russ smiled at Cherry again. She waved.

There was a lot for her to do after that. She wasn't avoiding Russ – but she couldn't go talk to him. This was her big day.

When she finally had a moment, she tracked him down. His kid was playing a game with rings and railroad spikes.

'Sorry,' Cherry said to Russ. 'I was ...'

'You're at work,' he said. *'I'm* sorry. I should have told you I'd be here. The mayor sent me.'

'You're welcome, of course.' Cherry brushed her bangs out of her eyes. 'It's good to see you.'

Russ winced. Just a little. After a second, he reached for Cherry's left hand. She let him take it.

He looked down at her wedding ring, nodded, then squeezed her fingers once before letting go.

'You were right,' Cherry said quietly. 'I wasn't divorced.'

Russ nodded again. His tongue was in his cheek.

'I was going to call,' she said.

He shrugged. 'Why?'

'To tell you that I'm sorry.'

'I'm the one who fucked it up.' He glanced around to see if any kids had heard him. 'I fucked it up.'

'I didn't give you much of a chance,' she said.

Russ sighed and ran his hand through his hair.

Then he made a determined face. He looked in Cherry's eyes. 'If we hadn't gone to that stupid movie ... If I hadn't seen that goddamn trailer ... It got to me, I'm sorry. It shook me up. I wish I could go back.'

Cherry didn't know what to say.

Could he be right? She *had* been crazy about him ...

If Russ had been more gracious, more certain of her – if he

hadn't lost his nerve – would that have been enough? Would she have finally let Tom go?

Cherry felt a wave of relief. A *riptide*. That she hadn't stepped completely out of her old life into a new one.

Even if that new life might have been lovely.

Russ's son pulled on his arm. 'Dad, I'm done. Can we eat now?'

'This is my son, Liam,' Russ said. 'Liam, this is my friend, Cherry. She's a robber baron and a good dancer.'

'It's nice to meet you,' Cherry said.

Liam nodded, immediately cutting his eyes away. 'Dad, can we eat?'

'Yeah.' Russ looked at Cherry and raised his eyebrows, like, *What're you gonna do?*

Cherry smiled. 'There are hot dogs on the porch. And hand-scooped ice cream.'

'It was good to see you,' he said.

'It was good to see you, too.'

Russ half turned. Then turned back. He looked earnest. 'I will always be happy to see you, Cherry.'

It might have been lovely.

Chapter 70

Cherry wanted to call Tom and crow about the museum opening, but he was out to dinner with movie people. It was a late dinner, and he was two hours behind Cherry on the clock – she'd be asleep by the time he got back to his hotel . . .

. . . *if* she could sleep.

Cherry had too much time on her hands again with Tom gone. Too much space. Too much quiet.

The ambient noise about the *Thursday* movie was getting harder to block out. Cherry couldn't look at any news sites. She kept getting ads for *Thursday* on Instagram.

She didn't like being reminded that Tom was important to so many people whom neither of them had ever met. That he was a titan. She needed to keep him man-sized in her head.

Seeing Russ at the museum had unnerved Cherry. '*That god-damn trailer,*' he'd said.

What had Hope said? That the first trailer was so much worse than the second. Specifically so much worse for Cherry.

How was it worse?

Cherry already knew about the actress and the fat suit.

She'd been so disciplined about this fucking movie . . . About not inviting it into her brain. Not giving herself extra content to obsess over.

'*The* first *trailer?*' Hope had said. '*Oh no.*'

Was there something egregious? A fat joke? (Beyond the walking, talking fat joke that was Baby herself?)

Cherry shouldn't watch it – she'd regret watching it. The way she always regretted looking at *Thursday*.

(She *had* to separate the art from the artist. The husband from the id. Her marriage from . . . whatever *Thursday* was. Figments. Jokes. Ideas.)

'*Oh no,*' Hope had said.

'*Don't watch it,*' Meg Jones said.

Stacia: '*You don't need it.*'

Faith: '*You're so much prettier, Cherry.*'

Russ: '*It shook me up.*'

Maybe it made Cherry more of a fool *not* to watch the trailer . . .

Not to know how the whole world saw her.

Not to understand why they were laughing.

She went downstairs to get her laptop. If she was going to do this, she was going to do it on a decent-sized screen. Stevie tried to follow Cherry back upstairs, and Cherry let her – she even helped the dog onto the bed. She'd make sure to change the bedding before Tom came home. He thought Stevie's new privileges were a terrible development – '*Her hair is already everywhere.*'

'So is mine,' Cherry had argued, '*and I'm allowed in the bedroom.*'

Stevie stretched out at Cherry's side. Cherry crossed her legs and balanced the laptop on her thighs. She rested a hand on Stevie's ruff and scratched it.

'It can't be that bad, Stevie,' Cherry said. 'He wouldn't let it be that bad.' (Tom wasn't cruel. Or careless.)

Cherry found the trailer on YouTube. She clicked to expand the window and pressed *play*.

The screen was black. White type appeared:

FROM THE STUDIO THAT BROUGHT YOU
"ALL OF OUR DAYS" . . .

A Christmas song started playing. Bells. Indie piano. A guy singing with a Scottish accent.

White lights twinkled on. A scene came into view:

Women in beautiful dresses swished past the camera, their faces cut off by the frame. Men in black suits drank cocktails. The camera was moving through them.

A girl appeared.

All in black.

Under an archway of fairy lights and flowers.

Faith had lied – the actress was very pretty. Thinner than Cherry (and Baby), even though she seemed to be wearing padding over her belly and hips.

The girl was underdressed for the party, but her hair was shiny and her cheeks were flushed. The lights shimmered in her eyes. She swallowed.

Across the room, under another arch – this house was even nicer than Meg Jones's – was Jesse Plemons. De-aged. Possibly also wearing padding. And a cheap-looking suit.

He was watching the girl. He waved.

She looked anxious. She waved back.

The Scottish singer hit a plaintive note.

This was apparently one of those trailers with one long scene instead of a montage or an overview.

Jesse Plemons crossed the room.

The song jangled. The backup singers *ooh*'ed.

'Nobody told you this is prom for rich white people,' The Guy said.

Baby shook her head. She looked luminous. They must have made her pupils bigger with CGI to add all those stars.

'Do you want me to help you leave?' he asked. 'Or do you want me to help you stay?'

'I'm not sure,' she said. 'Maybe if I stand really still, nobody will see me.'

Jesse Plemons squinted and grinned. He did that thing he does where only his top teeth show. 'I saw you,' he said gruffly.

Suddenly a word balloon dropped above them, and the rest of the scene dropped out. It was just the two of them and the balloon and Tom's handwriting:

I JUST MET THE MOST BEAUTIFUL GIRL.

The indie Christmas song crescendoed.
Jesse Plemons had never looked so quietly full of feeling.
That British actress with the big head had never looked so lovely.
Then the tempo of the song shifted up, and the trailer started shuffling manically through more scenes from the movie. The Guy and Baby – the two actors – were framed in panels that sped across the screen. Cherry recognized a few classic moments from the comics and a few memes.
The music got louder and more circular.
Then the title – more of Tom's handwriting – dropped in over all of the color and movement:

THURSDAY

And the screen went black.
Then, just when you thought it was over, Baby's face appeared again. In extreme close-up.
She winked.

Cherry closed the laptop.

Chapter 71

Today 6:03 PM

Hope
Cherry, there you are! We see you!

Joy
I don't see her!! What channel are you watching???

Hope
I'm not watching a channel. I'm watching some sort of social media streaming thing. Honny sent the link.

Faith
Cherry, you look so pretty! That dress!

Honny
Where'd she find a dress like that in her size?

Hope
Some dressmaker she found online. She bought it for work.

Joy
Send the link again!!

Faith

They're interviewing Tom!! I always forget he's famous. Even after all this time.

Honny

He's always so crabby in these interviews . . .

Chill out, Tom. You're prettier when you smile.

Hope

Look at Cherry's sparkly eyeshadow. Do you think she did her own makeup?

Joy

I can't open the link. I think I have parental controls on???

Faith

Has Cherry lost weight?

Honny

Maybe a little. She's still the fattest person in that zip code. (Sorry, Cherry. Don't worry – I'm still fatter.)

Hope

She's the only person there who isn't a size zero. That would be such a mind you-know-what . . .

Honny

Yeah, Hope – she must feel like you at Christmas.

Hope

So funny, Honny.

Joy

Somebody send me a screenshot!!!

Faith
Oh no!

Honny
NO!

Hope
She must be so mad.

Joy
What happened???

Honny
The red carpet person just called Cherry 'Baby.'

Joy
Is there actually a red carpet?

Faith
Aw. My heart!! Good answer, Tom.

Hope
He looks like he's crying a little bit.

Honny
Who knew that Tom was such a sap?

Hope
Literally everyone who's ever read 'Thursday.'

Honny
I should read 'Thursday,' but I get so bored.
There's no dialogue.

Faith
I'll bet the movie has dialogue.

Hope
There they go . . .

Faith

Bye, Cherry! You look gorgeous!

Honny

Dang, Cherry, you look even better walking away. Where'd you find that DRESS?

Joy

What's happening now??

Honny

They're interviewing the guy from Friday Night Lights.

Joy

Oh! Send me a screenshot!!!

Chapter 72

The *Entertainment Tonight* reporter was so skinny, you could thread her through a needle. Tom said that even the thin people in Hollywood were on GLP-1s.

'Baby!' the reporter shouted. She was all eyes and teeth. 'We're so excited to meet you! We all want to know – what's it like seeing yourself on screen?'

Tom leaned in before Cherry could answer. He reached out and pulled the microphone his way.

'Baby is a fictional character,' he said, frowning. 'She's two-dimensional – she's a shadow on a cave wall. My wife is infinite. If there are things you like about Baby, I probably stole them from her. But I could never fit everything she is, and everything she means to me, into a panel.'

Chapter 73

Cherry had shown up at his hotel.

Tom wasn't there. It was awkward. She sat in the lobby on a velvet sofa, with her suitcase and the coat she wouldn't need for a week, not wanting to just text him and tell him she was there.

She'd taken the week off work.

She'd boarded Stevie.

She'd known that she was stepping into something she wasn't ready for. Into light that might blind her.

Cherry saw Tom before he saw her. Walking in from the street. His shoulders were hunched. He was with another woman – probably Michelle.

Cherry stood up. She was wearing tight jeans and very cute yellow patent leather heels. (She'd worn heels on the airplane. She was in agony.)

Tom stopped.

He stood taller.

'Baby . . .' he said. She could read his lips.

Cherry nodded.

Acknowledgments

When you have a problem, in life, sometimes the thing that helps most is for a friend to truly pause and deeply focus with you on the matter at hand.

Do you know this feeling? When someone gives you their entire attention, and you feel like you are pushing together against an obstacle?

I am so incredibly lucky to have friends who will pause and focus while reading my books. Who will listen to my questions and truly consider them. I feel a gasping sort of gratitude in these moments. Like I am not alone under a mountain of words.

Thank you to Leigh Bardugo, Nicola Barr, Drew Davies, Joy DeLyria, Bethany Gronberg, Brian Guehring, Jessica Rowell, Lynn Safranek, and Elena Yip for your sincere consideration.

Thank you *especially* to Christopher Schelling and Ashley McCracken.

And thank you to my husband and sons, who solve so many of my problems around the dinner table.

Finally, I am very grateful to my editor, Jennifer Brehl, who is such a warm and insightful listener, and to the remarkable team at William Morrow and HarperCollins, people who authentically love and fight for books.